CHASING SUNRISE

PEOPLE ARE SAYING ...

Chasing Sunrise explores betrayal, friendship, integrity, and the life-changing gifts of love and hope.
—**Richard Paul Evans**, #1 New York Times Bestselling Author.

Chasing Sunrise is a fascinating story supported by wonderful story-telling and a well-woven plot line. This is a tale that will keep you turning the pages.
—**Ace Collins**, award-winning author of the *In The President's Service* series.

Opposite worlds, opposing ideals, and conflicting desires, *Chasing Sunrise* is an action-packed adventure.
—**Bill Myers**, multi-award winning author of the *Blood of Heaven* series and *Eli*.

Even the title of this soul-cleansing story by P.S. Wells has multi-leveled meanings. Alive in every conversation they share, these characters stay with you long after the book is finished. Read *Chasing Sunrise* for yourself and buy a copy for a friend.
—**Michele Howe**, reviewer and author of twenty books including *Navigating the Friendship Maze: The Path to Authentic Friendship*.

What an exciting story! If you like reading books set in tropical places and a big dash of danger, you'll love *Chasing Sunrise!*
—**Kathi Macias**, award-winning author of more than fifty books including *Red Ink* and *My Son, John*.

Riveting!
—**Jason Chatraw**, author.

Chasing Sunrise pulls you into a hurricane of betrayal and passion and danger. It won't let you go until the final pages.
—**Henry McLaughlin**, award-winning author of the *Riverbend Saga* series.

CHASING SUNRISE

P.S. Wells

Keep a
piece of paradise
with you

PUBLISHING THE POSITIVE
ELK LAKE PUBLISHING INC.
Plymouth, Massachusetts

Library Cataloging Data

Names: Wells, P. S. (P. S. Wells)

Chasing Sunrise / P. S. Wells

342 p. 23cm × 15cm (9in × 6 in.)

Description: Chasing Sunrise is solace worth seeking, adventure worth having, and a piece of paradise you'll take with you.

Identifiers: ISBN-13: 978-1-948888-63-9 (trade) | 978-1-948888-64-6 (POD)

| 978-1-948888-65-3 (e-book.)

Key Words: music, parajumpers, St. Croix, body trafficking, diving, art.

LCCN: 2018958421 Fiction

DEDICATION

"Son, the motto of the PJs and the Seals is *that others may live.*
That implies you are willing to give your life for someone else."

"Mom," he explained, "people need help. I want to be the one who shows up."

Sometimes a plea for help is verbal,
sometimes it is technologically communicated.
Sometimes it is a heart-cry in a desperate situation.

To those brave and dedicated people
—like my daughter—
who arrive when someone calls 911.
To my son. My favorite son.

To Garry Arasmith who said, "Why don't you write a love story?"

And to Patrick Kavanaugh and MasterWorks Festival who marvelously influenced my family and inspired the setting for this story.

CHAPTER 1

Captain Michael Northington looked toward the patient's room. The door was closed.

"There's a VIP patient at Bethesda." Corbin MacIntyre, the special ops commander had briefed him earlier. "Protect the room. No one is allowed access except medical staff, and they already have their orders."

"You're expecting an attempt on the patient's life?"

"Monitor the floor. Apprehend anyone."

The night watch in a hospital in the late 1980s was atypical for the parajumper accustomed to more active assignments. Establishing a runway before an invasion, rescuing a downed pilot, or descending from a hovering helicopter to a ship bucking like a bronco in a wildly choppy sea were customary fare for Michael and his four-man team. But tonight found his partner and him serving more as security guards in the upscale medical center than as trained rescue personnel. Still, orders were orders.

Now, Michael casually observed a gray-haired janitor as he lugged a wash bucket into the hospital corridor. *Mop. Slosh. Wring. Mop.* The overhead fluorescent lights gleamed off the man's glasses, and his name badge swung back and forth as he swept the mop from side to side.

"Evenin'," the custodian mumbled as he shuffled up to Michael.

As the old man swished the ammonia-smelling mop, Michael stepped away and let the man do his job. The janitor mopped his way into the room across the hall from the room occupied by the protected patient.

A thick-waisted nurse in soft-soled shoes walked toward the patient's room. She frowned when Michael stepped in front of her and flashed her identity badge and an irritated attitude. He nodded and moved aside. She brushed past and entered the room, closing the door behind her.

Suppressing a yawn, Michael checked his watch. In a couple of hours, the sun would rise and his shift would end. He anticipated a platter-sized breakfast at the twenty-four-hour diner followed by a nap.

Eager for morning and breakfast, Michael glanced out the window. A pale glow promised daybreak, and he could almost smell bacon spitting on the grill. He thought of the diner with its chrome and red vinyl seats that let him belly up to the counter. Early in the morning before the pert waitress arrived, the cook took orders and slathered the hot grill with margarine. Like a symphony conductor, the white-aproned expert simultaneously threw eggs and hash browns to sizzle, adding ladles of melt-in-your-mouth flapjack batter to the crackling, popping breakfast serenade. Michael's stomach growled and he looked again at his watch.

The nurse came out of the room, adjusted the stethoscope around her neck, and shut the door behind her. Michael watched as she entered another room, continuing her rounds. Turning his attention back to the patient's room, he observed the slightest movement as the door silently closed.

Jaguar-fast, Michael covered the space down the hall. He opened the door without a sound. In the darkened room, bending over the still form in the bed was the janitor.

Light from the hall spilled into the room behind Michael. The janitor whirled around just as Michael lunged at him. With well-trained maneuvers Michael quickly pinned the man's arms and muscled him into the hall.

"Send someone to collect." Michael spoke into his radio.

The janitor struggled like a wild man, surprising Michael with his desperate fight.

"Please," the man pleaded. "She needs water."

"Easy, old-timer." He gripped the man tighter.

From the stairwell, Captain Bryce Lassiter ran to meet Michael. "Okay, partner?"

"Yeah." The man in his grip stopped struggling.

Bryce's attention shifted to the elevator as the doors opened and four uniformed men stepped out and strode toward them. Suddenly, the janitor jerked from Michael's hold and ran back toward the patient's room. Michael dove and tackled the man, and the two fell hard on the clean linoleum.

"She needs me," the man rasped.

Without a word, Michael jerked the man to his feet. The janitor's glasses were broken from the impact and blood from his nose mingled with tears on his face as two special-forces officers roughly grabbed his arms and nearly carried him to the elevator.

"Let me care for her," he sobbed.

As the group reached the elevator, the old man craned his neck, the tendons standing out like cords, to look back toward the patient's room. The look of anguish on his face twisted Michael's gut.

"Verity," the man wailed. "My Verity!"

The two soldiers pushed him into the elevator and the doors whispered shut.

"Back to work." Bryce made shooing motions to the two remaining soldiers who turned toward the elevator.

"Back to my post." Bryce clapped Michael on the back. "Call if you need me."

He took several steps toward the stairway and then looked back. Michael stood rooted to the spot. His partner returned to his side. "What's up? You look like you've seen a ghost."

Michael spun on his heel and strode to the patient's room. Three paces took him to the bedside where he looked at the still form. The light was dim, but enough to see the spilled cup of water on the floor. Enough to see her.

The nurse brushed past to check on her patient, scolding everyone for the mess, and reminding them to keep quiet. In a rush of motion, two sets of strong arms grabbed Michael on either side and hauled him from the room. Too stunned to resist, Michael was unceremoniously dumped in the hallway.

One soldier closed the patient's door and stood in front of it. "I'm sorry, sir." He addressed Michael. "Orders are that no one goes into this room."

Bryce pushed his nose into the man's face. "He's your commanding officer, you moron."

"Sir, yes, sir." The soldier straightened his shoulders. "Our orders are *no one* goes into the room. Not even my commanding officer."

"I have to relieve you of your post." The second soldier took a position between Michael and the room.

Staring at the closed door, Michael murmured, "No problem, soldier. I was just leaving anyway." He turned and walked toward the stairway.

Bryce caught up. "Where we goin,' partner?"

A soldier jogged after the two and blocked their way. "Sir, I have to escort you out, sir."

"Knock yourself out." Michael brushed past him.

The soldier ran and blocked the way again.

"You're getting redundant," Bryce said to the man.

"By way of the elevator." The soldier spoke to Michael.

"I prefer to walk." Michael's hands were fists at his sides.

"I realize that, sir." The soldier swallowed. "Orders are that we use the elevator."

"Bloody orders." Bryce sighed.

Michael looked at Bryce.

"I love when you do that," Bryce said.

"Do what?"

"Raise one eyebrow like that."

"I can't believe you used that word."

The soldier cleared his throat. "Sirs, can we continue this conversation in the elevator?"

Bryce turned toward the elevator and started walking. "What word?"

Michael followed while the sweating soldier trailed behind. "My word."

Bryce's expression was the picture of innocence. "Your word?"

The elevator doors opened, and Michael stepped inside. Nervous and perspiring, the soldier stood to his right. The second soldier occupied the post Michael had kept near the patient's room.

"Yeah, my word."

Bryce remained in the hall. "Who said it's your word?"

The elevator doors closed.

CHAPTER 2

Elise Eisler lifted her hair off her neck and held it coiled in a bun at the back of her head. The trade wind blew through the open window and cooled her as she gazed out at the familiar view. The view she had known all her life. The Atlantic looked lively today—playing under the golden yellow of the warm sun like a child frolicking under the loving, watchful eye of a doting mother.

She shifted her weight, and the breeze made her sundress dance against her legs. Her own mother had been watchful and doting. Gentle and loving. Elise remembered sitting in this room, her tanned bare feet swinging from a Queen Anne chair much too big for her skinny nine years. Smelling of fairy stories and happily-ever-after, her mother bent over her, helping position the finely crafted viola in her young daughter's eager hands.

"Antonio did his usual fabulous job." With professional efficiency, a middle-aged woman bustled into the empty room, interrupting Elise's reverie. "Honestly, Elise, I don't know what this island did before he came here. Everything is moved out, the corners and closets are clean as the kids' stockings after Christmas. This is the only thing I found."

She held out a paintbrush.

"Thanks, June." Dropping her hair, Elise blinked away the sweet memory of her mother, took the brush, and drew the long, delicate handle through her fingers. Feeling the well-worn wood triggered a different remembrance, this time of her father. His blue eyes twinkling with success, he coaxed Robson, Ava, and Elise through the final movement of Beethoven's chamber piece. The four of them perched on the front of their chairs in a semicircle. Three adolescent music students and their instructor with music stands low so they could read the notes, like so much black confetti on the yellowed pages, and still make eye contact with one another.

"Why this piece?" Robson always needed the why.

Her father had placed the pages of music on each stand. "The String Quartet No. 14 in C-sharp minor, opus 131 was Ludwig van Beethoven's favorite of his chamber works."

Ava scanned her violin part. "How is it played?"

He bent to retrieve his conductor's wand, and Elise noted the whimsical curl of gray hair at the base of his neck. He placed the delicate wand in Ava's fingers and guided it to several places on the score. "The Quartet is about forty minutes in length and consists of seven movements."

"Seven pauses in forty minutes?" Elise could see Ava doing the mental math.

"Played without a break. And another mathematical inconsistency with this piece." He indicated the black letters of the title. "This is actually Beethoven's fifteenth quartet by order of composition but is titled the fourteenth based on the order of its publication."

Turning his attention to her, Elise's father put an affectionate hand on his daughter's head. "And you, *liebste*, you are your mother's daughter and want to know the story behind the composition." He hummed a few measures, thinking. Suddenly he brightened, and she knew he had matched the tune to the tale. "The illustrious composer dedicated this work to Baron Joseph von Stuttenheim—a gift of appreciation for finding a place in the military for his nephew, Karl, after an attempted suicide."

"Beethoven attempted suicide?" Elise couldn't imagine a composer like her father being anything other than fulfilled. He had music, after all.

Ava and Robson laughed.

"Not Beethoven." Robson's condescending tone reminded her that once again he understood something she didn't. "His nephew."

Under the tutelage of the conductor, the three young friends practiced separately and met together regularly at the cottage that served as a studio. Each week after the young students had gone, Elise's father put on a music recording and turned to his painting. Sometimes Elise's mother walked down from their house on the same property and joined him. From the time Elise was able to stand and hold a brush, her parents had set an easel between them for her to paint as well, encouraging her immature attempts.

Now she flicked the soft bristles across her palm. A round paintbrush of fine Kolinsky sable derived from a pale red weasel with fur—according to her father—"of superior strength, slenderness, and resiliency for the purpose of applying paint."

Savoring the sleekness, she drew the brush across her cheek and looked up to find June studying her. "Where did you find it?"

"On the top of the refrigerator. The brush must have rolled back out of sight. Probably when you closed the fridge door. I can just see you searching—"

Elise shook her head. "It's not mine." She sighed. The vacant room felt like the empty pit in the depth of her stomach. She hadn't been able to soothe the vicious acid of regret that burned in her core. Was there another way? Did she have to sacrifice one part of her parents' treasures to save the other?

June put a hand on Elise's arm. "This is a good decision, my dear."

"But—"

"Don't mistake good with easy." The older woman fingered her earring, and Elise recognized the jewelry as a set her mother had given to this dear family friend. "Sometimes the two are companions. Often they are polarized. Much like a grand marriage."

June surveyed the room and inhaled deeply. "Even empty, this special place smells like creativity. The salty sea, rosin, oil paint." She met Elise's eyes. "It smells of you."

"It smells like memories."

"You've made a lifetime of them here." June clucked her tongue. "And this is the beginning of new ones, my dear. You're making this into a goodbye."

"Isn't it?"

June flung open the glass double doors and beckoned Elise outside. "By the gods, no! This is a new beginning. A fresh new canvas. The beginning notes of a never-before-heard symphony."

Grinning, Elise twisted her hair into a bun once more and stuck the paintbrush through to hold the knot. Following June outside, she picked a smiling yellow hibiscus and tucked the bloom behind her ear.

CHAPTER 3

Corbin MacIntyre was on the phone when Michael barged into his commander's office. Corbin waved him to a chair, but Michael walked straight to the large desk and tossed his parajumper insignia across the dark wood surface.

"Listen, something just came up." Corbin spoke into the phone, but his eyes were still on Michael. "Call me later." He dropped the receiver into its cradle.

"You used me." Michael knew his tone was accusatory.

Ten years Michael's senior, Corbin was handsome and fit with a quick mind and an unending supply of Scottish witticisms. When agitated, he also had an unlimited string of Scottish insults and, as far as Michael could remember, never repeated any. Michael would know. He'd been the frequent recipient of the salty tirades during their years together.

Now Corbin regarded Michael. "I heard there was an incident on your last assignment."

"I didn't become one of America's fighting elite to kill women."

"My information was sketchy, Michael. We were ordered to protect the patient."

"Cut the crap, Corbin." Michael waved a hand at the television on a low coffee table. His boss kept it tuned to a news channel to stay updated on world happenings. Though muted now, the screen showed Senator Bennett Taylor wiping his eye as he told the press of his wife's passing. "The patient was a general's wife, mysteriously hospitalized."

"Don't you watch the news? Taylor's a senator now." Corbin crossed the room and closed the office door. "A general's wife or a senator's wife should receive extra protection." He returned to his side of the desk.

"Mr. God-and-Country barred all visitors and ordered life support withheld. That's not protection. It's a death sentence."

"But you did apprehend someone who was making an attempt on the patient."

"I apprehended her father, Corbin. Her father was attempting to give water to his only child."

Corbin sighed and rubbed the back of his neck. He indicated the chair again. "Sit down, Northington."

"No."

The phone rang. Corbin pushed a button on the display and spoke. "Saundra, hold all calls." The ringing stopped. "I'll look into things, Michael."

"Don't bother. She's dead." Michael slapped his palm on the desk. "She was murdered."

Corbin picked up the insignia and held it out for Michael. "Take some time off. Cool down."

The metal flash in Corbin's hand was the image of an angel enfolding the world in its wings. Michael ignored Corbin's outstretched hand. "I'm done." He turned and walked away. He had his hand on the doorknob when Corbin spoke again.

"Did you know her?"

Michael paused before he answered. "Yeah, I knew her." He slammed the door behind him.

CHAPTER 4

"Figured I'd find you here." Several days later, wearing a T-shirt tucked into worn jeans, Bryce dropped into a chair across the table from Michael.

Folding the classified section, Michael sat back and regarded his partner and friend. "Buy you a cuppa?"

A fit five-foot-ten, Bryce was more powerful in upper body strength while Michael was superior at distance running. He took in the scattered newspaper with several items circled in blue ink and Michael's empty glass. "Since I'm the only one here still employed, I'll do the buyin'. What's your brew?"

"Beer. A tall one."

Bryce signaled to the waitress who took his order.

Michael broke the silence. "Corbin send you?"

Bryce stretched and glanced around the restaurant, a small gem tucked among the bustling Washington, DC, commerce area. The island theme appealed to the two. Made them feel like they were anywhere but here. "You did get the Scotsman's underwear in a wad—an accomplishment few have been able to pull off." He smiled at the memory. "But I came on my own."

The beers arrived smelling thickly of malt. Michael downed half of his tall glass.

Bryce pushed his sunglasses up on his head. His brown eyes were flecked with gold which the ladies found attractive, particularly combined with Bryce's easy humor and ability to get along with just about anyone. He looked pointedly at the discarded want ads. "So, battle buddy, what's the plan?"

Michael clicked the pen absently. "I'm making this up as I go."

"This from the guy who was on a fast track to his goals when he was still in diapers." Bryce took a drink of his draft and licked the suds from his top lip. "Scary." Michael drained his beer and Bryce nodded at the empty glass. "If I get you another will you humor me with something more than monosyllables?"

"Deal."

Bryce signaled the waitress again and turned his attention back to Michael. "You were prepubescent when you joined Civil Air Patrol."

"I was fourteen, and you weren't."

Bryce casually rested his elbow on the back of his chair. "Being the older, more mature member of this dynamic duo, I was sixteen. And driving myself to meetings while your mom dropped you off in that stylish station wagon."

Remembering, Michael smirked. "You were driving that rust-fringed, dilapidated pick-up truck older than Methuselah."

"Don't poke fun at that ride, Mikey," Bryce warned. "It got us to a lot of great places."

Michael listed. "Training weekends, ground team practice, survival school, flight school …"

"Before it died on the side of a deserted highway. It's probably still there." The two sat in companionable silence as the waitress delivered Michael's beer.

He lifted his glass in toast. "To the Adventure Mobile."

Bryce raised his own and they drank. "Before you could shave, you had your eyes on the sky, Michael."

As a teenager, the sight of the military jets practicing formation in the sky above his house had stirred Michael's blood. "I only wanted to fly then."

"And I was gonna be your ground team."

"You were too chicken to get your sorry bohunkus in a plane."

Bryce folded his sunglasses and tucked them into his T-shirt pocket. "The plan was I'd watch your back as crew chief. 'Cept you got too tall to fly that fighter jet you dreamed about. So you switched to Plan B."

Michael filled in. "Parajumper."

"Heck, there's only five hundred of us in the nation. You passed the toughest training regimen in the world. Number one in your class."

"And drug you kicking and screaming the whole way."

"More like I carried you, partner." Bryce leaned forward on the table. "Parajumper is all you've wanted to be since you were sixteen. It's what you've been for ten years. Parajumper is who you are."

Studying his glass, Michael nodded.

"Come back, partner."

Michael spun his glass in slow circles, the condensation leaving wet rings on the table. After a few moments, he spoke. "I can't."

Bryce sighed. "This is about the general's wife."

Michael respected Bryce's keen sense of measuring a person, but hadn't come close to mastering his buddy's winsome knack for rarely allowing anything or anyone to annoy him. "It's about her murder."

His friend remained quiet. Waiting.

"What's our prime directive, Bryce?"

"So that others may live."

"Two people have done something for me in my life. One of them was Verity. They used me to kill her. I can't work for people like that."

Bryce locked his fingers behind his head and stared at the ceiling fan. "You know what this means."

"What's that?"

"Besides being there to see Corbin come unraveled." He grinned at Michael. "You'd have loved seeing that."

"Dinner and a show." Tipping back his chair on two legs, Michael finished his beer.

"You leaving means I gotta partner with Wingnut Wolcutt."

Michael grimaced. "Sucks to be you."

CHAPTER 5

Early the next morning, Michael sat at his kitchen table with a forgotten cup of coffee and a single classified heavily ringed in blue ink. After a process of elimination, this was the one possibility that remained. He had reread the newspaper ad so many times he had it memorized. There were details about the island of St. Croix, a description of the rental house, and a phone number. He punched the number into the phone and his call was answered on the second ring.

"I'm calling about a rental." Michael gave a description of the place from the ad.

"Yes, this is the management firm representing the owner of the cottage." The woman's voice on the other end sounded professional. "How did you hear about us?"

"Your ad in the newspaper." Michael took a drink from his cup. The coffee was cold and he pushed the mug aside.

"You must be on the mainland. How can I help you?"

"I'd like to see the place."

"Certainly. Let me look at my calendar."

In the brief pause, Michael could hear the background sounds of an office phone ringing and the rapid click-tick of an adding machine. Then, she was talking to him again. "When could I show the house to you?"

Michael did some mental figuring of travel time. "I could be there day after tomorrow."

"Fine," she replied cheerfully. "What's your name?"

"Michael Northington."

"My name is June." She repeated the date of his arrival. "Come to my office late afternoon, Mr. Northington. I'll take you to see the property."

He hung up and sat for a moment. "Let's check it out," he said aloud and dialed the number for the airline.

CHAPTER 6

Two days later, Michael gazed out the window as his connecting flight from Washington, DC, began its charge down the black tarmac. He felt the familiar surge as the speed reached the point of liftoff from the runway and watched as the famous Chicago skyline was framed in the small airplane window. The plane banked over the stockyards, a place he had read about as a kid when his mother tried to sell him on the benefits of reading and literature.

His mom had brought home a book she'd found for a dollar on a sidewalk sale rack outside their small-town bookstore. It had been his evening to do the dishes, which made him a captive audience when she seated herself on the barstool at the counter and began to read aloud.

The story was a well-written accounting of a desperate and brave bunch of Canadian livestock farmers who gambled their livelihood and their lives to save their drought-afflicted homesteads. In a daring last-ditch effort, the town's few able-bodied men decided to drive what remaining healthy cattle they owned to the Chicago stockyards during a brutal January winter.

Not ready to admit he was interested, Michael had worked slower and slower in the kitchen while his mom read on. At the crucial moment when the youngest drover, who was fifteen years old—like Michael at the time—had a threatening wolf in his shotgun's crosshairs, his mother closed the book.

"Hey, what happens next?" Michael protested before he could stop himself.

His mother laid the book on the counter. "Time for me to tuck your sisters into bed." Climbing the stairs, she tossed back over her shoulder, "And I've got laundry to do. I'm not sure when I'll get back to reading."

Stubbornly, Michael considered the small volume and turned away. He knew what she was up to, and he had no intention of giving her the pleasure. Or of reading. For pleasure. Then, with a sidelong look at the thin paperback, he decided he could at least find out what happened to the wolf before his mother came back downstairs.

Of course, after the wolf adventure, a blizzard broadsided the intrepid group on their impossible venture. That led to the daring rescue of one of his favorite characters who fell through the ice of a frozen lake. On his horse. Next, Michael read about the cocky teenager's impressions of the big city, its grand hotels with carpeted floors, and indoor baths offering the unbelievable luxury of hot showers, and flush toilets that could "shoot and reload." Heady stuff to the country-boy hero accustomed to dirt floors and an outdoor privy.

Even now Michael smiled at the memory—the first story that had awakened his appreciation of a well-told tale. And at his mother's shrewdness. He was still a slow reader but not nearly as reluctant. Choosy. But a reader, nonetheless.

Next his mother had brought home a recorded book by an author named Jack London. "These books on cassette are sure better than the ones you read," he informed her.

She had laughed at that.

But she'd been pleased that he accepted the audio projects more willingly than their hardcopy counterparts. The last couple years he'd been at home and finishing high school, she fed him a steady supply of literature including *Lord of the Flies*, C.S. Lewis's *Narnia* series, J.R.R. Tolkien's *Lord of the Rings*, *Moby Dick*, *The Hound of Baskervilles*, *Swiss Family Robinson*, and *A Tale of Two Cities*.

When he balked at yet another literary classic, she reminded him he was a student and knowing the context of so much of culture's sayings and behaviors would benefit him. She always followed the lecture with an offer that he could read them as ink on paper if he preferred. Which of course, he didn't. Returning to the present, Michael realized he'd been too distracted to do much reading on this trip. His book lay closed on the tray table.

At the Atlanta airport, he boarded his final flight that would travel east. The book he brought remained unopened while he stared at the beauty of the Florida coast fading from view and the intense blue of the Atlantic filling the airplane's passenger window. Multiple islands appeared below followed by the eastern rim of the vast Florida Keys.

Watching these islands pass beneath the wings of the plane, Michael considered investing several weeks on a boat exploring the seventeen hundred small landforms of raised coral reef. He figured he certainly could muster the time. After the debacle at the hospital, Michael had no choice but to resign. He imagined a casual exploration of the unique geographic landscape that extended south-southwest to Key West including the westernmost of the inhabited islands and ending with the uninhabited Dry Tortugas.

The flight pattern took the airplane over the large and populated island of Puerto Rico. Ahead, a smaller, less-inhabited island came into view. The ample tropical foliage gave the destination the appearance of an emerald set in the ocean. Single-story, flat-roofed homes dotted the low hills and areas close to the water.

Soon the small commercial airplane descended, dropping closer to the turquoise ocean and white beaches that wrapped like a lei around the island of St. Croix. "The jewel of the Caribbean," promised the newspaper ad for the rental.

The plane taxied to a low, sand-colored terminal building. "The winds are currently at eighteen miles per hour," the pilot reported. "The temperature is eighty-five degrees and the local time is three forty-five."

Michael stepped from the air-conditioned airplane into the tropical afternoon where the warmth and humidity hugged him like a wetsuit. Inside the terminal, the pulse of steel drums beat a musical welcome. Musicians and airport employees were casually dressed in shorts and flip-flops, many wearing silver and gold-hooked bracelets. Old black men in tropical print shirts stood near their taxis, talking together and trying to make eye contact with potential customers.

After tossing his backpack into a small car, Michael navigated out of the rental lot. "Drive on the left, Mon," reminded a large, bright sign at the airport's exit. Marginally awkward after spending his life driving in the right lane, he followed the signs leading him to the beach.

The golden sand felt warm and welcoming under his bare feet as he made his way to the water's edge and breathed in the salty smell of the rolling waves. Slowly turning, Michael tried to take in the vast horizon in front of him and the peaceful island behind. Tried to unclench his fists.

The frustration he'd wrestled to keep under control bubbled up like bile, and he began to run. Harder, faster. His feet pounded the sand and his fists punched the air.

After several miles, his breath was ragged and sweat stung his eyes, but still he ran, trying to excise from his memory the sound of the janitor's pleas. Those haunting cries of a father desperate to save his daughter.

CHAPTER 7

Pushing aside the hem of her calf-length lavender dress, Elise tied the ribbons on her sandals. She opened the front screen door, padded down the wide porch steps, and as she had all her life, followed the tabby path to the cottage. Growing up, she knew the cottage as her family's studio where they created music, art, and musicians through the regular lessons her parents taught. For Elise to continue to use the cottage as her own studio after her parents died and the large property with house and cottage, gardens, and view of the ocean had passed to her was a natural transition.

Today she went to the cottage for … for what? All of her supplies had been moved home, and June was showing the cottage today to someone coming all the way from the mainland. Inside, Elise looked through each room and felt satisfied. The cottage fit like her mother's pearls—soft beauty given from the soul. Renting the cottage was akin to lending her mother's cherished necklace to a stranger.

She checked her watch. Time to go. She assured herself the cottage was ready even if she remained reluctant to share this treasure with the world.

Outside in the well-manicured garden, Antonio Estrada layered mulch under a row of broad-leafed sea grapes. From their perch on the cottage roof, a pair of doves wooed each other with trilling love songs.

"Buenos dias." A man in his mid-thirties, Antonio was pleasant and industrious, though Elise suspected the gardener with the lyrical Mexican accent had experienced a deep sadness. She occasionally noticed him lost in thought as though his body were on the island and his heart somewhere else. And there was his son, Lisandro, an eight-year-old miniature of his charming father, but neither of them ever spoke of Lisandro's mother.

Elise gestured to the expansive gardens. "Everything is thriving under your skilled touch, Antonio."

He tipped his hat, accepting the compliment. "You are looking for a bouquet or a blossom?"

"Today a blossom."

"For your paint or your hair?"

"My hair."

He studied her appearance. "Purple." He led her to a cluster of bright blooms.

"How is Lisandro?" She plucked a violet passionflower.

Antonio beamed. "Brother Ned said he is a smart student."

"Like his father, I'm certain."

He stamped a shovel into the sandy soil. "If my son were like his papa, Brother Ned would not be so pleased."

Elise pretended to be shocked. "Surely, Antonio, you were a model scholar."

He put a finger to his lips. "It is our secret. Don't tell Lisandro, or he may get ideas to follow in his papa's wild footsteps."

"Your secret is safe with me." She lowered her voice. "Until I need material for blackmail." She wove the flower stem through the twist of hair near her face as a black Mercedes came up the drive and parked. Waving at the driver, Elise was about to go meet him when Antonio called to her.

"Miss Elise." The gardener brushed the dirt from his hands onto his pants. With a magician's flourish, he pulled a paintbrush from the back of her hair. "Yours, I believe."

She grinned. "I was looking for that."

Waving the paintbrush like a conductor's baton, Antonio welcomed the new arrival who had made his way from the drive to the gardens.

"You make the flower look pretty." Robson's Latin heritage reflected from his classic Castilian cheekbones as he held out his arm to Elise. He smelled of tangy soap and masculine cologne. "As always." Two years older than Elise's twenty-seven, Robson Carrillo nodded to Antonio with the confident manner of someone who thrives on competition and was accustomed to praise.

Elise linked her arm through his in their familiar way. "And you, Robson, look ready for the board meeting."

"Ready *for* the board? Or ready to *be* bored?" He glanced knowingly at Antonio. "Depending on the agenda and who is in charge, the meeting could go either way."

After they waved goodbye to Antonio, Robson helped Elise into his car. He started the Mercedes's throaty engine and drove into town. Robson found a rare parking spot among the picturesque and historic streets near the Christiansted Theater, and the two walked the short block to the building.

"She is such a grand and elegant dame." Elise tipped back her head to fully view the oversized structure that presided over the centuries-old city.

Robson opened the theater's front door for her. "I believe her undergarments may be in need of new elastic."

"Have you been peeking up a lady's skirt?"

"A gentleman such as I would never—"

"I can vouch for the cello player." Elise turned at the sound of the voice to see Brother Ned coming up the walk. "Remember, I take Robson's confessions."

Robson planted his hands on his hips. "What else do you not tell?"

Smile lines around the middle-aged black man's eyes deepened now with his ready grin. "Chronologically or alphabetically?"

Robson glanced at his watch.

"I know that gesture." Brother Ned fell into step beside them. "My parishioners use it when they have stopped listening to my sermons and have begun listening to their stomachs. My students use it whenever the sand and sun tug their hearts from their studies."

Inside the theater, Elise felt as if she were entering an immense seashell. Porous silence absorbed and cherished the music and rehearsed lines of concerts and stage plays, the practiced movements of graceful dancers, as well as the laughter and applause of eager audiences. Like the ocean embraced each raindrop, this magical place stored performance, sound, and memories. The three came into the ballroom where several others were already present.

"Let's begin this gathering of the Friends of the Philharmonic by taking roll." A round man with bushy eyebrows and a perpetual scowl held a pen poised over a clipboard. Trent Tucker, board president. Out of earshot, June called him Tedious Trent.

"Because he is tedious," Elise had asked, "or because he is trying on your nerves?"

June had waved away the question. "It's a toss-up."

In his monotone drone, Trent called their names. "Brother Ned?"

"Rejoicing in this day the Lord has made."

"Elise?"

"Hello, Trent."

"Robson?"

June interrupted the unnecessary roll call. "Trent, for Pete's sake, we are all here. Jacques and his wife. My husband, Karl, and me." June lifted her reading glasses from the chain around her neck and held them out. "Do you need to use these?"

"Just trying to bring some semblance of propriety to the session." Trent made a couple of marks on the clipboard and flipped the page. "Fine. If you will follow me, we'll tour the building as our first order of business."

"This is our *only* order of business." June followed Trent. "I put the agenda together."

The tour through the stately atmospheric concert hall and accompanying ballroom, conference room, dressing rooms, staging equipment, gift store, and lobby began as a delight for Elise. The theater had been her second home when she was growing up. In addition to administrative duties, her parents had spent a great deal of time rehearsing and performing here. Elise's first recollections were of falling asleep in a box of music scores while her father conducted the renowned symphony. As soon as she was able, she began playing music with her mother and father during rehearsal. Later, when she played well enough, she performed with the philharmonic.

Now, while she admired the art and exquisite design of the building's architects, Elise's mood as well as the glitter and glamour of her surroundings gradually dimmed as Trent whined on with his perpetual imitation of Winnie the Pooh's pal, Eeyore. Like the final notes of a concert, the hope in her heart faded.

According to building inspectors, there were several alarming concerns that needed to be addressed. As the list lengthened and the estimates for repairs increased, Elise stifled panic. How could she bring the theater to its former glory? Was restoring and preserving the lifetime of work her parents had poured into the community through their investment in the arts possible? She had lost her mother and father, but she was not ready to lose this last vestige of them. She refused to bury the building where they had imparted their spirits through their music.

With footsteps heavier than when they'd left, the board members filed back into the ballroom where two smartly dressed waiters were putting the finishing touches on a catered lunch.

Brother Ned inhaled the inviting aroma of salmon in a capers-and-cream sauce. "Jacques, my nose tells me you have gifted us again with your kitchen's cuisine."

The tall and gracious Frenchman pressed his wife's fingertips to his lips. "Credit for this particular specialty goes entirely to my wife, who won my heart the day she made this for me."

"Proving the way to a man's heart." Looking dapper with his carefully trimmed white beard, Karl held a chair at the large round table for his June and seated himself to her left. June patted the place beside her, and Elise dropped into the chair next to the outspoken redhead.

"I'm not sure I can eat after that depressing tour."

"Nonsense." June spread her linen napkin across her lap. "This is business, Elise."

"I'm in agreement with June." Robson sat next to Elise and the others joined them around the table.

Karl reached for an overflowing breadbasket and offered it to his wife. "Never mix business with pleasure. And eating Jacques' cooking is always a pleasure."

June chose a round, crusty roll. She opened her mouth to take a bite and froze when Brother Ned launched into table grace.

"For this food, Father, we give thanks." To Elise, the jovial Brother Ned seemed even happier when he talked to God. "And we ask that you guide this board to wise decisions regarding the care and safety of this place."

"Amen," June pronounced as she took a mouthful of the ample yeast roll.

"So what's the bottom line?" In his fifties with graying temples, Jacques was the consummate businessman as well as a dignified gentleman.

Trent thumped a stubby finger on the clipboard. "Bottom line is the board must deliver a boatload of money to execute the necessary renovations."

"What about our donors?" Jacques' deep voice, heavy with a French accent, poured over Elise's ears like the velvety coffee liquor that made his restaurant desserts famous.

The board president shook his head. "That income supports the day-to-day."

Robson finished his meal and pushed away his plate. "Perhaps the board can revisit the budget." Leaning back, he rested his arm across the back of Elise's chair.

Trent snorted. "Perhaps—if the board spent their money on the structure instead of fancy lunches?"

"Jewel by the Sea donated the meal." Jacques' tone was gentle as if instructing a child. "As always."

"Of course you did, Jacques, dear." June turned to the president. "Trent, why are you on this board?"

"Considering the stress," Trent rolled his eyes toward the ceiling, "I ask myself that every day."

June regarded him over her glasses. "And now we are asking."

"It should be obvious." Trent flipped to a page on his clipboard and turned the paper so the others could see the columns of estimated costs. "The only option this board has is to bow to the inevitable. The theater will soon be condemned. As a forward-looking group, we must accept this building is part of an era gone by."

Elise felt ill. Tedious Trent had voiced her deepest fear and tossed off the judgment as casually as if he were stating the day of the week. She swallowed back the bile that burned her throat. "There must be an alternative."

June patted her wrist. "We know how important this is to you, dear."

"Not just to me." Elise glanced around the table seeking agreement from the others.

"The pressing need," Brother Ned began, and waited until he had everyone's attention, "is to fund the necessary work to keep this majestic and historic site in good working order."

"To secure the amount necessary," Jacques interjected, "is a matter of leveraging what we have of large value."

"That's the point." Trent emphasized each word by hitting his fork on the clipboard. "We don't have anything worth this kind of money."

Elise leaned forward. "I can up my contribution as soon as the cottage rents."

Robson jerked his arm off the back of her chair. "Cottage? You're renting our cottage?"

"Our?" Elise felt herself flush.

"You didn't say anything about this."

She crossed her arms and met Robson's accusing gaze. "Nor do I need to."

"I practically grew up there." His voice raised an octave as he presented his reasoning. "The least you could do—"

"Oh, look at the time." June made a dramatic production of checking her watch. "We're due to adjourn, and I have an appointment this afternoon. Gotta run. Oh, heck, I'll take the jeep."

Elise turned to June, relieved for the change in subject. "To have your energy."

"Ah, but you do, *ma chérie*." Jacques pulled a thin cigar from his breast pocket. "Your energy overflows in your art."

"Come on, artist." June slung her purse over her shoulder. "I'll drop you off on my way."

Without a glance at Robson, Elise rose and followed June from the room. Behind her, she heard Trent bring the others back to the topic at hand. "When we meet next, I will move to raze the theater before the building becomes a hazard to the community. If this board wants to preserve the center, I suggest you present a viable plan to do so."

June pushed open the polished wood door, and they were once again in the lobby. Passing under unlit chandeliers, Elise felt the fresh air cool her cheeks. Her feet were silent on the thick carpet patterned in gold, greens, and red. The ballroom door whispered shut and she quickened her step to keep up with the purposeful June. She felt her heart pound a rhythm in her chest. *We ... don't ... have ... anything ... worth ... this ... kind ... of ... money ... We ... don't ... have ... anything ... worth ...*

Outside, June led Elise to where she had parked. Elise stared out the passenger side window as the jeep traveled through the narrow downtown Christiansted streets. Renting the cottage would bring in some dedicated income as a start toward chipping at the figure at the bottom of Trent's lofty column of necessary costs. Surrendering the cottage studio was an enormous sacrifice for her, and all Robson could think of was himself.

June's voice brought Elise back to the moment. "Am I taking you home, Elise?"

She tugged a decorative clip and the passionflower from her head. Her hair tumbled down her shoulders, and Elise felt the instant release of tension. "Drop me at the beach. I want to walk."

"And think?"

"And look for colors."

"Hmmm."

"He thinks he has some say in the cottage," Elise complained.

"Men are like that. They assume a lot."

"Nervy."

June waved a hand and her oversized bracelet jangled. "Men. Can't live with 'em. Can't live without 'em."

"Especially Karl?"

"He has his good characteristics." June sighed. "And his distractingly annoying traits."

"And you love him."

June slipped on oversized sunglasses "If you tell anyone, I will strictly deny it."

CHAPTER 8

Later that afternoon, Michael found himself in the passenger seat as a woman who looked old enough to be his mother expertly maneuvered her jeep over the narrow island roads. When she'd said her name was June on the phone, he'd expected someone slightly younger. But she had an easy way of making conversation, and Michael leaned back against the seat as she chatted about the history of the island.

"The town of Christiansted was founded in 1734. It was the Danish West Indies capital. The architectural quality and historic interest has made part of Christiansted a National Historic Site." She tucked her auburn hair behind her ear. "What about you? What's your history?"

She'd stumbled onto a topic he would not discuss. But he did want to know about this place where red hibiscus mingled with coconut palms and little black birds with yellow wings darted among the tropical plant life. "What's the basis for the island's economy?"

"The economy consists of exporting natural resources and importing in a manner of speaking." She chuckled at her own wit. "European planters made fortunes in sugarcane, molasses, and rum during the eighteenth century. The biggest moneymaker these days is tourism. Used to be what the island grew and sent out. Now it's who the island coaxes in." She adjusted her sunglasses. "What do you do for a living?"

The realtor had a knack for asking questions he didn't want to answer. Questions for which he didn't have answers. Not yet anyway. *Making it up as I go,* he had told Bryce. Once again he diverted the conversation away from himself. "What about the people of St. Croix?"

His chatty companion steered away from the coast and their jeep climbed the low rise.

"America's earliest treasury secretary, Alexander Hamilton, grew up here. His first lessons in money came as a teenage orphan handling foreign currency while Hamilton was working for a Christiansted merchant."

Michael didn't recall his school textbooks mentioning that Alexander Hamilton had been an islander before becoming a colonial revolutionary and a founding father. He was fairly certain he would have remembered that interesting tidbit.

At an intersection June turned onto another two-lane highway, exchanging a brief wave with the driver of a jeep traveling in the opposite direction. Michael noted the sign on the side of the passing vehicle read *St. Croix Adventures.* Not the first sign of commercialized tourism he'd seen since landing on the island. "Appears to be a lot to do here."

She bobbed her head. "There's a wealth of historical sites that attract outdoorsmen. Sunken ships to dive, kayaking, hiking, horseback riding. What about you? What do you like to do?"

If she asked one more "what about you" question, Michael thought he might open the door and jump out. But to deflect again would be rude. "I do a little deep sea fishing, a little surfing."

"Our waters are home to migratory fish like mahi, marlin, and the occasional sailfish." The bangles on her wrist jangled as she pointed east. "Surf season is November through March. The best waves for longboard and shortboard, windsurfing, and bodyboarding are on the east side of Salt River Bay."

After coming to the town of Christiansted, they drove past upscale shops that June described as popular with tourists and locals alike. The town's centerpiece was a large building June explained was one of only a handful of atmospheric theaters in the United States and in the world— halls with auditorium ceilings designed to give the illusion of an open sky.

The island's history seemed a safe subject for Michael, and he pursued that topic before she could ask another probing question about his life. "How long has St. Croix been an American holding?"

"The Dutch bought the island from France. After the slaves were freed in 1843, the sugar plantations declined. The United States purchased the Danish West Indies in 1917." With her right hand, she fished in her purse until she found a yellow pack of gum. "Want a stick?"

Michael shook his head.

Keeping one hand on the steering wheel, she unwrapped the gum and folded the piece into her mouth. "What about you? Have you been to the Virgin Islands before?"

At last, a question he could answer. "My first time."

Outside the town, his guide turned onto a private road. The tree-lined drive led to a sprawling home with a broad porch surrounded by well-tended gardens abundant with flowering plants and trees.

"This is a unique property. Been a private residence as long as I can remember, and I can remember as long as you are old." She glanced over and looked him up and down before returning her attention to the road.

Veering right, the jeep followed a second drive on the same property. In front of him and within view of the larger home, Michael saw the cottage. Though considerably smaller than the first house, the artistic design featured oversized windows.

"This has been home to a prominent couple." She pulled into a parking spot and turned off the engine. "They've both passed, but the family still owns the property."

Finding a set of keys in her purse, she exited the car and started toward the front door. Michael trailed behind. He spun in a slow circle, taking in the grounds around this haven on a hill. Two brown doves, purple spots like blush on their necks, cooed to one another under a manicured hedge of sea grapes. A fragrant trade wind reminded him he smelled like he needed a shower.

"Mr. Northington?"

He turned to see her standing beside the open front door.

"Are you ready to see the inside?"

He nodded and followed her into the cool interior. The cottage was roomy, neat, and inviting, smelling pleasantly of rosin, oil paint, and plumeria. The entryway led to a central room where open windows framed the Atlantic below. As Michael viewed the free and uninhibited expanse of the ocean, he felt the tension in his shoulders release and his fists unclench. June led him through the well-designed kitchen located to one side of the great room, and to the master bedroom with attached bath, a second bedroom, bath, and laundry room that occupied the opposite side.

"Each room's windows are positioned to catch the trade winds," his companion pointed out. "The wooden shutters can be opened to allow the breeze or closed against storms. Like I said before, this is not the usual rental property. Would you like to see the outside?"

He nodded, and she led him out the double doors onto the sun porch and around the section of grounds that would be his to enjoy.

"I'd like to take you to the outdoor café we passed on the way here." She checked her watch. "We can get something refreshing, and I'll answer your questions about the cottage and the area. Then if you'd like to think about it or look at other properties before making your decision …"

Her voice trailed off as Michael took in the secluded setting, the abundant view, and the welcoming cottage. He breathed in the fragrance of the garden carried on the salt breeze, and then turned to her. "I'll take it."

CHAPTER 9

As the final encore note of the Russian Rhapsody No. 1 in A Major echoed off the faux clouds in the high ceilinged Christiansted atmospheric theater, the appreciative audience responded with boisterous applause.

Seated at the center stage where she had a direct view of the animated conductor, Elise lifted her chin and perched her viola in rest position on her leg. The house lights came up and guest conductor Ava Kehl turned to face the audience and bowed. With a sweep of her music wand, she waved the orchestra to their feet and bowed again.

To Elise's left, Robson was his section's first chair. After skillfully drawing rich tones from his cello, he stood and bowed with the rest of the musicians, his hand relaxed around the neck of the tall instrument.

"Bravo!" The audience showed their enthusiasm with a standing ovation. Ava blew a kiss and bowed once more before leaving the stage. The house lights brightened, and the theater guests filed out of the auditorium while the musicians proceeded backstage to carefully pack their valuable instruments into protective cases.

Making her way through the orchestra members, Ava shook hands with each one and thanked them for playing. Elise loosened the tightly strung horsehair and packed away her bow. She turned the tuning pegs to add flex to the strings and laid her viola into the crimson interior of her case, spread the velvet covering over the instrument, and closed the lid. She pressed her fingers into the small of her back and arched backwards to relieve aching muscles. Straightening, she felt warm hands on her shoulders as Robson gently rubbed the tension collected in her neck.

"Ohh." Elise leaned into his therapeutic touch.

"This is how we do it in New York." Ava stood behind Robson, motioned to the other musicians, and began massaging his shoulders. Following the conductor's example, they formed a train, each rubbing the shoulders of the one in front.

"Just what the doctor ordered." From his tux pocket, Robson produced a bottle of aspirin and passed it down the line. "Hours of rehearsal. Hours of strenuous performance. Musicians are the unsung athletes."

"Let's form another train and go to Jewel by the Sea." Elise rolled her shoulders. "We'll celebrate Ava's return to St. Croix with something from Jacques' fine menu."

Ava nodded. "Seaside dining is the perfect coda, a worthy encore to the best concert I've had the opportunity to conduct."

Robson indicated the milling musicians. "Courtesy of the best music makers the islands have to offer."

Under a clear night sky dotted with bright stars, the lights of Jewel by the Sea were mirrored in the serene waters of the bay. Still dressed in formal black and exuberant with after-performance adrenalin, a dozen members of the orchestra arrived at the resort restaurant. The efficient staff quickly pushed together several tables near the large windows overlooking the night ocean.

Jacques bowed slightly as a greeting to his guests, and then took Ava's hand in both of his. "Having one of our own here on the island is wonderful. Your performance was stellar."

Ava blushed. "I am honored that you attended, Jacques."

He signaled to his wait staff. "On such an occasion allow me to introduce you to our new signature wine."

"Only if you'll join us." Elise moved her chair to allow for another seat at the table.

Jacques gave instructions to a waiter, who placed an additional chair between the two ladies. While orders were taken, the restaurant owner expertly uncorked a bottle of wine. "Ava, thank you for substituting for our conductor on such short notice."

"I wouldn't have missed the opportunity." Ava accepted a long-stemmed glass from Jacques and swirled the contents to inhale the full bouquet. She took a sip and closed her eyes.

Jacques waited patiently for her appraisal.

Finally, Ava swallowed and tapped her glass against the bottle Jacques still held in his hand. "A superior wine."

"As good as those in your big city up north?" Jacques filled her glass halfway.

"Better."

"I believe tonight's concert was better than anything on Broadway." Jacques poured for the others at the table and lifted his glass in salute. "To Ava, our guest conductor."

"To Ava," the others toasted.

"Guest *assistant* conductor," Ava corrected.

Robson rested his arm across the back of Ava's chair. "Surely only temporarily."

Ava shook her head. "Conducting is a man's world."

"But you have prepared for this all your life," the cello player insisted.

The conversation was interrupted as waiters delivered steaming plates with a variety of selections before the hungry musicians. "Nevertheless," Ava forked a buttery scallop, "there is a glass wall for women that has not been penetrated in this industry."

"Papa saw ability in you." Elise clicked her glass to Ava's. "Not gender."

"Exactly my point." Robson looked from Elise to Ava. "Elise's father was world-renown as a conductor, and he duplicated himself in you."

Several at the table agreed with Robson and the conversation continued around the possibility of a woman serving as conductor.

"And you, ma chérie." Jacques turned to Elise. "I see in you an answer to the board's financial concerns regarding our beloved theater."

"Me?" Elise wondered if she dare hope for a solution. "I've been awake at night trying to figure a way but the possibility seems as impossible as Ava becoming the world's first female conductor."

"Ava's time will come—such talent speaks for itself." Jacques poured wine into Elise's glass. "And your talents may provide the needed renovations."

"How?" Elise was torn between excitement that a solution could be in reach, and fear that she was pivotal to the plan's success.

Jacques indicated the guests around the table. "We will talk business another time, but I have thought about leveraging what we have of most value to bring in the funds for the theater."

After the late dinner, the well-fed musicians left large tips and bid farewell to Jacques and his efficient staff.

"Home then?" Robson nodded in the direction of the parking lot.

Elise paused. "Not yet. Let's walk on the beach."

A patio was set for outdoor dining on the seaside of the restaurant. Tonight a couple sat close together, their wedding rings bright in the candlelight at their table. Perhaps honeymooners. Several wide steps led down to the deck skirting a lighted freeform pool that gleamed clear and sapphire blue. A waist-high wall of black volcanic rock separated the pool from the sea and Elise trailed her fingers along the rough and porous stone.

Where the beach sand met the rock, they left their shoes and Elise raised her long skirt above her knees and tied the material in a loose knot. Their toes left shallow imprints at the water's edge as they strolled without words, each lost in private thoughts.

Robson finally broke the silence. "Are you avoiding going home tonight?"

She sighed deeply. "This will be the first time the cottage lights will be on. Not for Papa, or for Mama, or for me, or you, or Ava." She met his eyes. "A stranger will be there."

"That was not my idea—"

Her chin came up sharply, and he held up his palms in surrender. "Hear me out, Elise. I understand why you made your decision. I was just going to say that renting the cottage was not my idea of a fundraiser."

"Why not?"

"At that cottage, your father recreated himself in his students." He stepped closer to her. "Especially Ava. You. And me. The studio is a significant part of who we are."

She swallowed unsuccessfully against the lump in her throat. Blinking back tears, she gazed out at the play of moonlight on the dark water.

"We all miss your parents, Elise. Especially you." His hands were warm on her shoulders as Robson turned her to face him. "I can help you fill that hole in your life."

He pulled her close, and his arms encircled her. Elise rested her cheek against his chest. Robson smelled of the theater, of perspiration from hours of strenuous performing, of tangy cologne, and of Jacques' fine wine. Listening to the steady rhythm of his heartbeat, she allowed herself to relax against him, feeling the strong familiarity of this childhood friend and rival who probably knew her better than anyone else. They had grown up together and shared a vibrant history. A history that Elise strove to preserve. The effort began to leave her breathless. Exhausted. Now, Robson offered her a future. Would a lifetime together with Robson keep the safe and familiar world she had known from unraveling?

CHAPTER 10

The next morning, Michael ventured outside the cottage to greet the sunrise. Holding a mug of steaming black coffee, he perched on the porch rail. In minutes, the horizon above the far stretch of Atlantic Ocean began to glow. Brilliant color reached up to paint the wispy horsetail clouds first pink and then orange. Like a golden phoenix, the sun's bright orb rose out of the ocean and lit the island paradise of St. Croix.

The first day in his new home.

A white streak appeared from the right, underlining the low clouds. He stood to better take in the full view. The jet traced a straight path parallel with the horizon. The plane was too far out to hear, but the sight stirred Michael's blood.

Standing stock-still, trailing the jet with his eyes and heart, Michael was transported back to a similar sight from his childhood in the Nebraska farmland.

On a crisp Saturday, fourteen-year-old Michael had raked the musky autumn leaves in the yard. Earlier that day, his mother had declared a yard party, and now the four of them were sprucing up the outside. She was also known for frequent basement parties, garage parties, and barn parties. Mama thought big chores went faster and were more enjoyable when everyone did them together. And when the jobs were referred to as parties. Afterward, they'd celebrate their efforts and satisfactory results with hot fudge sundaes. Though no one liked the work, Michael begrudgingly admitted this was probably the best way to get the project done. At least he wasn't doing the outdoor chores by himself like a lot of other teenage boys.

Once he had the crackly leaves gathered into piles, his younger sisters, Marissa and April, scooped and spread them throughout the flower garden.

Michael could hear his mother sweeping cobwebs from the upper corners of the wide front porch. In the field next door, a tall John Deere combine harvested dry feed corn, but Michael barely paid the large machine any attention.

He heard the roar of the high-powered engines before he saw them. Focusing beyond where the sound told his eyes to look, he spotted the quick military jets. They flew in tight formation, then split and circled back the way they had come. He watched until they were out of sight, until the roar of their passing that raced to follow had died away.

"You wanna fly, son?"

Michael turned to find his mother standing beside him and watching the white trails left by the jets. Though she was relatively tall for a woman, at five-foot-ten, he'd passed her in height this year by three inches. She turned her gaze from the sky to meet his.

He shrugged and resumed raking. She put her hand on his arm. "You can, you know. If that's what you want to do."

He looked back at the empty sky. "How?"

"Let me check into it." Armed with her broom she went back to attack the porch.

The following week, they drove to the small private airport on the outskirts of the nearby town. "This is the Civil Air Patrol," she explained on the way. "The auxiliary branch of the Air Force. If you do well here, you have a good chance at the Air Force Academy. Short of that, your achievements count toward any branch of the military. The Navy also needs pilots."

"How did you find this?" Michael had never heard of the Civil Air Patrol.

"I'm a mom. Moms know stuff."

At the second weekly meeting, the CAP commander handed Michael's application form back to him. "Need your dad's signature."

Michael brought home the forms and dropped them on his bedroom dresser. The third week, when his mom hurried everyone through a spaghetti and green bean dinner so they could make the meeting, he finally said he wasn't going.

"Why not?"

"Just not."

She regarded him. "You wanna be in this or not?"

"I can't."

She picked up his empty plate, stacked it on top of hers. "Why not?"

"Something about the forms."

She carried the dishes to the kitchen. "Get them."

His mom had grown up in a broken home. As a result, she and her relatives were disconnected and estranged. Things hadn't gone much better when his mom and dad had married. When Michael's dad left, the tension in the home had left with him, but the emotional pain and the feelings of abandonment for the four of them were, at times, still suffocating. "When I married," his mom had explained, "I chose poorly."

His mother took only a nanosecond to spot the problem on the form. She picked up an ink pen and boldly signed her name where a father's signature was required. "That should take care of things." She handed him the completed form. "Now let's go."

Later that spring, a half-dozen members of the Civil Air Patrol stowed their gear in the rear and loaded themselves into the CAP's rickety passenger van. Michael suspected the white rust-pocked vehicle had been donated when it had outgrown its use for the original owners. Probably a donation and tax deduction. A senior member drove, and the commander, Major Matthews, sat shotgun.

Like an agitated hornet, Michael had awakened mad and stayed that way all morning. His mom drove him to the prearranged meeting place. Station wagons, pickups, and even one of those newly released minivans pulled up and deposited cadets and their fathers who drowsily climbed into the van and dropped onto the worn bench seats. Mentally, Michael sorted out the nicer family vehicles from the lower-income rides. "This's bloody awkward," he mumbled to no one in particular.

The weekend had been billed as a good opportunity for cadets to bring their dads for a father-son bonding time doing guy stuff. The thought made Michael sick to his stomach, and he wouldn't have come if he could have kept the information from his mom. Of course, she'd only seen the flyer with the trip details. She hadn't heard the commander tell the boys to bring along their dads. And Michael wasn't about to bring it up.

An older cadet who'd driven himself in an embarrassing excuse for a vehicle checked out the seating and swaggered to the rear bench where he squeezed himself between Michael and a father-son combo. The door closed and the van accelerated onto the road. Riding in the packed vehicle, Michael bounced like a nickel in a tin can.

Mid-morning, the driver stopped for gas at a convenience store. "This is your final opportunity to use civilized bathrooms and buy snacks," Major Matthews announced. "Be back in your seats in fifteen minutes."

Inside the convenience store, Michael watched the other cadets in a buying frenzy purchasing gummy bears, sodas, and donuts. Carefully adding the price tags in his head, he picked up beef jerky and granola bars. At the refrigerator aisle, he opened the glass door, and the cadet who had sat next to him reached in for a Gatorade.

"Thanks," the cadet acknowledged.

"Any bloody time." Michael retrieved his own bottle and followed the cadet to the checkout line where his seatmate purchased trail mix and beef jerky.

When Michael exited the store, the cadet stood outside opening his drink. Michael hadn't attempted to get to know any of the cadets, but he knew their last names from the name patches on their uniforms. This guy was B. Lassiter.

"There go Major and Little Major." Lassiter watched the commander and his son board the van. "Guess we better load up."

Two hours later, making clouds of dust, the van sped along a dirt road to a remote campsite on the backside of the reservoir that was part of an expansive national park. The cadets climbed out and filed into formation. Their dads stood aside rubbing their backs and complaining about the effects of the rough ride on their older bodies.

"Cadets, prepare for a one-mile run," the commander ordered. "Harch!"

Single-file, the group set out. A couple of dads, including Major Matthews, accompanied their sons. The rest, marshmallow-bodied, stayed behind to lounge.

Lassiter started out leading the pack and stayed there while other cadets on a sugar high sprinted ahead but quickly lost momentum. Michael—maintaining a strong, steady pace—gradually threaded his way past the others and came into step beside Lassiter.

"Looks like you've passed the root beer and donut diet crowd."

"Bloody sugar junkies," Michael growled.

When they returned, feeling stretched and breathless, there was a newcomer at camp.

"Gentlemen," Major Matthews introduced, "this is retired Lieutenant Colonel Garwood. He will be your instructor this weekend. Listen up."

His hands in parade rest behind his back, Garwood eyed the boys. Even though he was no longer active duty, he wore his training like an expensive suit. "You are training for ground team search and rescue. Planes rarely go down in easily accessible places. People get lost in remote areas. You won't do any of us any good if you can't survive without modern conveniences while searching for those who need your help. This weekend you'll learn a thing or two about living outdoors."

True to his word, Garwood taught the group to set up a base camp, use a compass, care for their feet, and take a dump in the woods. At dinner, he opened a large cardboard box and passed everyone a brown package.

"This is an MRE." Garwood held up a sample. "Military rations are designed for high performance. You're more active during field activities. You need to eat more calories and drink more fluids. Don't make us carry your sorry carcass to an emergency room."

He dumped the contents of his package consisting of several thin cardboard boxes onto the picnic table. "Eat some of each component to get a balance of nutrients. Eat the high carbohydrate items first. Save unopened snack items to eat when you're on the move."

From his 72-hour pack, Garwood pulled a nine-volt battery and a wad of steel wool. "A fire can be essential, and you don't have time to rub two sticks together. Carry these in your packs, but don't any of you numbskulls place them anywhere close to each other, or you'll be a flaming meteor on the trail."

He touched the battery to the steel wool and a fire ignited. A collective appreciative grunt went up from the cadets who were always impressed with fire, second only to explosive body sounds and anything else that blew up.

That night, several father-and-son duos bunked in pup tents. Michael spread his sleeping bag near the campfire. He was nodding off when movement roused him. In the dark, someone carried a sleeping bag from one of the larger tents to the campfire.

Michael groaned. He didn't want company. In the firelight, he watched Lassiter bed down across from him. "You bloody miss me or somethin'?"

"Don't flatter yourself. You better be quieter than the group in there." Lassiter jerked a thumb in the direction he'd just come from. "The wildlife is gonna report them for disturbin' the peace with all their burpin' and fartin'." He turned his back to Michael.

An unholy racket woke the camp in the middle of the night. Banging a flashlight against a tin plate, Garwood stood near the fire. "Rise and shine, ladies," he bellowed. "Consider this your oh-three-hundred emergency phone call. You've been activated for a search-and-rescue. You've got five minutes to get your twenty-four-hour pack and your pitiful selves ready to travel."

There was a mad scramble as unprepared cadets tried to assemble themselves and their packs and hurry into formation.

Major Matthews addressed the sleepy-eyed crew. "This is a mock training mission. An airplane black box has been hidden. You will track the signal and find the box. Our search-and-rescue plane has been deployed. Communicate with the plane that will be tracking the black box's signal from the air. As soon as the black box is located, you can go back to bed for your beauty sleep."

Cadets and their dads piled into the van. "You and you." Garwood pointed at Michael and Lassiter. "Come with me."

Inside his vehicle, Garwood handed Michael a high-powered flashlight. "You're our signalman for the plane. Lassiter, you'll man the radio. Buckle your seatbelts, boys."

The team quickly pinpointed an area. That had been the easy part. The plane flew above, and Garwood drove fast on a road parallel to the track the van had taken. They narrowed the target to a large open field. Cadets spread out and walked a pattern to cover the ground. An hour later, the black box still eluded the tired and frustrated squad of cadets.

"Can you hurry it up?" Michael overheard the search plane radio to Garwood. "This group can't find their way out of an outhouse."

"All they have to do is bloody sip coffee and fly in circles," Michael muttered to Lassiter.

"Will you bloody stop using that bloody word?" Lassiter blasted. "There are other bloody words in the bloody English language."

Michael shrugged. "It's a bloody multi-purpose word. It's a verb, an adjective, a noun, a comma, and an exclamation point."

Lassiter glanced up at the plane. "Could even be a pronoun."

Michael stood still and observed the other cadets. He watched where they walked and what they walked over. Then he went to a plastic grocery bag seemingly blown against the base of a power pole. He lifted the tattered piece of trash. There lay the black box.

The following morning, Garwood reviewed the night's mock mission and the proper packing of a twenty-four and seventy-two-hour pack. "Most civilian search-and-rescue missions hunt hangars. Some newbie pilot lands his plane too hard and unknowingly sets off the crash signal in the black box. While he's home having a barbecue and sluggin' down a beer, you'll spend several hours locating his parked plane. Every so often, someone really crashes or gets lost." Garwood held up the backpacks. "These two better be packed and ready to go at all times. When that call comes, someone needs your help, and they need that help now. Nationally, we average a hundred saved lives per year. Don't mess up."

The group broke camp and returned home in the rattling, rust-fringed van. Sometime along the drive, Michael learned that Lassiter's first name was Bryce.

Michael's mom and two sisters arrived as the group unloaded the last of the supplies. Michael shouldered his pack and hurried to the station wagon before his family got out and further embarrassed him with hugs in front of the guys. He climbed into the front passenger seat in time to see Lassiter toss his gear in the back of a dilapidated pickup.

"How was the weekend?" Michael's mom put the car in gear.

As the station wagon drove past Lassiter, Michael nodded to the cadet who nodded back.

"Better than I expected."

A lizard scurried across the porch rail, bringing Michael back to the present. The little reptile leapt onto a tree trunk. Glancing up, Michael saw the jet trails had evaporated from St. Croix's dawn sky. His coffee was cold. He poured the liquid into the mulch at the base of a yellow hibiscus. Glancing to his left, he saw he was not the only one up to watch the sun.

Outside the nearby large house stood a woman. Her back to him, she faced the sun. The morning light painted a glow around her shoulder-length blonde hair. For a long time, he watched her watching the sun until she turned and disappeared back inside the house. Soon, he heard music coming from the big house. Something grand. Something classical.

CHAPTER 11

A seductive trade wind blew from the east, keeping the humidity far below what Michael had grown up with in the Midwest. Showers came frequently, making music on the rooftops before collecting into cisterns. "We average fifty inches of rain each year. All our water must be caught in cisterns," the realtor had said. "We use it sparingly."

For the next several days, Michael explored. Frederiksted and Christiansted were the two cities that anchored St. Croix, a French word for The Cross. Throughout the island's two waterfront towns, distinctly European eighteenth-century architecture reflected a period of history when seven flags representing seven ruling nations—Spanish, Dutch, British, French, Knights of Malta, Danish, and American—flew at different times. Michael estimated the population was an equal division of whites and blacks. Natives of the island called themselves Crucians, often spelled Cruzan, and spoke a lyrical Creole dialect consisting of English with heavy influences of Portuguese, French, Danish, and Dutch.

In Frederiksted stood the historic Friedensthal Moravian Church, the oldest of its kind under the American flag. The beach adjacent to the Frederiksted pier was littered with battered conch shells, and countless sun-bleached conches were piled to mark paths along a seaside park. Furthest west, Michael stood on Sandy Point. On the eastern side of St. Croix, he gazed out across the ocean from Point Udall. In between were long stretches of inviting beaches.

Turk's Cap and Pipe Organ cacti were predominant on the dry terrain of the east end. Throughout the coastal areas, prickly cacti mixed with tropical flowers. Rain forests populated the island's interior. Low rolling hills in the cattle country were interspersed with the ruins of a hundred historic stone sugar mills and great houses, silent reminders of busier and more productive days in the island's past.

Of particular interest to Michael was the colorful Fort Christiansvaern. Standing sentry above the Christiansted Harbor and the Caribbean Sea, the imposing, yellow-brick marvel had been built by the Danes to ward off pirates and imprison those caught plundering the island's ports. In contrast to the fort stood the nearby Christiansted Steeple Building, the first church constructed by the Danes during their colonization of the island.

After allowing himself time to become familiar with his new surroundings, Michael decided to tackle the employment issue. *Time to get a job.*

Tourism was big business in St. Croix. Mercantile shops lined picturesque streets and cobbled alleys in Christiansted. Outdoors, brown and green pods dropped from tan-tan trees littered the streets of the shopping district while merchants inside the boutiques stocked bracelets and necklaces strung from the large and shiny tan-tan seeds.

Michael considered several companies that offered boat trips, scuba diving instruction, snorkeling trips, and off-road three-wheel adventures. He liked the look of one of these—St. Croix Adventures.

The captain was readying his boat in the Christiansted harbor early one morning when Michael approached. "Today's weather is eighty-eight degrees, sunny, with ten percent chance of rain," the captain reported as he wound a coil of rope.

"An ideal day for a tour to Buck Island."

The captain laughed. "It's always an ideal day. That's the weather forecast every day on St. Croix. Except during December when we can get Christmas winds."

Michael guessed the seaman was around fifty years old. His swim trunks doubled as shorts with a tropical print shirt buttoned above. Island work uniforms sure made military dress blues appear stiff and formal. Barefoot aboard his boat, the jovial man wore a Chicago Cubs ball cap to protect his balding head. Tanned from being outdoors year around, he had intelligent eyes that quickly weighed the measure of a man.

"Wouldn't mind a tour to Buck Island," Michael countered.

"Most beautiful snorkeling and pristine beach on the planet."

"St. Croix Adventures offers day trips to Buck Island, snorkeling, jet ski rentals …"

The captain tossed the circle of rope onto the deck. "And offshore scuba trips from that vessel." He inclined his head in the direction of a second, smaller boat anchored nearby. "And scuba diving from the beach at Cane Bay."

"Are you looking for a scuba instructor and guide?"

The captain put his hands on his hips and regarded Michael. "Military trained?"

Michael nodded.

"Thought so. Always the same dang haircut."

Self-consciously Michael ran a hand through his dark hair. He'd been letting it grow.

"I might be in the market if I like what I see. The name's Jerry." He extended his hand. "Jerry Todd."

Michael gripped the older man's strong hand. "Michael Northington."

"Come aboard," the captain invited. "We'll cruise over to the Dive Shack at Cane Bay."

Jerry maintained a respectful speed, barely tossing a wake within the harbor buoys. They motored past commercial boats and around the marked-off play area for jet-ski riders.

Passing three waterside hotels. Jerry pointed to several rows of boats tied to docks. "That's where the water babies live."

"Water babies?"

"People who live on their boats. A suburban water neighborhood."

A short cruise away, Jerry steered inland and anchored in the shallow water of Cane Bay. The two hiked up the serene beach, deep in white sand and shaded by mature palm trees. A couple of well-kept homes were visible to the east, Jerry's Dive Shop sat across the narrow coastal road at the center of the U-shaped bay, and a small bar and grill with a thatched roof occupied a sandy patch on the west end. Like most beachfront eateries, the top half of the walls were raised and latched in place by a long drop hook. Customers at the open-air restaurant ate burgers and seafood under the shaded protection of the extended roof.

"Best french fries on the island." Jerry held his hands apart to indicate a generous measurement. "Piled hot and high."

Inside, the Dive Shop was divided into two sections. Manned by a surfer transplanted from Hawaii, whom Jerry introduced as Makani, the front of the building was a store with select merchandise for divers. Michael noted the quality name brands. Rental gear was arranged and stored in the back half next to an office. Lined with wide benches, a broad porch ran the length of the low wooden building where locals congregated to drink beer and eat french fries while sharing news, and tourists sat to pull on wet suits and strap on their tanks.

"Pick what you want." Jack indicated the rental gear. From the office, he shouldered his own dive gear and walked to the porch.

With a practiced eye, Michael selected a short wetsuit. Not a fan of sea urchin quills, he added dive shoes and gloves.

Outside on the porch, Jerry and Michael suited up, hoisted their heavy tanks, and retraced their path back across the narrow road and down the beach to the boat. Jerry trolled out to deeper water and shut off the motor. From a supply container, he passed Michael a dive light and tucked a second one into his belt next to his dive knife.

Michael glanced down at the clear water and estimated he could see thirty feet below. "A dive light?"

Jerry nodded. "You'll need one where we're going."

Michael surveyed the clear blue water stretching as far as he could see.

"We're diving the wall," Jerry explained. "A mile straight down. Gets pretty dark pretty quick."

Michael secured the dive light next to his own dive knife. Equipped with tanks, regulators, and masks, the two dropped over the side of the boat.

The water was comfortably warm, nurturing colorful coral gardens. Bright fish leisurely went about their lives, keeping a wary eye on the approaching divers. Jerry led the way to a hollow in the rocks and coral. A young sea turtle dozed in the secluded spot while an eel peered at the newcomers from the protection of his rock den. Jerry swam to the bottom, about thirty feet below the boat, and picked up a large conch shell the size of the sea captain's head. He handed the superb specimen to Michael, who ran an appreciative hand across the beautiful surface and then turned the shell over to view the firm muscle of the mature creature inside.

Michael replaced the conch and turned to see a full-grown sea turtle cruise past. With an efficient kick, Jerry paced the turtle and reached for the top of his shell. The two swam on together like an underwater waltz before the hitchhiker released his hold and circled back to Michael while the turtle continued to swim on.

The divers swam north to a steep sand chute. Jerry aimed his flashlight ahead and descended. Michael flicked on his own dive light and followed.

Plate coral covered one side and large patches of elephant ear sponge occupied the other. At the end of the sharp drop was a natural doorway in the rock that Jerry easily slipped through. On the far side of the opening, both men turned off their lights, and Michael gazed in wonder at the rich expanse of deep blue.

Jerry glanced back, and seeing that his dive buddy was close, he paddled through the gentle current to a velvet cerulean opening. Once again following the older man's flashlight beam, Michael smoothly shot down this passageway like autumn cider through a funnel. He felt their speed and depth rapidly increase until the two swimmers emerged into the ocean and Michael looked at his depth gauge. One hundred feet.

At his side, Jerry pointed to the vertical wall they had just come through. From east to west, the majestic face stretched as far as Michael could see. As they swam west, he saw the wall was textured with spur and groove formations carved by the ocean's powerful and constant surge. Sand-chute doorways marked the wall nearly every thirty yards. Between the chutes, overgrown plate corals resembled petrified waterfalls tumbling down the abrupt precipice of this magnificent natural underwater formation to the abyss below.

Michael pointed down and used sign language to ask Jerry how deep. The older man shrugged and signaled about three thousand feet.

Jerry held his position, allowing Michael to admire the drama of the unique seascape. A pair of graceful french angelfish glided by a tiger tail sea cucumber in this silent wonderland where the only sound Michael could hear was his own even breathing. Dropping lower, the wall became a continuous surface no longer broken by openings. Intrepid wire corals grew straight out from the wall's exterior, balanced above the emptiness beneath. Unaffected by unique vistas, fish swam by, occasionally flitting to the wall to nibble.

Too soon, Jerry tapped his air gauge and pointed at the surface. Michael gave him the international okay sign, and the older man guided them toward the nearest sand chute. This passage was narrower, and with the bulky tanks strapped on their backs, the divers barely passed through the winding passage that dissected the reef. Bright yellow star-encrusted sponges lined smaller passages that branched off this channel in both directions. Passing the last porthole, Michael saw a porcupine fish gamely watch him go by much like a pirate guarding his cave of hidden treasure.

Then, they were back in the brilliant sunshine above the wall. Swimming east, they passed through a coral garden where schools of bright tinfoil barbs darted by a lone blue parrotfish. Sea urchin clusters covered rocks near fire coral. Something caught Michael's eye, and he swam over to get a better look. Half-hidden in the sand next to an aged brain coral specimen was a metal cylinder. Michael brushed away the sand. Jerry joined him and they uncovered an object six feet long and two feet in diameter. Curious, Michael ran his hand down the length and tried to lift it, but the man-made device was too heavy.

Once more, Jerry tapped the air gauge and pointed to the surface. Michael nodded, took a look around to mentally mark this spot and followed Jerry back to the boat. Surfacing, Michael spit out his regulator and pulled off his facemask. Jerry did the same, slid off his flippers, and climbed the ladder hanging from the back of the boat.

"That last patch," Jerry said, stowing his flippers and gloves, "is a good spot for training new divers. We also use it for night dives."

Michael swung himself into the boat that gently rocked under their weight. "What was that metal thing?"

"Sonobuoy."

"I've seen 'em." Michael held his hands close to indicate a length. "They're closer to four inches wide, not two feet."

"Modern ones." Jerry stored his tanks and opened a cooler. He tossed a juice bottle to Michael. "That one's from World War II."

Michael whistled through his teeth.

"Had a guy spend a summer diving with me to find those." Jerry peeled off his wetsuit. "He said when he was in the war he spit 'em out through a hole on the side of a P-3 Orion four-engine turboprop. An array uncoiled and hung down in the water for six hours. Then some dissolvable part ..." He paused, searching for a word.

"Dissolved," Michael offered the obvious.

"Dissolved, yes, and seawater flooded the compartment, and they sank."

"Why here?" Michael shook his head. "No German U-boats would waste their time near the island with bigger and better targets in the north."

Jerry swallowed the last of his drink. "This was the perfect place for the military to do deep-water testing close to shore."

"Did your friend find any of his buoys?"

"We salvaged one." Jerry smiled at the memory. "He was pretty happy with it, kinda like finding an old friend."

Michael finished his drink. "A tad big to take back as luggage on a plane."

Jerry secured the anchor. "Went to a museum."

Michael looked out to sea where they had just been. "That one would be valuable to someone."

Jerry grunted and started the motor.

CHAPTER 12

Perched on a stool in the living room, Elise yawned. She didn't sleep well these days. Though the board of directors for the theater and orchestra had a number of members on the roster, she felt certain she was the only one who cared deeply about the fate of the historic and cultural building.

Renting the cottage—hard as it was on her heart—delivered a tidy monthly sum that went directly to the refurbishment fund. She'd thought that would be the solution. Maybe even a heroic sacrifice. But she had been naïve. The board meeting that included the tour of the inspector's findings had showcased a far larger list of necessary repairs. The aging atmospheric structure required more than the cottage rent provided.

From the stereo, the *Brandenberg Concertos* by Johann Sebastian Bach filled the great room. She recalled her father telling her this collection of six instrumental works was widely considered the best music of the Baroque era. Viola in rest position on her leg, Elise penciled notes on the score spread across the extended music stand, but her thoughts kept returning to the problem of the theater. After all, she was practicing for an upcoming performance with the symphony.

The music transitioned to the second movement—this section featured the most difficult part in the entire repertoire for the trumpet. While the wind instrument was center stage, Elise decided now was a good time for the viola to take a break. She sighed and dropped the pencil onto the music stand. Maybe some fresh air would help her focus on rehearsing.

She walked outside and plucked a star fruit from a young carambola tree. Biting into the yellow skin, she chewed in time to the concerto music that could be heard outside. Glancing across the gardens, she considered the cottage. Elise had not met the renter, and he seemed to not be home now. More than merely going about her normal life, she had purposely avoided him. If she didn't like the newcomer, she wasn't ready to know that yet. She would be disappointed to have someone distasteful living in the studio where she had created art with her mother and father. Where rich memories with childhood friends still breathed.

Maybe Robson did have a say—albeit a small one—in her decision pertaining to the cottage. For a moment, she wondered what he would have said if she had discussed the idea of renting the cottage with him as a means of providing for the theater. Would Robson have been as adamantly against the thought as he had been at the board meeting lunch if they had calmly weighed the pros and cons together in the beginning? Had Robson objected to the renting of the studio or to being surprised by the news?

Elise turned her thoughts back to the renter. She had trusted June to connect with someone who would value the integrity of the intrepid little place that consistently remade itself to suit the developing talents of her parents and their students. But how much can a realtor discover about a person's core? What if the renter wasn't noble and honorable like her father had been? She shook her head to clear the fears. If her decision hadn't been a good one, she didn't want to know. Not yet.

The phone rang, pulling her from gray feelings of isolation. Back inside the house, she picked up the receiver.

"Elise."

"Jacques, *Chérie.*" She turned down the volume on Bach to better hear the phone conversation.

"I have been working on the details about what the Friends of the Philharmonic may leverage," Jacques replied. "Can you take a break from your work and come to Jewel by the Sea?"

CHAPTER 13

Several weeks later, Michael completed his work at St. Croix Adventures early and went home to change clothes and go for a run. Near the bottom of the drive, Antonio, the gardener who stopped in twice each week to tend the yard, turned the soil at the base of an orange crepe tree. A boy worked beside him.

"*Buenos dias*, Señor Michael."

"Hey, Antonio." Michael looked at the boy who had come to stand next to the gardener. The boy was handsome and bore a striking resemblance to Antonio. "Who's your helper?"

Antonio put a hand affectionately on the boy's shoulder. "This is my son, Lisandro."

Michael put out his hand for the young boy to shake. "Pleased to meet you, Lisandro. Looks like you're in business with your father."

The boy stood proud. "We're partners."

Michael thought of his partner, Bryce.

Just then, a shiny Mercedes came up the drive. The three watched the car park in front of the house. The driver, looking sharp in a tuxedo, strode to the front door. Moments later, he escorted a lovely woman in an evening dress the hue of the ocean to his car. He held open the passenger door while she gracefully collected her skirt and got inside. He took his place in the driver's seat and the sleek car motored by.

"Miss Elise is going out," Antonio said.

"She sure is pretty," Lisandro added.

Hours earlier, Michael had seen the same tall and slender blonde in the garden. Her hair in a ponytail, she had worn a paint-splattered apron over a summer dress as she collected flowers along the garden pathways of crushed seashells. If she noticed him watching her, she gave no indication.

"A private, prominent family," the properties management woman had said, describing the owners of the cottage Michael now rented. Presently, he felt rather private himself. As the weeks unfolded, the two neighbors had respected each other's solitude.

Michael said goodbye to the father-and-son team and set off running again. He hadn't gone far when he heard the sound of a vehicle downshift and turn onto the road behind him. The engine whined, and a car pulled up next to the huffing Michael. Strains of AC/DC's "Back in Black" played from the radio.

"Wanna ride?" A familiar voice called.

Grinning, Michael placed a hand on the door and vaulted into the passenger seat of the red convertible. "Nice wheels."

"Practicing being rich," Bryce explained. "Where to?"

Michael pointed, and Bryce revved the engine and popped the clutch.

Inside the cottage, Michael fished in the fridge for two cold beers. He tossed one to Bryce. "Been chasing the sunrise?"

"I knew you'd miss it."

Michael twisted the top off his bottle. "What's kept you busy?"

Bryce opened his own beer. "Some pilot got caught behind the lines so we snuck 'em out."

"And you snuck over here?"

Bryce winked. "Somethin' like that."

Michael led the way to the chairs on the porch. They sat outside and watched the sun paint the ocean gold as it disappeared below the horizon.

"The sun's going to spend the night on the other side of the world." Michael downed the last of his beer. "That's what my mom used to tell me."

Bryce laced his fingers behind his neck and studied the emerging stars. "You sure found yourself a spot to recharge."

Michael fetched a second beer for each of them from the refrigerator and a package from the cupboard. "Your batteries low?"

"Hadn't thought so 'til I got here." Bryce surveyed the scenery and then his gaze rested on the house. "Tell me about the neighborhood."

"Haven't met." Michael tossed a package of beef jerky to Bryce. "Some comings and goings. Mostly quiet, though I hear music."

Bryce twisted the top from the bottle Michael handed him. "I passed a nice-looking couple in a nice-looking Mercedes on the road."

"She lives there." Michael talked around a mouthful of jerky. "They occasionally go out."

Bryce put his feet on a chair. "You could use a woman in your life, mate."

"Funny coming from you. What I could use is something to eat." Michael stood. "I'll take a quick shower, and after, there's a great restaurant you can treat me to."

After a dinner of mahi-mahi, the two friends walked along the Christiansted harbor. The night air was pleasant. Michael noticed the Mercedes he'd seen earlier park in the harbor parking lot. The driver— still in his tux— made his way to a sleek sailboat, climbed aboard, and disappeared into the cabin. In a moment, lights came on inside, painting small squares of brightness on the water. The name on the boat read *Day Dream*. Jerry had called the residents who lived on their boats *water babies*.

Bryce appreciatively eyed Fort Christiansvaern as they walked a leisurely circle around the historic site. Tourists and locals crossed the grassy public area, coming and going from hotels and nightspots. Dance music drifted from a hotel plaza over the harbor water that glimmered black and shiny like obsidian.

"What do folks do around here for excitement?"

A nearby local answered Bryce's question. "We go to the crab races, *mon*."

Bryce and Michael looked over at the eavesdropper, who was keeping pace on his way to somewhere.

"Crab races?" Bryce echoed.

"You're new to the island." With brown eyes and an easy smile, the medium-built black man spoke with a lyrical Creole accent. He stuck out his hand to Bryce and Michael. "I'm Ned. Native to the island."

"Pleased to meet you," Michael gripped Ned's hand.

"Come along," Ned invited. "I'll take you to the races."

Bryce grinned at Michael. "Dinner and a show."

They fell into step with the energetic stranger and wove their way through the picturesque Christiansted streets until they reached an open-air pub on the pier.

A grubby homeless woman, her cart parked to the side and full of scrounged random belongings, led them to a small table under an expansive umbrella.

"How are you, Fran?" From his pocket Ned produced a couple of dollar bills and placed them in her eager, outstretched hand.

"Workin', as you can see." She gave him a toothless grin and greedily stuffed the money in her pocket.

As soon as Fran had gone to look for more customers, a waiter appeared, and Ned ordered a round of the restaurant's raspberry iced tea. It arrived in tall, frosty glasses and made Michael suck in his cheeks with the first large gulp.

"Not sweet tea," he warned Bryce.

Amused, Ned watched Bryce stir several packets of sugar into his glass.

Michael glanced around. "Where's the crab races?"

"Patience, my son. You're on island time," Ned reminded.

When their iced tea was nearly gone, more people began to assemble at the pub. Tourists with excited children made up the majority of the group. Michael recognized some locals, shop owners just off work, and several couples who laughed often and held hands. Honeymooners, Michael guessed. The chairs around the tables were quickly taken, and newcomers stood about with iced drinks in hand. Two busy waiters served glasses of beer, lemonade, and baskets heaped with cheesy nacho chips.

A commotion erupted when a man and woman arrived, jauntily pushing a handcart piled with two large plastic tubs and topped with a five-gallon bucket.

"Danny! Becky!" The pub owner stepped out from behind the bar, wiping his hands on his wrinkled white apron. He waved for the area in the center of the establishment to be cleared. Chairs scraped and tables were dragged to the outer edges.

Making their way to the space carved out for them, Danny and Becky exchanged greetings with those they knew and shook hands with new acquaintances. Ned confided to Michael and Bryce that Danny was an islander as well, though he had grown up in Cuba. Becky had come to St. Croix on vacation and never returned to the mainland.

Passing their table, Danny stopped and feigned exaggerated surprise at the sight of Ned. "Three times this week. I pray this penchant for gambling isn't an addiction for you."

"If it is, I'll see you in confession tomorrow," Ned countered. "Today I brought friends who want to know what locals do for entertainment."

"Besides drink rum, lay in the sun, and love a beautiful woman?" Danny proudly hooked a thumb in Becky's direction.

"They're new to the island," Ned explained. "I merely took pity on their lost souls."

Surveying the crowd, Danny beckoned a young boy to the center. Turning to his father, the boy got a nod, and bounded to Danny.

"This is the most important job," the Cuban told the boy. From his pocket, Danny produced a three-foot length of rope with a loop at each end. The boy slipped the larger loop around his ankle. Danny inserted a fat stick of sidewalk chalk in the smaller loop at the opposite end of the rope. With the boy's foot firmly planted at the center of the cement floor, Danny pulled the rope taut and walked around the boy, tracing a chalk circle on the ground with the boy in the middle.

"In return for your expert help, you may choose your crab first." Danny sent his young assistant to Becky, who was seated off to the side and in front of the now open plastic bins. She balanced a clipboard on her knee with a black marker poised above.

"Come on. Before all the fast ones get taken." Ned stood and herded Michael and Bryce to the line forming quickly behind the boy. "Just do what I do." When he came to Becky, Ned chose an active candidate from the box and gave the crustacean to her.

"There's no discount for being a regular," she teased.

"How about one for bringing new business?" He nodded toward Michael and Bryce. "These are on me."

"You're a big spender, all right," she agreed. "At two bucks per bet, you owe me six dollars for you and your friends."

When his turn came, Bryce considered the many hermit crabs busily crawling about the plastic cage but going nowhere fast. He selected a likely racer, and set the crab on Becky's clipboard.

"Name."

"Bryce."

"Crab's name?"

"We've not been introduced."

"Pick a name for your hot rod," she instructed, "so you can claim your prize if you win."

"Rover," Bryce declared.

Becky recorded the name of the crab and his optimistic gambler on her clipboard. Next, she penned the name of the crab on masking tape and stuck it to the crab's shell before depositing Rover into the adjacent plastic bin with the other hermit crabs already selected for the upcoming race.

"Lightning." Michael handed his racing contestant to Becky. She taped the name on the crab's shell, set him in the bucket, and looked to the next person in line.

Ned rubbed his hands together in anticipation. "Now, we find a good place to watch."

Soon everyone had chosen a crab. Some had wagered on several. Noisy with expectation, the spectators jockeyed around the circle for the best vantage place to watch the main event.

Danny carried the bucket of crabs to the center of the circle. "Is everybody ready?"

The audience cheered.

"Are you sure?"

They cheered louder. Ned hooted the loudest. Gently, Danny turned the bucket upside down in the center of the racing circle and blew the traditional Kentucky Derby theme on his kazoo. With the flare of a magician pulling a tablecloth from under a stack of breakables, Danny lifted the bucket that corralled the crabs.

The crowd went wild as the crabs sped off in every direction.

"Go, Rover," Bryce yelled.

"Faster, Flash," Ned instructed.

Crabs scrambled across the swept floor. Those who had money riding on the small racers yelled as if their volume would guarantee a winner.

"Run, run!" The boy who had helped draw the circle called to his crab through cupped hands.

A petite woman with a large voice on the far side of the circle bounced on tiptoes. "Move your little arse!"

Too soon, a spunky specimen had crossed the finish line, quickly followed by runners-up. Danny scooped up these fastest crawlers and called their names to Becky, who wrote their places on her clipboard.

After twenty crabs had crossed the line to the winners' circle, and their names had been recorded, Danny and Becky collected the pokey contestants and deposited them into the bucket with their faster counterparts. When all the crabs were accounted for, Danny returned to the center of the chalk circle.

Clipboard in hand, he read the names of the winners while a smiling Becky handed out prizes donated by island merchants. Michael recognized two trips to Buck Island and a jet-ski rental donated by Jerry. Good for business, Michael concluded, as exuberant tourists collected the vouchers.

Rover was good for 80-proof rum from the Cruzan Rum distillery. "Manufactured right here on St. Croix." Danny handed the golden bottle to Bryce.

"Ned, you won two tickets to the St. Croix Theater for the event of your choice." Danny regarded the smiling black man. "You seem to win something every time. You must know someone."

The locals laughed at this. "Someone indeed." Ned collected his prize. In the center of the crowd, tickets in hand, Ned faced the large group. "And to all of you, I invite you to join us this weekend at St. Elizabeth's. I promise the message will be good."

"You just can't resist a crowd, can you?" Danny ribbed. "Well done, Brother Ned. Well done."

Bryce opened his bottle. He offered first to pour into Ned's half-empty glass. "Father, is it?"

Ned nodded and held his raspberry iced tea under the bottle while Bryce splashed the rum into the glass. Next, Bryce tipped some of the contents into Michael's glass, and then his own. When he offered the bottle to the adjacent table, several fellow gamblers accepted a topper for their drink. The bottle made the rounds and returned to Bryce as Becky and Danny joined them at their table.

"This, my new friends," Ned spread his arms, "is what islanders do for fun."

CHAPTER 14

Something niggled at her. Elise stepped back and critiqued her work. She liked the piece, but was it good enough? Could this extra-large landscape bring in the funds necessary to refurbish the theater?

The idea belonged to Jacques. Drawing on Elise's growing popularity as an artist, the businessman had proposed she create a sensational painting for auction. "To secure the amount necessary," Jacques explained, "is a matter of leveraging what we have of large value. I see in you an answer to the board's financial concerns regarding our beloved theater."

There was something intimate about this first painting done in her childhood home rather than in the cottage studio she had shared with her parents. The piece was a coming-of-age work. No longer merely the daughter of her illustrious parents, she was a property holder, landlord, part-time musician, and full-time artist. She studied the unique colors, carefully created, mixed, applied, and blended. An island sunrise was common subject matter, but even to her critical eye, this canvas appeared exceptional. The work was a fusion of her father's enthusiasm to interpret the heart and her mother's delight in hues to fashion a soul-nurturing setting. A place. An environment.

To think a piece of art she created could be a vital aspect to preserving the legacy of her parents was an intriguing plan—and a great deal of pressure. Her painting would be the featured piece at a grand auction hosted by Jewel by the Sea. Marketing beyond the confines of the island, the resort owner introduced the upcoming art opportunity to select guests that stayed at Jewel by the Sea and sent invitations to art galleries, dealers, and collectors around the globe.

If no one valued her talents, she would feel humiliated and mortified that she could not provide for the theater. Suddenly, she felt that the ability of the historic theater to continue providing excellent music and imaginative performances rested squarely on her shoulders.

Carefully grasping the edges of the oversized picture, Elise moved the completed painting to the drying stand. Oils took months to dry. For the painted images to be completely safe from marring required a full year. Tipping her head, first one way and then the other, she felt the tight muscles release. Next, she set a fresh, clean canvas on her easel. She mixed the mango color of the sunrise over the ocean and began a fresh work.

CHAPTER 15

The next day, Michael and Bryce ran on the beach and swam in the ocean. After wading onto the shore, they collapsed on the sand. "There was a time I hated the ocean," Bryce confided.

"You didn't hate the ocean." Michael propped himself up on both elbows. "You hated the proctors ordering endless butterfly kicks on the beach with the waves crashing over us."

"And I thought I hated the inflatable boat-surf passage." Bryce rolled onto one elbow and looked out at the horizon. "Unwieldy inflatable boats. A crew of miscreants. Countless push-ups in sandy, soaking wet BDUs until we looked like Christmas sugar cookies."

Michael grinned. "They can kill you, but they can't eat you. We passed Superman School just so we could enroll in the Pipeline."

"Scuba school, jump school, free-fall school, survival school, paramedic school, helicopter-dunker training," Bryce listed.

"Meeting the Wonderful Wizard of Wig."

"More like being introduced to him." Bryce passed one hand over another to illustrate. "We're doing crossovers, my team swimming near the bottom of the pool, the other team crossing over on the surface—"

"Instructors pouncing, pushing, kicking, punching, ripping off our masks—"

"Until at least one of us wigged out." Bryce shuddered. "Tell you what, though. None of that was any rougher than the ocean in a storm."

"Or trying to rescue a stronger guy who's panicking."

"After underwater laps in our fatigues," Bryce continued, "the instructor tied our hands behind our backs—"

"And our ankles together—"

"Tossed us in the deep end to learn how not to panic. To teach us how not to drown."

Michael shook his head. "That one son-of-a-gun instructor used to say, 'If you live, you can be a parajumper.' Some days were just about staying alive."

"Sink to the bottom, push to the surface for a breath, and relax back down. That was the only rest we got in PJ." He knocked Michael's elbow out from under him. "Longer for you since you set the record for holding your breath. Two minutes, ten seconds."

"Fifteen seconds," Michael corrected. "Two minutes and *fifteen* seconds."

Bryce's tone turned serious. "I'd stand there, arms crossed 'cuz my biceps were too tight to straighten my arms. My pecs were shaking."

Michael reached a hand to the level of his ear. "In the shower, I couldn't raise my arms high enough to soap my hair."

"They'd shout the scenario, 'You're gonna take it in the butt. You gotta pick up a pilot from the water. People are shooting at you. Maybe you'll die …'"

"So, what?" Michael mimicked. "At least you die doing something worthy."

They both were quiet with their memories. After a few minutes of silence, Bryce asked, "Did you ever think about signing the self-initiated elimination paper? They passed those out every night during Superman School." He dropped his voice an octave to imitate the orders. "Ninety percent of you who survive Superman School are tough enough to graduate Pipeline. But only ten percent of you will pass Superman School. Just sign. In an hour you can be at a strip joint eating steak and watching girls dance."

Michael remained quiet.

"Did you ever think about quitting?" Bryce repeated.

Michael sat up, his back to Bryce. "Didn't everyone? Every day?"

Watching the waves, the two were quiet while their thoughts remained in the past. Until Bryce's stomach growled.

Michael checked the position of the sun. "Must be past your eat-every-two-hours mark."

Bryce patted his middle. "Like clockwork."

Michael stood. "Let's get lunch and I'll show you around."

"I want the grand tour. Here." Bryce tossed the keys to the convertible. "Practice being rich."

Michael drove along the coast and parked at Cane Bay. At the outdoor bar and grill next to Jerry's Dive Shop, they ordered burgers, fries, and freshly squeezed lemonade.

"This is the place to snorkel or dive." Michael nodded toward the bay's calm waters.

Bryce added catsup and salt to his fries. "This island is nearly surrounded by a barrier reef. What's special about here?"

"The largest living reef in the Caribbean." Michael pointed. "There's a coral garden a hundred feet offshore. And the wall."

"The wall?" Bryce smiled his thanks to the waitress who refilled his lemonade.

"The wall starts at thirty feet and plunges over thirteen thousand feet."

Bryce whistled.

"It's the steepest wall in the world," Michael continued. "In some places, it's like looking down an elevator shaft."

"I'd like to dive that."

Michael paid their bill, leaving the money under the catsup bottle. "Tomorrow?"

Bryce shook his head as they returned to the car. "Next time. Gotta get back tomorrow."

"Next time it is." Michael put the car in gear and pulled onto the road.

CHAPTER 16

Two months later, Michael, Makani, and five students surfaced from the azure waters at Cane Bay. With Michael as their dive instructor, the dive with St. Croix Adventures had been a rewarding excursion for these first-timers. Clear skies with bright sunlight provided enhanced visibility, and there had been plenty of finger pointing as divers showed each other brain coral, schools of brilliant and curious fish, and a toothy barracuda.

As they swam toward shore, the group shared superlatives about what they had just seen and experienced. Listening to the exuberant exchange between the divers, Michael spotted two familiar figures sitting on the beach.

Michael took his time while he and Makani helped the students out of their air tanks. With the bulk of the equipment stored, he bid a short good-bye to the group and went to meet the newcomers. The two stood as Michael approached.

"Look what the tide washed in." Bryce clasped his hand warmly and pulled Michael into a backslapping embrace.

Stepping back, Michael looked at the second man.

"You're looking good, Michael." Corbin offered his hand.

Michael accepted his handshake. "I doubt you came all this way to check on my tan."

"You underestimate me," Corbin countered. "Be slow in choosin' a friend but slower in changin' him. We've got a lot of history together, my friend."

"And …?"

"And Corbin's buying lunch." Bryce tossed Michael the key to the rented convertible. "So take us to the most expensive place on the island."

Driving along the coast, Michael pointed to a small bay where a freshwater stream met the ocean. "This is the only US-owned soil where Christopher Columbus landed. That was November 14 in 1493."

"That would've been his second voyage to the New World." From his vantage place in the front passenger seat, Corbin pointed to a dolphin that lazily surfaced and blew, the sun glinting off its sleek, gray skin.

"Columbus only saw the top half," Michael continued. "Underwater, that bay borders a canyon that's three hundred feet deep. The west wall's topography is a series of mini canyons. The east wall is a hot spot for marine life, coral, sponges, and gorgonia."

In the backseat Bryce sighed. "He was a fool for leaving."

"More like lucky to get out alive." Michael turned off the highway. "The natives didn't exactly roll out the welcome mat."

"Columbus would have claimed the island for Spain," Corbin considered. "But hasn't this been a Dutch holding?"

"Columbus named the island Santa Cruz or Holy Cross. He anchored off this natural bay called Salt River." Michael motored past a quiet harbor filled with anchored boats and stopped the car where they had a view of the bay. To the north, Salt River opened to the ocean. To the south, the bay meandered inland. "Two-dozen armed men from Columbus's fleet went ashore to explore, probably looking for fresh water. Carib Indians greeted them with arrows."

"Not known for their hospitality." Bryce observed.

"Didn't play well with others." Michael agreed.

Bryce lowered his sunglasses for a better look at Michael. "All this from the guy who barely passed history. Now you sound like a tour guide."

"Part of the job. Jerry insists his scuba instructors be able to give the tourists an overview of island history." Back on the road, Michael slowed so Bryce and Corbin had a chance to view an abandoned stone tower in a field. "Sugarcane was the island's economy during the eighteenth and nineteenth centuries. Then the governor abolished slavery in the summer of 1848, and the islands never recovered economically."

"Until tourism," Bryce put in.

"And you are tourists." Michael drove into the resort parking lot and switched off the engine.

Seated at an outdoor table at Jewel by the Sea, the three ordered lunch. Corbin picked up their conversation. "Were the Carib Indians that attacked Columbus known to be hostile?"

Michael shook his head. "The island was originally home to the Taino or Arawak Indians. In the fourteen hundreds, the Carib people came over from the Guiana region at the north tip of South America. They established a system of coexistence with the Spanish on Puerto Rico until a Spanish adventurer raided St. Croix for Carib slaves."

"Adventurer?" Bryce countered. "Sounds more like exploiter."

"There's nothing new under the sun," Corbin quoted. "Methods change, and evil takes different forms, but it's still evil."

Lunch arrived, and Michael continued his narration as they ate. "To fight back, the Caribs joined efforts with the Tainos of Puerto Rico against the Spanish. The Spanish responded to the uprising with legalized extermination. A short while later, the Caribs abandoned St. Croix."

"And the Dutch moved in." Corbin took a roll from the basket of bread.

Michael held up a finger for each of the five nations. "The Dutch and English and some French Protestants. Britain and the Netherlands coexisted until the Dutch governor killed his English counterpart."

Bryce nodded knowingly. "So the English retaliated and killed the Dutch governor."

"Right. The Danish West India Company purchased St. Croix from France in 1733. The nearby islands of St. Thomas, St. John, along with St. Croix became royal Danish colonies in 1754." Michael pushed away his empty plate and eyed his former boss. "Which brings us to today. What's up, Doc?"

"What brings me to the largest of the United States Virgin Islands?" Corbin waved an arm indicating the surroundings. "It's seventeen point seven degrees north latitude, sixty-four point seven west longitude, eighty-two miles in area, anchored by two distinct towns, Frederiksted and Christiansted. Hurricane season is June first through November thirtieth, peak season being mid-August through mid-October."

"So you did your homework," Michael acknowledged. "Being prepared has always been your strong suit."

Corbin finished his iced tea, and Michael looked at Bryce. "You're enjoying this."

His old friend tipped his chair back on two legs. "Dinner and a show."

Michael turned back to Corbin. "Except you didn't do your homework on that last assignment you gave me."

Corbin's jaw tightened. "Things aren't always what they seem. You know that."

"Are you telling me her death was justified?"

Corbin shook his head. "No."

"Then you made a mistake?" Michael heard the anger in his voice.

Again, Corbin shook his head.

"Well, if you're not here to apologize, what did you come for?"

"I came to ask you—"

"No, you didn't," Michael interrupted. "I'm not doing your dirty work again."

Bryce dropped the front legs of his chair to the floor. "I think you should hear him out."

Michael glared at him. "Whose side are you on?"

"Not fair, buddy." Bryce's voice was gentle, but firm. "You know I've always had your back."

Michael studied Bryce, who gazed back levelly. At last, Michael ran a hand through his hair, stiff with Atlantic Ocean salt. "Okay."

"I'm not asking you to come back, Michael." Corbin laced his fingers over his middle. "I already know the answer to that."

Bryce watched the hostess seat a couple at an outside table and nudged Michael. "Isn't that your neighbor? The lady I saw in the Mercedes?"

Michael glanced behind him. "Yeah," he acknowledged and turned back in his seat.

Corbin leaned his elbows on the table. "I'm asking you to think about doing an occasional assignment."

Michael's chin jerked up.

"You choose the jobs you do," Corbin assured him.

"You'll freelance. So, don't give up your day job." Bryce signaled for the waitress. When she came to their table, he nodded to the other table. "The blonde lady who was just seated with that older gentleman. What is she drinking? Send over a bottle of whatever she likes."

Michael blinked and focused on Bryce. "What are you doing?"

"Being neighborly."

"On my expense account," Corbin noted.

Bryce grinned and shrugged.

The three sat quiet for a long time. Finally, Corbin broke the silence. "Look, this is a lot to think about. Why don't you two drop me at my hotel? You guys go share a bottle of whisky and chase women, or whatever you young men do. We'll talk again tomorrow."

Corbin paid the bill and left a generous tip. As they exited the restaurant, the three stopped in the lobby to view a display featuring an oversized oil painting. A placard invited art collectors to the rare opportunity of bidding on the work at an upcoming auction hosted by the resort—proceeds to benefit the home of the St. Croix Philharmonic.

Michael stepped closer to the painting. The horizon glowed above the far stretch of Atlantic Ocean. Color reached up to paint the feathery clouds pink and orange. Like a golden Icarus in his chariot, the sun's bright orb rose seemingly out of the ocean itself and lit St. Croix. In the bottom right hand corner was the artist's name.

Elise.

CHAPTER 17

"It's good, ma chérie." Jacques stepped back and rested his hands on his hips.

Elise noted his long fingers and knew she would find a way to one day include in a painting the hands of this kind friend.

Jacques studied the oil painting that rested on a gold easel and nodded. "Very good."

Jewel by the Sea displayed Elise's art in a prominent place in the cool and welcoming lobby. A small light at the top chased away shadows and illuminated the canvas. She had experimented with textures, adding thickness and dimension to the curling waves. The delicate sprinkle of gold dust brought playfulness to the lively yellow of the sun that danced on the ocean surface.

"Fine enough to tempt an investor to give us the money we need for the theater?" The weight of this gamble made her stomach flip.

"I believe so." Jacques took her elbow and steered her to the table set for their lunch. He had promised to prepare something special to celebrate the completion of the painting that had captured her attention and kept her indoors with her oils these many weeks. "I do believe so."

CHAPTER 18

After the three men left Jewel by the Sea, Michael and Bryce dropped Corbin at his Christiansted hotel.

Bryce jumped from the back into the front passenger seat.

Michael eyed his friend. "Any more surprises?"

"You mentioned the world's best scuba diving last time I was here."

Michael put the convertible in gear and returned to Cane Bay where he outfitted the two with equipment from Jerry's Dive Shack. They pulled on knee-length wetsuits, flotation vests, and rubber boots, then shrugged into the heavy air tanks. The divers slipped masks on their heads. Before grabbing fins and heading for the water, each strapped a knife to his ankle, with an MK13 day/night flare taped to the knife sheath. Once they were properly equipped, they made their way across the beach and quickly disappeared under the turquoise surf.

Dodging prickly sea urchins in the shallows, they swam into deeper water where they paddled among schools of fish and underwater gardens of brain coral. Dropping down the wall, Michael guided Bryce along the best displays of coral and sponge life. When the air in their tanks became depleted, the divers made their way back to the beach. The sun was setting as they stowed the equipment. From the clump growing next to the Dive Shack, Michael showed his friend how to break off a piece of the fleshy, spear-like aloe plant.

Avoiding the spines and pointed tip, Bryce smoothed the soothing inner gel over the back of his sunburned neck.

"Works as mosquito repellent, too." Michael surveyed the group gathering along the beach.

Someone had lit a bonfire, and people were drawn to the flame like moths to a porch light. Several pannists set up steel drums, and the trade wind carried the chromatically pitched tunes across the sand. Within minutes, a net for volleyball was in place and players in shorts and bathing suits reached for the ball that bounded off their fingers.

"Looks like a party," Bryce observed.

"Nearly every night. The locals. And tourists." Michael elbowed Bryce in the ribs. "C'mon. Let's get a sandwich, and I'll take you to the party."

At the thatched-roof café, Michael bought Reuben sandwiches made with dark pumpernickel bread stuffed with thick slices of pink corned beef, tangy sauerkraut, and melted cheese. The waitress, wearing a bikini top and shorts, who knew Michael encouraged his diving students to eat there, threw in two paper plates mounded with the café's signature hot french fries. From the small refrigerator in the office of the Dive Shack, Michael retrieved a six-pack of Coke. Stopping at the bottom drawer of Jerry's desk, he lifted out a small bottle of Cruzan rum. Satisfied to see the bottle nearly full, he tossed the rum to Bryce. The sandwiches disappeared in a couple of bites as the two made their way to the bonfire.

The Pythagorean cycle of fourths and fifths from the steel drums mingled with the crackle of the bonfire and the shouts from the volleyball players. Michael and Bryce sat in the circle of light cast from the flames. Michael popped the top of a Coke can, drank several swallows, and then filled the can to the top with rum. Bryce did the same. When a drummer came over and held out his can, Michael poured.

"They play for rum," he told Bryce as the drummer nodded his thanks.

"What about you?" Bryce watched the drummer pick up his sticks and begin a new tune. "What will you play for?"

"I'm not sure I want to play."

"You're not sure you don't want to, either." Bryce swallowed the last of his drink. He crushed the aluminum can in his fist and threw it into the bonfire. "I love camping. Burn the dishes."

Hand-in-hand, a couple in swimsuits held out their Coke cans to Michael who topped them off with the native brew. They smiled their thanks and went walking along the beach, the waves washing over their tanned bare feet.

Michael pushed his own bare feet into the sand until his toes were covered. "What do you know about all this?"

"I know there are good people who really need our help." Bryce met his gaze. "I know who I partner with best."

"So your motives are purely mercenary."

"You underestimate me." Bryce grinned. "My motives are only partly mercenary."

Michael tossed his empty can into the fire. "What do you know that you're not telling me?" He handed a new can to Bryce and opened one for himself. After the required first drink of Coke, the two topped off the beverage with the bottle from Jerry's supply.

"I know I'm leaving on a job that I don't want to do without you watching my back."

Michael shrugged. "Thought you were partnered with Wingnut."

Bryce winced. "On normal days, that's difficult. In this instance, it's disturbing."

CHAPTER 19

The following morning, Michael and Bryce went running. On the return lap along the beach, Corbin jogged down and joined them. The three of them had often trained together. "A tree is not a mast until it's hewn," Corbin would say as he ordered ever-tougher workouts. Keeping pace with Corbin reminded Michael of the day when he'd first met his boss.

On a summer afternoon ten years before, Michael's squadron had stood in formation on the base's grassy parade grounds. Under the merciless heat of the full sun, Michael felt like an egg in an iron skillet. "Hurry up and wait" was the military's motto, so they waited.

The unit commander liked everyone in alphabetical order, and that placed Bryce slightly in front of and to Michael's left. To his right, the sun gleamed off empty aluminum bleachers. The only other objects that broke up the monotony of the open field were a pathetic clump of three scraggly trees with barely ten leaves between them—too thin to cast a shadow, let alone offer any shade.

He estimated they had fried there for an hour when the commanding officer returned, a cold drink in his hand. "Your instructor for this afternoon has been delayed," the CO announced.

No kidding. Michael fought the urge to roll his eyes.

"He should arrive anytime." After finishing his soda in front of the sweltering men, the commanding officer strode over to the empty bleachers and sat.

Maintaining military bearing, Michael felt the sweat drip down his back. Somewhere behind him a man threw up. That caused the guy next to Michael to throw up. The chunky, vile-smelling vomit splashed on Michael's boot.

Chunks. I hate chunks.

Still the group stood at attention.

During the next hour, the smell of sunbaked barf filled the air. A guy in front passed out and fell to the ground. Two others threw up. Unpleasant as those events were, Michael thought the distractions at least made the wait go faster.

Then Michael saw Bryce's head move—barely perceptible, but his friend had spotted something to the left. Moving only his eyes, Michael glanced that way. Unfolding out of the wiry trees was a soldier, camouflaged to blend perfectly with his sparse environment.

He dropped from the tree without a sound and walked to the front of the unit. Michael inwardly groaned. This clown had sat frozen in a cramped position for more than two hours with virtually no cover and none of these experts in training had detected him.

The CO got up from his seat on the bleachers and met the stranger in front of the men. They shook hands.

"Ladies," the CO yelled, "this is Major Corbin MacIntyre. I think you can learn a thing or two from him."

During the past decade Michael had learned a lot from Corbin. His grandparents had emigrated from Scotland and settled in a Scottish community in the Pacific Northwest. Probably because the dank, rainy climate was the closest weather they could find to their native origins. Between them, Corbin's parents had a mere dozen years of formal education but were well read. Corbin had been the first in his family to get a college degree, a feat that made his relatives immensely proud.

"There's a world of difference between being educated and being stupid," Corbin had yelled at his men in one form or another during training, always after one of these bright stars had screwed up.

Corbin's hobby was Scottish history. From the stories he'd shared, Michael learned that Corbin was descended from a noted—or notorious, depending on whose history you read—line of fierce fighters. Even the bloodthirsty Viking conquerors steered clear of the Scots who were perpetually rough and ready from ongoing conflicts with the Norman kings of England, bitter struggles between their own clans, and surviving everlastingly bad and foggy weather. Michael figured ferocity ran in Corbin's blood. Live or die with honor was that man's motto. When he was given his own special-forces team, he had requested Michael and Bryce be part of the roster.

"I only work with people I like," Corbin had stated. "Life is too short to partner with people I don't like."

Michael didn't trust easily but he had grown to trust the Scotsman. Until Corbin betrayed that trust.

Now Corbin was back in Michael's life, invading his island retreat. Returning to the starting point where they began their run, Michael took the lead. He turned uphill, leaving the beach and the sound of the rolling waves behind. Bryce and Corbin followed as he ran through the streets of antique Christiansted, past the outdoor restaurant on the corner, and up the narrow winding road to the private drive. Rounding the corner, the three runners veered past the main house and arrived at the cottage.

Inside, Michael mopped the sweat from his face with a towel. He threw towels to the other two and pulled three chilled Gatorades from the fridge.

Corbin looked appreciatively around the cottage. "A guy could get used to this."

"A nice place to run away to," Bryce agreed.

"I wasn't running away." Michael pushed a cold bottle into Bryce's middle and handed a second to Corbin. He tuned the radio to a rock station, led the way to the back patio, and perched on the wooden rail. Bryce collapsed into a wicker chair and propped his feet in another.

Corbin sat across from his host. "Have you thought about my offer?"

Michael took a long drink before speaking. "Thought about it."

Corbin nodded. "What are your terms?"

Michael leaned forward. "I want full disclosure."

"Things have to be engineered to a fare-thee-well." Corbin set down his drink.

"I know the company line." Michael crossed his arms.

Bryce laced his fingers behind his neck as he watched the other two volley words.

"Many others are involved. Assignments arc layered." Corbin fished for the right word. "Complicated."

Michael didn't want a repeat of his last experience. "I want to know everything you know."

Corbin folded his hands across his firm abdomen. "What else?"

"I decide whether I go." Michael was aware of Guns N' Roses on the radio singing "Welcome to the Jungle." "I can turn down any assignment."

The Scotsman didn't flinch. "Anything else?"

Michael glanced at Bryce and back to Corbin. "I pick my team."

There was a long silence while Michael and Corbin regarded one another. At last the CO nodded. "A fair offer is *nae cause fur feud*." Corbin stood and extended his hand to Michael. "Or in English, no reason for an argument. We have an accord." The two men shook hands.

Michael took a chair at the table between Bryce and Corbin. "Now suppose you two tell me what is so all-fired important that you came all this way to wine and dine me out of early retirement."

CHAPTER 20

The next morning, Elise was outside clipping flowers when she saw the man who rented the cottage start out for his usual run. He was frequently outdoors, and even from a distance, she could see he spent regular time involved in physical activity. Though he didn't entertain much, he had lingered outside on the patio with two others yesterday evening. After "Don't Stop Believing" by Journey had played out, occasional laughter had carried on the gentle winds as Elise had set up her easel outdoors to better capture the changing colors of the brilliant sky.

Working on the painting now displayed at Jewel by the Sea had caused her spirit one moment to wing at the opportunity to use her art and in the next instant to plummet under waves of insecurity and doubt. With that effort complete, she allowed herself with this new painting to play with color, texture, and whimsy. Doing a lighter project proved to be therapeutic, and the easy subject matter seemed popular with art galleries that sold her work.

The new neighbor jogged past the gardens of her home, and Elise decided now was the time to officially say hello. To do anything else today would merely be rude, so she waved him over. His running shoes made a crunching sound as he followed the tabby path through an explosion of yellow and pink blooms nurtured by Antonio. A breeze ruffled his hair, now much longer than when he arrived, and she had observed him from Robson's car. As he came closer, she estimated he was a few years older than she. And taller.

"Thank you for your gift yesterday."

He frowned. "My gift?"

"The waiter at the restaurant delivered a bottle of my favorite Moscato, and said the wine was from your table. Of course, I've only seen you from a distance, but I thought the man was you. Perhaps I was mistaken."

He thought for a moment and brightened as he seemed to recall the previous day's lunch. "You're welcome."

"I trust you are comfortable in the cottage."

"That's an understatement." He inclined his head in the direction he had just come from. "It's quite a place."

She was relieved. He did have an appreciation for the setting.

They were quiet, and she fished for polite conversation. The only thing they had in common was his address. "The cottage was my father's studio," she volunteered. "After he died, I made it my own."

Michael looked from the house to the cottage. "Not a bad commute."

"My commute is even shorter since I brought my work home."

"You know what they say about bringing work home with you," he teased.

"What about you?"

"Leaving later today, actually. On business." He gazed out across the Atlantic and then his eyes came back to her. "My first trip since arriving."

"Perhaps you can take a piece of paradise with you."

He studied her upturned face, and she noticed his eyes were dark like his hair. "How?"

She pointed toward the ocean view. "Imprint the picture in your memory. Then it goes with you."

He shrugged. "I'll give it a try."

She snipped a hibiscus and added the bloom to her basket of flowers. "Well, you must have things to do before you leave. Thanks again for your kindness yesterday."

He resumed his run to whatever awaited him. Elise was already on her way back to the house when he turned and caught up to her. He held out his hand. "By the way, I'm Michael."

For the briefest moment, her hand was in his. "Elise."

CHAPTER 21

Bryce and Corbin had left the cottage yesterday evening after Michael and Corbin reached their agreement. Michael lingered on the porch, watching the sun go down and the bright stars boldly take their place in the evening sky—all the while his thoughts raced over the mission his friends had laid out. He was still mentally sorting facts and assembling a supply list the next morning when he finally met and spoke with his neighbor.

Elise. She had called him over. Looking into her blue eyes, he recognized the familiar fragrance of plumeria that had been so prominent on his first visit to the cottage. She smelled like an island flower.

Now aboard the unpressurized C-130 Hercules along with Bryce and fellow parajumpers Wingnut and Meatloaf, Michael breathed pure oxygen. Built to transport parachutists and cargo for long hours in all kinds of weather, the tanker was anything but comfortable. In turbulence, the plane bucked like a rodeo bronco.

The only light inside the plane was red. As they flew at twenty-six thousand feet, the four PJs thoroughly checked their own equipment and each other's. Preparing for a HALO—high-altitude, low-opening jump— each wore an oxygen mask, carried a fifty-pound rucksack, and had an M-16 strapped to his side.

"Two minutes to target." The pilot spoke to Michael over the radio inside his helmet. "Air speed one-twenty-five. Twenty-six thousand feet. Cloud deck below."

"I hate clouds," Meatloaf said.

"I hate power lines," Wingnut said.

"I hate power lines in clouds," Bryce put in.

Dressed in Gore-Tex jumpsuits designed for cold weather protection, the four men stood by the open door. The signal they waited for came. Serving as jumpmaster, Meatloaf gave a thumbs-up, the ready signal. Next, he pointed out the door, the signal for the team to jump.

Together, the four stepped backward off the plane and into thin, cold air—ten degrees below zero. The rush was immediate—one of the great perks of being a PJ. Free falling thousands of feet stirred butterflies in Michael's stomach that flew throughout his body. This was the ultimate high.

In the sudden quiet, he looked up at the star-studded sky that appeared much nearer at this height. Dropping a thousand feet in seconds, Michael felt like a falling star.

"Number one, okay." Bryce reported over the radio in Michael's helmet. Number two and three followed suit.

"Team leader, okay," Michael responded.

Peering through the boogie goggles that protected his eyes, Michael checked the altimeter on his wrist. Nearing five miles. He glanced around for the other men. The glow of the Cyalume ChemLight on the back of each helmet indicated their positions.

Hearing only the sound of the wind and his own breathing from the bottle of compressed air, Michael took his spot in formation. The other three fell into place, forming a circle some thirty feet across. Facing center, the four could see one another.

"Cloud deck ahead," Michael warned.

At twelve thousand feet, they slammed onto the top of a cloud. From below, these sky residents looked like friendly cotton balls and the rounded raindrops from an island rain felt refreshing. Crashing onto their pointy tops from above at one hundred twenty-five miles per hour stung like dropping onto a bed of nails, and despite his waterproof suit, Michael's skin was quickly damp. In the foggy turbulence, Michael struggled to maintain his position in the circle. Holding his bearing was vital to avoid a fatal collision with another team member.

In the dense cloud, he felt cold, disoriented, and alone. Staring below, he waited impatiently for the lights of the world to reappear. Michael checked his glowing altimeter again. The circling hand whirled toward zero. Fear jolted through his body. Instinctively, his hand reached to pull his chute. Then he caught himself. The altimeter only went to thirteen thousand. When he jumped from twenty-six thousand feet, he had to remember that the altimeter must make two rounds from thirteen thousand to zero. This was merely the halfway mark. He fought panic and the fear of hitting the earth like a bug on a windshield. The altimeter circled to thirteen thousand, and he was relieved when the count began its final cycle to zero.

"I'm free," Bryce announced. Simultaneously Michael, Wingnut, and Meatloaf dropped out of the cloud. With minimal maneuvering, the foursome reformed their inward facing circle.

The group held this formation until they reached six thousand feet.

"Break off," Meatloaf ordered.

The men turned one hundred eighty degrees away from the circle's center. Michael checked the air space around him. Certain that all was clear, he began his pull sequence. He reached to his right shoulder, grasped the steel ring, and yanked. Still he fell. He rolled his body left to break any vacuum that had formed above his back. The chute refused to open. Michael rolled to the right and tried again.

"Michael!" Bryce called through the radio.

"Workin' on it." Michael gritted out the words as he pulled a cutaway handle with his right hand and grasped the reserve ripcord with his left.

"Arch!" Bryce commanded. "Arch your back. Now!"

Michael twisted as he was told and felt the comforting jerk, swing, and reverse of his downward plunge as the chute at last flared.

"I'm good," Michael reported into his radio.

"You scared the crap out of us," Bryce admonished. "I think I wet my pants."

"Same here," Michael admitted.

"Check in," Bryce ordered.

"Jumpmaster okay," Meatloaf returned.

"Nav okay," Wingnut said. "But team leader is now below me."

"Just tell me the way home," Michael responded.

"Watch for planes or movement on the ground that says we've got company," Bryce said.

In the next few moments, Michael calmed his breathing and racing heart and focused on his surroundings.

Wingnut spoke again. "Nav's got the drop zone. Ground wind from the south."

"Team set up for landing," Meatloaf called.

Following the klicks called by Wingnut, Michael descended at half-toggle, riding the wind current like a bird. At four feet, he stalled his chute and dropped heavily to the ground. He quickly turned to watch the approach of his teammates and dodged to allow the others to come in behind him.

In quick succession, the other three regained terra firma. Shedding their gear, Wingnut and Meatloaf called in.

"Three's in."

"Nav's in."

Bryce dropped to the ground, rolled like a puppy, and was up and at Michael's side. "Sweet Mother of Moses, what was that?"

"If that's your idea of a welcome back gift," Michael groused, pulling free of the reluctant parachute, "you need to find a new place to shop."

CHAPTER 22

Elise ran her palms discreetly against the smooth linen of her skirt. She felt more anxious than she had expected.

Sitting next to her, June gently caught Elise's hand and gave a reassuring squeeze. "Relax." She spoke barely above a whisper. "All will be fine."

Elise took and held a breath. Straightening her shoulders, she slowly exhaled. She wanted to appear peaceful and confident. Her paintings had sold in galleries in several nations. She was one of the rare artists who made a living with her art. Yet Elise had strong emotions around this sale. The future of the atmospheric theater depended on this painting selling for a goodly sum.

The evening's benefit auction had begun with a reception where guests were invited to drink fine wine, sample culinary specialties from Jacques' kitchen, and peruse the exceptional items to be sold.

"Make sure everyone gets generous amounts to drink." June had instructed the waiters and waitresses. "People loosen the ties on their wallets when the wine has loosened their resolve."

Elise mingled near her painting, available to meet with potential buyers. That had been Jacques' idea. Her preference would have been to stay out of sight. The process of creating a piece of art was intense and a pouring out of her spirit through the medium. Selling her pieces involved connecting her heart to a home. But selling this painting felt like being measured, weighed, and critiqued. Would a buyer pay the amount she must have to restore the theater? Was her work worth enough?

Several items had already been auctioned. A honeymooning couple purchased gold and silver hooked bracelets from a jewelry designer on the island. Jacques' week at Jewel by the Sea created a bidding war between two travel agencies, and Jacques had the winning bid on a boutique run of rum from the Cruzan Rum factory. The oil refinery purchased a day of snorkeling at Buck Island from St. Croix Adventures for their company picnic.

Waiters kept the drinks flowing for the guests who filled Jacques' resort for the gala event. As each item came up for bid and sold, Elise felt the moment inch closer when her painting would be the center of everyone's attention.

June's warning to her had been delivered earlier. "Wear your thick skin. They'll be judging a work of art, not you."

Her friend was right. Each piece Elise created included something of the artist in the concept, color, and subject. And she released each one for sale. Today's auction wasn't about the painting, Elise mentally justified. While immensely fond of the project, she was attached to the goal. Would the sale of this painting garner the finances needed to preserve the legacy of her parents in the historic Christiansted atmospheric theater?

Robson must have read her thoughts—he slipped his arm along the back of her chair and softly squeezed her shoulder. With June on her left and Robson smelling of soap and cologne to her right, she unknotted her nervous fingers. Also at her table was Karl, along with Jacques and his serene wife. Each appeared hopeful.

The auctioneer signaled to his assistants, who carefully brought the painting on its easel to the front of the room. To Elise, the framed work embodied all of her immediate hopes and dreams. The tuxedoed auctioneer swept his arm toward the painting that now stood before the crowd, vulnerable and raw, like a reflection of her soul. "Now, ladies and gentlemen, the grand moment we've been awaiting."

CHAPTER 23

Shanghai was China's most populous city and one of the first to adopt the one-child population-control policy. The metropolis slept as Michael located the aged ambulance. From his vantage point, he watched the box-shaped vehicle pull up to a back door at the orphanage. Like many civic structures in this crowded center, the dilapidated building had enjoyed a former life as an ancestral hall or temple.

An armed guard got out of the passenger side of the ambulance and banged on the building door three times. The door opened, and several children were ushered from the building to the wide double doors at the rear of the ambulance. They disappeared inside the vehicle. After a moment, a slightly taller figure was escorted from the orphanage. The figure seemed to take stock of the guard and the ambulance and refused to move until the guard pressed his gun into her back.

Claire Taylor.

"Since when do we go after private citizens?" Michael had asked that evening on the island porch as Corbin briefed them on the mission.

"Since this one is Senator Bennett Taylor's daughter," Corbin said.

"That guy makes Ted Kennedy look like a bunged-up conservative," Bryce had put in.

"Last time I was involved with Taylor's family," Michael looked meaningfully at each of them, "I had a bad experience."

"And that's why we need to do this." Bryce paused. "You know Verity Marshall would want us to help her stepdaughter."

Now, in a commandeered garbage truck, their skin and Bryce's hair tinted to avoid suspicion, Bryce and Michael followed the ambulance to a military hospital. The ambulance parked near a nondescript door in an alleyway. Bryce maneuvered down the narrow passage and idled the noisy garbage truck between the ambulance and hospital door. While his friend ignored the irritated tirade from the ambulance driver, Michael kept his hat pulled low and carried an offensive-smelling trash can past the driver's nose to the back of the truck which was lined up parallel to the rear of the ambulance. Under the bullying of the guard, the passengers were just beginning a slow trek from the ambulance to the hospital. The alleyway door opened, and two hospital staff waved them inside.

Stamping and cursing, the ambulance driver followed Michael who shrugged, stumbled on, and bumped the trash can against the truck. The odorous contents sloshed over the top and spilled onto the man's pants and along the street. Retching, the man turned and ran from the smell, searching for something to wipe the offensive waste from his legs. Michael slung the trash can around so the toxic mix splashed on the stocky guard and the two at the door.

In that moment of chaos, while everyone held noses and scurried from the putrid odor, Bryce revved the garbage truck's engine and added a cloud of blue smoke to the mix.

Michael clamped a dirty, gloved hand over the mouth of the last figure in the group from the orphanage—the tallest one they had identified as Claire Taylor. "Shhhh," he hissed into her ear. "We're good guys."

She stopped struggling but remained tense. Slowly, he released his hold on her. "Come on," he whispered. "We're getting you out of here."

Sheltering her from sight with the oversized trash can, he shoved her into the back of the garbage truck as Bryce lurched the vehicle forward. Throwing the can into the back, and covering her from anyone who dared to look, Michael jumped aboard as the truck rumbled away.

Making several turns, Bryce wove through dark streets. From his lookout in the rear of the vehicle, Michael was confident they had not been followed.

Claire pushed herself free of the trash and took in her surroundings. She spoke to Michael. "I can't go without the children."

"My orders are to get you out of here."

According to plan, Bryce drove to a designated spot where he stopped long enough for Michael and Claire to exit the stinky truck. Once they were out, Bryce drove away. He'd meet them after stashing their getaway vehicle.

Claire stood her ground. "I can't leave them there."

"You don't have a choice." Michael grabbed the girl's upper arm in a vise grip.

She struggled to pull free and swung around. Her face inches from his, she looked past his greasy face paint and into his eyes. "They will be killed."

"That's not my problem." Michael steered her forward. "Now move."

"Their bodies will be harvested for replacement parts for moneyed men."

Michael stared at her. He knew from his training not to get distracted from the assignment. Distractions always presented themselves, and they were the undoing of any successful military operation. His single assignment was to bring Claire home.

"Do I have your attention?" She spoke each word carefully. "Leaving them is their death sentence."

Michael tightened his grip on her arm and pushed her ahead of him.

"Did you notice? They're all girls." She flung the words at him. "Girls are sold as a commodity. Orphans are worthless in their society. Orphan girls have it worse, if that is even imaginable."

The faces of his two sisters filled Michael's mind, and he cursed. Still, he relentlessly pressed forward. Orders were orders. Right now, he had to get Claire out of sight until night fell, when they would leave the city under cover of darkness.

Claire planted her feet. "You have to listen to me."

They were nearly at the safe house. Michael didn't have time to debate nor could he chance attracting attention. Too soon, the city would be awake and teaming. Quickly, he slung her over his shoulder and carried her the short distance to their destination.

Inside, he set her down and kicked the door closed behind him. When she wavered on her feet, Michael guided Claire to a couch. He checked their rooms, and satisfied they were secure, locked the door. He downed a glass of water and brought one to Claire where she sat on the couch with her head in her hands.

"You are a brute." She drank the water and handed the glass back to him. "I should have screamed."

He refilled her glass. "You're not the screaming type."

Michael checked for supplies and offered Claire first use of the single bathroom. She returned to the main room showered, and in fresh, though worn, clothing. Brooding, she showed interest only when he offered food. Too thin, the girl ate eagerly. Michael noted symptoms of malnutrition. Her hair was dull, and her eyes were overly bright.

After ditching the garbage truck, Bryce stopped in long enough to clean up, eat, and nap. Then he went ahead of Michael and Claire to make contact with Meatloaf and Wingnut for the return trip.

After his own shower, Michael ate for high performance as he had been taught during his early days in the Civil Air Patrol. "You're more active during field activities," Commander Garwood had instructed. "You need to eat more and drink more fluids."

Michael said as much to Claire so she would be physically prepared for the night's extraction. "Get some sleep," he added. "Rest now because you'll need to be alert tonight."

Later, Michael felt more than heard a stirring. Despite his exhaustion and hours without sleep, he hadn't been able to do more than doze anyway. The pitiful figures of that handful of adolescent girls haunted his thoughts, and he had jerked awake from nightmares several times. He hadn't been there to help his sisters, but helping these girls would be a serious breach of orders.

Silently, Michael rose and pursued the faint sound. He knew it was Claire and didn't relish dragging her back. Following behind her, he suddenly felt intense pain on the back of his head. He swayed, and for a moment, his vision went black. Once steadied, he whirled to see Claire standing behind him with something large in her hand.

He wrenched the object from her and tossed it away. "Some thank you for saving your life."

Instead of shrinking from his anger at her missed attempt to knock him unconscious, she stood fearless. "I'm going back for them. Are you coming or not?"

"I don't get you." Michael rubbed the back of his head. "Your daddy is the biggest proponent for harvesting organs from society's lower echelons, and you're asking me to risk my life and career to save some nameless orphans."

Claire bit the inside of her bottom lip.

"When you look up liberal in the dictionary, Bennett Taylor's photo is there." Michael pressed. "When you look up chip off the old block, your picture is the visual aid."

"You forgot abortion proponent who preached women should sell their fetal material for stem-cell research." Each word came like a bullet.

"Berkeley grad, hippie daughter," Michael fired back. "Whose number one hobby is drink fests and whose number two hobby is verbally crucifying conservatives and the brutish military in the name of free speech."

Claire worried her lip some more.

"But when daddy's girl gets in trouble, he sends those military *bullies*." He recalled Claire's words earlier. "Those military brutes."

Claire narrowed her eyes. "Sends you to do what?"

"Save your pretty little ass," Michael returned.

"Right."

Michael grabbed her shoulders. "Is there something you're not telling me?" She glared defiantly back at him. He leaned closer and repeated his question. "Is there something you're not telling me?"

The two stared at each other for several moments before Claire shrugged against his grip, and he released her.

"I'm going back for them," she repeated. "Are you coming or not?"

Michael's emotions warred with what he knew was right, the orders he knew he was to follow. But the memory of the heartbroken father in the hospital trying to get water to his dying daughter flashed through his mind and his resolve melted. No doubt they would both die in the attempt, but he couldn't let her go alone.

He clenched his jaw and gave a curt nod. "Let's go."

CHAPTER 24

Midday, clean and professional, Michael accompanied Claire back to the military hospital. According to a hastily concocted plan, inside, she power-walked both of them into a crowded department. Foreign patients, talking in languages he did not speak or understand, filled the rooms and lay in beds shoved against hallway walls.

From his gurney, a jaundiced Malaysian man reached out and clutched Michael's sleeve. He spoke one word or maybe twenty. Michael tried to shake off the man, but his fingers clung claw-like and desperate. The man licked parched lips and spoke again, this time in heavily accented English. "Soon?"

Claire appeared and placed a cup of water into the man's hand. "Soon," she assured and pushed Michael along.

She glanced sidelong at him. "Your bedside manner stinks."

"This morning, I stunk," he muttered. "Right now, I suck."

Through another door, Michael sensed they had entered a surgical area. Backing out of a room with a tray of bloody instruments, a nurse turned and faced them. Behind her came a doctor. Seeing them, the doctor's eyes narrowed.

Before he could speak, Claire stepped closer. "I'm with International Dialysis Corporation. Someone was to meet me. We have an agreement for a transplant."

The doctor silently regarded her. When he glanced past her, Michael met his glare and pointedly looked the man up and down. "From the pile-up in the hall," Michael challenged, "it doesn't look like we'll get what we paid for."

The doctor dismissed the nurse with a slight wave of his hand. In heavily accented English, he responded. "During the Lunar Festival, many prisoners volunteer for the New Year celebration."

"We're not waiting until the festival," Claire stated. "Your representative said today."

"Very well." With a nod, the doctor led them to an office. The room was sparse except for a metal desk across from two chairs and a filing cabinet against a wall. On the narrow windowsill was a small pot with a pink orchid. "Please wait here. Someone will be with you shortly to discuss your arrangements."

As soon as the man was gone, Michael stood. "I'll look for them. Keep serving that bologna you're dishing."

Ducking into a closet, he found a cleaning cart. *By the looks of this place, no one uses this much.* Pulling an apron over his clothes and snapping on rubber gloves, Michael reached for the mop and froze. Visions of the custodian and his ammonia smell as he mopped the floor in front of Verity's room flooded his mind. The irony of this disguise knotted his stomach.

In a room above the alley door where they had been delivered by the ambulance in the early morning hours, Michael found the orphans. Lying on crude cots, the girls had been sedated enough to keep them quiet but, luckily, not asleep. Only four. One was already gone. Michael cursed under his breath.

He hurriedly undid the rappelling ropes strapped around his middle underneath his clothes. At the window, he signaled. As preplanned at the safe house, Bryce moved the odorous garbage truck into position below. Too groggy to protest, the first adolescent girl allowed him to fit her into the harness. Michael dropped out the window with her. On the ground, Bryce loosed the girl from the lines and quickly stashed her among the smelly trash. Michael swiftly pulled himself back up to the third story window. He repeated the process three more times, feeling slower each time. The dead weight of the girls caused the ropes to knife deeply into his flesh where the taut lines burned his thighs and backside. Sweat stung the raw skin. Still, he worked until the last girl was down.

"Go!" Michael ordered.

"Where's Claire?"

"I'll find her. Get them out of here."

Bryce nodded. Blue smoke belched from the truck as it turned out of the alleyway.

Michael ascended the wall again. Inside, he rewrapped the ropes under his clothing. Suddenly, the door opened, and he ducked out of sight. A nurse and an orderly surveyed the empty cots and hurried out, calling an alarm.

Stealthily, Michael slipped out. He did his best to look like a janitor, but knew everyone in the vicinity would be suspect. Running footsteps told him several people had gone into the room previously occupied by the orphans.

He took advantage of the brief moments they would spend to investigate the situation to get clear of the area. Down an adjacent hall, he resumed his depressed mopping of the floor, taking a chance that the last place the hospital personnel would look for suspects was in plain sight. Systematically, he made his way back to the office where he hoped Claire was still serving verbal hash. Instead, he watched as a gurney was pushed from the room. He knew the form under the sheet was the senator's daughter. Either they had figured out Claire was the missing body from yesterday's transport, or they guessed she was part of the reason four bodies were missing today. Neither option was good.

His only consolation was that she wasn't dead. They wouldn't waste good body parts. That blood sucking industry would harvest her marketable attributes and then incinerate the evidence. He had to get her. Fast. Bending the rules would not be a popular decision with Corbin, and Michael didn't want to think about what the Scotsman would have to say. He certainly didn't want to explain to Corbin he'd sacrificed the person he was sent to recover in order to bring home four nameless adolescent orphans.

With the doctor at the head and the nurse at the foot, the gurney disappeared behind double doors. Two armed guards stood sentry in the hallway. Michael had to act quickly. These guys were greedy to grasp a supply. They wanted their pound of flesh, and Claire was going pay for five. Peeling off the janitor's coat, Michael slicked back his hair and retraced his steps to the crowded waiting area filled with wealthy internationals awaiting promised transplants.

He stopped beside the man who had grabbed Michael's sleeve earlier and leaned close to the yellow man's ear. "They won't give you a transplant. They just take your money and let you lay here until you die. Then they sell your body parts."

The man cried out and grabbed for Michael, but he was out of reach and already murmuring the same ghastly news to other hopefuls. Instantly, the waiting area was in an uproar. Many panicked and scrambled to leave.

Those too sick to move wailed. An angry group of patient representatives charged the hall, demanding to see the doctor.

The pandemonium brought the two guards running, and they were soon swept into the hysterical circle of paying customers demanding satisfaction. Summoned by a panicked nurse, the doctor and his assistant appeared from the surgery room. Terror showed in his eyes as the doctor attempted to quiet the riot. Unsuccessful, he backed away, flanked by a guard. Then, across the room, the doctor's eyes met Michael's.

Ducking, but not before seeing the guard start in his direction, Michael skirted the bedlam—close enough to be confused as part of the crowd, but enough on the fringe to drop aside when the opportunity presented itself. Seeing the guard coming for him through the hysterical people was reason enough. Swiftly, Michael traveled adjacent hallways to arrive at the surgery room where they had taken Claire.

Inside, a surgery tech monitored Claire's vital signs. He turned as Michael entered, and his quizzical expression rapidly dissolved into disdain. The tech grabbed a syringe and ran at the intruder. Blocking the man's thrust with his forearm, Michael wrenched the tech's other arm tightly behind his back, causing the man to spin around. Michael deftly applied more pressure until he heard the shoulder dislocate. The man screamed and dropped, sticking the needle into Michael's leg on his way to the floor. A quick blow to the head silenced the man's cries.

Pulling the needle from his leg, Michael was reassured when the syringe still contained plenty of fluid. But a growing wooziness told him some of the sedative, or whatever filled the syringe, was coursing through his system.

Michael breathed a sigh of relief to find Claire unconscious yet still breathing. He removed the surgical prep of tubes and monitors, lifted her body, and carefully folded her into a wheeled cart used for soiled sheets, hiding her under folds of fabric.

He undressed the tech and pulled on the hospital scrubs. The shirt was tight, and stitches tore as he hoisted the tech onto the gurney in Claire's place. A guard stuck his head into the room and asked a question Michael did not understand. Assuming a position of busyness over a tray of instruments, he kept his back partially turned and gave a casual wave in hopes the guard would believe that all was well. His tactic worked, and the bulky guard left as quickly as he had come. On the gurney, the tech groaned and stirred. Michael reached for the abandoned syringe and injected the tech. Immediately the man's head lolled back and he sank into a medicated sleep.

Michael rolled the laundry cart toward the swinging doors just as a nurse entered. She held the door until he had his load in the hall. As he kept his face averted, he was grateful for his naturally black hair. A blonde and blue-eyed American would be at a disadvantage trying to blend in here. But he had only taken a few steps, when the nurse began a tirade of harsh dialog.

Was she calling guards? Did she recognize that he didn't belong here? He turned slightly to see her pointing an impatient finger in the opposite direction. Michael mumbled enough for her to hear a response but not to hear what he said, turned and wheeled the cart in the direction of her wagging arm. With a satisfied grunt, the nurse disappeared inside the room he had just left. Before long, she would realize something was amiss. He whirled the cart in a different direction and nearly fell as a nauseous dizziness swept over him.

Down the hall, he could hear the mini-riot he'd instigated still providing some diversion and clearing most of the halls. His vision began to blur. That tech must have gotten more medication into him than he thought. Michael angled the cart into an empty room, closed and locked the door. Leaning back, he slid down the door to the floor as he lost consciousness.

CHAPTER 25

The moment had come. When the next to last item sold, everyone's attention turned to her painting.

The auctioneer began by introducing the painter. "Elise Eisler's work has recently received international notice. Critics have listed her among the top emerging artists to watch."

After a pause for effect, the mustached narrator continued. "The Christiansted Theater is honored to feature Elise's work at this worthy event. Those familiar with the island's historic atmospheric theater also know that the talented Ms. Eisler is an occasional musician in the St. Croix Philharmonic and that her parents were instrumental ..." He chuckled appreciatively at his own pun and nodded to those who laughed with him at their shared humor, "... in making the concert hall and the symphony a destination for travelers from both Eastern and Western continents."

He swept his arm toward the gold stand where the completed canvas rested under a mini-spotlight aimed to display the work to best advantage. "Whether you are an established collector or are just beginning a collection, this is a monumental opportunity in the art world."

The auctioneer named the reserve price. Several sealed bids were opened, the amounts read, and the highest number announced. The auctioneer added several thousand to the standing bid and looked across the roomful of attendees. "Who will top this?"

Elise dared a hopeful glance at June as several bidders were acknowledged and the purchase price increased until a voice from the back doubled the amount.

"That's better," June approved.

Elise heard murmuring among the others in attendance but the amount from the mysterious bidder remained unchallenged.

Calculating quickly, June whispered. "This may work, Elise, if we keep this momentum."

Elise held her breath, waiting for a response as the auctioneer called for someone to outbid the current number. After a considerable lull, Robson answered the challenge with a raise of his hand. Karl came next with a greater amount, and Jacques quickly topped his. He leaned to Elise. "She would look splendid in Jewel by the Sea if these others don't recognize the opportune moment."

Elise couldn't respond. Her voice wouldn't work, and words collided in her throat. Her inability to speak was probably a benefit, she decided. Who knows what embarrassing statements would be born of her nervousness. What would she say anyway? Any conversation would merely draw attention when the last thing she wanted was people watching her. Instead, she sat straight and composed while her emotions crashed against her chest and flamed her cheeks.

Robson's effort had the desired effect and a few others added their bids, steadily raising the price. But to Elise's mind, the increase seemed painfully slow. Then the voice from the back bid a second time. Heads turned in his direction, there were a few whispers, and the bid stood unchallenged.

The amount remained below the sum the painting had been anticipated to bring and not even near what Elise needed to make the essential repairs to the theater that held so many rich memories of her parents. She couldn't bear losing this calculated gamble to redeem the Christiansted Atmospheric Theater.

CHAPTER 26

Voices. Shouting words he didn't understand. Pounding. At his back.

Fighting to regain consciousness, Michael felt like he was clawing up from the dark bottom of the St. Croix underwater wall. Had he blacked out while diving? Did he still have sufficient air to reach the ocean's far distant surface?

At last, he cracked open heavy eyelids. Instead of a vertical wall textured with overgrown plate corals that cascaded toward the abyss below, Michael saw wheels. His vision followed the wheels to find the cart they supported. He squeezed his eyes closed in an attempt to align his senses with reality. The vibration at his back continued. He blinked again and focused on his surroundings. He was in an unfamiliar room with stark and curious furnishings.

Then he remembered. He remembered where he was at the same time the assault on the locked door at his back stopped.

Whoever wanted in would have left temporarily to arm themselves with tools and a gun. He better be out of this place before they returned.

Michael stumbled to his feet. Swaying, he considered giving in to the seductive pull of returning to his bed on the floor. But a glance at the linen cart reminded him that he had to get Claire safely home. Squinting about the room, he noted a sizable air vent and an even larger window. Working fast, he opened the grate to the vent system in the ceiling. Lifting Claire from her cramped position in the cart, he threaded her unconscious form into the overhead passage. Michael's arms shook with the effort of hoisting her dead weight. She was the fifth female he had carried since beginning the early morning rescue and the muscles in his arms were dissolving into spasms. He was grateful she wasn't built like a football linebacker.

Tearing sheets from the laundry cart, he tied the strips together. After securing one end to the doorknob, he opened the window and dropped the other end of the makeshift rope outside, cascading down two floors.

Two floors. He was on the third. Claire was now in the duct system above the third floor. He fought to think clearly as the sedative warred with his determination to get himself and Claire free from their pursuers and reunited with his team. Gambling that those hunting them wouldn't notice that the decoy fell short of a reasonable escape from the window to the ground below too soon, he squeezed himself into the air vent. The too-tight hospital clothing taken from the tech in the surgery room made maneuvering difficult. A seam ripped and his elbow tore through the fabric.

He settled the grate back into place as the door burst open, and three men poured inside.

CHAPTER 27

Had she been too egotistical to think her work would reap the large sum required to restore the theater? As the auctioneer recounted the stellar reviews garnered by the St. Croix Philharmonic, Elise fought an urge to bolt. June must have read her mind because she gently patted Elise's leg.

"Faith, dear." June's voice was soft and full of comfort. "It's not over until it's over."

Elise's heart felt like a runaway horse. She took a deep breath and slowed her breathing in an effort to rein in the rapid pace. Perhaps there was another option if the auction didn't have the desired results. If Jacques' idea to preserve the theater didn't work, she would find another way.

The auctioneer puffed out his mustache and recounted the quality of the artwork. He barely finished reading a glowing review of Elise's talents by a renowned critic when another bid was made and quickly topped by the same confident voice from the back. The crowd quieted.

"Someone wants the painting." Karl sounded hopeful.

"For a ridiculously low number considering the value," June countered.

"Why does the bidding stop after Mr. Back Row speaks?" Robson raised his paddle and craned his neck to find the man in the back that once more called out a top bid.

"And why doesn't he just use his paddle like everyone else?" June turned and scanned the crowd.

"Whatever the reason, his strategy is working." Thoughtfully, Karl smoothed his white beard. "Must be someone people know."

"Ladies and gentlemen," the auctioneer stepped to the side and rested his elbow on the podium. "Sotheby's came rather late into the field of auctioning art. Established in 1744, the founders initially contented themselves with selling books including the library Napoleon took with him to Saint Helena. Now headquartered in New York, we experienced our first major art success with the sale of a Frans Hals work in 1913. As I said, we are come lately to the field of auctioning art."

He gave a slight bow to those who laughed at his humorous exaggeration. "Of course, since adding art to the portfolio Sotheby's does auction, we've seen an impressive number of world treasures." The auctioneer moved close to Elise's painting. "Not only is this a one-of-a-kind by a talented and upcoming artist, the sale of this piece preserves another, and far larger," he paused once more for his audience to chuckle at his double meaning, "work of art. Our involvement with auctioning Ms. Eisler's work, in a heightened sense, is Sotheby's first excursion into the field of artistic architecture. All proceeds from the sale of this painting titled *Chasing Sunrise* benefits the preservation of the cultural center of the island, the Saint Croix Atmospheric Theater."

With a grandiose sweep of his arm, he indicated those in attendance. "Rarely has the sale of magnificent and collectible art had the added benefit of supporting a worthy cause. Who will boldly invest and take our bid to the target amount?"

Now everyone within Elise's limited view turned to see the man in the back. Expectant. Her face resolutely turned toward the front of the room, Elise heard murmurs behind her as a white-suited figure came forward. The audience seemed to hold their breath as he crossed his arms and considered the painting. Elise regarded him. Mid-fifties and handsome with an air of confidence. She had noticed him earlier when others approached her to talk. He had lingered in the background, watching. Studying the painting from a distance, she had judged.

Robson leaned to Karl. "Who is that?"

"Don't you watch the news?" His Santa beard barely moving, Karl spoke in a stage whisper.

Robson shrugged.

"That's Senator Bennett Taylor."

"Does anyone else want to take a closer look?" The auctioneer moved to the side, making room near the display.

The senator stepped back. "I bid the amount needed to reach your goal." In the cover of the immediate burst of applause, he crossed to Elise. Bending over her hand, he lifted his eyes to hers and spoke so only she could hear. "If you agree to have dinner with me."

CHAPTER 28

Statue-still in the circulation vent, Michael listened as footsteps ran to the window. There was another flurry of words he couldn't understand, and then footsteps pounded back down the hall. He turned his attention to pushing Claire ahead of him through the tight metal tunnel.

After a sluggish progression through the vent system, Michael came to an intersection. By pushing Claire past the T, then pulling her back down the adjacent passage, he could take the lead in this two-person parade and see what he'd be jumping into when he exited their above ground railroad to what he hoped would be freedom. Traveling in the aluminum vents, pulling Claire's body, made him sweat. The sweat reminded him of his rope-burned rear and thighs. Once he maneuvered into the new tunnel and dragged Claire in behind him, he laid his head against the cool metal to rest.

Michael wasn't sure how long he slept, but he woke with a start and cursed himself for giving in to the sedative. Powerful stuff, whatever it was. He wondered when Claire would wake. Then he wondered if she would. Inching forward, he came to an opening in the air system. Peering down through the grate he couldn't see much except a window. Nighttime. Fewer personnel to contend with.

Hearing activity from somewhere in the room below, Michael traveled farther along the restricted passage. At the next grate, he lay quiet for a long time, listening for anyone in the room. There was a queer humming from some type of machinery and a strange, burnt odor, but no human movement that Michael could detect.

After a deep breath, he pushed against the grate. It didn't budge. He pushed harder. No movement. He took several deep breaths and shoved against the grate with all his strength. The grate held. He wished he could kick it out, but he was head first in this situation with no possible space to turn around. Nor did he want to be at a disadvantage if he encountered someone. He needed to be able to face and deal with the unexpected, and so far the whole day had been unexpected. He shoved on the grate with all his might, followed by pushing steadily for long periods. Sweat blurred his vision and his muscles protested, but ever so slowly, the grate began to give under the pressure. Slowly, slowly, the grate moved until falling to the floor with a loud clang.

Using surprise as his only strategy, Michael pushed himself out of the vent and somersaulted onto the floor where he crouched, poised to meet any attacker.

No one seemed to be in the room.

Or was there? Michael looked around. Nearby stood a rack of narrow bunk beds, four shelves high. Michael walked to the form lying on one of the shelves. As he pulled back the sheet, he was shocked to his core. An adolescent Chinese girl. Or at least she had been a girl before so much of her young body had been removed. Stolen. The fifth orphan. She had been someone's daughter. Maybe a sister. Michael thought of his younger sisters Marissa and April, and he retched.

Turning, he eyed the machine that sounded of motors, fans, and filters. Radiating heat. An incinerator. For people. Or for what remained of them. A fast way to dispose of the evidence. The fourteen-foot oven reduced a human body to a few pounds of dry calcium phosphates with minor minerals of salt and sodium potassium. But there were no pretty urns to serve as a final and honorable resting place for these dead. A common trash barrel held ashes and bone fragments. All that remained of the deceased— all mixed anonymously together.

In a scrap bin lay salvaged jewelry, assorted metals from dental work, and a titanium hip replacement that would not burn. Michael didn't want to think about how that procedure had been done. Medication reservoirs comprised the next collection. Salvaged pacemakers drew his attention. If subjected to high heat, they could explode and damage or destroy the furnace. Perfect. Michael gathered three of the discarded heart stimulators and tucked them out of sight on the dead orphan's body. If he couldn't stop this heinous crime, he would inflict enough damage to cause a halt to the process.

He glanced at the air vent. He had to get Claire out of there before she awoke to see this grisly site. Previously, he'd wanted her to wake, but now, he prayed the sedative would last long enough for him to get them free of this house of horrors before they were discovered. Were the monsters that worked here gone for the night or simply on a break?

He checked the room for options. No windows, only a vertical chimney pipe that vented the oven. Cautiously, he cracked open the door. The adjacent room was vacant except for a smoking cigarette in an ashtray next to a deck of playing cards on a table. Someone would be back any second.

While considering his options, he heard footsteps in the hall. Silently, Michael crept back to the crematory area and slid the vent's telltale grate out of sight. The only exit was through the door, and that would bring him face to face with a guard or technician. He ducked onto a shadowy bottom bunk and covered himself with a sheet. As the door opened, Michael held his breath, something his training allowed him to do for several minutes.

Footsteps neared the machine.

Checking the cooking time.

Then to the bunks, stopping in front of the place where Michael still held his breath.

Like a snake striking its prey, Michael's hand darted out and grabbed. The reach was blind, but he made contact and squeezed. Hard. A scream of pain erupted from his victim. Jumping out, Michael hammered a fist into the surprised man's jaw. His aim was true, and the man dropped like a rock.

Michael stacked the unconscious worker on the bunk and returned to the other room where he'd noticed a small window. He decided against climbing down the building. He'd attempted to lead the hospital staff to believe he used the same method to escape earlier and there was no sense chancing heightened security around the ground level of the building.

He tore off the overly snug hospital scrubs. From under his shirt, he pulled out the ropes and clips. After securing a line to a ledge above, he returned to the incinerator room. Awake but unsteady, Claire stood staring at the orphan's body.

"Claire! Don't!" Michael bounded to her side just in time to catch her as she fainted.

Hands under her arms, Michael pulled Claire into the next room. At the window, he wrapped the ropes around both of them and fastened her to him. Confident she was secure, he stepped to the window ledge and began his climb. The ropes burned the already sore rope tracks along his legs, rear, and waist as he pulled them both onto the lowest level of the two-tiered roof—hopefully not guarded. Thankful for the cover of darkness, Michael undid the ties that held them together. He secured Claire by anchoring her to a stable fixture in the roof while he explored the terrain. He needed to craft a new plan.

Back at Claire's side, he reattached her safety line to himself and carried her along the sloping roof and around the corner. Once more, Michael affixed the ropes that held the unconscious Claire to a strong pipe rising out of the building's interior. With a practiced hand, he swung the end of a line across the alley and roped a fixture on the roof of the neighboring structure.

Then, with the senator's daughter retied securely against him, hand over hand, he laboriously pulled them across the gulf between the two buildings.

CHAPTER 29

"You have some fungicide?" Michael spoke over the throaty drone of the military cargo plane as it ferried the weary team west.

Dressed in his BDUs, Bryce looked up and grinned. "Mikey got a personal problem?"

Michael shifted uncomfortably. "Ropes and sweat are not a good combination."

"My old friend crotch itch." Bryce dug in his pack and produced the desired tube of medicine. "Never leave home without it."

"Didn't." Michael sighed. "Used mine up."

"Serious case." Bryce winced and then brightened. "Speaking of serious, how's your neighbor?"

"This is a rescue, not a fishing expedition."

"Just tossin' in my line in case I get lucky."

Sinking down into a seat, Michael rolled his shoulders in an attempt to stretch the aching muscles. Carting a still groggy Claire, Michael had finally made the rendezvous point in Shanghai. Relief had shown in Bryce's eyes when he arrived, but Wingnut and Meatloaf, assigned to get them across the border, hadn't expected four additional people. Nor had they expected to be behind schedule.

"Flex and go," a fatigued Michael had ordered. Now the four PJs, Claire, and the four Chinese orphans were safely on a military transport back to the States where the girls and the spunky senator's daughter would receive much-needed medical attention. Michael closed his eyes to rack up as much sleep as he could before he had to debrief with Corbin. He could only imagine what the fiery Scotsman would say.

Back in the United States, Michael reported matter-of-factly on the assignment to his boss. Corbin barely heard him out before launching into a heated lecture featuring the long list of areas where the team—and

Michael in particular—had acted outside the specified parameters of the mission.

"The Scottish people have a saying, Mr. Northington."

Braced for the verbal onslaught, Michael maintained strict military bearing.

"God takes care of the poor and the stupid." Corbin pushed his face close to Michael's and thrust his finger into Michael's chest, emphasizing every word with a thump against his breastbone. "And you, Mister, are the visual aid for the latter."

Standing under Corbin's tirade was akin to facing down a Nor'easter. When his boss had at last exhausted his dissatisfaction, Michael was dismissed. As he passed by the desk of Corbin's receptionist, Saundra tossed him a cold can of root beer.

"Nicely done, Michael." She lifted her own drink.

Michael inclined his head toward Corbin's office. "Glad someone thinks so."

Down the hall, Michael found Bryce waiting for him in the lounge. An empty root beer can sat on the coffee table next to a discarded newspaper. Bryce soberly regarded his partner. "How'd things go?"

Michael raked a hand through his hair. "Got my ass sufficiently chewed."

"Did you expect otherwise?"

"Nah." Michael dropped into a chair. "I deserved it."

"The senator should be glad you brought his daughter home safe and sound."

"As long as no one tells him I also nearly got her killed and pieced out."

Bryce stood and stretched. "I won't tell if you don't."

Michael rubbed the back of his neck in an attempt to relax tense muscles. "Something still doesn't feel right."

"Our job," Bryce yawned, "is not to solve the problems of the world, buddy. Remember?"

Michael remained quiet, studying the ceiling.

Bryce walked behind him and leaned his face over into his friend's view. "We just do the job and let guys like Corbin handle the big stuff."

CHAPTER 30

Elise still felt conflicted several days after the auction. What had happened?

When the auctioneer closed the bidding, people had gathered around to congratulate Elise. "Your parents would be so proud," she heard from several encouragers. Mentored under their expert tutelage, the talents she inherited from her mother and father had saved the theater. The funds from the painting would keep their legacy in splendid working condition for at least another generation.

So why didn't she feel good about the results?

Restless, she threw an oversized sketchpad, Conté crayons, and set of charcoals into a beach bag. In minutes, she was driving her dad's BMW convertible to the ruins of a sugar mill. Parking at her destination, she pulled a floppy hat over her windblown hair and set out on foot. From a kumquat tree, she plucked a handful of overly yellow fruit that smelled of concentrated sunshine, added them to her bag, and hiked to the historic structures that stood solid against the centuries of wind and weather. Tall grass grew along forgotten pathways where raw sugarcane had once been transported, and an aged key lime tree faithfully produced though no one came anymore to collect.

At a place where she could see the terrain that stretched beyond the mill's shadow, she took out her drawing pad. Imagining what this ancient factory might have looked like, Elise sketched women in cotton skirts with worn bandanas tied over their hair. She added a rutted road where men in open-neck shirts guided a wagon stacked with mature sugarcane freshly harvested from one of the island's two hundred sugar plantations.

In its day, the mill was a large, though simple, contrivance designed to harness the great force necessary to overcome the tough resistance of the fibrous cane as it was pressed and ground to release the tightly held sweet nectar. Liquid gold. Looking like a giant's sewing thimble, the mill's hull resembled a puzzle of fitted rock and shells. With bold strokes, Elise brought to life on paper the great canvas sails that had been removed more than a century ago. When powered by the wind, the axle mechanism atop the tower had rotated the middle of three upright rollers within the oversized machine. By means of cogs, the automated movement turned the other two iron-plated cylinders. Elise imagined the voices of dark-skinned slaves singing over the heavy sounds of machinery as they fed stalks of nectar-rich sugarcane into the rhythmic dance where the cane passed to and fro through the efficient, though oversized, roller system.

Extracted by grinding, the clear juices ran downhill through a leaded trough to factory buildings where male and female laborers produced the moist brown sugars preferred by British customers, as well as molasses, and clear 140-proof rum. In the humid boiling and curing house, the liquid flowed into large metal pans called clarifiers. Ashes and lime had been added and the mixture heated to remove impurities before the juice was ladled into the first of a line of wide-mouth iron basins called coppers. The leftover fiber refuse—called bagasse—fueled fires under the copper pots where the juice reduced and thickened. At the last of the train of coppers, a skilled workman watched for the precise stage when the syrup became ready to set. At the point of crystallizing, the new sugar was poured off into large wooden hogshead barrels.

For six months of the year, the hot, dangerous, and labor-intensive work of the sugar mill continued day and night. On a breezy day, the tangy smell of sour mash would have permeated the air from the lees pond where the dregs from the manufacture of rum was disposed.

Elise thought about the people who had worked in this place so long ago. She closed her eyes and listened for the echoes of their lives. Determined and robust Dutch settlers introduced these sugar mills—much like their domed cousins in Holland—to the West Indies in the early 1600s. In later years, the sugar farmers replaced the billowing canvas sails with more efficient wooden louvers. During the last half of the 1700s, St. Croix had been acclaimed as one of the richest sugar islands in the Caribbean.

Elise drew the owner of the mill, handsome and middle-aged, his arms crossed over his chest. He would have been wealthy. Like the fitted cogs that turned the rollers, her thoughts spun back to Senator Bennett Taylor—the very person she was trying not to allow into her mind and heart. Initially, she had felt relief and joy, even gratitude, that the stranger in the white suit had swept in and bought the piece for the hoped for and necessary price. Selling her painting to benefit the theater had proven to be a worthy idea and the concert hall's salvation. The funds would cover a number of immediately necessary repairs and upgrades.

But what had happened that day at the auction? She was still sorting impressions from facts. Many guests had attended, presumably with the intent to purchase. Yet the others appeared to have felt hindered in the senator's presence. People who had indicated to Elise and to Jacques that they had come expressly to bid on the art had remained quiet and reserved. Their intended bids were never offered.

With light lines, Elise sketched a young girl stirring a great pot of sugar with a long-handled spoon. Wisps of hair escaped from the girl's loosely knotted scarf and curled in the island humidity. Right now, Elise felt like a little girl herself, unsure of what to do. Despite his purchase agreement, several days had lapsed and the senator had yet to complete his half of the bargain. The painting remained on display at Jewel by the Sea. The sold sign declared Bennett Taylor as the owner of her best work even though he had not paid for his purchase. Elise suspected he was withholding payment until she agreed to have dinner with him.

Why had he made such a strange request? Initially, she had not put stock in the words he said before he pressed his lips to her hand. Surely, as a politician, the senator planned the gesture of flattery to provide a show for the crowd. Now, as quickly as he'd arrived, the man was gone again from the island, leaving behind his investment and a theater still desperately in need of his money. The transaction should have been simple. Today, she and the theater board ought to be pouring over plans to move forward with renovations. Instead, she was tramping through abandoned remnants of the island's history, hoping the theater would not soon be listed among the pieces of a richer past. Had she been successful or not?

Elise considered the now hollow mill that stood as a hushed sentinel over the abundant era when sugar was king—a time before slavery had been abolished, and Europe turned to sugar beets. Then World War II had overshadowed the Western world and stripped the historic factories of their iron for scrap to build weapons and ships. Sighing, she tipped her charcoal sideways and shaded the shadowed side of the rum building in her drawing. When would the senator return? Would he expect a dinner date as the final transaction of exchanging the longed-for finances for her painting?

Elise withdrew the sunny kumquats from her bag. Popping the rounded fruit into her mouth, she bit through the thick, sweet skin into the tart flesh beneath. The sweet and sour tasted refreshing when eaten together. She brightened the blouse of the girl in her portrait with a yellow blending into orange as she considered what she would wear on a dinner date with the career politician. She was accustomed to socializing with people of position. Her parents had regularly included her in many of their gatherings with musicians and patrons.

This time, however, she would not be with her parents, but with a man, a senator, who was old enough to be her father. Why did he want time alone with her?

CHAPTER 31

Michael would return to St. Croix tomorrow. He looked forward to adjusting back to island time, the smell of plumeria, and the sound of classical music in the breeze. He was ready to watch the sun rising over the ocean. And maybe he would see his neighbor, Elise, again, watching the same sunrise.

That night, Bryce and Michael visited their favorite haunts for good food and live music. As he had many times before, Michael crashed on the couch at Bryce's tidy condo. The next morning, after a satisfying workout and shower at the gym, Michael stuffed his sweaty clothes into his duffle.

"This is it, then?" Bryce shook his friend's hand.

"Until the next time."

"Need a ride?"

"Thanks." Michael shouldered his bag. "But I've got a stop to make on the way."

Later that morning, as he entered Bethesda National Naval Medical Center, Michael felt the old anger boil. A setting that killed under the guise of healing was not a place he could trust. In answer to his request, a receptionist with tightly permed hair gave him directions. Finding the patient's room, he tapped politely on the open door and stepped inside.

"You're real?"

Michael smiled at Claire, who lay in the hospital bed. "'Fraid so. Was there ever a doubt?"

She reached for the bed control and raised herself to a sitting position. "Lying here in clean sheets, being served good food, I began to wonder if I imagined you. Or maybe you were an angel sent to supernaturally help us."

"Not sure hospital food fits under the category of good. And I've been called a lot of things." He shrugged. "But never an angel."

"My ancient literature course covered biblical writings. The Hebrews believed God's warrior angel is named Michael."

"I'm sure a pair of wings would have lessened the bumps and bruises."
She looked him over. "How are you, then?"

"Like you, on the mend."

She indicated a chair. "Please sit down. I've a thousand questions."

"Got a few of my own." He turned the chair backward and straddled it.
"Isn't anything the Bible says a bit far to the right for you?"

She lifted her chin. "Don't confuse educated with religious."

Michael shook his head. "No one is accusing you of being religious."

A hospital volunteer came into the room and refilled Claire's water
pitcher on the bedside table. The volunteer poured a glass for Michael and
left again on silent shoes.

"I want to know how you found us." Claire returned to the topic.
"After I arrived here, I learned the only person I'd confided my plans to is
dead."

"I'm sorry."

Claire adjusted the hospital sheet across her lap. "Our lives and beliefs
were polarized, but she was truly interested in my ideals. We had great
debates."

"Debating with you sounds like as much fun as getting hit by friendly
fire." Absently, he rubbed the spot on his skull where Claire had bashed
him with something hard.

"She was more of a mentor than a friend. Patient." Claire wound the
sheet around her finger, unwound and wound the fabric again. After a
moment, she continued. "She said someday I'd get it."

"Get what?"

"I'm not sure." Claire swallowed hard. "After what I discovered overseas
…" She didn't finish her sentence.

"And she died?" Michael thought about Verity. Seems Claire had
recently lost two people—her stepmom and this mentor she was talking
about.

"Very strange." Claire frowned. "She never mentioned any health
issues. Though he did—her husband, that is. He had a condition. Liver.
A souvenir from Vietnam. I tried to contact her as soon as I could get to a
phone. They said she was dead." She shook her head. "I can't believe Verity
is dead."

Michael jerked as if a thousand volts of electricity had gone through
him. "Verity Marshall?" Exactly the topic he didn't want to talk about. He

had been relieved that Claire hadn't talked about her stepmother during the assignment, and he certainly wasn't going to. The girl was as tight-lipped and private as he was.

"My gosh, you knew her?"

I helped kill her. "Not many people named Verity."

"Marshall was her maiden name actually. She kept it though, I think, because she was an only child and did it to honor her dad." Claire puffed out her cheeks and exhaled slowly. "Funny the things we do for our dads. But it was one of the things I liked about her. Before …"

Michael spoke as much to himself as to her. "You could have helped care for her."

Claire's eyes filled with tears. "If only I had known she was sick."

"She was your stepmom, for Pete's sake." There was no hiding the harsh tone in his voice. If Claire and her family had properly cared for Verity, Michael would not have gotten involved. He wouldn't have been at this hospital that had smelled of antiseptic and ammonia that night to keep Verity's father from his daughter. Michael wasn't proud that he had physically and forcefully prevented her devoted father from caring for Verity. "Even if your family doesn't communicate …" Michael thought of Bryce's disconnected clan but dismissed the image, "… which is unlikely since your dad spends his career communicating—her death was announced over the television news."

He read the same angry determination in Claire's face that he'd seen when she declared her intent of going back for the orphans. Unapologetic for clobbering him on the head, she had seemed disappointed the effort hadn't succeeded in knocking him out cold. Now her words were like jabs from a stiletto. "In case you missed it, where I was didn't exactly serve apple pie with the evening news."

He considered the possibility that it had taken Claire several months to get herself so lost overseas that he and Bryce had been sent to retrieve the senator's missing daughter. Perhaps she was already in the bowels of China before Verity had been hospitalized.

Now Claire seemed to be doing some figuring of her own. "You must know her through the military."

"Not exactly."

She leaned forward, keen for information. "Were you close? Do you know what happened to her?"

He shook his head. "Only saw her a handful of times."

Interrupting their conversation, a doctor, accompanied by a nurse, entered the room. "How are you today?"

While the doctor talked, the nurse expertly wrapped a blood pressure cuff on the patient's arm. Ignoring Michael, the physician proceeded with his abrupt bedside manner. "Let's get some vitals and discuss your progress."

The nurse pushed a thermometer into Claire's mouth. Relieved to end the uncomfortable conversation, Michael rose to leave.

"Wait," Claire called. He turned back. Waving the thermometer in her hand, she said, "I'd like to talk to you again. I have more questions."

Conversing with Claire, Michael estimated, was akin to hugging a porcupine.

"Maybe later?" Noticing the glare from the nurse, Claire glared back but obediently stuck the thermometer back under her tongue.

Answering the inquiry in her eyes, Michael nodded, though he doubted they would ever see one another again.

CHAPTER 32

As he left Claire's hospital room, doubts about Verity chased themselves in Michael's mind like hamsters on a wheel. She'd been a lighthouse during the dark days he'd drifted through life like a rudderless ship tossed in stormy seas.

His conversation with Claire about her stepmom resurrected another memory he had worked hard to stuff far into his subconscious and keep buried. The unthinkable had happened just before he'd met Verity. Michael had returned from a deployment and like he always did, had found a phone as soon as he could and telephoned home to catch up with his mother, the girls, and the goings-on back on the Nebraska farm. He kept in regular contact except when an assignment prevented communication. In those instances, he called home as soon as he could. On this day, the phone rang several times followed by a strange click and two more rings.

"Hello?" The voice on the other end of the line was not his mother's.

"I must have dialed the wrong number." Michael had apologized, about to hang up.

"Michael? Is that you?"

Confused, he answered the question. "Yes. Who's this?"

"Oh, Michael. I'm so glad you called. This is Rachel Carolynne."

Still puzzled, Michael had smiled. Rachel Carolynne Thieme had been his mother's best friend for as long as he could remember. Ninety pounds soaking wet, she was the most gracious person he knew. "Hey, Rachel. How's everything at home in Nebraska?"

"You're so good about keeping in touch. I knew you'd call as soon as you could so I had your mom's calls forwarded to me."

This confusing conversation wasn't making any sense. "Forwarded? Why?"

"This is very hard, Michael—"

"Where's Mom and the girls?"

"Michael, I wish I could—"

"What's wrong?" Fear washed over him. "Are they okay?"

"I'm so very sorry, Michael."

Panic raised his voice an octave. "Rachel Carolynne, what's going on?"

"They were killed—"

"Killed? Mom?" He shook his head. "That's not possible."

There was a sob on the other end. "I wish it weren't true."

He struggled to comprehend her words. Desperate for hope, he asked, "The girls? The girls too?"

"Yes."

His lungs refused to breathe. "How?"

"I tried to reach you, but—"

"I was on assignment." He choked out the words through a throat that no longer cooperated.

He heard her sigh. "I figured that was the case."

Tears rolled down Michael's face. "I want to see them."

After a pause, she answered. "My news doesn't get any better."

It was all he could do not to scream at her now as he repeated his question. "What happened?"

Rachel Carolynne's voice broke as she explained Michael's mother and his two younger sisters had been on their way home one night. From the opposite direction, a semi-truck, whose driver had fallen asleep, careened into their lane and hit the midsize car head on.

Michael tried to force oxygen into his unforgiving lungs. "I'll get right home."

"Please try to understand, Michael. I didn't know what to do. They were so hurt—"

He wiped his nose on his sleeve. "What are you saying?"

"Their bodies, I mean. The paramedics said they died instantly. No suffering. But their bodies ..."

"Where are they?"

"I tried to wait as long as I could."

"I want to see them," he cried. "I need to see them."

He could hear his mother's friend weeping on the other end of the line. Finally, she spoke again. "I wanted you to see them. Truly, I tried. But the days piled up. I didn't know how long you'd be away, and we really couldn't wait any longer."

He didn't think he could take any more bad news. "What are you telling me, Rachel Carolynne?"

"I'm trying to tell you they're already buried."

"Gone? All of them are gone?" Michael dropped his head against the wall. With his free fist, he beat against the unyielding surface. "No, no, no! Oh God, oh God, oh God."

Rachel Carolynne's gentle voice was tearful. "I'm so sorry, so very sorry, Michael."

He cried for a long time before he could momentarily dam the emotion. "When did this happen?"

She provided a date.

"That's the day I left."

He waited while Rachel Carolynne cried. Finally, she managed to speak. "The funeral was yesterday."

When the call ended, Michael had pressed his hands and face against the cold wall while his body shuddered with deep sobs. He didn't know how long he'd stood like that when two hands gripped his shoulders. Michael opened his eyes to see the concerned face of the chaplain. Then, he had collapsed under the immense grief.

The military had granted Michael a few days to return home where Rachel Carolynne met him at the airport. Exiting the plane, he saw her scanning each passenger, her expression brightening when she saw him. She stood still, hesitating, as if unsure how he would respond to her. When he reached her, Michael saw the deep compassion and genuine love in her eyes. Tears blurred his vision as he wrapped her in his arms like he would his mother. The two had held each other and wept.

Practical and efficient, his mother had put her affairs in order shortly after his dad left. She had worked hard to be a strong parent and free the children from additional pain and responsibility resulting from her husband's abandonment. One of life's rare treasures and a soulmate kind of friend for his mother, Rachel Carolynne had taken care of most of the remaining details. She helped Michael walk through the lingering items that needed his attention, and he spent hours at the cemetery, weeping and telling his mother and sisters all the things he needed to say. That's where he had been when his friend showed up.

"Figured I'd find you here."

Sitting at the gravesite, his head in his hands, Michael looked up. Silhouetted against the Midwest sun stood Bryce. Michael wiped at his face and moved to get up. Bryce held out his hand, and he accepted the help. Once he was on his feet, Bryce pulled again, locking Michael in a brusque embrace. His friend thumped his back and stepped away.

"How in—?"

"Some big shot needed a ride to the Pentagon." Bryce grinned. "I volunteered."

"This's a long way from DC," Michael pointed out.

Bryce shrugged. "He's in meetings all day."

"So what's a bored pilot to do?"

"Precisely."

"Been to see your mom?"

"Maybe later." Bryce regarded the headstones. "This stinks, man. Worst sight I've ever seen."

Michael nodded.

"How are you holdin'?"

"I don't know." Michael swallowed hard and brushed at fresh tears. "Not good."

"Your mom was a rare good woman, you know. She trusted me. Made me want to live up to it."

"She taught you manners, you hillbilly."

"A hillbilly with teeth, mind you." Bryce smiled, but then sobered. "Sure ate a bunch of good meals at your place."

"Slept on the couch a bunch, too."

"Sometimes for fun." Bryce stuffed his hands into his pockets. "Sometimes 'cuz it was better than the war zone at home."

"You brought the war with you. The only videos you brought over were battle flicks."

"She sat in her rocking chair and watched 'em with us on that postage stamp-sized thing you guys called a TV. No big screen for the Northington family." He paused. "Your sisters ..." Bryce brushed his sleeve across his face.

"They were there for the popcorn."

"They idolized you, bro'. I thought they'd marry well and give you a lapful of nieces and nephews."

This time he couldn't stop the tears. Dropping onto the plot of fresh dirt, Michael pulled his knees to his chest and pressed his face against his arm in an attempt to block the stream of tears and slow the raging sorrow that churned his belly. He felt Bryce's hand on his shoulder as waves of grief buffeted his body.

Much later, spent from weeping, Michael lifted his head and looked around. There were bouquets of wildflowers on each grave, and on his mother's headstone was a challenge coin from the Civil Air Patrol. Under the coin was a dollar bill on which Bryce had penned, "Gotta fly."

Michael slipped the challenge coin into his wallet next to his own identical one. They had each received the traditional coin when they earned rank in the Civil Air Patrol. He folded the dollar to fit beside the matching coins.

CHAPTER 33

Too soon after the loss of his family, Michael had returned to base for the next level of training.

"Do not mistake this for a training course," the proctor had warned. "This is a testing ground. June 16, 1964, Petty Officer Billy Machen was the first SEAL to die in the Vietnam War. He was caught in a firefight in the Rung Sat Special Zone. By the time that conflict ended, forty-seven SEALs were dead. We conduct all types of missions behind enemy lines. We work jointly with Special Forces of all branches. There will not be another Rung Sat Special Zone on *our* watch."

Previously, Michael thrived on pushing himself beyond what he thought he could do physically and emotionally. Despite the ever-increasing challenges, his heart remained back at a cemetery in Nebraska.

"You will risk your life to save another." The proctor's voice had boomed like cannon fire. "You will go behind enemy lines to set up on a drop zone or airfield. You will call in fire support to troops who need it. If you wear the maroon beret of a PJ, it is because you provide around-the-clock emergency and life-saving services to airmen, soldiers, and civilians in both peacetime and combat environments. When a plane goes down in the jungle or ocean, PJs search, locate, and save the pilots and crew."

PJ training was Pain 101. Only a few would survive to the end. The brutal physical conditioning included sleep deprivation and plenty of time in cold water. "Water. Learn to like it. For most special forces groups, water is an obstacle at worst and an inconvenience at best," the instructor had stated. "For PJs, water is a refuge, a transportation system, and sometimes a threat. A lot of our rescues involve water. Get used to being wet. For a PJ, water is your second home. Learn to like water, use water, and find safety in water."

There was as much ground training as time in the water, and on one particular day, Michael was having a tough day on land.

"Who gave you permission to puke on my asphalt?"

Bent over, hands on his knees, Michael heard the proctor's question before the big man's shadow eclipsed the sun. Pulling himself erect, Michael assumed military bearing as the instructor pushed his chest close to Michael's. Bile heaved from his stomach, but he choked it back. He didn't dare mess up this man's uniform. "Drop and give me fifty. I want to see your nose touch what you left there every single time."

Michael's pectoral muscles shook with the strain of additional push-ups. The proctor towered over him. "Brigadier General Hal Moore led the First Battalion of the Seventh Cavalry into and back out of the bloodbath in the Ia Drang Valley in 1965. Three hundred and five Americans and eighteen hundred North Vietnamese died in that battle. Moore promised he would leave no man behind and he kept that promise." The proctor rested a booted foot on Michael's back for the final ten push-ups. "Even the dead were brought home to their families. That is the way of the military brotherhood."

Guys he had worked out with, sweated with, and stayed awake with quit. Sometimes several quit in a day. Sometimes one at a time. On previous occasions, seeing someone give up strengthened Michael's resolve to succeed. That day was different.

He knew better than to even think about quitting. "As a man thinks, so is he," his mother had often quoted from Proverbs. Avoiding the guys who hung out in the back of the run column to complain, he stayed with the leaders in the front who refused to think about how hard each day was. Instead, he focused on the end of the day when, sore and bone weary, he laughed with those who made it through.

"Man, can you believe that stuff?" Bryce recounted the toughest training of the week.

"Yeah." Michael returned. "We did it."

But the days spent at home had cost him. Bryce and the men Michael began training with had continued on to their next revolution during his absence. To compensate for time lost in Nebraska, Michael had been reassigned to a squad who began one segment of training behind his own. As the new kid in an already established group, hostility and vicious pranks replaced the familiar camaraderie previously shared with Bryce and the others.

The training process for parajumpers included combat diver school, underwater egress training, survival school, and free-fall parachutist class. Once those were passed, every parajumper wannabe entered the PJ Pipeline which included the special operations combat medic course and the pararescue recovery specialist course.

But since the terrible news that his family was dead, day after grueling day, he began to let his thoughts slide to that single piece of paper. Just scribble his signature on the line, and the pain would all be over. He could walk away. No one would hold him back. No one would make him stay or even try to talk him out of it. "If I want one good man, I start with five good men," the proctor had stated. "I will sift you until I find that man who would rather die than quit."

Michael recalled when one buddy had walked off the day's regime. Instinctively, he had reached to grab his fellow soldier and pull him back. The words were already forming in his mouth.

We can do this. Stay with me.

Like a striking snake, his instructor knocked back Michael's hand and yelled in his face. "Let him go," he hollered. "You hear me, Mister? You let him go. Get your head back where it belongs. You've got a job to do. You got me?"

The fierce man stood between Michael and his retreating battle buddy. One glance at those determined eyes, and he knew this was a defining moment. He had turned his attention forward once more.

Lying on his rack that night, hands clasped behind his head and staring at the ceiling, Michael knew a PJ could never quit, never walk away from his team on a mission. If someone was going to walk away, it had to happen here. Now. The ones that stayed the course and made it through would be the men that he could count on when his life depended on it. The betrayal of a buddy giving up on himself and his team was part of the training. But the fire in his own gut that had burned hot and focused was waning. What did it matter anymore if he stayed or if he quit?

"You have two hours to shower, shave, and do your laundry," the proctor instructed the next day. "Dismissed."

At the base laundromat, Michael slid quarters into the designated slots and the washer began to fill with water. Two machines away from Michael's, a woman fumbled to do the same, but the quarters slipped out of her fingers and rolled under the row of washing machines. She fished in her pocket for a coin and slipped it in the slot, and then dropped to her knees to peer under the washer. She tried to slide her fingers underneath, but her hand wouldn't fit.

"Here." Michael produced a quarter from his pocket. "Quarters under the machines are donations to the base."

She stood and accepted the coin. "Thanks." She started the washer. "I'll trade you for a Coke. The vending machine gave me two for the price of one."

"Typical military." Michael accepted the can she pulled from her laundry basket and held out to him.

"It's stuffy in here. Want to sit outside and tell me what a gentleman like you is doing in a place like this?"

He followed her outdoors to a shady spot on the cement steps. An attractive woman, she appeared older than himself but younger than his mother. Judging by the ring, she was married. "The bigger question is what you're doing in a place like this. You look more like officer country than enlisted laundry status."

She nodded. "My husband's an officer. He's away at a meeting and the washing machine fritzed."

"You gotta be desperate to come here."

"I'm entertaining some other wives in the morning."

"Show me a woman who's cleaning and I'll show you a woman who's expecting female company," Michael quoted. "One of my mother's sayings."

"Smart woman." She popped open her drink can.

"She was a smart woman." That sharp reminder pierced his gut.

"Was?"

He looked out across the parking lot. "She died a few weeks ago."

"I'm truly sorry."

They watched two soldiers carry bulging drawstring bags into the laundry building. Michael took a gulp of the cold soda, swallowing against the sudden tears that unexpectedly sprang to his eyes.

"Tell me about her." Her voice was gentle—like she really wanted to know.

Until the washer finished, he spoke the words that had burdened his thoughts. When he ran into memories that gripped his heart like a vise, he drank hurriedly and let the liquid dissolve the lump in his throat. All the while, she listened. Later as he folded his fresh laundry, his emotions felt washed as well.

The next day, Michael felt stronger. The heaviness that had dogged his every step had eased.

A week later, Michael dragged his exhausted body and stinky laundry bag back to the base laundromat. Ahead of him, two guys from his unit mimicked the drill instructor. Michael walked behind, half listening to their crude humor until they disappeared into the building ahead of him. He had his hand on the doorknob when a voice to his right asked, "Can I buy you a drink, soldier?"

Sitting on the same step they had shared before was the officer's wife.

For the first time in weeks, Michael smiled. "Your washing machine still on the fritz?"

"Thankfully, the repairman got it working the next day."

"Then what's a nice girl like you doing in a place like this?"

She stood, her hand outstretched. "I owe you a quarter." She dropped the coin in his palm.

He adjusted the bag over his shoulder. "If you have time, I'll buy you a drink."

"If you're lucky, the vending machine is still giving two for one."

Minutes later, his clothes were washing, and he returned outside to the cement step with two Cokes.

"How was the wives' club?" He handed her a cold can.

"Fine." She popped the top and took a drink. "My husband came home and left again. More meetings. He's not feeling well which worries me."

"I understand." Michael opened his own soda. He drank deeply and the bubbles stung his nose.

"I'm glad to see you, actually," she said quietly.

With his thumb, he rubbed the condensation off the can. "Thought about dropping."

"I know."

He looked at her, questioningly.

"I've seen the look before." She regarded him thoughtfully. "You look better today. But still thinking about it?"

"Occasionally."

"What would your mom want you to do?"

His head jerked up. "My mom?"

Talking around the candy bars they were stuffing into their mouths, the two loud soldiers came out of the laundry and passed between them down the steps.

"And your sisters?"

He swallowed the remainder of his drink and crushed the can in his fist. "You have children?"

She shook her head. "Just kids like you."

He tossed the crumpled aluminum into a large trash can.

"From what you told me," she continued, "your mom and sisters cheered you on to this point."

He nodded.

"Stop thinking of quitting. Start looking at them. Accomplishing this is a dream the four of you shared."

Deep emotions swelled in his chest. These sad emotions were pushy companions that made their appearance at unexpected moments.

"Tell me about your sisters."

Until the washer finished, he talked about those two shiny-eyed girls who thought he was a hero. All the while, she listened, occasionally asking a question and often smiling as if she could picture Marissa and April coercing their big brother to join them for yet another tea party. Little glass cups with Disney characters on the side and filled with tiny servings of Jasmine tea. Returning to his unit that afternoon, his step once again felt lighter after sharing a Coke at the laundromat.

Weeks later, Michael landed his plane after practicing evasive maneuvers. As he walked out of the aerodrome, a car stopped in front. The driver hurried around and opened the back door. As she stepped from the car, Michael recognized the officer's wife. He went to the trunk where the driver was retrieving a single bag.

"I'll take that." Michael dismissed the driver.

"Hello." She smiled at him.

"Where you headed? I'll bring your bag."

She motioned toward a plane. "My husband collapsed while he was away. He had emergency surgery."

"You mentioned he wasn't feeling well."

"He's been brought back into the country. I'm going to meet him while he recovers."

She pulled papers from her purse and showed them to a flight staff member. She turned to Michael. "Been looking at civilian life anymore?"

"No, ma'am." He handed the luggage to the attendant.

"Good." She walked toward the plane.

"Wait," Michael called.

She turned.

"What's your name?"

"It's Verity."

"Mine is——"

"M. Northington." She laughed. "It's been on your shirt all along."

"Of course." He glanced down. Carefully stitched above his pocket was the patch with his name.

"We're ready for you, Mrs. Marshall-Taylor," the staff member said. "You can board now."

Halfway to the plane, she tossed a quick wave over her shoulder. He waved back and slowly dropped his hand.

Mrs. Verity Marshall-Taylor.

A general's wife had taken the time to share a soft drink. Twice.

CHAPTER 34

Corbin was on the phone when Michael barged into his office. The Scotsman waved him to a chair but Michael walked straight to the large desk, planted his palms on the polished surface and leaned toward him.

"We had a deal."

Corbin covered the phone with his hand. "Jings and crivvens, Michael. Shut up and sit down." He put the phone back to his ear. "I'll call you back," he said into the receiver and hung up.

Michael paced as Corbin pressed a button on the phone and spoke to his receptionist. "Saundra, you know the drill. Hold my calls."

"Full disclosure." Michael pointed his finger at Corbin's chest. "That was the deal."

"Part of the deal, actually," Corbin countered. "So if you're here to apologize, just get it over with so I can get back—"

"You didn't tell me Verity was connected with the China mission."

Corbin held Michael's challenging gaze. "I'm not sure there is a connection."

"Why don't you tell me what you are sure of?"

"Don't you get tired of barging into my office like a bull in a rodeo?" He indicated a chair. "Do you want to sit or continue to pace and glare?"

Knowing he wouldn't get anything unless he gave Corbin some semblance of authority, Michael reluctantly sat. "Claire knows—is related to Verity. One is dead, and the other almost was, and you're telling me it's all a coincidence?"

Corbin leaned back in his chair, lacing his fingers across his flat stomach. "Verity is ..." He stopped himself and began again, "... *was* Claire's stepmother."

"Verity Marshall-Taylor."

"Bennett Taylor divorced Claire's mother when he returned from Vietnam." Corbin summarized the facts. "Later in his career, he married Verity."

"What about Claire?"

"She lived with her mom until her mother died of cancer."

Michael winced. He had lost his own mother, but Claire had lost a mother and a stepmother she was fond of. "When was that?"

"Her mother died when Claire was about thirteen. Claire attended the best boarding schools and graduated college not too long ago."

"Long enough to get herself in trouble overseas. And while Claire was away, Verity died."

Pushing paperwork aside, Corbin rested his arms on the desk. "That's where the connection ends."

Michael studied Corbin's face. There was no guile. He knew Corbin to be a straight shooter who provided his team with as much information as he could compile. When Michael asked beyond his rank, Corbin traditionally responded, "You're getting left of yourself." Scottish for privileged information Corbin had but was not at liberty to confide. Michael could be satisfied that his CO was aware of his concerns and had considered the possible options and consequences.

Still, Senator Bennett Taylor's family was occupying a lot of real estate in Michael's life. Too much. And Michael had plenty of questions and no answers.

"If it walks like a duck and quacks like a duck," his mother used to say, "then I'm calling it a duck."

Corbin must have guessed Michael's thoughts. He broke the silence by repeating his conclusion. "That's where the connection ends."

Michael stood. "Or maybe that's just the beginning."

CHAPTER 35

He was back.

Elise saw lights illuminating the cottage one evening and felt the familiar stab of regret. Had she made the right decision to give up her parents' studio? She longed to turn back the clock to those bright years when familiar and secure defined her life. Now she felt as if she were clutching a handful of sand. The more she grasped onto the familiar, the faster it slipped through her fingers. She had rented the cottage to provide for the theater, and while helpful, the regular income did not equal the need. Now she missed the sanctuary for her family's creativity but the longed for place no longer existed because of her decision. Perhaps the loss would have been worth the cost if the theater could have been renovated. Instead, she was losing the two places that had defined her and her family.

As he had when he initially came to St. Croix, Michael kept to himself—an arrangement that served as a relief for Elise. Not that any of this was his fault, but she needed time to shake off the remorse that dogged her. The first morning after his return, she saw him go for an early run. His steps on the paved drive hit like staccato notes. In the evenings, when the trade winds were right, she heard the driving beat of rock and roll music coming from her former studio. Guns and Roses mostly. Occasionally Bon Jovi and Aerosmith.

But after a few days, the music became softer with songs from Journey, Bruce Springsteen, Foreigner, and the mystic songs voiced by Robert Plant of Led Zeppelin. She noticed his steps were lighter as he settled back on island time. Elise had observed the same phenomena in guest musicians who came to perform at the theater. Some took longer than others to shed the off-island tension in favor of the tropical rhythm. Those who came often, like Ava, opened their hearts quickly to the island's tempo. Similarly, Elise settled into a companionable acceptance of the guilt she felt over her decisions.

Together, her parents had created an environment that nurtured their daughter, the arts, and the island. What they had accomplished, seemingly as naturally as the plumeria bloomed beauty and fragrance, threatened to unravel in Elise's hands.

Several days after he came back to the island, Elise was clipping ginger leaves into her teapot when Michael returned from the day's activities. He nodded to her, a grocery sack in one hand, and she waved him over. As he drew near, she could see his face was tanned under hair that appeared stiff from the salty ocean.

She took a deep breath. June had pressed her to invite him. Reluctant, Elise had promised she would do as June suggested only if she crossed paths with Michael naturally. Nothing forced. She would not knock on his door.

Elise swallowed and forged ahead. "Would you be interested in accompanying me to a gala at the philharmonic Saturday evening?"

He looked surprised. Suddenly, Elise didn't want her neighbor to think she was pursuing him. In her haste to justify the invitation, her words tumbled out quickly. "June suggested you might enjoy getting to know more about the island's culture."

"June?"

"She owns the property management company. I believe she showed you the cottage."

Michael shifted the grocery sack into his other arm. "The jeep driver."

"Right." She clipped two more green leaves from under the bright yellow flowers and let them fall into the teapot.

"Tea leaves?"

"Ginger Thomas." She handed a blossom to him. "Our territory flower, good for a number of things including headaches."

He nodded at the teapot. "You have a headache?"

She held a hand to shade her eyes. "Occupational hazard. Sometimes the paint fumes are bothersome."

"Sounds like you've been working too hard."

She smiled. "Then the party is just what the doctor ordered."

"What about the gentleman who usually picks you up?"

"He's meeting the guest conductor at the airport just prior to the beginning of the events." She waited as he seemed to consider. Just as she was beginning to regret asking, he spoke.

"What time should I come by?"

"Five-thirty. There's a dinner that night."

He nodded. "Five-thirty then."

CHAPTER 36

On Saturday, Michael knocked on Elise's door promptly at 5:15 p.m. In a moment, she welcomed him inside.

"Come in. I'm nearly ready, and you're stylishly early."

"In my business, early is on time and on time is late."

Still barefoot and in a sundress, she led him into the living room. "Make yourself comfortable." She waved him to a chair and disappeared down the hall.

Like his cottage but on a larger scale, a great room with large windows framed the ocean view that served as the center of the house. The furnishings were a mix of light tones in a variety of textures where vintage intertwined with contemporary. On the sound system, Glenn Miller's swinging sax played "In the Mood." Breathing deeply, Michael took in the scents of plumeria, rosin, and oil paint.

An easel stood to the right of the windows. Michael stepped closer to the rectangular painting. On the canvas, the brilliant sun burst fresh above the horizon, gleamed on the ocean, and lit the island. The signature at the bottom read *Elise*. This painting was nearly identical to the one Michael had seen on display at Jewel by the Sea—with a single exception. Under the low clouds, a jet traced a white line parallel with the horizon.

He was staring at the painting that vividly captured his first morning on St. Croix when Elise returned to the room. With her hair loosely swept up, she wore a floor length dress the color of ocean foam. The painting left him speechless. She took his breath away.

"I'm not sure what to call this one," she offered conversationally.

"I saw another just like it—"

"The day you sent a bottle of wine to my table. But that one—"

"Doesn't have the jet."

Elise stood next to him, her arms crossed as she regarded her work. Michael studied the canvas again. "Why two paintings?"

"I agreed to do a painting for the benefit." She absently pulled on a curl near her cheek. "I painted this one first, but I couldn't let it go. Something about it stirs my heart."

"Chasing sunrise," he murmured.

She turned to him.

"That's what pilots do." He pointed at the straight line the jet created above the horizon.

"Is that what you do? Chase the sunrise?"

"Sometimes. Sometimes, I chase the sunset." He checked his watch. "Five-thirty. We'd better go."

Michael escorted Elise to his car. Picturing the spic and span Mercedes that was her usual ride to these events, he had vacuumed and washed his vehicle earlier just for this occasion. Having sand scattered on the floors wouldn't do.

The trip from the house to the historic downtown was short. Though he had often driven by the Christiansted Theater, he'd never been inside. A valet parked his car. Michael and Elise followed other well-dressed attendees to the large ballroom where round tables were draped and set for dinner with white and lavender orchids arranged in the center. Michael noted the dance floor gleaming in front of the elevated stage where the musicians played pop tunes with an island flavor.

From the bar, Michael purchased Cokes without rum for both of them. Turning, he nearly collided with his boss at St. Croix Adventures.

"Well, well." Jerry grinned, his teeth white against his handsome, tanned face. "After exploring the treasures of the sea, you've come to discover the treasures of our island culture."

"That I have."

"Well done." Jerry wholeheartedly slapped him on the back causing the Cokes to slosh over their rims.

Elise introduced Michael to a variety of people including several musicians and the owner of the resort where Michael had taken Bryce and Corbin for lunch. Michael recognized Jacques as the man Elise had been having lunch with when Bryce sent over a neighborly bottle of wine.

Jacques' attention shifted to someone behind them. Michael turned to consider the newcomer as Elise turned and found herself nearly against the man's chest.

She squared her shoulders. "Senator Taylor."

Senator Bennett Taylor. Michael pushed back thoughts of Verity.

"I'm glad you've returned for your painting." Elise indicated the room. "The Friends of the Philharmonic are eager to begin remodeling."

"We have much to talk about." The senator placed a hand on her elbow. "Why don't you join me at dinner?"

"I took the liberty of including you at our table." Jacques inserted himself between them and quickly made an introduction to Michael. While shaking Senator Taylor's hand, Michael wanted to loosen his tie. He hoped Claire hadn't shared too many details about their time together. He sure wasn't going to bring it up.

As the guests took their seats for dinner, Elise's friend with the Mercedes arrived. On his arm was a beautiful woman dressed in a flattering black suit. Elise excused herself and crossed the room to greet her friends. Engaged in animated conversation, Elise led the trio back to their table. Michael stood.

"Robson, this is Michael," Elise introduced. Robson gave Michael a wide grin, and the two men shook hands. Elise continued. "And our special guest tonight is Ava."

Michael nodded to Ava. "Pleased to meet you."

Michael held Elise's chair, and she took her seat next to him. Robson helped Ava to her place next to Elise and sat next to her.

"We're all delighted you are here," Elise said to Ava. "How was your flight from New York?"

"Far too close timewise." Ava's words were tinted with a Scandinavian accent. "I prefer to settle in before a performance. But it couldn't be helped."

June, with a man in tow—who looked like Santa Claus on vacation—bustled over to the table. Taking the empty place next to Michael's left, June introduced her husband, Karl, and warmly clasped Michael's hand. "Good to see you. How are you enjoying the cottage?"

"It's everything you said it was," Michael acknowledged.

"I spent my formative years there," Robson put in.

Michael looked from Elise to Robson. "Elise mentioned the cottage served as a studio."

"Robson studied under my father." Elise rested her hand on her friend's arm. "He was Papa's best cello student."

Ava leaned forward. "Elise's father was a world-renowned conductor. A number of top cellists studied under him as did several conductors."

"Including Ava," Robson said. "She's the first female conductor in a man's world."

"Congratulations," Michael said.

"Assistant conductor, actually," Ava corrected. "Seems the world is still not quite ready for a woman conductor."

The resort owner and his wife claimed two of the last three chairs at the table. "Though Michael is relatively new to the island, he has dined at your restaurant," Elise told them.

The middle-aged man gave a slight bow. "I hope it was to your liking."

"My compliments," Michael returned. "There was also a beautiful painting there that day. One that did justice to the island sunrise."

"I was honored to display Elise's work," Jacques answered.

Waiters placed steaming plates of prime rib and coconut shrimp at each place as Senator Taylor returned and took his place next to the resort owner.

"You have a noted guest, Jacques," June said.

Jacques nodded. "The senator is staying at Jewel by the Sea."

"Superb accommodations," Taylor acknowledged.

June's husband lifted his glass and leaned forward. "Jewel by the Sea has partnered with Cruzan Rum to serve their own label rum for occasions like Elise's display and for their distinguished guests."

"Karl does the marketing for Cruzan Rum," June explained to Michael and Ava.

A waitress refilled Michael's water glass.

"And you, Mr. Northington," June said. "What about you? What have you found to do on St. Croix?"

Michael looked around the table at the expectant faces. "I'm a scuba instructor."

Throughout dinner, Elise and her friends talked and laughed the way longtime friends do. After dessert, the band switched to dance music. Ava excused herself to prepare for the upcoming concert.

Robson stood and reached for Ava's hand. "One dance before business?"

She smiled her agreement. Their faces close, Robson and Ava talked as they danced, and then he held her close for the final notes. At the song's conclusion, the couple left the dance floor in the direction of the theater's backstage. The next song was upbeat. June's husband escorted his wife to the dance floor, and the two spun dramatically around the polished wood. Michael caught Elise's glance and held out his hand to her.

"One day, you'll be glad you know how to do this," Michael's mother had promised when he'd been a teenager, and she drove him week after week to ballroom dance lessons.

"I doubt that," Michael had groused, sullenly staring out the passenger window.

"At least you'll be able to dance if you want to when the occasion presents itself." Confident she was right on this subject, she added, "Too many people sit on the sides because they don't know the steps."

"Or because they're smart." Michael was just as unwilling to be wrong.

During the final lesson, the dance class was one girl short, so Michael's mother stepped in as his partner. "Practice for when your sisters get married, and you dance with me."

Circling the dance floor with Elise now, Michael allowed himself to recall the memory. He was grateful for that class and the time he had danced with his mom—the way they should have danced at his sisters' weddings.

At his high school prom, Michael had discovered how easy being a hero was when he asked several beautifully-coiffed wallflowers to dance. The other guys had razzed him until they observed the heightened attention Michael received from all the girls who noticed his kindness. Dancing came in handy at Meatloaf's wedding—and at the dance following their graduation from Superman school.

"Teach me how to do that," Bryce had demanded that evening, falling into step beside Michael. The band had taken a break and Michael left the dance floor, headed to the refreshment table. Like all the other graduates, Michael and Bryce looked sharp in their dress blues.

"Do what?" Michael feigned ignorance as he surveyed the lovely ladies in attendance and downed a glass of sweet punch.

Bryce grabbed Michael's elbow and steered him outside. Under the starry night sky, Bryce released Michael's arm and faced him. "Show me how to dance." He took several clumsy steps.

A guy and girl, her arm linked through his, passed by. Bryce's feet tangled. He stumbled and looked imploringly at his friend. "I've watched you all night, but I just can't make it work."

Michael folded his arms across his chest and smiled at Bryce's awkward movements. "Dancing is for sissies, remember?"

"Guys dance so they can touch girls. Call me a sissy." Bryce watched another couple strolling in the moonlight. "Just teach me enough steps to get in the game."

Now, holding Elise in his arms, Michael moved easily in time to the music. *You were right, Mom,* he acquiesced silently. He felt a tap on his shoulder.

"May I?" Robson didn't wait for an answer. Smiling magnanimously, he slipped an arm about Elise's waist and stole her away.

Michael returned to the table where the older couples sipped after-dinner cordials. "Those two have practically grown up together," June remarked as she watched Elise and Robson. Michael had to admit they made a stunning pair.

Karl and Michael discussed underwater wildlife until June changed the subject. "The senator certainly has good taste. Has a habit of taking up with young women since his wife died."

Michael followed her glance to the dance floor. Robson was nowhere in sight. Instead Senator Taylor's arms encircled Elise as the couple circled the dance floor.

"I think he had a wandering eye before she died," Jacques wife confided. "The news said she overdosed on weight loss pills."

"She wasn't overweight," Jacques stated. "The man was more than lucky to be married to such a beautiful woman."

Michael recalled the gentle Verity who had invested several afternoons sharing a Coke and conversation with him. Lithe and willowy, she certainly hadn't appeared to be the diet pill type.

"They never had any children," June remarked.

"He did," Jacques' wife said. "A daughter from his first wife. He kept her enrolled away at boarding schools."

"So much for family life," June critiqued.

Jacques' wife added, "Though they were only the best and most expensive schools."

"Liberal, no doubt," Karl stated.

Michael matched the liberal moniker with stories and photos of Claire he had viewed in the media as he recalled her determination to rescue the orphan girls. The Claire who had walked into an overseas hospital she'd barely escaped from to liberate the most vulnerable in that culture showed little in common with the flaming liberal of her public reputation. The senator's daughter was an enigma.

The group watched the dancers until the song ended. Elise politely attempted to excuse herself as the next number began, but the senator gave her a polished smile and held her hand firmly. In a moment, the two were stepping in time again to the music, but each time Elise's face came into view, Michael thought she looked strained. The way his sister had looked when a pasty-white, pimply-faced adolescent had cornered her at the church youth group bonfire.

Recalling his sister's appreciation when he had stepped between them and led her to join his friends, he excused himself from the table.

"May I?" As Robson hadn't, Michael didn't wait for an answer. Smiling beneficently at the senator, he slipped an arm about Elise's waist and danced away.

She smiled her thanks. Her hand soft and relaxed in his, she intuitively followed his lead as they waltzed to the "Blue Danube." When the next piece of music began, Michael expected Robson to cut in at any moment.

Elise must have read his thoughts. "Robson went backstage to prepare for the concert."

Sorry about your luck.

Michael put all of his attention into the moment. They danced three more selections before the band stopped. As people made their way from the ballroom to the concert hall, Michael recalled the musical scores his mother used to sing around the house and suddenly understood her favorite lyrics from *My Fair Lady.* Michael could have danced all night.

Entering the theater, Michael's attention went first to the boxes that lined both sides of the concert hall. Styled like Mediterranean villas, circa 1600, the balcony seats resembled outdoor patios complete with flowering rose and ivy vines. Several levels of plush red chairs stretched from the stage to the back of the lengthy hall. Above, in a ceiling of Baltic blue, floated a scattering of clouds.

"I feel like I'm in Italy," Michael said.

"It's Old World elegant." Elise led the way to two seats in the center of the second row. "I never tire of coming here."

On the stage, the musicians were individually practicing in subdued timbres. A horn player ran a cloth through his gleaming instrument while a violinist rubbed a layer of rosin onto his bow. The timpani player lightly tapped the skin of the polished copper drum and leaned his ear near the taut vibrating crown. On the right side of the stage, Michael spotted Robson, his cello the one nearest the audience. Robson winked at Elise.

Soon the musicians quieted, sat ready in their seats, and the oboe sounded a single note. The concertmaster tuned his violin to the A, and the orchestra members matched the sound. The lights dimmed while the ceiling transformed into a violet and cobalt blue star-studded evening sky.

"Amazing," Michael commented.

"This is one of only five atmospheric theaters in the world," Elise told him.

From backstage, someone began to clap, and the audience joined in as Ava walked out on stage. She bowed to the audience, shook hands with the concertmaster, and took her place on the podium at the center of the orchestra. Silent, the audience waited as she held her conductor's baton poised in midair. With a theatrical sweep, the baton descended, and music dramatically burst forth.

Glancing at the program, Michael read that the first piece was "Karelian Rhapsody" by Finland's most noted composer, Uuno Klami. All the music selections of the evening reflected Ava's heritage and represented Finland, Denmark, and Sweden. The back page provided history about the theater designed by architect and visionary, John Eberson.

After the concert, Michael and Elise went with members of the orchestra to a backstage party. Ava looked weary but happy as Robson brought her a glass of champagne.

"A toast." In the silence of the moment, Robson smiled at Ava. "To Ava's return to our island and to the first female conductor to direct our humble philharmonic."

Ava returned his smile and held up her own glass. "And to those who have made this possible including the foresight of Elise's parents who breathed life back into this elegant theater and mentored many of us."

"And to Elise's painting that provided funds for the continuation of this culturally rich enterprise," Jacques put in. "The Christiansted Theater is the centerpiece of the island's art, culture, and entertainment."

As the crowd of musicians and their friends murmured their approval, Robson, Ava, and Elise formed their own threesome and clinked glasses. Glancing his way, Elise pulled Michael into the intimate circle within the larger group.

In the early morning hours, the adrenaline-filled musicians began to wind down. Robson took Ava to her hotel while Michael drove Elise home and walked with her to her door.

Elise stepped inside her front door and turned. "Thank you. You're a courageous man to brave an evening with strangers on their own turf."

Comfortably elegant and confidently undemanding, Elise made a pleasant companion to a surprisingly enjoyable evening. He tipped a make-believe hat. "I'd say the evening was worth the risk."

CHAPTER 37

Antonio was carefully grafting a slip of a plant onto a grape stem when Elise came into the garden.

He glanced up and smiled. "You're just in time for the wedding ceremony."

"Who are the bride and groom? I don't recall an invitation."

The gardener pressed the tender fibers of the two plants together. "Now for the ring." Expertly, he wound several layers of plant tape around the place where the two plants were now joined and ran a thumb over the seam to assure the end was neat. He stood and examined his handiwork. "A good union."

She compared the two. "They are both grapes?"

He brushed dirt from the stem. "This one is strong." With a finger, he gently lifted a small leaf of the graft. "This plant produces a light and sparkling fruit, but is far too delicate to survive the island storms. Together, I believe, they will create an abundance of sweet grape clusters."

"Where did you get the slip if it doesn't grow on St. Croix?"

He indicated a row of six other plants with matching tape. "Seven altogether. I ordered these starts after seeing how well the native grapes grow on this hill."

"And if your experiment is successful?"

"From table grapes to wine, these will make the palate sing." He turned his attention to her and nodded at her elegant dress. "Music with Mr. Robson this evening?"

She shook her head. "Not this time."

Antonio smiled warmly. "Ah, a second date with Mr. Michael?"

Elise wasn't surprised Antonio knew that Michael had been her guest at the Philharmonic Gala. She learned long ago that living on an island meant everyone knew a lot about everyone else. "Senator Taylor is taking me to dinner."

Antonio frowned. "Has he purchased the painting?"

So Elise wasn't the only one who had questions around the senator's delay in completing the purchase. "No. He wanted to talk about the work first. I hope tonight will see the arrangement finalized."

With trimming shears from his pocket, Antonio snipped a clematis. He repocketed the garden tool and wove the flower's stem through her bracelet. She thanked him and turned to walk back to the house as a car came up the drive.

"Miss Elise?"

Looking back, she saw the gardener following her. "Yes, Antonio?"

"I wanted you to know I'll be working late in the greenhouse this evening."

"All right."

"I'll probably still be here when you return home tonight."

She nodded and went to meet her guest. Elise had to admit that even though he was old enough to be her father, Senator Bennett Taylor was a handsome man. He held the passenger door for her and then navigated the car down the drive.

"I made reservations at the Bougainvillea." Bennett Taylor pulled sunglasses from his shirt pocket.

Elise nodded. "They have a rotating display in their art gallery, though I've not been there recently."

"Then I made a good choice."

The shadows were growing long as they parked. His hand at her elbow, Senator Taylor guided Elise up several stone steps original to the 1763 Sugar Mill. After years of being vacant, the historic site had been refurbished into a vacation experience. A popular wedding and honeymoon destination, the unique bed-and-breakfast was near Frederiksted and offered three floors with private suites that overlooked flowering gardens and a pool.

Still bearing the original Danish tile floor, the entry served as an art gallery in the round. Warmly welcomed by the couple that owned and managed the establishment, Elise and the senator were invited to tour the art gallery while the chef completed their dinner. Elise made a mental note to come by the gallery more often. Being among the work of other artists was like sharing ideas with friends. She was reminded of techniques she had forgotten and brushes she had put aside. The fresh subject matter stirred her spirit, and she felt eager to get home to her sketchpad.

The senator was complimentary of the paintings on display. One in particular caught his eye. "My wife would have liked this."

Elise thought of how much she missed her parents. "I'm sorry for your loss."

He brushed at his eye. "I miss her."

"I understand."

"Thank you for joining me this evening." He turned to meet her gaze. "Being with you helps ease the loneliness."

Their hostess arrived to seat them at their table, and they followed her up a circular staircase that led to an outdoor terrace at the top of the mill. Tables were set where diners had a view of the ocean.

They dined on plates of beef medallions, mushroom tarts, and asparagus in butter and lemon, but Elise couldn't help feeling ill at ease. What should she say to this man? She decided to steer the conversation to the subject that was foremost on her mind.

"Where do you plan to hang your painting? Work or home?

"That's a good question." He sipped his wine. "Once I know you better, I will know exactly where it belongs."

"Oh?"

"Perhaps you can visit and see with your artist's eye where my investment would look best."

Elise pushed an asparagus around on her plate.

He lowered his voice. "I thought about you while I was back on the mainland."

"I hoped you were thinking about the reconstruction of the atmospheric theater." She warmed to her topic. "One of only a few of its kind, the place is valuable as a historic monument, not to mention a center of culture and art for the islands. And for the many visitors from the mainland to the east and the west of us."

He smiled. "When you talk about the concert center, I see your artist's passion. I would like to host you and a showing of your art in the Washington, DC area. International ambassadors as well as other world-changers will fall in love with your talents. As I have. They will take your art to the four corners of the globe."

Elise was speechless. The scope of what he suggested was beyond anything she had dreamed. Jacques offered a bold plan when he proposed a single work of art to be auctioned from the comfort of her St. Croix surroundings. This was grandiose.

"Imagine, Elise." The senator leaned forward. "You could generate sufficient funds to do whatever you wanted with the Christiansted Theater."

She allowed her mind to visualize the possibilities as her dinner companion pressed the idea. "There are a number of top galleries in the Capitol neighborhood. And always parties where I could introduce you to those who appreciate art."

The waiter refilled their water glasses. The senator picked up his glass and considered the contents. "Like water, the quantities of many commodities on the island are restricted. Land, of course, is limited. Reduced number of buyers results in decreased funds and that leads to scarcity in income."

"The island attracts a lot of visitors such as yourself."

He drank from his water glass. "On the mainland, and throughout the continents, is an infinite supply of new people with plenty of money. And, most importantly, the unencumbered ability to generate additional funds."

"The idea sounds promising." She met his eyes. "But I have obligations here."

"To?"

"To the philharmonic, the community, my friends …" Suddenly her cozy life sounded lifeless and dull.

The senator poured wine into both their glasses from the chilled bottle. "You have an infinite talent just beginning to emerge. What a shame to stifle your potential by keeping you isolated here."

"Updating the theater before I consider other opportunities is very important to me."

He sat back in his chair. "So this theater is where you have given your soul."

She frowned. "I would hardly describe my feelings in those terms."

He waved away her objection. "Everyone gives their soul to someone. Or something. Sometime. You are delightfully young. Even naïve." Her hand rested on the base of her wine glass—he reached across to place his fingers over hers. "I will be your guide and introduce you to the successful people in the world."

Elise realized they had drifted far from the subject of his money and her painting. She struggled to grasp the nuances of his suggestions. Dessert arrived with crystal glasses containing a cordial. She tasted, anticipating the flavor to be something rich and smooth like the selections that made Jacques famous, but this was completely different. The deep port warmed her throat.

"Michelangelo and Bach had sponsors—a common occurrence in the arts." Her dinner companion dabbed the linen napkin to his lips. "As your contemporary sponsor, I can open doors for your future nationally and internationally."

After dessert, Senator Taylor led Elise on a walk through the grounds of the converted Sugar Mill while they continued to talk.

"Consider what you could do with an ever-expanding income from your art." He plucked a pink bloom from a bush. Stepping close, he smelled the flower before tucking the rose behind her ear and letting a wisp of her hair flow through his fingers. "Have you thought of establishing a trust that could provide perpetually for your historic structure? The board could serve as trustees, which would free you to be other places."

Much as she steered the conversation to the painting he had promised to buy, she consistently found herself contemplating larger possibilities. Perhaps through innovative opportunities to benefit the theater long term, the troublesome problem could be solved permanently.

Returning through the gallery, the senator lingered in front of the painting that had earlier caught his attention. Then he quickly wrote a check and purchased the piece. The director of the boutique gallery wrapped the painting in protective layers of newsprint. Returning to the car, the senator settled the new acquisition in the backseat of the rental luxury car for their drive back to Elise's home.

"I know just where this will go." Bennett Taylor turned to Elise. "Think about coming back with me and choosing the best setting to display your painting."

This man baffled her. He instantly bought a piece of art he took a fancy to yet still hedged about paying for hers. "We can talk more about destination when you truly own the work."

He laughed. "I gave Jacques a check today."

Relief flooded Elise. At last the Friends of the Philharmonic held the money to begin repairs. They could begin tomorrow.

Bennett Taylor drove up the low hill, parked in front of her house, and came around the car to open her door. Briefly, the overhead light illuminated the interior of the sedan and the newly purchased painting that rested in the back. He helped her from the car and drew her close as he tucked her hand around his arm. Still warmed by the port, Elise finally felt at peace regarding the theater. The cottage supplemented unexpected costs and the senator's check that he said he'd submitted today would be the solution to the remainder of her concerns.

The handsome older man waited while she unlocked and opened the front door. "So now you understand that there are several advantages for you to come to Washington with me." He bent, and just as his lips brushed hers, she heard a voice.

"Miss Elise."

Antonio. Elise remembered that the gardener said he would be working late.

"If you would like, Mr. Michael, Lisandro, and I are on the cottage terrace. Come and join us?" Antonio's eyes went briefly to the senator. "Of course you are welcome, too, sir."

"That's quite a group." Elise glanced up to the cottage, aglow with light and beckoning. Only a short walk from her own home, but she had not taken the well-known path since Michael moved in. After her bewilderment this evening, her spirit longed for the safe and familiar. The cottage had always been that for her.

"Brother Ned, too," Antonio added.

So Michael had made friends with the cheery priest. That spoke well of his character. "Yes, Antonio. Thank you." She turned to Senator Taylor. "Would you like to come along?"

"Pour Some Sugar on Me" by Def Leppard played from the direction of the cottage as Bennett Taylor considered. Wistfully, he shook his head. "I have business to catch up in the morning."

"I understand."

The senator slipped the clematis from her bracelet, and put the bloom to his nose. "Good night."

CHAPTER 38

The five of them lingered on the cottage patio that night until after midnight. For the first time since Michael had come to the island, Elise returned to the former studio. A deep joy filled her as she found solace once more in this sacred place. Watching Brother Ned teach Lisandro magic tricks, she saw the same ease on the kindly priest's face.

Brother Ned had known her parents and the cottage over the years. As if understanding her thoughts, he looked up from playing with Lisandro and smiled. "I'm glad you joined us."

She returned his smile. "Me too."

Glancing out at the ocean, Elise felt she could tiptoe with the moonlight on the tops of the waves. Jacques held the senator's check for the restoration of the atmospheric theater, and repairs could begin right away. Elise had been pleased to find Michael neat and considerate. While seeing someone else's belongings in what had previously been an art studio took getting used to, Michael and the cottage seemed to fit together. June had chosen well when she'd signed him as a tenant.

Elise listened as Antonio and Michael talked about favorite foods and restaurants from different places on the mainland. When Lisandro yawned, Antonio checked his watch. "It is past your bedtime, *mi hijo.*"

The boy did his best to look awake. "I'm not tired, Papa."

The adults glanced at one another. No one appeared eager for the night to end.

"It is the weekend," Michael pointed out.

Brother Ned tapped his chest. "Sleeping in is exactly what I intend to do tomorrow."

Elise laughed. "You are an incurable early riser, Brother Ned."

The priest winked at Lisandro. "Just like the student is not sleepy tonight, the teacher will sleep in tomorrow."

Noticing the boy's heavy eyelids, Michael stood. "I have an idea." He went inside and returned with a pillow and something under his arm.

"Wow." Lisandro watched, fascinated, as Michael turned the small parcel into full-size bedding

"Tools of the trade." Michael tossed the pillow to Lisandro. "Sleep on the couch or on the ground."

"That doesn't look like standard-issue scuba gear," Elise noted.

Michael told them he had been in Pararescue with the Air Force.

"What's that?" Suddenly, Lisandro was not so sleepy.

Michael repeated by rote. "Pararescuemen—also known as PJs—are United States Air Force Special Operations Command and Air Combat Command operators tasked with recovery and medical treatment of personnel in humanitarian and combat environments."

Lisandro frowned. "But what do you *do*?"

"In English," Ned coached. "For the boy."

"Well ..." Michael reworded the job description. "... we are trained medically to search for and help military and civilian personnel, who are lost or injured and need to be brought to hospitals."

"Like an airplane ambulance." Lisandro made a connection to something he understood.

"Like an airplane ambulance." Michael nodded.

Antonio guided his son into the bedroll on the couch in Michael's living room, tucked the boy in, and returned to the patio with the grown-ups. Minutes later, Lisandro made his way back outside and placed a hand on Michael's arm.

Michael lifted the boy onto his lap. "Your rack not comfortable?"

Antonio moved to put Lisandro back to bed, but the boy asked, "What's a rack?"

"Military term for bed." Michael hooked a thumb in the direction of the couch. "I asked if your bed is uncomfortable."

"I like it fine." Lisandro nodded. "What else does a PJ do?"

Antonio spoke up. "Remember your manners, Lisandro. Now, back to bed."

The boy turned questioning eyes to Michael.

"If it's okay with your father, perhaps we can do both," Michael suggested. "I'll answer a question, and then you go back to bed."

"It's called a rack," Lisandro corrected.

"So it is, and when PJs are not in their rack, they recover the astronauts when they return from space with a water landing. They rescue downed pilots and crews, establish airstrips, and rescue anyone lost or in harm's way."

Stifling a yawn, Lisandro slid off Michael's lap and returned inside to go to sleep.

Michael turned the conversation, asking about activities on the island. "Besides crab races, eating at Jewel by the Sea, and the Philharmonic."

Brother Ned, Antonio, and Elise listed favorites until a sleepy-eyed Lisandro returned and tugged on Michael's sleeve.

Michael turned his attention once again to the boy. "Another question?"

Antonio stood and picked up his son. "Too many questions are not polite, my son."

Lisandro looped an arm around his father's neck. "Mr. Michael, how do you do that all by yourself?"

"Well," Michael grinned. "Since I don't have a cape or superpowers in my 72-hour pack where that sleeping bag came from, I need a lot of help."

Lisandro leaned his head on Antonio's shoulder. "Do you have a partner?"

Michael nodded. "We work in teams."

"Like our baseball team at school?"

"Not that many. Four technicians trained in medicine, survival, rescue, and tactics.

The explanation made sense as Elise recalled Michael's recent absence. *Chasing sunrise.*

CHAPTER 39

Michael surfaced and surveyed the sky above the secluded St. Croix beach. An advance team of two scuba instructors from the San Francisco Bay Area swam below. After familiarizing themselves with the island's best places to dive, they would return in several months, leading a commercial dive trip. As their guide, part of Michael's job included making sure they weren't surprised by a turn in the weather. Presently, the predicted storm stood a long way off.

Today's leisurely morning reminded Michael of another beach trip. His first experience in the ocean, actually. The day after high school graduation, Michael had found himself on a commercial airliner with Bryce seated next to him. Mom and his sisters occupied the row behind. He didn't know how she'd pulled it off, but they were on their way from their Midwest home to a Florida vacation.

Michael had his suspicions. His mom had picked up a side job in recent months, sold the car for a smaller model, and made arrangements for Bryce to come along on the trip. The fact that she secured an agreement with Bryce's mom was worth a commendation.

"We're going to make a memory before you jet off to your training," his mom had announced. They stayed a week at a condo on the beach. While the girls sunbathed, swam, and shopped, the boys took surfing lessons.

That first morning eight students, smelling strongly of suntan lotion and armed with oversized, soft-topped surfboards, followed their instructor to the beach.

"Before we hit the waves," the surf instructor outlined, "you get a crash course on paddling, catching a wave, and standing."

He dropped his board flat on the sand and they followed suit. Lying on their bellies on the padded fiberglass boards that smelled of sweet coconut wax, the surfer wannabes watched the instructor demonstrate how to quickly jump to their feet in one fluid motion.

"Don't look at your feet. Keep your eyes focused ahead and your center of gravity low," said the tanned forty-something with a gray-streaked ponytail. "To go faster, lean forward. To apply the brakes, put more weight on the back foot." He showed the technique a second time and then pointed to each student in turn who did their best imitation of what they'd just observed.

"Push yourself up, pull your feet underneath, and stand," the surfer coached. "Keep your weight on the back foot and your knees bent. You'll be able to move with the ocean when you connect with it."

One by one the students jumped to their feet. The instructor made minor adjustments to the way several stood on their stationary boards. Then he came to Michael.

"A goofy foot," the instructor pronounced.

"He's goofy, all right," Bryce quipped, balancing on the board next to Michael.

"Uncommon, actually," the surfer explained. "I only get a few each season. Look down the line."

The parade of surfing students resembled a chorus line. Except for Michael.

"The rest have their left foot in the forward position," ponytail pointed out.

Michael switched his feet around.

"Feel awkward?"

"Yeah," Michael admitted.

"Everyone automatically puts their best foot forward, literally, on that first jump from laying down to standing. Your best is opposite most of the rest of us."

Michael wasn't sure he wanted to stand out in the crowd.

The instructor bent and picked up the point of the large board. He lifted it slightly and rocked the board back and forth. Michael quickly lost his balance. "Surfing teaches you to go with the flow. To take life as it comes."

Great. The surfer is a philosopher. The next time, Michael put his best foot forward and was instantly more stable.

"Don't sweat it. Being a goofy foot won't hinder your ability to surf the Hawaiian pipeline." He grinned and moved on with the lesson.

Finally, Michael leashed the board to his ankle, slung it against his left side the way he had carried his schoolbooks, and trotted to the blue-green surf. As he waded in waist-deep, the cool water washed the sticky sand and heat from his body. Sliding belly first onto the surfboard, he paddled with the other students after their teacher. Leaving the shore, they'd floated over the rhythmic waves destined to roll up on the land.

Soon, the class bobbed like a line of corks along the break where shallow waves made their run for the beach. Aboard a blue-striped surfboard, Michael floated on his stomach. He didn't have to look back to feel the wave gather behind him.

"Paddle," the instructor yelled. "Paddle, paddle!"

Powerfully, Michael dug his hands into the water to move the surfboard forward, yet the more powerful swell drew him back. Then, with a surge, he was part of the wave, gliding swiftly atop the roaring surf. Behind him, Michael heard Bryce's whoop and knew he'd caught the same wave.

"Push up!" The instructor's voice already sounded far away.

Just ahead of the curl, Michael pushed up and pulled his feet beneath him. Easing into a low stance, his hands splayed for balance, he firmly planted one foot across the backbone of the surfboard, then the other. For those few magnificent moments, the world whisked by, the sky bluer than before, and the sandy beach rapidly drawing closer. The exhilarating ride lasted only thirty seconds and was the biggest rush he'd experienced so far.

During that last idyllic week before he packed his bags for parajumper orientation training, Michael surfed with Bryce and spent time with his mom and sisters.

On the flight back home to Nebraska, his mother had asked, "Was this a good graduation present?"

"The best," Michael told her.

The low rumble of a boat's motor brought Michael back to the present. Nearby, a private yacht cruised purposefully toward the beach and dropped anchor. About one hundred and sixty-four feet in length with three decks, the name on the gleaming side identified the vessel as *Al-Leatto*. On land, a black luxury car parked near the water's edge and a man emerged. Something about his movements seemed familiar to Michael.

A rigid-hulled inflatable boat carrying two passengers launched from the yacht and sped toward the beach. Faint diesel fumes from the yacht's tender reached Michael's nose as he watched the boat reach the shore.

While the guy operating the motor stayed with the inflatable, a dark-haired man got out of the tender and shook hands with the waiting man. After some conversation, the two ashore stepped aboard, and the runabout spun around.

Still low in the water, and careful not to draw attention, Michael swam closer. As the boat zipped by on its return to the sleek ship, he could make out two Asian men from the yacht with their Caucasian passenger. Senator Bennett Taylor was still on vacation in St. Croix.

CHAPTER 40

Concentrating on the musical score, Elise drew the bow across the tuned viola strings. She stopped, paused, and began again. The voice of a single instrument, clear, deep, and hauntingly beautiful—or would be once she got this section practiced well enough. "Practice makes permanent," her father would say as he encouraged his music students to stop after each wrong note and correct to the proper tablature.

At the agreed upon time, she thought she heard a step on the porch. She and Michael were going to Frederiksted to listen to live jazz on the pier at sunset. On the cottage terrace that night after her dinner with the senator, Elise, Antonio, and Brother Ned compared their list of things to do on the island with the activities Michael had so far experienced. When they found Michael had yet to picnic on the pier while local musicians played, a date had been arranged to include Antonio, Lisandro, and Brother Ned.

With renewed vigor, Elise returned her attention to her music. She began at the beginning to see how long she could travel the notes without needing to redo a few. She played several pages through before tangling on the trouble spot once again. Glancing at the clock, she realized Michael should arrive any minute. On cue, she heard the knock she had been listening for that signaled the end of this practice session and the beginning of an evening with friends.

Viola in hand, Elise went to the screen door.

"Beautiful," he pronounced.

"The music or me?" She swung the door open for him to enter.

"Both." Standing close in the entryway and wearing shorts, T-shirt, and flip-flops, Michael smelled of sun and the ocean. He followed her to the living room and noticed her music stand in front of the large picture windows. Oversized sheets of music scores lay strewn on the floor. "What are you working on?"

Elise gathered the scattered sheets and stacked them on top of the pages on the stand. "I'm playing with the orchestra for their big concert in September. Occasionally, they need additional musicians, and I fill in."

"Play something for me?"

She went to a cupboard and pulled a music book from the stacks of dog-eared volumes. She flipped to a page and set the opened score on the music stand. "Romance for Viola and Orchestra in F major, Op. 85" by Max Bruch. She played a couple of notes, then stopped and turned two tiny screws near the bridge. She passed her thumb across the strings. Satisfied with the sound, she began again.

Taking a seat on the couch, Michael watched and listened. Elise found performing in a crowded concert hall as part of the orchestra easier than to play as a soloist for one person. But she quickly forgot about her guest as the familiar notes filled the room and the warm timbre of the instrument sang.

"Like the sirens serenaded Odysseus," her father had coached her. "When the music becomes part of you, you play from the heart."

After the final note, she moved the viola to rest position and waited for Michael's response.

He sat forward. "Your music is talking without using words."

"There isn't much that can't be said through music," she agreed. "When I play, I hope for you to feel what I feel."

He indicated her easel by the windows. "And when you paint?"

She smiled. "Art is communication between artist and those whose hearts are open. Receptive. Painting is talking with shapes, colors, and textures instead of words. Music is connection through sound."

"Did you learn cello?"

"Papa taught me. But I did better with Mama's viola." She tucked the instrument under her chin and lightly played a quick scale. "More my size. Or maybe I just didn't want to be in competition with his star pupil."

"Robson?"

She nodded. "He was a competitive kid. When I excelled with viola, the competition dissipated and we played duets instead."

"I'll bet that was popular with audiences."

"People began pairing us together when we were children." She shrugged. "We probably reminded everyone of a younger version of my mama and papa."

"Reasonable," Michael admitted.

Elise sighed. "I remember the first time we kissed." She paused, reminiscing.

Michael stood and crossed to the window. The movement reminded her that the sun was setting. She placed her viola in an open instrument case resting in a wingback chair. The polished wood nested in red velvet. "Time to go." She snapped the case closed. "We don't want to keep the others waiting, and the view of the sunset from Frederiksted is not to be missed."

CHAPTER 41

Still learning about the island he now called home, Michael frequently chose a different beach to explore. Each place had its own unique flavor, and today, he sought the seclusion of Gentle Winds beach, not far from Christiansted. The snorkeling was interesting near the quiet condo complex with a beachside pool surrounded by vibrant bougainvillea.

After running and swimming laps, Michael lay back in the sand to let his muscles rest in the warm sun. Propped on one elbow under a slate blue sky, he watched a large tanker make its slow, steady pass toward the Hess Corporation oil refinery.

He found himself thinking about Elise. Again. Her authenticity disarmed him and he felt comfortable in her company. "You could use a woman in your life, mate," Bryce had said. "Speaking of serious, how's your neighbor?" Contemplating his friend's words, Michael was surprised to see a familiar figure come into view. Wearing a one-piece bathing suit with a wrap-around skirt tied about her waist, Elise walked ankle deep in the surf.

Michael jumped up and jogged to meet her. "What brings you to this beach?"

She smiled when she saw him. "Grab your shoes and I'll show you."

Carrying her sandals casually by the straps, she led the way. At the west end of the beach, the white sand gave way to a rocky terrain. Like pockets, tide pools filled and emptied with the ebb and flow of waves that broke against the black, unforgiving crags. Elise slipped on her sandals and climbed. Michael followed her onto the bed of rough rocks. After only a few steps, he put on his beach shoes too.

No bigger than a silver dollar, black crabs skittered sideways from under foot. Elise inspected each tide pool, pointing out spotted fish the size of his fingernail, brilliant blue ones with tiny yellow tails, and an occasional hermit crab. Chitons, sea anemones, and sea snails hugged the sides of rocks as the waves washed back and forth over them. Clusters of black and red prickly sea urchins reminded Michael of his earlier snorkeling and scuba instruction.

Several years earlier, with their parajumper-issue snorkeling equipment, Michael, along with Bryce and a few other trainees, had caught a military transport to the island of Hawaii. In possession of a three-day pass, the guys wanted to see the height of a volcano and the depth of clear water with snorkeling said to be second to none.

Bryce and Michael had snorkeled along the top of the volcanic reef on the island of Hawaii. When a sea turtle casually swam past, Bryce had grabbed onto the large shell. Kicking in time to the turtle's languid strokes, the two moved easily out to sea. Michael leisurely followed, fascinated with the abundance of colorful sea life. Farther from shore the underwater volcanic rocks quickly rose, narrowing the space for a swimmer between the coral and the surface. A powerful wave pushed Michael across the sharp surface. Feeling the coral slice his stomach, he had thrown out his hand to brace himself against the next wave that carried him back toward the razor sharp edge. Like fire, sudden pain seared through his hand and he forgot the cuts on his abdomen.

Shoving off the rocks with his flippers, Michael swam into deeper water. There he held his hand in front of his facemask. A million black sea urchin spines protruded from the length of his little finger like countless needles in his grandmother's pincushion. Instinctively, he grabbed with the finger and thumb of his right hand as if extracting a thorn. But the moment he touched them, the fragile spines broke off. Gingerly he tried again. Again the needle-thin spines snapped, leaving the hurtful tips deeply, painfully, and solidly embedded in his flesh.

Michael kicked to shore. Carrying the fins and mask in his good hand, he held his left hand above his heart in an attempt to dull the unrelenting sting. He hiked back to the hotel's front desk where the tanned and shapely clerk sat on a stool, reading a magazine and chomping gum.

He held out his hand. "Do I need to take this to a doctor?"

She leaned across the desk for a closer look. "That's almost as bad as the girl who was in here earlier." The clerk turned a page in the fashion magazine. "She stepped on an urchin and her entire heel looks like your finger."

"And a doctor cut out the spines?"

She shook her head. "They'll dissolve."

"Dissolve." Michael raised his hand above his head again in hopes of easing the throb. "And what about the pain?"

"Pee on it."

"Excuse me?"

She popped her gum. "Really."

He tried to read her expression. "Is this the advice locals give gullible tourists?"

"Take it or leave it." She shrugged. "I dive too. It's what we all do."

Towel over his shoulder and carrying snorkel and mask, Bryce stepped up beside him. "Do what?"

"Pee on it," the clerk repeated.

"Why would I do that?" Michael had been in no mood for guessing games.

"I'll do it," Bryce offered.

"It's the pH," she explained. "It neutralizes."

Bryce looked at him expectantly.

"Don't even think about it," Michael growled to his friend.

"Did you do it?" Marissa had asked at this point in his story during his next visit home.

"Yeah," April added. "Did you let Bryce pee on your hand?"

"Girls," his mother admonished at the unladylike word. But she looked at Michael, her eyebrows raised in humored question.

Michael let the question linger, enjoying their full attention and the suspense he had created. "I went to the restaurant and asked for a cup of apple cider vinegar."

"Good thing the restaurant was open," his mother said.

"Eventually."

His mom's eyes widened and he'd winked at her.

Now, Elise spoke as she bent and pointed to a tide pool. Michael realized he'd been so immersed in the memory that he'd missed what she said. He squatted across from her to better see what she showed him.

"My mother liked tide pools," he said as a way to reengage in conversation with Elise. "She approached them like an Easter egg hunt. Everything she found she called a treasure. I followed along until I'd put in a polite amount of time. Then I made some reason to go about my own business."

Her eyebrows went up. "You weren't interested in tide pools?"

"Because she was interested in them, I wasn't." He paused. "I don't think anyone was ever really interested in anything my mom was interested in."

They stood and continued across the rocks.

"That must have been lonely for your mother."

He nodded solemnly. "There are some things I'd do differently if I could."

Elise picked up a shell. "I trailed my mother through these tide pools, fascinated with the creatures she showed me."

Michael pictured a little blonde girl with a swinging ponytail.

"My mother made her peace here." A wave broke against the rocks and threw water on Elise's ankles.

"Wasn't she happy?" Michael wondered how anyone would not be content living on the sea with perpetually pleasant weather, plenty of outdoor activities, and local rum.

"Mother was raised in the United States. Papa was born and grew up in Austria. They met playing in a symphony in Europe. English was their common language, but they said they fought in French."

"Your dad knew three languages?"

"Just Austrian and English. Neither spoke French, so they didn't argue." Elise watched his face and smiled when she saw he understood the joke. "They lived in Europe until Papa took his position here. One day, I followed my mother across these rocks, through the low coral along the cove in front of us, along the next beach rough with chunks of coral and shells, until I said, 'Mama, we could walk around this whole island.' She stopped and contemplated the coast before us for a long time. I remember watching her hair blow in the wind, thinking she reminded me of the slender and beautiful white egret. Then she relaxed and gave me her biggest smile. She took my hand and swung it as we turned back toward home. She said, 'We could walk around this whole island if we wanted to.' After that day she was comfortable to be here—to be *all* here—with Papa and me."

As they rounded the rocky point, a small cove lay before them. The broad black rocks transitioned to smaller, lighter stones. They stepped down into the calf-deep water and walked carefully through leafy sea plants that swayed with the rhythm of the ocean. Navigating the uneven footing was slow going.

"I can't imagine what it was like to grow up on this island." Michael watched schools of small fish dart away from their feet in the clear water.

"What was it like growing up in Nebraska?"

He harrumphed. "Different from here."

"How so?"

At the middle of the cove, they waded ashore. Far from a sunbather's pick, cantaloupe-sized chunks of brain coral lay scattered across the beach. Elise stooped to dig a partially buried piece from the sand and traced the patterned surface with her fingers.

Hands on hips, Michael watched a boat far out on the horizon. "The only seas in Nebraska were seas of tilled and turned earth. Seas of crops. Soybeans one year, feed corn the next. Winter wheat in between the two summer crops. Some fields of alfalfa. In years when the corn grew tall in the fields around the house, everything felt closed in. Claustrophobic."

Leading the way, Elise picked her way through the rough terrain. On the west end of the cove, rocks littered the coarse sand. She found a stone and placed it in his hand. "What color is this?"

"Purple." He studied the smooth, egg-like specimen. "A purple rock."

She dropped a second rock into his hand. "I come here when I'm looking for colors." Blocky with stripes of gold against charcoal, this stone looked more like a piece of wood.

Michael had never considered identifying and naming colors of rocks. He wasn't sure he had noticed that rocks were anything other than colorless gray. With fresh eyes, he studied the landscape and noted a variety of colors. A bright piece, partially buried in the sand, caught his attention and Michael picked up the stone.

"Sea glass or sometimes called beach glass." Elise showed him the polished edges. "Occasionally shards of bottles from a shipwreck come to shore. My mother said they were sea gems. Sailors call them mermaid tears."

Michael gazed at the play of the sun on the vast ocean. "What makes a mermaid cry?"

"According to legend, mermaids have the ability to influence the weather, but King Neptune forbade them from using their powers to intervene with the lives of men. Mermaids often swam with ships, and one mermaid, accompanying a schooner on the ship's ocean travels, fell in love with the daring captain. When a violent storm threatened to destroy the ship and drown the crew and captain, the mermaid calmed the seas and saved the life of her beloved. For her disobedience, Neptune banned the mermaid to the depths of the ocean, far from the travels of ships and men. The tears of the mermaid who misses her captain make their way to shore as these soft-colored bits of sea glass."

"Not much of a happily ever after." Michael thought his sisters would have liked the story but not the ending.

"Bittersweet actually. The mermaid loved the captain more than herself. She provided for his life and happiness at the cost of her own." Elise thought for a moment. "My parents said that true love is more invested in what's best for the other than in oneself."

That sounded like something his mother would have said. "And today, the glass is a fresh color for the artist." Michael placed the sea glass in her palm.

"The rocks, the water, and the sky." She swept her arm toward the countless rocks of various shapes and sizes crowded together, washed, softened, and polished by the sometimes gentle, sometimes pounding waves. "They are unlimited sources for colors. Some I can copy. The delicate hues of others elude me."

"Your mother needed to conquer the island, but you make peace with the colors."

"And you conquer the ocean and the sky?"

He was silent, considering this.

"Isn't that why divers dive?" Shading her eyes from the sun with her hand, she looked up to see him. "And pilots fly?"

He studied her. "That's what you were thinking when you included the plane in your sunrise painting?"

Elise took the two stones from his hand. "I was intrigued by the designers, builders, and pilots who dared to triumph over the once unreachable. By that pilot who belonged to the dawn sky." She rinsed the stones and the beach glass in the salty water and inspected their colors anew. Then she slipped the rocks into her pocket but held onto the glass, running a thumb along the edges smoothed by years in the ocean. "Imagine long ago, people who created and molded the glass into bottles, filled them—"

"With beer for the sailors."

She smiled. "Or rum. Or oil or perfume. Someone loaded this bottle and others onto a ship crafted by engineers who understood tides, currents, and winds. Then bold adventurers cast off to travel to new lands."

"And some ships along with their scurvy crew were conquered by the elements that transformed the bottle into beach glass."

"Mermaid tears." Soberly she pocketed the sea glass, and they began their walk back.

"Sea gems." Climbing away from the water, Michael went first this time. He knew the way and turned to offer his hand for the climb. "You know, some sea glass may be from careless picnickers who left soda bottles on Buck Island's beach. Or from water skiers who dropped a beer bottle over the side of their boat. Maybe even from a hurricane that blew trash into the ocean."

From her pocket, Elise retrieved the sea gem Michael had found and examined the glass. "Maybe from a rum bottle that carried a love letter written by a sailor shipwrecked on an island."

Michael and Elise retraced their steps back to Gentle Winds beach. Elise studied the coconut palms clustered above the sand. "Have you had a fresh one yet?"

"Coconut?" He eyed the cluster, like a bunch of giant grapes just out of reach under the lofty palm branches. "Only the ones from the grocery. My sisters were fond of them and of chewing on segments of sugarcane from the produce section."

"Only your sisters?"

He grinned. "Okay, maybe I liked them too."

She glanced around. "If we find a long branch, we can knock one down."

Michael rooted through a collection of scrub until he found a lengthy dead branch. By jumping and swinging the long stick, he made contact at last with a coconut husk and sent the nut crashing to the ground along with its neighbor.

The size of a volleyball, the thick green husk had brown splotches like a banana transitioning to overripe. Elise led him back to the rocky part of the beach and balanced the coconut upside down between sturdy stones.

She handed Michael a rock as large as the coconut. "This is the easy way to open a coconut. Just drop the rock on the point of the husk."

The first blow produced three cracks in the thick covering.

"This time," she coached, "put some *umph* in it."

A second blow split the husk, revealing a hairy, pale brown nut neatly within. A softer hit on the eye of the nut from the weighty rock poked a sizable hole in the top. Inside, the fruit was nearly full of cloudy sweet milk. She drank half the contents, and he drank the rest. Hungry and thirsty, Michael found the fresh coconut milk satisfying after their trek.

A final strike from the rock easily split the soft nut into two pieces. Elise showed him how to run his thumb under the thin white flesh and peel the meat from the shell. Sitting cross-legged in the sand, they ate the tender coconut meat that tasted new and resembled the texture of sushi.

"Juicy," he declared.

"Anything like this in Nebraska?"

Michael watched the coconut palms sway in the breeze. "Soybeans are flavorful right off the plant. My sisters and I picked handfuls of the pods as soon as they formed. The feed corn was edible when young. Wheat kernels off the winter wheat have a nutty flavor. Chewing alfalfa stems has that fresh grass flavor."

"Fruit trees?"

He considered. "Mulberry trees. Wild blackberries, woods strawberries, gooseberries, Concord grapes."

"Those are rare imports in our markets."

"St. Croix's normal fruits are labeled exotic by the time they reach the Midwest. Pineapples, mangos, papayas, dates, key limes. Coconuts. All the fruits growing in your garden."

She nodded. "Many of those were native. Mama and Papa crafted their garden the way Papa conducted a symphony. They added colors and flavors like a composer weaves instruments, tempos, and sounds."

"And Antonio?"

"He's an artist in the garden. When Papa and Mama were unable to maintain the property by themselves, Antonio came to us from California where he used to manage a winery. He spends a day or two at our place, and the rest of the week, he creates landscapes for others."

Michael swallowed the last bite of his half of the coconut and stacked the pieces of outer husk. He reached for the unopened coconut, and tossed the nut up and down like a football.

"When the husk turns brown, break that one open to eat," Elise said. "The coconut will be more mature and the texture will be firmer."

He tucked the coconut under his arm, and they made their way back.

CHAPTER 42

The harsh jangle of the phone jarred Michael from sleep. He glanced at the bedside clock. Five minutes before the alarm would go off anyway. The phone rang again and Michael reached for it.

"Yeah."

"We have a Red Cat." Corbin's voice was all business.

Adrenaline coursed through Michael's veins. "How soon?"

"A plane is on its way to pick you up. Meet your ride in an hour."

"Roger that." Michael bounded out of bed and into his BDUs. Shouldering his 72-hour pack, he tossed back a canned energy drink and headed for his jeep.

Opening the passenger door, he pitched his pack onto the passenger seat, then turned to survey the ocean view. The sun hovered just above the horizon. Peace. Beauty.

He glanced over at Elise's house. Shaded by the glossy leaves of a majestic mahogany tree, she sat at the table in her garden, sketchbook in hand, drinking tea in the quiet morning. He must have sounded like a raging bull because she looked his way and waved.

He jogged over to her. "Great portrait of Robson," he observed as he took in the drawing she'd been working on. The pang of jealousy he felt surprised him.

She stood, tipped her head sideways, and considered her work. "Actually length is the longest part of the canvas, width is the shortest. If the design is horizontal, the picture is called landscape. A vertical design is portraiture. Since I drew this likeness horizontally, maybe it's really a landscape of Robson's face."

"You're not following the rules."

"Artists are more about asking questions than following rules." She regarded his clothing. "You're probably better at following the rules."

He winced. "Most of the time." He directed the conversation back to safer ground. "Even horizontal, you sketched a good likeness."

"I wanted to catch that look from the dance the other night. The beauty haunts me so I knew I had to purge it onto paper."

"That look?"

"Of being in love."

Michael rubbed the back of his neck and wondered at the fresh rush of emotion. What was that about? Elise and Robson had already spent a lifetime together. He was the newcomer in this equation. He cleared his throat. "Well, no one accused Robson of being blind or stupid."

She looked at him quizzically. Then she swept the charcoal to accent the cello player's generous eyebrows. "He looks good in love."

Michael thought of Meatloaf and his wife, Diane. Their love for one another reflected on their faces. When one walked into the room, the other lit up like a Christmas tree on Christmas Eve.

She continued. "And Ava is a worthy choice."

Michael blinked. "Ava?"

She added highlights to Robson's cheekbones. "Surely you noticed the attraction between them the other evening."

Michael studied her face.

She tipped her head. "What?"

He shifted his weight. "I thought …" He shifted his weight again. "Robson came here so often for you …"

"And?"

She wasn't making this easy. "I assumed you and Robson …"

Elise turned those blue eyes directly on his. "Assumed what?"

"That you liked each other."

She smiled. "Of course we like each other."

He bobbed a quick nod. "Of course." Feeling confused and awkward, he turned his gaze to the safety of the ocean.

"We practically—"

"Grew up together." He finished the sentence with her. "I heard that."

She held the sketchpad at arm's length. "But Robson's in love with Ava."

Michael looked back at her upturned face. "In love?"

She held the sketch at arm's length. "He hasn't said so. But I know. He's in love."

"With Ava." Michael ran a hand through his hair, trying to take in this surprising information. "But you said you and Robson kissed."

Elise burst out laughing. "After that kiss, he asked what I was thinking. I said, 'Kissing you is like kissing my brother.' For a moment he looked hurt, and then we laughed until we cried. It was funny because everyone expected us to fall in love. We love each other all right but not the way they expected."

His loss. My gain.

She propped the sketchbook on the table and turned back to him. The sun danced off her necklace. Michael recognized the sea glass he had found when she'd taken him to the rocky beach where she looked for colors. *Mermaid tears. Sea gems.*

"I turned the memory into jewelry." She took off the necklace for him to examine.

Once again he held the beach glass, but Elise had added a row of fresh water pearls held by a delicate silver wire that attached the pendant to a slim cord. He ran his thumb across the pearls. "It's even prettier like this."

She turned, and he put the necklace around her neck and did the clasp. He lifted her hair, letting the jewelry settle against her neck.

Facing him again, she eyed his camouflage clothing. "This doesn't look like a normal scuba day."

He shrugged. "A different kind of normal."

"Chasing sunrises?"

"I hate to leave." Michael waved an arm toward the ocean. "This island is home now."

Elise followed his gaze to the horizon. "Keep a piece of paradise with you."

He took in the ocean, the gardens, and imprinted them in his memory. As Beethoven played from the house, he stepped back, pretending to get a better view but now inserting Elise's shapely form into the picture. Michael inhaled the fragrance of plumeria, frangipani, night jasmine, and gardenia hedges the trade wind blew to him and watched her hair wisp about the sea-glass necklace and across her cheek.

She turned to face him, He knew in that moment he'd take with him this picture, this piece of paradise.

CHAPTER 43

Computer specialist Rob Hancock needed to be taken off a nuclear submarine in the Pacific—an unusual rescue, as Hancock himself wasn't in any danger. But a computer system at a nuclear power plant was. The system needed to be fixed right away, and Hancock was the man to repair the problem.

"You'll trade your space in the helicopter with Hancock," Corbin outlined during briefing. "The 'copter will get the computer man, a couple other experts, and some equipment to their assignment."

"What's my destination?" Michael had wanted to know.

"The sub will make port in the Philippines. You'll catch a ride home from there."

A familiar scenario, PJs frequently traded their spot on the mode of transportation for another to be evacuated to necessary medical treatment. In this case, Michael would trade his seat so Hancock could be evacuated to provide essential technical expertise.

On schedule, the submarine surfaced in the midst of heaving seas. From a helicopter hovering above, Michael descended on the penetrator. During Superman school, Michael learned the forest penetrator was developed to pierce the dense jungle canopy. The need to drop into thick forests of unforgiving trees led to the employment of a second piece of equipment, a reinforced jumpsuit, a first cousin to the ones worn by smokejumpers in mountainous Montana and Idaho where firefighters fly in to fight forest fires. Heavy nylon straps stretched from the wearer's feet up the inside of the legs to form a low crotch. Inside the reinforced suit, a PJ could take a direct kick in the groin or drop onto a sizeable tree branch without suffering injury.

Though initially designed to safely drop parajumpers into solid jungles in Vietnam, PJs continued to use the suit and the penetrator in other scenarios. The shape of a milk can, the device was lowered from the helicopter by a hoist to deliver a rider or extract a passenger—in this case, both to deliver Michael and extract Hancock. The penetrator was a popular option for unpredictable open seas situations like this one.

According to plan, Michael rode the penetrator down to the sub. The helicopter's loudly thropping blades were deafening. The roar of the wind and sea were just as loud. Michael tried to time the rise and fall of the deck below. Stepping off when the ship fell into the next wave trench meant he could drop fifteen feet. If he stepped off when the sub rose, the blow would feel like getting hit by a truck. Despite opportune timing, his legs smarted with the impact.

From the sub's turret, a seaman helped Hancock to Michael.

"Don't touch the cable." Michael yelled to Hancock above the roar of the wind and the chopper's fiercely spinning blades.

"Static electricity?"

"'Copter generates enough to light up your world." Michael cinched Hancock firmly into the harness. "Enough to knock you into the next time zone."

After concise instructions from Michael, Hancock rode the penetrator up to the waiting chopper. In a moment, Michael saw the thumbs up from the crewman through the open door, signaling Hancock was securely aboard. The helicopter banked left and flew off into the night.

Following the gesture of the seaman who waited inside the open hatch, Michael climbed down several rungs of the metal ladder while the seaman slammed and secured the hatch behind them. This was his ride to the next port of call.

In Manila, Michael linked up with Wingnut, Meatloaf, and Bryce who had also completed an assignment in the area. Tomorrow, the PJs would catch a flight home. Tonight, the balmy air of the large island beckoned, and the guys were eager to shed the stress and accompanying tight muscles of the recent mission. Strolling downtown, the foursome wandered past tourists and locals.

"I'm hungry. Let's eat there." Bryce indicated a busy storefront where delicious smells clung heavy around the doorway.

"Must be good," Meatloaf noted. "Packed with locals."

After they were seated inside, the young Philippine waiter brought plates piled with *malagkit*, a long-grain translucent rice grown in Central Luzon and Tagalog. The glutinous grain tasted sticky and sweet next to the generous portions of roast pork. Another bowl held *ginataang galunggong*, a fish dish made by soaking grated coconut meat in hot water and then squeezing the moist coco through a sieve to create a gata cream used to flavor the fish. Caramelized bananas topped generous portions of bread-and-butter pudding.

Their stomachs full, the foursome returned to the streets. A few blocks down, Wingnut led the way into a bar where a scantily clad waitress with too much makeup brought them a round of beers.

Settling back in his chair, Michael let the beer course through his system. He was ready to unwind. While a seedy-looking band played poor arrangements of old American pop tunes, Michael watched a customer follow a girl to the back of the bar where they disappeared through a door.

The waitress returned to their table. "Gentlemen want something else?"

Wingnut's eyebrows went up. "What else is on the menu?"

She smiled and turned away.

"Nice view." Wingnut watched the girl leave their table. Glancing back over her slender shoulder, the waitress winked. After serving another customer, she returned with a second round of beers and deposited the mugs on the table. Wingnut opened his arms, and she slid onto his lap.

Meatloaf polished off his first brew. "I'm bushed, guys."

"You're married," Wingnut countered. The girl ran a finger suggestively around Wingnut's ear.

"Those who can, do." Meatloaf grinned and stood. "I'm heading back."

"Don't be rude. She just brought you a beer."

"Help yourself." Meatloaf indicated the full beer that had just arrived.

"You're with the boys," Wingnut urged. "We won't tell your wife."

"Won't need to," Meatloaf tossed over his shoulder.

The waitress signaled and two girls came to their table. One slid onto the bench beside Bryce. The second sat next to Michael.

Meatloaf disappeared out the door in the direction of their hotel. Wingnut shifted under the weight of the girl in his lap and whispered something to her. Tucking a strand of long dark hair behind her ear, she whispered something back.

A hand on his thigh brought Michael's attention to the girl who sat next to him. She looked at him with lovely, dark eyes.

Bryce tried to talk to the girl who sat next to him. To her broken English and his elementary Filipino, Bryce added pantomime—the two laughed awkwardly.

Michael looked back at the girl at his side. Her lips smiled suggestively, but her eyes were solemn. Sad.

Bryce found a pencil and played tic-tac-toe on a napkin with his companion. Michael offered Meatloaf's abandoned beer to the girl at his side and then felt stupid for doing so. She was small, like his youngest sister the last time he saw her. She was young, probably too young to drink. Definitely too young to be in a place like this.

The girl made a polite motion of taking a sip of the beer and set the glass back on the table. She reminded him of the little wren that accidentally flew into the mud porch of their farmhouse in Nebraska. After a frantic chase, he had cupped the quivering bird in his hand and walked outside. Just before he released the tiny creature, he'd looked once more at the frightened dark eyes.

Wingnut and his seatmate were getting chummy. Michael cleared his throat and indicated to the girl he wanted her to move. Reluctantly, she slid from the bench and stood, eyeing him expectantly.

Michael stood. "I'll see you guys later."

Wingnut leaned toward him. "C'mon, Michael. Relax. You can get a lap dance here for less than a burger and fries back home."

Michael looked at the young girl beside him. She should be anywhere but here. "No, I can't."

"What's wrong with you, man? You're too uptight."

Bryce stood and made his way around the table. He stopped between Michael and Wingnut.

"Unlike you," Michael's words were like daggers, "I can't save somebody one day and use someone the next." He took the girl's arm gently and guided her through the entry door. When the older woman with too much makeup followed, Bryce calmly positioned himself between her and the door.

Outside under the stars Michael could hear strains of the band's mediocre attempt to play Elvis's "All Shook Up." He fished money from his pocket and pressed the bills into her palm. "Go home," he told her kindly. "Find another job."

She looked from him to the bar. Bryce still filled the doorway, his back to Michael and the girl. Her eyes met Michael's again, and he saw the same fear there he had seen in the eyes of the little bird.

He indicated the bills in her hand. "Should be enough until you find something better."

She counted the money in her hand. When she looked at him again, hope shone where fear had been a moment ago.

"Now go." Michael spoke gently.

She gripped the bills tightly and stuffed them inside the front of her dress. As Bryce stepped backwards out of the doorway, the girl turned and fled.

Standing beside Michael, Bryce stuffed his hands in his pockets. "Mama-san was curious about what was happening with her girl." The two watched the girl disappear into the night.

"And?"

"I gave her some money for her trouble."

Michael grunted and turned toward the hotel. Bryce fell into step beside him. They were nearly back to their hotel when Bryce finally broke the silence. "You okay?"

"She probably wasn't any older than Marissa."

"Probably not."

"She should be playing with dolls."

"Or picking on her older brother's best friend."

Michael smiled, remembering the good-natured pranks his sisters used to pester good-natured Bryce. "Remember that first snow when April—"

"Yep."

"And the time you slept over and Marissa—"

"Don't remind me."

They walked on, each lost in his own thoughts. Stopping outside the hotel, Michael stared at the stars. "Think she'll do something better with her life?"

Bryce shrugged. "Well, I'd say that's up to her." He slapped Michael on the back. "But you gave her the option."

CHAPTER 44

Their flight brought Michael, Bryce, Wingnut, and Meatloaf back home to the Washington, DC, airport where Meatloaf's very pregnant wife, Diane, greeted them.

"You certainly married up," Michael said to him as Diane released her husband and hugged him too.

"Don't I know." Meatloaf's eyes were full of pride as he looped a strong arm around his pretty wife's expanding waist.

"Be sure to name the baby after me," Bryce instructed.

"Especially if it's a girl," Wingnut taunted.

Diane gazed up affectionately at her husband. "If it's a boy, we'll name him after his father."

"Meatloaf Junior?" Michael winkled his nose. "That's pretty harsh to saddle a baby with."

Meatloaf looked offended. "What's wrong with my name?"

"Yeah." Bryce tossed his duffle bag and the burly man caught it. "What's wrong with Meatloaf? It's a good name."

"Not his nickname," Diane assured. "His real name."

"He has a real name?" Bryce was incredulous.

Meatloaf tossed Bryce's duffle bag back to him. "Meatloaf is good enough for you clowns."

Bryce grinned. "So what's the embarrassing handle?"

Meatloaf put his arm around Diane's shoulders and pulled her forward. The airport exit was in sight. "Never mind."

Diane looked over her shoulder at Bryce. "His name was on the wedding invitation."

Bryce threw out his arms. "Did we get an invitation?"

"You were part of the wedding party," Wingnut reminded. "Duh."

"Precisely," Michael agreed. "The wedding party just shows up. We don't get an invitation."

Bryce ran in front of Diane and Meatloaf. He turned and faced them, blocking their path. "Okay. Uncle. What's the big guy's real name?"

The automatic doors were mere steps away. Determined, Meatloaf brushed past the grinning Bryce.

"Diane. Please." Bryce implored as the couple swept past and the sliding doors parted in front of them. Sultry air blew in from the street.

"Merritt Lockhart," Diane called back. "A family name. Old South."

The doors closed behind the departing couple. Bryce stood frozen. Michael watched his battle buddy digesting this news. He blinked and looked at Michael. "They'd be better off naming a boy Bryce."

Back on base later that afternoon, the four PJs submitted to routine physicals and vaccinations. A civilian employee and a familiar face, Dr. Richard Evans owned a pharmaceutical research lab often contracted to supply the unit with inoculations.

"What's up, Doc?" Because everyone else had duties to return to, Michael waited to be the last patient.

"Well, well, look who's back." Dr. Evans extended his hand and warmly clasped Michael's. "It's been lonely here without you."

"Your business must be doing well," Michael countered. "You work less and less."

Dr. Evans grinned. "That's like asking a mother about her new baby. The business is indeed growing and allowing me more free time for my other love."

"Your wife."

Dr. Evans brightened. "Keri continues to be the love of my life but—"

Michael felt his stomach tighten. In an unbidden flash, he remembered the day his dad left. "But?"

"I have a new passion."

Michael clenched his jaw and regarded the door.

Dr. Evans continued. "Keri and I have more time to spend boating."

Michael exhaled. "Boating?"

The doctor looked at his watch. "You're my last duty of the day. I'd like to hear about your new island address and what you're doing to maintain your excellent health. If you have time, why don't you come back to the yacht and have dinner with Keri and me?"

"Deal."

Dinner that evening with the doctor and his wife led to a cruise. Scheduled to meet with his company's board, Dr. Evans invited Michael to sail with them from the Annapolis berth to New York. He checked with Bryce, who agreed to cash in a couple of vacation days and meet Michael when the boat docked. With the last minute arrangements made, Michael helped Dr. Evans cast off.

CHAPTER 45

Elise was looking forward to today's board meeting of the Friends of the Philharmonic. At last, the group would be together to finalize plans to initiate the remodel.

As usual, Robson picked her up. She could drive herself, but the monthly meeting had become an excuse for the childhood friends to get together.

At the single table set up in the ballroom, the board members gathered, and Trent distributed the agenda. The top item was the ever-present securing of necessary finances for the repairs.

Elise allowed herself a slight smile. After much mental and physical energy, today's agenda item could be checked off as complete. During their dinner at the Bougainvillea, Senator Bennett Taylor had assured Elise that he had given Jacques a check for the painting. Their funds for the renovation would be adequate. At last. Since that awkward evening with the senator, Elise had felt like the weight of the atmospheric theater no longer pressed down on her shoulders. Relaxed, her creativity spiked as evidenced in her work, and she once more slept well, which had a profoundly positive effect on her disposition and outlook on life.

Today, these fellow board members would approve the proposed agreement with the contractor, and within a year, the historic concert hall would be structurally sound. She could barely contain her excitement.

Trent opened the meeting and asked Karl to give the treasurer's report.

"The auction brought in one-third of our financial goal." Karl directed their attention to a line item on the budget. "As you can see, two-thirds remains outstanding although …" He smiled at Elise, "I anticipate those funds coming in at any moment."

Elise turned to Jacques. "I understand Senator Taylor gave you the check."

"Why didn't you just deposit that into the building fund?" June intercepted the envelope Jacques passed to Karl and quickly took out the check.

Jacques nodded in the direction of the paper in June's hand. "I wanted you all to see the document so no one would question the amount."

June pursed her lips and passed the check to Elise. The artist's exuberance to hold the long anticipated funding quickly dissolved into disappointment. She read and reread the figure the senator had penned on the line. Elise reached for the envelope that June still held and searched inside for a second check. But the envelope had held only one piece of paper. The number on the lone check was a dismal half of what the senator owed for the painting he had boldly purchased at the auction. Half.

CHAPTER 46

"Ah, the Big Apple." Bryce greeted Michael's late afternoon arrival in New York harbor. "Think we can squeeze in a Broadway show?"

"Sure," Michael replied. "A stroll through Central Park, a meal at—"

"Dinner and a show."

With the yacht secure at her docking, Dr. Evans and Keri invited Bryce aboard.

"Not a rough ride, Mikey," Bryce approved.

"A step up from riding with you in the Adventure Mobile."

Bryce nodded. "We've moved up in the world in more ways than one."

Following a gourmet meal and several high-spirited games of ping-pong with Dr. Evans and his wife, Michael shouldered his bag. "Thanks again for the ride."

Keri wrapped an arm around her husband's waist as the couple walked their guests to the dock. "Please don't think we take on just any hitchhiker."

"Well, you're not too particular if you took this guy aboard." Bryce elbowed Michael.

The men shook hands, and Michael and Bryce made their way up the pier toward the bright lights of New York City proper. Content after a delicious steak and Merlot dinner, Michael surveyed the calm harbor and the expensive boats that rocked in their berths.

"By the by," Bryce said. "The boss flew in this evening."

"What's up?"

"Corbin's meeting with Dr. Evans and his board. Something about a missing virus from Dr. Evans's pharmaceutical company."

"Missing? Like lost?"

"More like stolen is what they think."

The two grew silent except for their steady steps that sounded muffled on the wooden pier.

Along a stretch of occupied berths, Bryce spotted the names of the boats as they walked past. "*Bay Baby, Worth the Bucks ...*"

"Shopping for a yacht?"

"I'm practicing being rich." Bryce read the name of another yacht. "*Lea.*"

Michael followed Bryce's gaze to the yacht anchored apart from the ones in berths. Estimating the length to be about one hundred and sixty-four feet with three decks, he stopped and studied the vessel's long elegant lines. He had seen the vessel before in St. Croix. Senator Bennett Taylor had boarded this yacht in that secluded island bay. But the name on the boat in the Caribbean had been *Al-Leatto*. Some white tape could have easily masked a few letters to leave *Lea*.

"Let's check that one out." From his bag, Michael retrieved his radio.

"Have you completely flipped? You don't just board a boat because it's pretty."

Michael secured the small radio to his ear and handed the mate to Bryce. "I've seen that one before. But this time the name's partly concealed. I want to know why."

Before Bryce could attempt to inject any semblance of reason, Michael made his way closer to the yacht.

Silently avoiding the watchman posted on the sundeck, Michael used the shadows to cover his movements as he boarded. On the main deck, he found a salon, the dining room attached to the galley, and a stateroom suite. The place dripped opulence. Forward, he discovered the owner's suite and a large room that appeared to be an office. A cherrywood desk occupied the center. Atop, a computer hummed, the screen hibernating. A handful of files were neatly stacked on the glossy desktop, and a highly polished matching cabinet stood against the wall. A large painting of an exotic woman with perfect skin caressed in gossamer veils hung on an interior wall. No doubt a safe lay behind the frame.

Glancing toward the door, Michael pressed a key on the computer keyboard and the screen sprang to life. He moved the mouse to page through past history, noting files that had been recently opened.

He felt more than saw the movement and turned just in time to see the guard aim a nine-millimeter at him. Instinctively, Michael ducked. Despite the silencer on the gun, he heard and felt thunder as the bullet creased the side of his head. His vision swam and his ear rang, but he whirled quickly and charged the man like a bull charging a matador's red cape.

A second shot whizzed past his ear as Michael slammed his body into his assailant. The two wrestled for several minutes until Michael delivered a sharp blow to the man's jaw. The man's head flew backward and he sprawled limp and unconscious under Michael's weight.

"Michael!" Bryce's voice came over the radio in his ear. "Someone's coming."

"Roger that." He picked up the man's handgun and tucked it into his waistband, surveying his surroundings for a place to duck out of sight.

"Michael? Can you hear me?"

"I hear you," he answered. "How many are coming?"

Bryce's voice was urgent. "You're about to have serious company. Do you read me?"

Michael tapped the radio at his ear and felt warm, sticky blood across the side of his face. He pulled the radio from his ear. The bullet had damaged his ear and the earpiece. "Can you hear me?" He spoke directly into the device.

"Michael!" Bryce's voice talked over his own. "Big, ugly guys are piling out of this limo, and they have guns stuck in the ribs of two people with bags over their heads."

Michael quickly straightened the furniture that had toppled during his scuffle with the unconscious man. Then he half carried, half dragged the guy into the bedroom. Closing the door behind him, he studied his surroundings. A queen-sized bed flanked by matching nightstands occupied the left side of the room. Straight ahead was a bathroom. To his right were mirrored closet doors.

Like he had in China, Michael quickly removed the unconscious man's clothes and put them on. This time the broader man's clothing easily went over Michael's own without the sound of tearing stitches. He bound the man with an electric razor cord he found in the bath, gagged him with a washcloth, and stuffed him onto the floor of the closet under a cascade of hanging clothes.

Bryce no longer talked to him through the now one-way earpiece. Probably even the receiving aspect was broken. Michael quietly slipped out the door. Trying to resemble the man whose clothes he wore, he headed down the hall past the office. Behind him, he heard the scrambling of footsteps and knew the group Bryce had warned him about was coming down the stairs.

Rounding the hallway corner toward the far side of the boat, he waited to see the direction the group would take. Instead of stopping, the peculiar parade steered for another set of narrow stairs. Michael caught a brief glimpse of two hostages with bags over their heads being manhandled by four others. Moonlight flashed on a gun barrel pressed against the covered head of the first hostage.

"Move." The gun's owner pushed the weapon harder against the prisoner's temple. Trembling, the second hostage walked into the first, and the two tumbled down the stairs. The sound of a woman's cry told Michael one of the hostages was female.

Spewing profanity, the others ran down after them. From the stairwell, Michael heard commotion as the sounds continued to midship, and then he heard a door slam and lock.

Two additional sets of footsteps calmly made their way to the office where Michael had been earlier. Through the open door, low voices drifted out. "This is a mess."

"He'd better make sure we get out of here," said a gruff voice, heavy with an Asian accent. "Things won't look good if he's implicated."

"Bringing two people onboard complicates things," a second voice responded coolly.

"Idiot! I couldn't kill them there."

"Killing them anywhere isn't what we came for." The cooler voice sounded oily and American.

"We came for business. We walked into a setup."

"She was only asking questions. You're too nervous."

Michael heard a sound that could have been a fist pounding on the desk. "There was only one reason she would ask such questions."

"It's a moot point now," said the cool voice. "We have to deal with the present."

There was a long silence. Then, "Something is wrong about this room."

"You're too jumpy. Relax."

"Where are the guards?"

"All accounted for."

Michael heard glass clink against glass. "Here, have a drink."

Two men came quickly back up the stairs and went into the office.

The phone rang and the gruff voice picked it up before the second ring. "Talk to me … A tanker? … Very well." The phone was slammed down. "We'll shadow a departing tanker. Ready the boat."

Michael retreated farther into the shadows as the two men who had been downstairs left the office, most likely to set sail.

"And the two below?" asked the cool voice.

"Once we're away from here, we'll feed 'em to the sharks."

"A waste of good commodities."

"I'm not taking any more chances."

"Too bad."

Michael silently calculated how many people were aboard. A guard topside. The guard snoozing in the closet. The two chatty men in the office. Two men downstairs with the hostages. Two men readying the boat. Probably a cook and a captain. Eight to one. He wondered what Bryce was up to.

Michael called downstairs. "Hey, boss wants you topside."

"Both of us?" came a voice from below.

Michael chose not to answer. In a moment, steps echoed on the stairs. Standing out of sight, he waited. A man came up the steps and continued toward the office. Stepping quickly and silently behind, Michael clubbed him. Before the man hit the ground, Michael caught and dragged the unconscious body to a storage closet. He took the man's gun.

Footsteps pounded down the hall and down the stairs. "Where's Lenny?" the man called. "The boss wants him." In the small closet, Michael pulled the door closed and straddled the unconscious man.

"Not here," came the reply.

The man cursed and headed down the hallway.

Opting for a surprise frontal assault, Michael opened the closet and then confidently strode down the stairs and approached the guard standing in the hall, his back against a door.

"Lenny," the guy spoke. "They're looking for you up …" As Michael came closer, suspicion clouded the man's face, and he reached for his gun. Michael launched himself at the man, hitting him full force with his body before he could fire. The two fought desperately until Michael delivered a knockout punch to his temple. Three down.

As Michael took the unconscious man's gun and checked the ammo, the yacht's engines hummed to life. The boat would put to sea soon, and

Michael didn't want to still be aboard when that happened. Patting down the guy's pockets, he found a key and inserted it into the lock.

Pushing open the door, he stepped inside and then everything went black.

CHAPTER 47

Michael groaned and opened his eyes. His head throbbed. A woman bent over him. She looked familiar.

Brandishing the leg of a chair above his already damaged head, she demanded, "Whose side are you on?"

Michael blinked and sat up. He studied her face. "Claire?" Putting his hand to the back of his head he found a large goose egg. "Your aim is improving."

"You know this guy?" A man standing to one side looked from Claire to Michael.

"What are you doing here?" Michael tried to stand—the man extended a steadying hand.

She stepped forward, her nose inches from his. "What are *you* doing here?"

"I'm really confused," the man said.

Michael put a finger to his lips. Listening, he heard the pounding of footsteps above followed by shouts. "They'll be back soon." He looked at Claire's confused friend. "Drag that guard in here."

Feeling the boat begin to slowly troll away from the docks, Claire's eyes grew wide. "We have to get off this boat."

"Get moving." Michael led them out of the room. He stopped long enough to close and lock the door in hopes the locked door might buy them time if no one knew they weren't inside.

Sticking to the shadows, the three made their way topside. From his vantage point on the sheltered exterior deck, Michael noted they were well underway. He motioned the two to duck down out of sight while he studied the situation. Gaining on the yacht's starboard side was a cargo tanker. Coming even with the yacht, the larger vessel dwarfed the smaller one as the two made their way through the New York harbor toward open sea. Overshadowing the smaller boat, the tanker blacked out the lights from the passing shore. In the direction of the tanker, Michael scanned the night sky. For the briefest moment, where the tanker and the night sky met, a couple stars blinked out. Michael stared hard into the darkness. Again for a moment those stars blinked out.

"Company," Michael murmured. At least two people had dropped from the big ship. The one-sided phone conversation he'd overheard earlier said nothing about additional personnel coming aboard. Someone was headed this way to come aboard or to eliminate this potentially embarrassing ship and its inconvenient hostages. Tapping the damaged earpiece, Michael winced. His ear was damaged too.

"Hey, buddy," he whispered. "Can you hear me?"

Trying to raise Bryce had been a long shot, and receiving no response, he knew his partner was still out of communication. His eyes intent on the water between the two boats, Michael calculated the length of time for underwater skids to bring two divers to the yacht. The time came and went without newcomers boarding. He recalculated to measure the time for divers to reach the underside of the yacht and attach an explosive device. That time also came and went. Still the tanker traveled a polite distance away. Michael doubled the time mentally and eyed the large vessel. Just as he suspected, three minutes after he figured, the tanker began to gradually pull ahead of the steadily trolling yacht. He had to get the three of them off this boat.

Urgently Michael pushed the other two along the deck. "Keep the boat between you and the shore so you're harder to see."

Surveying the water around them, Michael spotted a tugboat on the opposite side of the yacht from the tanker. The tug steadily progressed their way. In that moment the *Lea*'s topside outer door inched open. Crouched behind his aimed gun, a man slowly stepped outside and went searching along the shore side of the deck. A second man followed, his search focused on the side where Michael and his two companions ducked in the shadows.

Michael clutched the upper arm of Claire's friend. "Get over the side. Swim strong away from the pull of the boat's movement." He pushed the guy forward. "Now go!"

The man stepped to a dark area at the railing. He set his hands on the silver rail in preparation to vault himself over.

Michael pushed Claire forward. "Get over the side. Go!"

She was following her friend when someone yelled, "Freeze!" From behind the boat's tender, a gunman leveled his weapon at the would-be diver.

Her friend froze and then slowly put up his hands.

Spotting Claire in the shadows near her friend, the gunman leveled his pistol in her direction.

Jaguar-fast, Michael sprang from the shadows between the loaded gun and Claire. He clapped his hand across her neck, spun and locked her in an iron grasp, her back against his chest. "I've got her," he bluffed, jamming his gun into her temple.

"Michael, can you hear me?" He heard Bryce's voice once again in his ear.

Claire went rigid momentarily and then pulled hard against his grip. "I knew I couldn't trust you," she hissed.

"Where are you?" Michael tightened his hold on the struggling girl. But no reply came from Bryce.

His gun trained on Claire and Michael, the armed man peered from behind the ship's tender.

"Michael, are you there?" Bryce asked again.

Michael heard Corbin's voice through his earpiece. "Tell him we're on the tug."

"He's not responding," came Bryce's voice, still in his earpiece.

Claire kicked painfully at his shins.

"Trust me," Michael growled into her ear.

Rising from his crouch, the guard pointed the barrel of his gun directly at Claire. "Hold still," Michael loudly commanded the struggling girl.

When her thrashing subsided, the gunman trained his weapon on Claire's friend who raised trembling hands higher above his head and pleaded, "Don't shoot! Don't shoot!"

The cautious gunman stepped away from the tender and shifted the direction of his aim to Michael's head.

"Shoot!" Michael heard Corbin's distant order through his earpiece.

In front of the threesome, the gunman slowly moved forward. Behind him, Michael heard the second gunman coming in their direction.

"Shoot!" Corbin commanded a second time in Michael's ear.

"Somethin's not right." Bryce's voice sounded unusually nervous.

"If he gets any closer, it'll all be over," Corbin insisted.

Warily, the gunman approached Michael, Claire, and her friend. Michael scanned his options. They were close to the deck railing. The tugboat kept pace while maintaining an acceptable distance. No doubt, from his hiding place, the second gunman behind Michael had them in his sights.

"It's Michael!" In his ear, Bryce's voice was incredulous.

"Impossible." That was Corbin.

"Michael's a goofy foot."

"A what?"

"Surfing term." Bryce spoke fast. "Right-handed and leads with his right foot."

"Mixed dominants."

"Whatever."

Michael heard Corbin's steady words, "If that's him, then ..."

From the doorway to his left, Michael glimpsed four armed men who came purposefully onto the deck and spread out in a search pattern. The cautious gunman stepped closer and Michael partially hid his face behind Claire's hair. Another step closer. The gunman recognized him at the same moment Michael recognized him as the guy he had earlier left tied in the bottom of a closet. In that instant, a bullet sang behind Michael, and a man dropped to the deck. Michael fired his weapon and the man in front of him fell. Claire screamed and turned her face into his chest.

Michael whirled to confront whoever was behind him. His eyes wide with terror, Claire's friend spun to see the rapidly approaching foursome. His sudden movement spooked an edgy trigger finger and a violent onslaught of bullets tore into his body. The force threw him so hard into Michael and Claire that he bowled them over the side of the boat.

Suddenly submerged in inky cold water, Michael instinctively went limp to allow his body and the air trapped in his lungs to point him toward the surface. Getting his bearings, he kicked strongly until he broke the surface. Gulping in air like a thirsty man gulps water, he searched for Claire. From the railing, several gunmen rained bullets into the water, shooting in the dark.

Michael spotted Claire too near the churning wake of the yacht. He dove in her direction, grabbed her leg, and pulled her down and away from the bullets and the boat. She quickly began moving with him and they swam as hard as they could away from the bullet-spitting *Lea*.

Surfacing, Michael rolled to his back to float and suck in air. Struggling for breath, Claire did the same. Not far away, he spotted something, or someone, floating. He swam in that direction. Claire followed. Coming closer, Michael realized the shape was Claire's associate, floating face up. When he reached the man, he felt his wrist for a pulse. Either he had a pulse or Michael was starting to shiver in the cold water. From the bullet wound in the man's torso, blood flowed into the water. That wasn't good.

Glancing back, he saw Claire paddling toward him. But the silhouette of the man proved an inviting target and bullets cut through the water near Michael's head.

"Get down," he hollered to her, but she had already ducked below the surface. Michael looped an arm around the neck of the prone man, dove, and kicked to pull him away from the gunfire.

Out of air, Michael rolled to his back and allowed only his nose and mouth out of the water. He inhaled deeply several times and continued kicking and dragging his passenger, seeking shadows and steering an erratic pattern. Bullets trailed them but were less accurate. Close enough to see him but far enough away to minimize their appearance as a target, Claire paddled a parallel route ten feet away.

"Michael!" Claire called in a voice high-pitched with fright. "Something big just brushed under me."

Fear flooded Michael's veins. "Be calm," he instructed softly. "Very, very slow and calm."

Vainly he tried to see into the water around him. Did something move nearby? Behind him? He steeled himself against a new wave of trembling chills that had little to do with cold. Then something brushed his shoulder. For a split second, the tip of a fin glinted above the water and then disappeared so fast he wondered if he imagined it.

A sudden jerk on the body of the man Michael towed made him sick. Every instinct screamed for him to swim as hard as he could away from this concealed and sinister menace. But his training told him that too much movement would only serve to incite a prowling shark. Clenching his teeth against their chattering, he moved steadily away from the *Lea* as another bullet sang past.

A second sickening jerk against the body pulled Michael backwards.

"Michael?" Horror filled Claire's voice.

The dark lurking presence brushed Michael's leg. Violently he kicked, hoping to connect with the shark's only weak spot, its sinister eyes. He wasn't sure where the blow landed, but the water roiled and the demon circled and attacked the body again.

The movement brought a fresh volley of bullets from the *Lea*. Michael felt the body jerk as several bullets penetrated. With frozen fingers, he felt for a pulse. The man was no longer alive. But Claire was. He released his hold and slowly, deliberately, dove down several feet and swam in her direction. Surfacing, he called and motioned for her to follow him away from the feeding shark.

"Slow," he directed. "Easy. Calm."

He heard her teeth chattering and a stifled sob. He spotted another fin, maybe two, occasionally flashing above the ominous waters. Their only chance of escape lay in the cruel hope that the sharks were content with Claire's unfortunate associate.

Suddenly, with a thunderous blast, the *Lea* exploded into a blistering ball of orange flame.

CHAPTER 48

Elise trailed through the tabby paths of the garden. In the greenhouse, she saw that Antonio's fledgling grafts were taking well to one another—like a good marriage, according to the gardener. As well as the grounds surrounding Jewel by the Sea, her yard served as Antonio's privileged studio. Elise's parents had arranged for him to keep the gardens and had given him the freedom to design as he liked. Her parents understood the creative process better than most and encouraged art in all its forms—which Elise found unlimited. The more she observed, the more her opinion grew that everyone was an artist in some area.

Her walk outdoors served to stretch her legs prior to this evening's rehearsal and provided an excuse to be near the cottage. But the former studio remained dark. Quiet. Michael had been gone for quite a while, and Elise missed him. Where once she felt dread that another would occupy the sacred space, now she eagerly watched for the windows to once more be alight at night and for rock and roll to play loud enough for her to hear he had returned home. The newest addition to her circle, she felt safe with Michael. When he looked at her, she knew she was lovely.

Despite the obvious dangers of his job that required training at a level she could not imagine, Michael held an easy sereneness born of confidence. She recognized the same quality in her father, Robson, June, Jacques, and Jerry. Especially the lively Brother Ned. These people were exactly where they were created to be in life. They had found their fit and significance. No need for striving or questioning or self-aggrandizement. She felt on the verge of finding that place in her own soul.

Renting the cottage had been the catalyst for a mix of emotions. Hope for the Christiansted Atmospheric Theater. Trepidation around her decision-making skills. Reluctance to meet the new renter who shared her small, secure patch of the world. Surprise that the new person, Michael, intrigued her. Humor to finally understand Robson's place in her heart as a dear big brother rather than a potential lover.

At first, Elise had felt a light flattery from the senator's attention. Now, she realized she had relied on him to be the easy solution to the problems with the theater. There was a danger in needing someone as the sole key to a dilemma. Completely unpredictable, the politician used his payment for her painting as manipulation and control. Yet his suggestion that she expand her horizons to establish a trust fund for the theater had merit. With such a fund in place, the theater's future would be secure.

As he had done many times before, Robson arrived at Elise's house and picked her up for rehearsal. The tradition had become an opportunity for her dear friend to have someone to talk to about his feelings for Ava as he considered what their future could look like even though, with Ava in New York, they lived on opposite ends of the nation. This turn of events made Elise happy. Robson and Ava were her dearest friends and knowing they would be together filled her heart with an extra-large scoop of comfort that the three of them would do life together from now until they were babbling about grandbabies. And great-grandbabies.

"So where's Michael?" Driving to the theater for their evening rehearsal, a smile accompanied Robson's question as if he were privy to a secret.

"Off island. For his other job is all I know."

He nodded. "There is more to that man than is initially obvious."

She recounted Michael's brief explanation to Brother Ned and Lisandro of his time as a parajumper.

"And?"

"And what?" Elise felt her cheeks grow hot.

"And what else?"

Strangely wanting to change the conversation she blurted, "And Senator Bennett Taylor has invited me to DC."

"The guy who hasn't kept his financial agreement to the Friends of the Philharmonic?"

"He says he can help my art become popular in larger circles."

Robson's eyebrows went up. "At what price? What does he expect in return?"

"What do you mean?"

"Elise, his ethics and morals are polar opposites from ours—yours. There's a trail of dead wives in his wake. Both young and beautiful women."

She turned to him. "But imagine, Robson. I could establish a trust and never have to worry again about the theater being condemned."

"Slow down, Elise. The theater hasn't been condemned yet." The cello player parked behind the theater in the area reserved for performers. He shut off the engine and turned to her. "Look, probably more than anyone else on the island, I understand how important this place is to you." He gestured to the building. "Like you, I have a lifetime of memories that happened here. Your dad, mom, Ava, you, and me. Elise, we learned to dance in the ballroom. We played our first concert on the stage. We saw every theater and ballet produced. We've performed the Nutcracker Suite each Christmas since we could walk without help—first as children in the opening scene, and then as musicians when we could actually make music come from our strings."

"Not just us, Robson." Resting her head against the seat, she studied the car's ceiling. "June, Karl, Jacques, Brother Ned—"

"Mrs. Nelthropp, Becky and Danny, Jerry and Reta ..."

Tears sprang to her eyes. "What will childhood be like for the Todd children without the theater and all the opportunities associated with it?"

"What will the honeymooners, tourists, visitors to St. Croix, and the populations of the surrounding islands do without this single vein of culture?" Robson waved an arm to indicate their surroundings.

"Now you're making fun of me." Angry, Elise got out of the car.

Robson got out and came around to her side. "No, I'm not."

From the backseat, she grabbed her viola case and marched to the theater's backstage door.

Robson reached the door first. "Listen—"

"Move out of my way." She jerked the strap of her case over her shoulder.

"Elise, I know you probably better than anyone on this planet, and right now, I'm asking you to hear me out."

She narrowed her eyes. "Move. Now."

Robson raised his hands in surrender and stepped aside. Elise pulled open the door.

"I think a trust fund is a smart idea."

She turned back to face him. "You do?" Behind her the theater door closed.

"Who wouldn't?" Robson's voice remained calm. "And renting the cottage was a surprise, but also a smart step toward your goal."

Elise waited to hear him out.

"Your parents had a partnership that worked so seamlessly, it appeared – well – effortless. They instinctively encouraged others to do what they do best. Ava sees the composition of the music so your father taught her to conduct. I am prideful and competitive so he pushed me always to invest my energy in challenging myself rather than judging others. When their island version of the secret garden they created for you became too much for them, your parents invited Antonio to do what he does like no one else, and the place has never looked better."

Elise took a deep breath and exhaled the anger she had wanted to unleash on Robson only moments ago.

"And they established a board to oversee the theater, populated by people with specific talents."

"What's your point, Robson?"

"My point is you are a strong-willed and capable woman. You grew up in an environment where you were free to pursue your talents, and now, you feel you have to take over all that your parents once naturally accomplished together." He stepped closer. "But, Elise, that is not what your parents intended for you."

"Since you are such an expert on my parents ..." She heard the possessiveness in her tone. "... what did they intend for me after they were gone?"

"They intended for you to work within a community. To trust the board to have the same goal you do."

She waved an arm in the direction of the ballroom where the board regularly met. "No one on the board cares about keeping the theater going. Not like I do."

"You're wrong, Elise. We do care."

"Then prove it! I rented the cottage, and I spent weeks on that painting. Now, I have an invitation to take my art to powerful circles on the mainland. But I've not seen anyone else doing anything to raise funds for the renovation." She planted a hand on her hip.

"Maybe because you keep running ahead and doing, doing, doing but not with the board. You leave us trying to catch up or fill in the gaps left in your wake."

"What are you saying, Robson?"

"I'm saying that for you to be a good board member, you have to be a part of the board. Presently, you disdain the rest of us while you dash ahead without allowing us to work as a team—to help you make a plan and follow through."

Elise felt her anger flame again. "Is that all you wanted to say?"

Robson nodded.

She pulled open the theater door and power-walked inside. Tears threatened, which made her angrier. She went straight to the women's sitting room and splashed cold water on her face. Confident the involuntary urge to cry had passed, she collapsed onto an aged chair of green velvet. For several minutes in that sweet old room, she allowed the crushing responsibility she felt for the building to overwhelm her. Could Robson be right? Was the board as invested in the theater's welfare as she was? Had she indeed run ahead of a community that she could trust to work together toward a shared goal?

Trent's words from an earlier meeting echoed in her mind. *The only option this board has is to resign to the inevitable. The theater will soon be condemned. As a forward-looking group, we must accept that this building is part of an era gone by.*

Glancing at her watch, she realized she needed to pull herself together. Standing, she smoothed her skirt and went to take her place in tonight's rehearsal.

CHAPTER 49

Flaming shards from the *Lea* hailed down on Michael and Claire, burning their clothes and skin before they dove beneath the fiery current. Dodging the sizzling materials floating on the water, Michael and Claire swam toward the shadowy tugboat that meticulously patrolled the vicinity of the exploded boat. Michael watched the pattern of floodlights as they searched the waterway beginning in the area where he and Claire had gone over the side.

If there was a bright side to their situation, it was the explosion probably discouraged the sharks from staying in the area. "Come on," he urged the tired girl who treaded water behind him.

Wearily, she pointed herself in the direction he indicated. She gave two great kicks, then gasped and disappeared under the waves in a violent movement that made Michael think she had been grabbed by a shark. The water swirled and boiled as a man broke to the surface while he held Claire under.

Michael dove below the melee and came up behind the guy. Throwing both arms across the man's head, Michael forced him underwater. Thrashing and kicking, the opponent released Claire and desperately flailed against Michael's grip.

Holding the man's head below the surface, he glimpsed the flash of a wicked blade as his foe deftly lurched and swung. Michael rolled away from the intended slash. With surprising agility, his antagonist grappled onto Michael's back and thrust him away from life-giving oxygen. Michael twisted around and caught the arm that now pressed the sharp knife against his throat. With his knee, the man viciously kicked Michael's side, forcing the last bit of air from his lungs. He kicked again and again and again, forcing his weight and the weapon against Michael's neck. The muscles of Michael's arms bulged and shook under the strain of holding the death-wielding blade from severing his jugular. His lungs burned from lack of air, and his vision exploded in blots of neon color. Then he lost consciousness.

CHAPTER 50

Following the rehearsal, several musicians, including Elise and Robson, went to Jewel by the Sea for late-night appetizers. Robson and Elise rode together in silence. Though Robson had been an intuitive and effective substitute conductor for tonight's rehearsal, neither he nor Elise wanted to rekindle hostilities by taking up their earlier conversation.

But upon entering the resort, they immediately saw the lobby looked different.

"Hey." Robson spun in a slow circle. "Where's your painting?"

Elise had already noticed the absence. She felt a glow of accomplishment each time she'd viewed her art at Jacques' resort. Having her painting on display had given her the gift of distance. Her personal criticisms and "I should haves" had dimmed, and she finally felt satisfied with her effort. Especially when the piece sold.

"Senator Taylor must have taken the painting home." Now she smiled. "That means he paid the remainder of the purchase price."

"Time to celebrate." Robson put an arm around Elise's shoulders. "Now you can relax. All will be just the way you wanted."

Relief washed over her like the gentle waves that met her feet when she walked on the quiet beach.

The hostess seated the rehearsal-weary musicians outdoors, and once everyone had given their orders to the waitress, Elise excused herself from the group and went back inside. Jacques had long since retired for the night, so Elise sought out the night manager who informed her Senator Bennett Taylor had checked out and arranged for the painting to be shipped. Mr. Taylor had left something for her at the desk.

The manager retrieved an envelope with Elise's name written in rounded letters on the front. Quickly, she slid open the flap, but inside was not the hoped-for check for the outstanding balance owed on the painting. Elise allowed herself to believe the senator had given the final balance to

Jacques as he had with the first half of the payment. Unfolding the resort stationary, she read Bennett Taylor's words.

My dear Elise,

I look forward to your visit to Washington, DC.

My heart is better when you are near, and I look forward to sharing you and your work with people of influence. You will show me where to hang your painting. Enclosed is your plane ticket.

With anticipation,

Bennett

CHAPTER 51

Michael coughed and choked, convulsed, and vomited. He had never been so scared in all his life. Impressions of darkness and danger drowning life from his lungs caused him to thrash explosively.

"It's over, Michael," came a strong voice. "You're safe."

That had been too close. In that immediate moment, he'd thought of Elise. He wanted to see her again more than he wanted anything in the world.

"Yo, Dog." Bryce's familiar voice danced at the edge of reality. He felt strong hands grip his trembling shoulders, and then his friend's thumbs kneaded Michael's trembling arms.

Feeling waterlogged and heavy, he opened his eyes. Bryce's grinning face was as welcome as a cold beer on a stifling day. His buddy floated at his side in the dark water. Michael's head rested on a flotation ring supported by Claire whose teeth chattered violently. A tugboat idled next to the sodden trio. Looking up, Michael watched Corbin and the boat's pilot securing the underwater attacker, who had obviously been gaffed and hauled aboard thanks to the tug's towing equipment.

"Breathe," Bryce coached. "In slow."

He inhaled and held a lungful of oxygen in an attempt to calm his quaking body.

"Exhale," Bryce instructed. "Nice and slow."

Obediently, Michael released the air in his lungs. He squeezed his eyes tightly closed and pictured Elise as he had last seen her—facing him, her blue eyes framed by her blonde hair as the trade wind carried the fragrance of plumeria, frangipani, night jasmine, and gardenia to him—the piece of paradise he'd brought along when he'd left the island.

"You okay?" Bryce patted his cheek. "Stay with us, Mikey."

Michael groaned and opened his eyes. He felt Claire shuddering next to him. "Get her warm."

"Already tried that." Bryce turned his attention to the girl. "He's gonna be fine. Now get aboard."

Claire allowed herself to be hoisted out of the frigid water. Then Michael and Bryce were lifted to the tug's solid deck and wrapped in warm blankets. The tug's captain brought mugs of hot, black coffee generously laced with whiskey for Michael and Claire, and then set a course back to civilization.

Once on land, Claire, Michael, and the only survivor of the *Lea*, were taken to a hospital for examination and care. Then the PJs transported the prisoner to a nearby military base. Michael was glad the details and red tape were someone else's responsibility. His job was to put this guy in a safe and contained place for the people who did that stuff to be able to question him. The intelligence guys had more than a few questions about what and whom he knew. On base, Michael insisted on accompanying the military police as they escorted his would-be killer to confinement.

"Here's your cell." Michael had shoved the guy inside. "Try not to mess it up. I don't want to clean your blood off the walls."

"I'm a soldier." The man glared defiantly at Michael. "I demand to be treated like a soldier."

Michael wanted to slam a fist into the belligerent prisoner's mouth. Instead he grabbed the man's shirtfront in a white-knuckled grip. "You are not a soldier. You are a terrorist. I am an American and Americans don't negotiate with terrorists. We hunt them down and bring them to justice." He sent the man sprawling into the lockup and slammed the door.

Debriefing took longer than usual, and Michael walked through the days and the process detached. In between duties, paperwork, and meetings, much like a ship returns to the harbor, his thoughts continually returned to Elise.

"From what we can piece together, this was a high-level hostage situation," Corbin explained. "Intel tracked the funding for a training facility for international subversives. There was a meeting between internationals and Americans at the Ritz-Carlton."

"I hate cheap hotels," Bryce said.

"Apparently they did too," Corbin replied, "because something spooked 'em. Guns appeared, and they fled with hostages."

"Claire and her friend," Michael put in.

"They were transported to a private yacht in the New York harbor."

"Obviously not American," Michael said.

"This boat had diplomatic immunity." Corbin scratched the day's stubble on his chin. "There're still a lot of unanswered questions."

Michael rocked back in his chair. "Does Claire have your answers?"

Corbin laced his fingers across his abdomen. "Apparently, she has questions of her own."

"She's got a knack for getting herself and us in trouble," Bryce observed.

Michael snorted and rubbed the bump on the back of his head. "All you have to do is drive a garbage truck and a tug. I'm the one who keeps getting whacked on the head."

Corbin finished the dregs of a long-cold cup of coffee. "She was nosing around and nosed herself right into a hornet's nest."

Michael nodded. "A senator's daughter is a weighty hostage."

"What about her friend?" Bryce stood and stretched. "Who was he?"

"An employee of the International Dialysis Corporation."

"High up?" Michael wanted to know.

"Purchasing."

"Purchasing what?" Putting a few facts together, Michael didn't like where his suspicions were leading.

Corbin turned the questioning. "Michael, we'll talk about how you ended up onboard later." He frowned. "That explanation should be as entertaining as a Siamese cat wearing a plaid kilt and dancing the Highland fling."

Michael shifted under his boss's scrutinizing stare.

Corbin cleared his throat and returned to the topic at hand. "So, Michael, while you were aboard ship, did you see anything that would be helpful?"

Michael recalled the computer files he had briefly scanned. They didn't mean anything at the time, but now they were food for thought.

"What's the common thread between Claire and that yacht?" Bryce asked.

"I think they arrange materials for transplants." Michael thought about the Chinese orphan girl he had been too late to protect from a grisly fate.

"That would fit with Intel's suspicions. They suspect these guys market body parts for big price tags to fund training of international terrorists." Corbin sighed. "We just don't know who's backing this."

"Claire is the common denominator in this scenario and the last time I got bashed over the head." Michael looked from Corbin to Bryce. "China would be my guess."

"Definitely a supplier," Bryce noted.

Corbin raised an eyebrow. "Which leaves us with the obvious question—who's the American connection?"

CHAPTER 52

"Very good." Elise looked over the shoulder of Lisandro as he spread bold colors on the newsprint. During the school year, Elise gave art lessons weekly to the students in Brother Ned's school. Though she told each child that he or she was her favorite artist, she had to admit Lisandro held a special place in her heart.

"These are my father's flowers in the gardens at your house." The young artist drew circles of pink and yellow over bright green leaves.

Elise showed him how to roll the bristles sideways to layer the paint on his brush—first pink, and then yellow on top. When he applied the brush to the paper, his eyes shone bright with delight at the two simultaneous colors that appeared on the paper. He began to bounce on his toes, and the other students gathered around to see. Elise demonstrated the technique again for everyone to learn. Soon the developing subject matter became practice for layered strokes and swirls. The young students giggled at their surprising results.

Brother Ned left a teacher-in-training to oversee the remainder of the class time, helped Elise gather her supplies into her oversized portfolio, and walked with her outside. "Do you have time for tea?"

Elise considered her schedule. "I have time for your famous raspberry iced tea."

He led the way, stopping in the kitchen to pour two glasses from the pitcher in the refrigerator. In his office, he took a chair across from her in the little sitting area near the window.

"So," he began, "how are you?"

Elise took a few M&Ms from the dish on the coffee table. "So, this is not about the art classes for your students?"

"You are the only instructor the children will skip recess for." Brother Ned gestured toward the classrooms. "If we talk about art classes, the subject will be to see if you can come and teach more often."

"My secret is that I don't teach. I play with them."

"Your papa and mama used the same successful technique with their students—and with you." He folded his hands. "And your parents asked me to check in with you occasionally."

She raised her eyebrows. "My parents?"

"And Robson." The priest grinned. "Remember, I take his confessions."

"I don't understand."

"He is concerned you are taking too much responsibility on yourself for the theater."

Elise recalled her last heated conversation with Robson on their way to rehearsal. "And I wish other members of the board took more responsibility for solving the problem." She could hear the frustration in her voice. "We must renovate the theater before it's too late."

He stood. "Let's walk while we talk."

They left the school, and Brother Ned led them toward downtown Christiansted. "With the bulk of the funds for renovations coming from your painting, you must feel like the future of the theater rests on your shoulders."

Elise nodded. "And later the building will require other work."

"Such is the way of the world. Each person and object is either growing or deteriorating. There is no status quo, though we exert a lot of energy striving for that impossible state."

"To hedge against ever being in this situation with the theater again," she explained, "Senator Taylor recommended the board establish a trust fund with the board as trustees."

Brother Ned pulled on his ear. "We are still in process of procuring immediate funds. How will we fund the trust?"

Having this wise mentor ask the question she had been wrestling was like poking a hole in a sack of sugar. The hopes, ideas, concerns, and possibilities surrounding the senator's offer came pouring out. As was his way, Brother Ned listened without interrupting. When all the words were out, he asked a few more questions for clarification, and Elise answered as best as she could. The idea, after all, was still theoretical.

They walked a few minutes without speaking while the priest mulled over the situation. Their steps took them near enough to the pier that she could hear the seagulls. On the east side of the bay, Robson's boat, the *Day Dream,* rocked gently alongside other vessels. On the west side, rows of docked boats swayed with the ocean's movement. Seeing Jerry's boat in port reminded Elise of Michael.

I'm a scuba instructor. That's what he said at the philharmonic dinner when June asked what he did on the island. Elise smiled. That was true. On St. Croix, he guided water and adventure sports. But off-island, he had another job description altogether.

Brother Ned turned up the quaint narrow streets of Christiansted's downtown and soon the theater came into view. The stately old building stood over the smaller adjacent structures like a grandmother watching over children at play.

"Elise, what do you think concerns Robson about your potential trip to the capitol?"

"Whether it's what I do with the cottage or my art, Robson thinks he has a say in my life."

In the shadow of the theater, Brother Ned stopped at the counter of an ice cream store and purchased two cups of gelato—fruity for him and dark chocolate for her. "Robson does have naturally strong opinions. But what could be behind his opinion about this?"

"Besides that he likes to tell me what to do?"

Brother Ned sat on a bench under the shade of a tan tan tree. "Yes, besides that."

With the emotion removed from the decision, Elise slowly paced and considered. "What could be wrong with my art creating enough money to support the theater?"

"Nothing." He ate a spoonful of the raspberry ice cream. "But there are other parts in the equation. Jacques presented a good idea to auction your painting—a way to weave your talents with the art you enjoyed doing with your family. If the sale raised the desired amount, that would be good. If not ..."

She swallowed a spoonful of chocolate. "I would have failed."

"And so we have come to the root of Robson's concern. And quite honestly, mine as well."

She faced him. "What do you mean?"

"My dear, you have taken this entire challenge over the theater and turned the upkeep into a burden that you cannot possibly carry. Nor were you ever supposed to. Your parents would never have wanted that." He patted the bench and she sat down beside him. "Close your eyes for a moment and think about your mama and papa. How did they live their days?"

Obediently, she closed her eyes and went with him back in time. "They laughed a lot." She tried to recapture the sound. "They had fun. They encouraged people to do what they were best at."

"What were they like together as a couple?"

She recalled her parents in the studio, the garden, and the theater. "They loved each other deeply. Their love was freedom and inspiration for each to be more together than either could be when alone." She opened her eyes and saw her companion was gently rocking back and forth in agreement.

"The theater belongs to the community. No one person carries the weight of such a, well, such a weighty project." He shrugged apologetically at the pun. "Whether or not the theater continues for generations does not depend solely on you. You must trust the process. Remember how you teach the children through play, not drudgery?"

"I envision the parties in DC as being fun." She also felt a twinge of apprehension about entering a completely unfamiliar environment.

He tapped his breastbone. "That depends on your motivation. Why are you there? Who are you there for? Who are you there with? These questions help assure that you are aligned with your principles. That your soul is at peace."

Elise thought about the senator's statement that she had given her soul to the theater—or at least its preservation. "I would be there to promote my art worldwide."

He acknowledged the answer with a single nod.

"Initially, I would be there for the theater. Maybe for my own ego."

Brother Ned studied her. "How do you feel about being with the senator—dependent on Bennett Taylor for your success or failure?"

Elise shook her head. "I'm not comfortable with him."

"Has he proven trustworthy?"

She thought of the promise to pay the full price of the painting and the half still outstanding. She weighed the impudence of the letter and travel ticket he left for her. "No."

"Before a large crowd, he made a declaration to purchase your painting. Senator Taylor signed a purchase agreement, yet paid only half and took the painting when he left the island. At best that is stealing. At worst, I believe he is using your desire for the promised funds as bait to manipulate you to come to DC."

She recalled her conversation over dinner at the Bougainvillea with Senator Taylor. "So this theater is where you have given your soul," he had said. He had masterfully focused on what was important to her and purposefully withheld what she wanted. Elise was unaccustomed to unraveling convoluted thinking. "But why?"

"I can only guess, my dear, and none of the possibilities bode well for you." Brother Ned scraped the last of his gelato from his dish. "Going to the mainland and expanding your circle of influence is fine. But being lured is completely different. Would you go if the senator had paid in full for your painting?"

She shook her head. Her art was steadily producing a growing income. If funds for the theater's renovations were in the bank, Elise would not be thinking about art shows at the nation's capital among the world's leaders. Having raised the money for the renovation, she and the board—she thought of Robson's challenge to be a team player on the theater's board—would have time to plan and develop a trust fund that would finance the theater's future.

"In my experience," Brother Ned continued, "people act out of two motivations—ministry or manipulation. Regrets come when we are so enamored with our own pressing agenda that we ignore the manipulations of others with equal, or more powerful objectives."

"Ignore or excuse or compromise."

The priest placed a hand over his heart. "That inner check in your spirit is the Lord. He often tells us when we need to be cautious. The danger, Elise, is when you don't listen to that prompting. In ministry, I have heard more confessions than Danny and Becky have crabs. Yet, I've never met anyone who could say that going against that intuition ever turned out well."

She tossed her empty ice cream cup in the shop's trash.

"Being a world-renown artist is a good goal to have, Elise, but not at the expense of your peace and joy. Your soul. Honor yourself and your principles. Do what you love and the money will come. And your art can still prove successful with the right connections at the right time."

She sighed. "But not now and not with the senator."

"Truthfully, I fear the company you would be with." Then he brightened. "Unless you had someone with you like Michael."

She smiled at that, and they began the walk back to the school.

"Tell me the things that are going right," he invited. "Your good decisions and the places in your life that bring serenity."

Elise considered. "Robson and Ava are in love, and they will live happily ever after."

Brother Ned cast his eyes to the heaven in thanks.

"Antonio does the outside work I could not begin to do."

"As he does for me." He smiled. "Your music and art?"

"Going ever better because there is always something to learn." She touched his arm. "I have a collection of dear friends."

"Then you are truly rich."

"The most surprising thing …" She paused, suddenly feeling shy. "… is that renting the cottage turned out to be an excellent decision—for the theater and because it brought Michael to the island."

"He is a fine addition." Arriving back at school, they found the students on the playground involved in a rowdy game of dodge ball. A wide grin lit his face. "Come on. It's time to play!"

CHAPTER 53

Mentally, Michael was standing in front of Elise's portrait again. He remembered her in a dress the color of sea foam as they danced across the ballroom floor. She was breathtakingly beautiful in a larger world that had an ugly underbelly.

"Did you hear me?"

Michael came back to the present and saw Corbin staring at him. "What did you say?"

"Precisely." Corbin gave his shoulder a firm yet friendly slap. "I've never seen you so distracted. The loose ends of this puzzling event are finally all government tidy. Get yourself back to your island retreat. You need it."

Before either of them returned home, Michael caught up with Claire. He had lots of questions, few answers, and suspected Claire knew far more than she shared.

"All those things you accused me of in Shanghai are true." Claire looked tired and troubled. "I championed my father and his liberal politics."

"And you work for International Dialysis Corporation, the forerunners of trading in human commodities."

"Most of their business is conducted overseas because the United States has some semblance of ethics against ..." She struggled for words.

"Against trading in human flesh." Michael finished the sentence for her.

She swallowed and pressed on. "My goal in going to China was to shadow a prisoner through his process of regretting his crimes against his fellow man and nobly choosing to make restitution by volunteering to give his body for the good of others."

Michael fought a powerful urge to laugh. "Are you serious? Are you that naïve?"

"I was that idealistic. That's the rhetoric my dad preached all my life. I believed it and planned to vindicate his ideals by documenting the story …" Her voice trailed off and her expression told him she was remembering something.

Michael waited.

"Only …"

"Only what?"

"Only," she began again, "that wasn't how it really is."

"What's the truth, Claire?"

She shuddered. "The prisoners are political prisoners, many gentle people brutalized because of their religious beliefs. The most vulnerable and powerless members of their society are subjected to the worst kinds of abuses. Then, the market expanded to pad the palms of those who ran the orphanage." Her eyes reflected horror as she met Michael's steady gaze. "They traded children for money."

"And how is that different from selling fetal material? Children are children, no matter what age."

Claire looked away and chewed her lip before facing him again. "I championed that philosophy. I was wrong. Rather than protecting the powerless, those in leadership exercise arbitrary and unconstrained power. In China, my words had faces. The faces were beautiful—my words were ugly—as hideous as what I saw in that hospital morgue."

Michael recalled the orphan he had been too slow to protect and prayed the medical devices he'd placed in her body had blown the place to Mars. "Kinda makes the ol' United States of America look pretty good." Michael couldn't resist the verbal jab.

Her eyes flashed anger. "Don't patronize me with your patriotic flag-waving. There are some gross mistreatments of liberty here too."

"Like what we do to unborn babies? Like powerful men who take license to blow away anyone who might disclose their repulsive deeds done in the dark behind closed doors?"

Wearily, Claire rubbed her eyes. "Something like that."

"Who were you meeting with and why?"

She eyed him fiercely. "I've already been through all that with your bosses. I don't think I have to do it again with you."

"Fine," Michael fired back. "But someone tried to kill you. And me. Twice. You might want to figure out who that is."

"Or what I'm doing that puts me at risk," she mumbled thoughtfully.

"No problem there," he said sarcastically. "You're not exactly home baking cookies. You're putting yourself in the middle of nasty business."

She met his eyes. "Whose business?"

CHAPTER 54

The next day, seated in the airplane's window seat, Michael was glued to the view below as the long Florida coast faded behind. He studied the countless small islands that inhabited the fluorescent turquoise sea. Farther from the mainland, the calm Atlantic flattened out to resemble the woven texture of Elise's canvasses.

The sun had set when the plane began the descent into St. Croix. From the air, Michael watched the lights of the island emerge from the surrounding sea. He stepped from the air-conditioned plane into the tropical evening, thick with warmth and humidity.

Inside the terminal, the pulse of steel drums beat a musical welcome. After serenading arriving tourists, these street musicians would soon follow the twilight to beach parties and bonfires like he and Bryce had attended at Cane Bay.

Finding his car, Michael navigated the narrow streets to the cottage on the hill. His heart thudded as he turned into the driveway. He wanted to see Elise. But at this late hour, he knew he'd have to wait until tomorrow—the morning seemed an eternity away.

At last, he could see the big house. Light shone through Elise's living room curtains. He parked at his cottage and got out of the car. He stared at the lighted window, checked his watch, and then looked back at the large house. He wanted to see her more than anything in the world. Just see her.

He strode to her front door. Would she be offended when he knocked this late?

Michael stood on her porch, breathing in the perfume of the night-blooming Queen of the Night. The curtained light from inside was enough for Michael to see the center of the oversized bloom in the shape of the manger under the star. Growing up, his mother had woken him and his sisters on those special nights to see the wonder when her carefully nurtured epiphyllum cactus bloomed. On the island, Antonio cultivated this one near Elise's door and another near the cottage. Rich and full, the rare fragrance filled the night.

The screen door was open. On the days Elise nurtured her gardens, she propped the wood-framed, squeaky screen with a large conch shell. He'd watched her, with an armload of blossoms held in dirt-encrusted hands, shove open the front door with her foot, then open it wide with a bump of her hip. Tonight, from the other side of the closed front door, he could hear the faint melody of Antonin Dvorak's Symphony No. 9 *From the New World*.

He knocked.

In a moment, the door opened. Framed in the light, Elise wore a flowing nightgown that reached to the floor and was as white as the cactus flower petals. The ribbons of the matching robe hung untied at her throat. Her hair fell loose about her shoulders and she was even more beautiful than he'd remembered.

"Elise." Unexpected tears stung his eyes and he swallowed against a sudden lump in his throat that threatened to betray him.

She tipped her head slightly.

"I know it's late ..." His words were husky.

Graciously, she stepped back. He followed her into the house and closed the door behind him. Elise led the short way into the great room. The low table near the couch held a tray with a teacup and teapot. A pink hibiscus bloom sat next to the pot and he smelled the aroma of steeping hibiscus blossom tea. An open book, turned facedown to hold a place, lay on the couch. Dvorak's "Largo" filled the room with expectancy. In the circle of brightness from the floor lamp, stood Elise, looking at him.

"I wanted to see you." He paused. "I missed you, Elise."

Then she was in his arms. With her head on his shoulder, her body warm against his chest, he breathed the plumeria fragrance of her hair. He held her for a very long time, feeling at home.

As Dvorak's scherzo notes danced about them, Michael gently kissed the top of her head. He kissed her forehead. Cupping his hand under her chin, he tipped her face and slowly, lightly, kissed her nose, her left cheek, and then her right. As he looked at her face, so close to his, Elise opened her eyes. He watched her search his face, his eyes. He knew she could read his raw vulnerability.

Then she smiled. "Michael," she whispered.

He kissed her, his lips tender on hers. Her mouth was welcoming, and her arms slid up around his neck. He kissed her for a long time, never wanting to stop. Michael kissed her chin. His lips tasted the lovely skin of her neck and the curve of her shoulder. He could feel her heartbeat under his lips.

As he slowly traced her collarbone with his kisses, the gathered neckline of her nightgown slipped off her shoulder. Oh, God, she was beautiful! He'd never wanted anything so much in all his life as to love Elise.

Easily, he lifted her into his arms. His eyes trailed the path his lips had taken from her lips, down her neck, and across the bare silken shoulder. He pressed his lips to her shoulder, her neck, and her mouth. Drawing back, he met her eyes—Elise's trusting eyes.

He carried her down the hall to her bedroom. The glow from the living room light illuminated the four-poster bed. Michael pulled back the covers and carefully laid Elise in the sheets. He kissed her lips, feeling her breath against his face. Summoning all his self-control, he reluctantly stood. Reaching for the white down comforter, he tucked it around Elise.

"Good night," he whispered.

Retracing his steps back down the hall, Michael turned off the living room light. The final notes of Dvorak's "The Allegro con fuoco" movement of the *New World Symphony* played as he stepped into the night and closed Elise's front door. Bending, he moved the shell and allowed the squeaky screen door to whisper closed behind him as he stepped off the porch. The fragrance of the Queen of the Night followed him into the starlight toward his cottage. He had just done the toughest and the noblest action of his life.

CHAPTER 55

The next morning Elise played the *New World Symphony* again, memories of Michael's late-night visit sweeping over her. She savored each moment.

The headlights of his car had briefly reflected against her window, and her heart had leapt to know he had come back to the island. To the cottage. She looked forward to seeing him, talking with him again.

She had not anticipated he would visit immediately upon his return. But the knock so soon after his car had come up the drive was enough to assure her that Michael was at her door. At first, she had searched for a reason. Perhaps something amiss at the cottage?

But before she could ask about anything as mundane as had he lost his key, she saw something in his eyes and demeanor. A shyness combined with purpose. Then his words, and the way he'd said her name. The naturalness of being in his arms. Feeling like she belonged when he kissed her. What a wonder to realize he felt about her as strongly as she longed for him. And that he was worthy of her trust.

Now, she hummed along with Dvorak, skipping paint onto a new canvas in time to the butterflies that danced in her stomach each time she remembered his kiss. The front door stood open to allow the paint fumes to air, and she heard Michael's flip-flops on the porch as he came to her door again just before noon.

"May I take you to lunch?"

She wiped mango-colored paint from her hand onto her apron. "That would be lovely."

He grinned. "I'll pick you up in an hour." He turned to leave and then turned back for another look. "Casual. Very casual."

Knowing an *hour* meant he would be back fifteen minutes before the arranged time, Elise had changed and was ready when he returned to her door. "Where are we off to?"

"A picnic." Climbing into the driver's seat, Michael started the engine and turned on the radio. A familiar melody filled the space between them.

Elise recognized the music. "This is the *New World Symphony*, but different."

"The difference is the electric guitars."

She listened. "Innovative."

"Rock and roll."

"Who's the artist?"

"Artists, with an 's' actually." He held up five fingers. "A group called Yes."

As he drove to the beach, Elise felt happy. Michael had returned home, and they were together. At a scenic spot bordered by flowering blue plumbago, they settled on a blanket. He unpacked sandwiches from the nearby cafe.

"You were away a while."

He turned his gaze to the ocean and watched the rhythm of the waves. "Some trips are longer than others."

"I sense a change in you," she said softly.

He met her eyes. "I realized what is truly important."

She nodded. "You invest your life protecting what is important."

Michael shook his head. "This time I understand what is important in my own life."

"And what's that?"

Standing, he held out a hand to her. After he helped her to her feet, he kept her hand in his as they walked barefoot in the sand. At the water's edge, the salty Atlantic washed away their footprints and swirled around their ankles.

He stopped and faced her. "I love you, Elise."

His words made her knees feel weak. "I love you, Michael."

Taking her other hand in his, he dropped to the sand on one knee. A low wave splashed over his shorts. "Will you do me the honor of becoming my ..." He swallowed and began again. "Will you marry me?"

She studied him for a moment. His dark hair. The sincerity and vulnerability in his eyes she had seen last night. He was handsome and strong in deep ways she could rely upon. He lived large and risked with intention for the sake of others. Michael stirred her soul and captivated her heart. "I'm honored, Michael," she answered at last. "Truly honored."

She pulled him to his feet and stepped close. "I'll give you my answer soon." Sliding a hand behind his neck, she tipped her head and kissed him tenderly. Elise lost herself in his answering kiss as another wave crashed against their legs.

CHAPTER 56

Those deep emotions that Michael had shelved since his family had died were thriving once more. Letting down his guard and being transparent with Elise involved risk. To allow himself to love her meant releasing a range of emotions he had worked hard to control. Yet, after that nightmare in New York, Michael had relived over and over every moment of his time with Elise. And he had made a decision. He wanted her to be his wife.

Waiting for her answer felt a bit unnerving, yet she had a lot to consider. They had met so recently, and he hadn't been anywhere on the radar as she had considered her future. The gift of time was a protection for his soul and hers. The time helped him to be certain he wasn't reacting or being impulsive.

In the mail that week, Michael received an envelope from Bryce. Inside was a short note in his battle buddy's scrawl. *This seemed too coincidental not to pass your way. Corbin has been as uptight as a long-tailed cat in a room full of rocking chairs.*

The Nebraska saying his grandmother had often used brought a smile. But the grin quickly faded as Michael read the enclosed newspaper clipping—the obituary notice of the doctor who had overseen Verity's care. Lack of care was a more accurate description. Michael didn't like the guy or the brand of medicine he practiced, but reading the physician died from contracting a rare disease not seen since Dr. Evans's research lab contained the virus a decade ago was unsettling. Michael's thoughts went to New York when Bryce met him at the pier.

By the by, Bryce had said. *The boss flew in this evening.*

What's up?

Corbin's meeting with Dr. Evans and his board. Something about a missing virus from Dr. Evans's pharmaceutical company.

Missing? Like lost?

More like stolen is what they think.

Too much of a coincidence. He could hear Bryce's voice in his ear, "We just do the job and let guys like Corbin handle the big stuff." Corbin and Dr. Evans were aware and already working on handling the problem.

Michael laid the article on the table, knowing he would reread the clipping later. Mulling over the news, he searched for connecting threads as he drove to his island job.

He found Jerry hatless in his Christiansted office, across the wooden pier from where the two St. Croix Adventures boats were docked when not on adventures.

Jerry placed a thick finger on a square of the month's calendar. "We've got a free day." He looked up and grinned at Michael. "Let's play."

"What do you have in mind?"

"Buck Island. Snorkeling. Picnic," Jerry listed. "Lazing on the most pristine beach on the planet."

Returning to the cottage, Michael found Elise in the garden. She sat at the outdoor table, dipping a large, flat paintbrush into a pot and swishing soft color across an oversized canvas.

Peering into the pot, he saw what looked like wet red Kleenex with steam rising above.

"Making your own colors?"

"Umm-hmm." She concentrated on the evenness of the strokes.

He watched quietly while she brushed the textured surface several times. She sighed and rested her brush across the top of the container. Balancing the canvas against the chair, she stood back, crossed her arms and regarded the product. She dipped the brush two more times and swept over areas that appeared to Michael to be just fine.

Satisfied at last, she turned her attention to him. "I like the color. Do you?"

"Very nice. How did you make it?"

From the pot, draped over the brush and dripping miserably, she lifted a limp blob into view. "Red hibiscus blossoms."

"At least they used to be."

"Poetic, really. In this altered state, the lives of these blooms will far exceed that of their comparatively short-lived peers."

"I'm impressed." He shifted his weight and plunged ahead. "How about a day trip to inspire new color creations?"

She let the lifeless hibiscus slide back into the pot. "What do you have in mind?"

Michael repeated Jerry's list. Elise quickly agreed.

With beach towels, sunscreen, and flip-flops, Michael and Elise met Jerry, his wife, Reta, and their three children at the boat. In short order, they had loaded the picnic lunch and cast off. From the top deck, Jerry navigated through the harbor. The sound of a cello caught their attention, and Elise pointed to the docked boats. Sitting on the deck of the *Day Dream*, Robson drew his bow across the tall instrument's bass strings.

"Bet the neighbors love that," Michael voiced.

"They're an eccentric group, those who live on boats," Jerry observed. "I doubt they mind."

When Robson failed to notice Elise's wave, Jerry blew a short blast on the boat horn. Looking up, Robson saw them grinning and waving. He stood, his hand around the neck of his cello, and bowed as he did onstage.

Once past the caution buoys, Jerry accelerated into the open sea. The trip to Buck Island was punctuated by sightings of sea turtles and playful dolphins. The shyer turtles kept to their steady courses while the dolphins frolicked alongside the boat as if excited to have playmates.

Arriving at Buck Island, Jerry anchored the boat knee deep in the clearest turquoise water Michael had ever seen. While Jerry and Michael secured the boat, Reta and Elise laid out lunch on the white sand beach. Jerry's children piled over the side of the boat like a litter of exuberant puppies and waded ashore. They were off to hunt for the small sharks that sunned in the shallow waters along the little island's coast.

"Remember to stay away from the manchineel tree," their father warned. "Don't touch it or pick up any of its fruit."

The three explorers acknowledged his warning and sped on to their explorations. Soon there were squeals from the youngest. She padded with fast feet back to the boat.

"We found them! We found little brown sharks!" She grabbed Michael's hand.

Feigning reluctance, he let her pull him along the way she'd come. She waved for the other adults, and they followed behind her like a small parade. To Michael's right, the thick forest stopped where the beach began. Near the dense tree line lay occasional coconuts—some were old while others were the current year's fruit. Where the beach curved, the sand melted into rocky terrain. Shells of all shapes and sizes were randomly cast up on shore. More were visible between the large flat rocks under the shallow water that lapped at the island's edge.

Catching up to her older siblings, the girl stopped.

"Shhh." Her older brother pressed a finger against his lips. He pointed. A dark shadow glided slowly out of sight.

"You scared it off," he accused, turning on the newcomers.

"Look," said his sister. "There's another one."

They searched in the direction where she pointed. Barely visible, another dark shadow moved slowly toward shore. As the shape came closer, Michael could make out the head of a small shark, the top fin, and a body that tapered back to a finely shaped tail. Then, with a quick flick of that tail, the shark slipped out of sight into deeper water.

"Did you see it?" The girl's eyes were bright with excitement.

"I did," Michael assured her.

"Look at this." Her older brother had already moved on to new discoveries. He stood over a large, hollow tree trunk. Bleached smooth by water, sun, and rain, the weathered and colorless wood had anchored itself in its present location long ago. The ten-year-old boy crouched and peered into a wide crack.

Michael caught up and looked inside. A small black crab stared back. The boy pushed a stick near the crab that skittered sideways just out of reach but didn't run away. As soon as the stick was pulled back, the crab retook his territory. Like a little black pirate, the crustacean swaggered closer to these giant intruders. He appeared to puff himself up, fiercely daring them to challenge his ownership of this piece of island real estate.

When the boy angled to tease the defiant inhabitant with another poke from the stick, Michael offered a distraction.

"Step back and see if you can bat with that weapon." Glancing around, Michael grabbed up a small greenish-yellow fruit near the tree line.

"Drop it!" Jerry yelled, as the two little girls screamed.

Obediently, Michael dropped the offending pseudo baseball. But the damage was already done. The fruit had broken open when it fell from the tree and from that crack, a drop of milky sap now clung to his hand.

"Oh, Michael." The first to his side, Elise peered at the damage. The skin was inflamed and blistering.

Jerry pushed him toward the water. "Rinse off the sap. Carefully."

"Let me guess," Michael said flatly. "That's a manchineel tree."

"Tourist," Jerry accused.

"A little something you forgot to include in my job training," Michael shot back.

"Manchineel are usually found near the beach," Jerry intoned. "An attractive tree with shade and apples, but they are very dangerous."

"Poisonous?"

"Deadly to everyone except a species of land crab."

Michael thought about the intrepid little crab holed up in the tree stump.

"The fruit is fatal if eaten," Jerry continued. "Columbus discovered the danger after several of his men died."

His hand afire, Michael wondered how anyone in Columbus's crew managed to eat one. He couldn't imagine what the fruit must have felt like going down. The salt water stung when Michael stuck his hand into the ocean.

Jerry squatted next to Michael at the water's edge. "Carib Indians used the sap to poison their darts. They poisoned the water supply of their enemies with the leaves. They tortured their victims by tying them to the trees and leaving them exposed to the rain."

"Quite a weapon."

Jerry nodded. "The Saladoid Indians used the sap on their arrows."

"They look similar to the seaside mahoe tree," Elise added. "The best way to tell them apart is by the leaves. And the mahoe fruit floats."

"They look like a blasted apple tree," Michael complained. "The kind Johnny Appleseed brought to the Midwest."

"Who?" The boy wanted to know.

"Pay attention in history," his dad suggested.

"Ask Michael about him later," Elise recommended.

Michael examined the extent of the damage. "If it's so dangerous, why not get rid of the tree?"

"That's just as dangerous." Jerry shook his head. "Maybe more. The tree and its parts contain strong toxins. Standing beneath the tree during rain may cause blistering. Cutting the tree gets the poisonous sap everywhere. Burning the tree causes blindness if the smoke reaches the eyes. Inhaling the smoke blisters the nose, mouth, and respiratory system."

"Nuisance," Michael groused.

Reta enlisted the children—the four of them prowled the nearby greenery. She returned to hand Jerry a bright pink frangipani bloom.

"Along the coastal beaches of the Caribbean and Central America, the manchineel trees provide windbreaks." Jerry squeezed the milk sap of the frangipani onto Michael's wounds. "The roots prevent beach erosion by stabilizing the sand." Jerry held the spent frangipani flower up for consideration. "If you ever work hard enough to blister your hands, say by working the ropes on the boats, this little specimen has healing qualities." He tossed the lifeless bloom into the receding wave. "There are quite a few manchineel trees on the west side of this island. The sap can cause blindness and severe burns on the skin. Be sure to caution tourists not to picnic under one."

Michael flexed his hand. "I'll keep that in mind."

The medicinal qualities of the salt water and the frangipani soon reduced the pain caused by the manchineel sap. Michael wrapped more frangipani around his hand as the picnickers ate their lunch. With bellies full, Michael and Jerry lay on the beach while the three Todd children covered them in sand. The group snorkeled, played volleyball, and ate again. As the sun dipped low on the horizon, and the captain pointed the boat back home, a dolphin swam alongside the picnickers. Jerry allowed his son to steer, and the two girls dozed in the cabin leaning against their mom. On deck, where an occasional wave crashed against the bow and sent saltwater spray across his face, Michael took in the view of the surrounding Atlantic. Elise came to where he stood and wrapped her arm around his waist. When she smiled up at him, her face tanned from their day in the sun, Michael decided that even despite his sore hand, the day had been perfect after all.

CHAPTER 57

Weather was always a consideration for parajumpers. On the island, Michael didn't pay attention as much as he used to, but extreme conditions typically meant someone needed to be rescued somewhere. On September 10, the weather watchers reported a depression had formed three hundred miles southwest of the Cape Verde islands. "A classical Cape-Verde tropical cyclone," the report said.

Two days later, the westward-moving depression reached tropical-storm strength. On September 13, based on satellite images, the storm had become a minimal hurricane. By September 14, the winds of the intensifying cyclone were estimated at one hundred and fifteen miles per hour. With the dangerous weather swirling a thousand miles away from any land area, Michael wasn't concerned. Only curious.

Locally, the island prepared to welcome the Christiansted Philharmonic's new conductor. Having officially accepted the baton as leader of the orchestra, Ava would conduct her first symphony as the first female conductor in the United States at the Christiansted Theater on Sunday afternoon. The schedule included a formal luncheon with speeches prior to the concert followed by a less formal party for the musicians and their families as well as the symphony's patrons after the musical event.

Season ticket holders for the New York Philharmonic, Dr. Evans and Keri were familiar with Ava and had come for the double purpose of sailing to St. Croix in their yacht and being present for the festivities. They had collected Corbin on the way. Dr. Evans, as Corbin's physician, had ordered Michael's boss to take some time to rest. Michael suspected a story there somewhere. Corbin rarely took time off, and Michael knew the Scotsman was more than overdue.

Early on the morning of September 15, as Michael drove to town, news reports predicted the hurricane would hit St. Croix. On the way, he saw Brother Ned who taught at St. John K-12 School. Though the Midwest was strongly Catholic, Michael's background was nondenominational when he needed to put something on the line about religious preferences for military forms.

Calling a man 'brother' or 'father' felt awkward for him, but he made an exception in Brother Ned's case. "What's on the assignment book for today?"

"The first order of business," the kindly priest looked meaningfully up at the heavens, "is to say a prayer asking the Almighty to direct the course of Hurricane Hugo so the storm comes only close enough to fill our needy cisterns."

"If they're anything like I was as a kid, your students will be asking for Hugo to come close enough to give them a day or two off school," Michael predicted.

Brother Ned grinned. "I might include that in my own petition— though silently of course—appearances and setting a good example and all. Even Jesus regularly took time for rest and solitude with his heavenly father."

"My mother used to say if you don't come apart, you'll come apart."

"Insightful woman."

Michael nodded thoughtfully. "I hear that a lot."

Shifting books to his other arm, Brother Ned made the sign of the cross as a blessing for Michael and fell into step beside two students on their way to class.

Michael continued on his way to Jewel by the Sea where he picked up a couple who had booked a scuba adventure for that morning.

"What do you think about the weather reports?" The honeymooners wanted to know. Michael could see they were nervous and hoping for reassurance.

"St. Croix has weathered storms before," Michael answered vaguely as he turned left toward Cane Bay. In truth, he hadn't experienced a newsworthy storm since moving to the island, so he had little to base an opinion on. "When's your flight home?"

"Tomorrow morning." The woman reached for her husband's hand.

He grinned. "No worries then. You'll be watching the storm on television back in the States. Where do you live?"

"South Carolina," the man replied.

After their dive, Michael returned the honeymooners to their hotel and met Corbin for a run on the beach. Noting the clear blue sky, Michael found it hard to believe a hurricane swirled aggressively out in the Atlantic. Listening to his boss puffing air beside him, Michael felt that familiar competitive rise and upped his pace. Corbin did the same. Michael pushed harder, and his legs pounded up and down like pistons. Corbin matched his stride until they both were running full out. Now the competition was all about who dropped behind first. Michael ran until his lungs felt like exploding—he knew if he kept going he'd embarrass himself by throwing up. There was a time and a place for that, but not on a beach in St. Croix while trying to best his mentor. Still, Corbin kept stride beside him, though when Michael glanced over to signal their slow down, Corbin looked like he was about to be sick, too.

Their feet pounded heavy prints in the sand as they slowed and bent to rest their hands on their knees.

"I'm getting too old for this," Corbin said between breaths.

Sweaty from their strenuous endeavor on the Caribbean sand, Michael followed his boss ankle-deep into the refreshing surf.

"At forty-four, I'm the oldest guy still doing this."

Michael scooped handfuls of the salty water across his neck and chest. The sticky Atlantic mingled with his sticky sweat. "It's been workin' so far."

Corbin studied the horizon. "Except different thoughts are going through my head these days."

With damp fingers, Michael raked his hair back from his face. "What kind of thoughts?"

"When I was young, I never considered the potential pain." Corbin splashed water over his head and face. "The risk. Living on the edge. Pushing the envelope merely gave me an adrenaline rush."

Michael nodded.

"Now I think about how much the pain will hurt if things go wrong."

"And?"

Corbin's jaw tightened as he studied the view, and Michael knew he weighed the risk of becoming too vulnerable. Michael shifted so he stood side by side to Corbin and focused his eyes on the distant waves.

After a long pause, Corbin spoke again. "Suspicions. Wondering if I'm pushing my luck. Never thought I'd look in the mirror and admit I'm getting old."

Michael didn't know what to say, so he didn't say anything. Corbin sighed and began to walk along the beach. Michael kept pace. They soon cooled off and their breathing returned to normal. Corbin bent and picked up a baby conch shell no bigger than his thumbnail.

Michael finally spoke. "What are your options?"

Corbin slipped the tiny shell into his pocket. "That's a good question."

CHAPTER 58

Late the night of September 15, Michael's phone rang. Meatloaf, acting in Corbin's place while the CO took some time off, had orders.

"NOAA reconnaissance aircraft penetrated the eye of Hurricane Hugo," Meatloaf reported. "From satellite estimates, we expected the usual one hundred mile-per-hour range. But the crew clocked sustained winds of one hundred and ninety miles per hour."

Michael knew these daredevil pilots. "Did they make it out?"

"Miraculously. Though I doubt any of them chance it again."

"How did they survive?"

"Those hot dogs pulled off a dangerous low altitude penetration into the eye wall. The barometric pressure was twenty-seven point ten," Meatloaf explained. "The pilot dumped fifty thousand pounds of fuel to escape the hurricane."

Michael rubbed the back of his neck. "Unbelievable."

"With one hundred and sixty mile-per-hour sustained surface winds, Hugo is a category five hurricane. And he's headed your way."

"Orders?"

"Prepare and buckle down."

The next day, the news around the island centered on the weather and that Senator Bennett Taylor had returned for another island retreat from Washington, DC, politics. Michael didn't like the guy and wished he'd find another place to vacation. He felt territorial about St. Croix. And about Elise. He remembered how the senator had attempted to dominate Elise's time on the ballroom dance floor. And any other time he visited the area. The creep. Old enough to be her father, the guy paid too much attention to Elise. In Michael's opinion, the senator could be a more attentive father to his own daughter, Claire. Perhaps if the senator tended to his own family, Michael wouldn't have to.

On Saturday, Michael went for an early morning run. When he returned to his cottage, Bryce was sunning on his porch while listening to a recording of "Shook Me All Night Long" by AC/DC.

"The weather guessers predict the brewing tropical storm will spin into a newsworthy hurricane." Bryce patted the 72-hour pack leaning near the door. "I was close, so Meatloaf sent me here in case things get dicey and you needed expert assistance."

"Thoughtful." Michael clapped Bryce on the back. "Can't think of any other expert assistance I would rather have. But things look pretty tame at present."

"Tame enough that you can take me for the Cruzan Rum factory tour?"

Michael eyed the sky. "Let's go."

The Cruzan Rum plantation consisted of several structures. Turning into the drive, Michael pointed out the old stone sugar mill that had been converted to a cistern. A nineteen-century chimney stood tall above a wide building, a reminder the factory had made changes to keep up with the times. They parked near the only other car in the small parking lot in front of a large home, obviously once the Estate Diamond's great house, and now the factory's main office.

At the welcome center, the owner of the Cruzan rum distillery, Mrs. Nelthropp, offered to give them the tour. "At one time there were over a hundred and fifty plantations producing molasses and making rum on the island. Now we're the only one." She told them the story of how her mother had scandalized her teetotaler Methodist parents stateside by marrying into the Cruzan Rum family. Eventually the parents had acquiesced and come to visit their daughter, the island, and their grandchildren.

"Drinking is viewed differently here than in the States," she continued. "Legal drinking age on the island is eighteen though it's not uncommon for kids to accompany their parents to places that serve alcohol."

"Everything is open air anyhow," Bryce observed. "Hard to tell where the beach ends and a pub begins."

"We're pretty casual on St. Croix." The owner led them from the center toward the operations beyond. "We don't treat drinking as a big deal and we don't have much problem with underage drinking or people overdoing. Except for some of the tourists, of course, but they're only here for a week and then the problem catches a plane back to where they came from."

"With a case of rum as carry-on." Michael followed their hostess up a set of stairs.

"This is the base of our rum." On a metal catwalk, she paused where they could see into the giant swirling vats of molasses. "Sugarcane is grown and harvested by hand with machetes. Molasses is extracted from the sugarcane. We'll go anywhere in the world to get the highest grade, high-test molasses. It's so sweet it's more like maple sugar."

The three watched the churning mixture in the large distillery tank below them. "The molasses is diluted with rain water and boiled to four hundred degrees. After it cools to room temperature, the mixture is moved to these seed tanks."

Bryce inhaled the thick malty smell. "Looks like it's in a large blender."

"There's no stirring mechanism," she said. "The motion is caused by the ingredients reacting with each other in the process. To the molasses is added five pounds of yeast and rainwater to total five hundred gallons of mixture. We use only pure Virgin Island rainwater. That's one ingredient that makes our product different from the competition. The movement you see in the tank is natural chemistry."

"A lot like what the weather photos are showing right now," Michael compared.

"In sixteen hours, seven hundred and fifty billion living yeast organisms are working in each gallon. Once the yeastie beasties are doing their work, the mixture is transferred to fermenters. Water is added and the yeast eats the sugar, converting it into alcohol."

"Converting?" Bryce wrinkled his nose. "They eat the sugar and it comes out—"

Michael elbowed him. "Don't even say it."

"As alcohol," their guide finished for Bryce, a smile playing on her lips. "I have sons. There is something about bathroom humor that never stops being funny to boys—of any age." Glancing down from the catwalk, she spied a worker shaking hands with another man. She waved as the second man glanced up at her and then hurried toward the parking lot.

Next they went through the fermentation room. "The remaining mix is three parts water and one part molasses. Foamy and brown, it's called beer though it's not the type served at taverns. Ten percent of this mix is used in the rum. Now the alcohol is removed from the fermented mash."

Michael and Bryce followed their guide to the next area of the factory. "This first column boils the beer at two hundred and twenty degrees until the alcohol evaporates and floats to the top where it's trapped and cooled back to its liquid state. Light rum is highly rectified to remove impurities, hence the lighter color. At this stage the rum is at one hundred and eighty-nine proof."

Bryce whistled. "High test."

"Water is added to reduce it to one hundred and forty-two proof. The third column cleans the rum and it emerges clear as rainwater. We use only ethyl alcohol," she pointed out. "Our distillation process assures purity and cleanliness."

They walked through the warehouse filled with rows of corked wooden kegs in various stages of aging. "The Cruzan rum is diluted to forty percent and poured into corked barrels. We house twenty-seven thousand aging barrels. There's no shortcutting. The aging process is key to the quality of our product. Every barrel must age for five to twelve years."

She slapped a barrel that sounded full and solid. "When the rum's ready to be de-barreled, the barrel is rolled and beaten until the cork pops."

"Roll out the barrel…" Bryce hummed the polka.

With a smile, Mrs. Nelthropp stepped the polka's heel, toe, dance step, and then continued. "The aged contents of the barrel are drained into a holding tank and diluted to eighty-proof. Charcoal filters remove any remaining impurities. The light rum remains in the filter system longer to remove color."

Michael surveyed the rows of casks. "How much do you get from each barrel?"

"The yield is thirty-six cases per barrel. Daily eleven-hundred cases are bottled and labeled for disbursement."

Michael added these facts to his island trivia to share with tourists. "How much remains on the island?"

"Fifteen percent remains here. The rest goes to the mainland."

Back outside, the threesome first looked to the sky for signs of impending storms. The clear sky belied the weather reports.

"We've been a family business for two-hundred-fifty years. Hurricanes are a part of life on the islands." She shaded her eyes with her hand. "St. Croix gets brushed every three and half years. Rarely do we take a direct hit. The storm usually isn't the worst. The problem is being without electricity and water for the following weeks. Some places are equipped with generators as backup. Jewel by the Sea, for instance. Jacques has the best equipment so his guests are assured of a comfortable stay. We label one of our rums for his hotel."

"He does attract some famous guests," Michael acknowledged. "Senator Bennett has taken a recent fancy to the place."

"The senator has ordered his own label of Cruzan Rum," she reported proudly. "Someone was here just before bottling to check on the quality."

"Some guys have it all," Bryce observed. "Money to purchase their own label and lackeys to taste-test it."

Bryce bellied up to the bar at the welcome center. "The locals say the gold rum doesn't kick like the clear rum."

Their guide nodded knowingly. "That's been the rumor for as long as I can remember." She set two glasses on the counter. "The dark rum is aged in bourbon barrels, charred white ash barrels purchased from Jack Daniels."

Bryce watched her pour. "Recycled barrels?"

"On arrival they're steamed to remove any residue flavors from their former use. The rum is stored in the barrels from two to twelve years to take on the golden color." She pushed the two glasses across to her guests. "The third column removes the fusel oil that causes hangovers."

"No wonder Cruzan rum is the drink of choice."

Bryce and Michael drank the sample.

"Our flavored rums are popular." She began to blend something new. "We have coconut, banana, citrus, orange, pineapple, and rum cream."

"What do you call that brew?" Bryce leaned forward to watch.

With a practiced hand she prepared her recipe. "One part Cruzan coconut rum, one part Cruzan mango rum, and top the glass with pineapple juice." She handed new glasses to her guests. "Cruzan Confusion."

While Michael and Bryce sampled the signature drinks, the television at the bar gave an updated weather report. "The tropical storm has developed into a full-grown hurricane," the announcer stated.

"The key will be water," Mrs. Nelthropp mused. "If the cisterns are damaged, water is doubly precious."

"Surrounded by the entire Atlantic Ocean and thirsty for water," Bryce noted. "That's what I call ironic."

Their hostess countered. "That's island reality."

CHAPTER 59

Very early the next day, Michael rechecked his 72-hour pack. He and Bryce secured the patio furniture and prepared the cottage as best they could. Then Bryce went to meet with Corbin, Dr. Evans, and Keri while Michael made certain everything was prepared at Elise's family home.

With Elise's help, Michael secured shutters across the large windows. "What else?"

"The last hurricane to come to St. Croix was Hurricane Hazel in 1954." She propped open the screen door with the weathered conch shell. "Before my time, so I'm not experienced. I'm relying on what I remember from the storm drill we were taught in school."

Michael carried her outdoor drawing table inside. "Water's crucial."

"Food, lighting, and first-aid supplies." From a cupboard, she produced an emergency pack with the essentials.

Antonio arrived to help Elise board up doors, something he was doing for his landscape clients. Lisandro puffed out his chest as he worked to keep up with his father. The young boy's face was flushed with excitement to see the anticipated Hurricane Hugo.

Satisfied that Elise was prepared, Michael went to Christiansted where parishioners were making their way to St. Elizabeth's. The open-sided structure made of steel beams could hold twelve hundred people and likely would be filled today. All the churches on the island were holding traditional Sunday services as usual including the Moravian church, the Lutheran Church, Lord God of *Sabaoth*—the oldest of its kind under the American flag—the Seventh Day Adventists, and the Assembly of God.

Downtown, merchants secured anything that wasn't nailed down, stacking outside tables and chairs inside, and boarding up windows and doors. Michael realized this type of weather was the reason for the iron bars across the windows of most businesses.

At the harbor, he found Jerry busily securing the two boats that made the tours to Buck Island. "What about the Dive Shop at Cane Bay?" Michael asked.

"No problem, mon. I locked that down first."

"What else?" Michael surveyed Jerry's clean boat.

"Every so often we get a hurricane warning." Jerry pulled against a taut rope to make sure it held firm. "We always over-prepare, but that's okay." He glanced out to the other boats anchored in the harbor. "Let's take a couple crotch rockets and see if any other boaters need an extra pair of hands to batten down their hatches."

The sun bright overhead, Michael turned the throttle and powered his jet ski forward. Churning water in the usually placid harbor warned of the hurricane spinning toward them. As the jet ski bounced over the waves, spray doused his sunglasses and pelted his face.

He trailed Jerry, who knew these boats and their owners like Michael had known the neighbors on his country road in Nebraska. They waved to several boat owners busy with storm preparations for their vessels. Jerry pulled alongside one double-bowed sailboat and offered some suggestions. When his recommendations weren't well received, Jerry proceeded to cuss the sailor who suddenly seemed to grasp he was in the presence of an expert. After a second failed attempt to follow Jerry's instructions, the lifelong seaman told Michael to hold his jet ski while he climbed aboard and did the job himself.

"Idiot." Grumbling, Jerry got back aboard his jet ski. "These guys land a good deal, make some money, buy a boat in the islands, and think they know what they're doing. Guys like that will get all our boats in a knot if a strong wind blows through."

Jerry pointed his craft toward the residential section of the harbor. "Come on. There are a bunch of boats over here that people live on part of the year, but they're stateside during hurricane season."

As the two moved on through the harbor, Michael spotted Robson with another couple he recognized as the cello player's neighbors. Like Robson, their address was a floating one. The trio worked topside on a boat near Robson's own.

Jerry pulled up alongside the threesome and idled the jet ski. "Need a hand? Or four?"

Robson stood, pressing his hands against his lower back where he'd been bent over. "Wouldn't turn them down." He nodded a greeting to Michael. "There's five boats we need to check to make sure they're secure. Their owners aren't here."

Jerry and Michael tied their jet skis to the boat and jumped aboard.

"What about your boat?" Michael asked.

Robson nodded. "I secured the *Day Dream* first. She's fast." He checked his watch. "And I've got to get dressed and pick up Ava soon."

They worked steady and efficiently and soon Robson left to clean up for the afternoon's event at the theater.

"Good enough?" Michael asked Jerry.

"We've done all we can." The seasoned seaman surveyed the surrounding harbor dotted with rocking boats. "Let's get ready for those big doin's in town."

Later, the weather had turned decidedly blustery when, showered and dressed, Michael arrived to take Elise to the theater. "All set?"

Dressed in professional black to perform with the orchestra, she nodded. "As prepared as I'm going to be. How are things in town?"

"The same. Folks have tied down anything that couldn't run away first. If it did run away, they clubbed and then secured it."

Outside, they both took a moment to look across the Atlantic. The ocean whipped and tossed as the eastern sky darkened. As Michael drove to the theater, their conversation turned to the upcoming event and the anticipation of having Ava as their fulltime conductor.

Parking had always been in short supply in Christiansted. Today proved no exception. Michael dropped Elise at the theater and went to park on another block. The winds blew stronger as he walked the short distance to the theater.

Inside the ballroom, guests lined up for lunch at the buffet tables heaped with conch fritters and clawless Caribbean lobster, baked and sugared sweet potatoes, coconut pudding, and salad with sweet prickly pear. Key lime pie and rum cake filled the dessert table. Michael recognized these dishes as specialties served at Jewel by the Sea and knew Jacques' award-winning restaurant had done the catering. That chef sure knew how to cook some of the best meals Michael had ever eaten.

Finding their seats at a round dining table, Michael noted that Senator Bennett Taylor wouldn't be sitting with them. Michael didn't think he could force polite conversation with that guy. Instead, Robson and Ava joined them, as well as Dr. Evans and Keri, Corbin and Bryce. Michael suspected Elise had something to do with arranging the pleasant company for lunch.

Jerry stopped at Michael's table to good-naturedly pound him on the back.

"These are fellow boat lovers." Michael indicated Dr. Evans and Keri, and then turned to Corbin. "Corbin, this is Jerry. My boss."

His old friend stood and extended his hand. "I'm pleased to meet the man who can tell this guy what to do."

Jerry looked sidelong at Michael. "Same haircut." He shook Corbin's hand and returned to his seat beside Reta, their three children, and the jaunty Brother Ned.

Glancing at an adjacent table, Michael smiled at June and Karl, Jacques and his wife, Mrs. Nelthropp and her husband. Michael spotted the senator a short distance away. Next to him was a young woman, and even from the back, she looked familiar.

Bryce leaned forward. "Did you see Claire?"

Michael spun back to face him and Corbin. "Claire?"

Bryce shivered. "I don't know whether to say hi or pull on my combat gear."

"The senator's daughter?" Elise followed his glance. "You know her?"

"Something like that," Michael mumbled.

With a polite nod to those at their table, Ava excused herself to prepare for her first official performance as the conductor for the St. Croix Philharmonic Orchestra. At that moment, an excited stir rippled through the guests as the calypso band began to play. The steel drums beat an intoxicating rhythm and four *mocko jumbies* made their long-legged entrance. They were dressed entirely in white. Under a wide-brimmed hat, each face was masked. Below a flowing blouse, loose cotton pants extended for yards from the dancer's waist to the floor. Balancing on stilts ten feet high, the mysterious entertainers gamboled among the attendees.

"They look like the Ku Klux Klan on stilts." Bryce sat back to take in the scene.

"Mocko jumbies represent a spiritual, ancient African art form," Elise spoke above the music. "They are an icon of Virgin Island culture."

Towering above their audience, the limber mocko jumbies expertly spun, skipped, and swayed to the irresistible percussion.

"In Africa, the mocko jumbies were people who lived among the villagers, but they remained anonymous by wearing a mask and covering their body in traditional clothing." Elise turned their attention toward Jerry, who jumped to his feet and moved expertly with steps that wove him between the stilted legs of his white-camouflaged dance partner. "The same applies on the island, except this is the first troupe to include women."

Keri swayed with the rhythmic drums. "Why so tall?"

"Their height and dominating presence symbolized the power and protection of God." Elise tipped her head toward one of the troupe who circled their table like a frolicking daddy-long-legs. "The Africans brought their religious ceremonies with them to St. Croix, but the European slave masters forbade the practice. So they disguised the practice as a festive event."

Dr. Evans leaned closer to ask above the music. "What does mocko jumbie mean?"

"It means another social studies lesson when we were in school." Robson nodded knowingly at Elise. "Mocko means to mock evil spirits. The name translates as seeker, protector, healer, good spirit."

"Some people attain new heights by pursuing careers in law, business, and medicine. Others attain real height as a stilt-dancing mocko jumbie," Bryce joked.

Following the energetic performance of the stilted dancers, Robson and Elise left their table to join the orchestra members assembling for the concert. Robson would lead the cello section, and Elise filled a place with the violas.

In time for the afternoon concert, Michael led their group of visiting friends from the ballroom. The St. Croix Theater regularly attracted concertgoers from the neighboring islands, but today the lobby and theater were far from full. The usual island-hoppers had elected to stay home due to the weather. While the orchestra tuned, the islanders would be tuned to the weather station.

Michael's glance swept the lobby where guests met and mingled. An oriental-looking man entered. Oblivious to the ornate décor, he studied the people until his eyes fell on Senator Taylor, who had just ordered a cocktail. The newcomer approached the senator, who airily tried to dismiss the stranger. As the senator turned away, the man caught his elbow. He leaned close and spoke to the politician. The senator pulled his arm free and casually sipped his drink, his eyes on the crowd while the man said something else.

Michael continued to watch the scene unfold. Coming from the ladies' room, Claire stopped at the bar and ordered two drinks. Her father tensed as she stepped to his side. Sipping her own drink, she offered the other to the newcomer. The man glared at her. She pushed the drink into his hand, but he refused to accept the glass. Leaning close to the senator, the man spoke something into his ear and then moved away.

Michael heard Keri sigh appreciatively as they entered the historic auditorium.

"This is spectacular." Corbin took in the ambiance of the Old Italian décor.

"Playing in such a historic and beautiful performance hall is an added benefit to Ava's promotion to conductor," Dr. Evans agreed.

Remembering his first visit to the grand theater, Michael looked about the now familiar setting, this time trying to see it as he had then—as Corbin, Keri, Dr. Evans, and Bryce viewed the theater for their first time now.

Michael ushered his guests to their seats as the musicians on stage tuned. Nearest the audience on the right side of the stage, Robson bent his head near his cello as he lightly played. To Robson's right, Elise tucked her bright viola under her chin and jigged her bow across the strings.

Then the concertmaster stood, and the musicians fell silent. The audience also quieted as each orchestra section tuned to the oboe's A-note. From behind the stage, someone began to clap. The orchestra and the audience joined in and Ava, baton in hand, walked purposefully to the conductor's music stand. In tailored tails and black high heels, she stopped to shake the hand of the concertmaster and bowed to the audience.

Ava turned to the orchestra and poised the slender baton in midair. Michael could see Elise's welcoming and expectant expression as she watched for Ava's cue. Sitting forward on the edge of his seat, Robson beamed.

The baton descended. Music burst forth and filled the air with Beethoven's overture "Leonore." Michael knew the stories behind the classical pieces she played were important to Elise, and he silently read the description in the program. *Fidelio was the only opera Beethoven wrote, though it reflects its share of music drama full of heroic themes. The work proved Beethoven was skilled as a music dramatist in genres beyond his symphonies. His mini-music drama had an inspiring effect on future composers including Berlioz, Liszt, Wagner, and Mahler, each who paid tribute to Beethoven's earlier works.*

During the brief moment between selections to set the stage for the second piece, Robson took the soloist chair placed in front. He tuned his cello and settled the instrument's position. Ava lifted her baton and the orchestra began "Cello Concerto No. 1 in C Major." Michael glanced back to the program to find the story behind Haydn's composition. *Haydn composed this concerto around 1761— 1765 for longtime friend and principal cellist of Prince Nicolaus' Esterhazy Orchestra, Joseph Weigl. The work was presumed lost until a copy was discovered in Prague.* Playing center stage, on Ava's left, Robson's solo performance brought the audience to its feet.

Following the intermission, to Michael's delight, the second half of the concert featured Dvorak's *New World Symphony*. The lights dimmed and the music began. He sat back in his chair, letting the rich music and treasured memories wash over him. He watched Elise, saw passion for the music in her face as she followed the parade of notes on her music stand, occasionally glancing up as Ava guided the musicians.

The orchestra launched into the Allegro con fuoco movement of Dvorak's spectacular score—now Michael's favorite classical piece. He remembered that night when he knew he loved Elise. The night he first held her, kissed her, felt her surrender in his arms. The night he chose to honor her.

He was watching her play the memorable notes, concentrating, being part of the orchestral whole, creating the sound and allowing the notes to carry her as part of the music, when an usher startled him. Seeming to appear from nowhere, the man passed a note to Michael and disappeared again in the semi-darkness.

Michael looked at Elise once more, then at the envelope in his hand. Sliding his thumb under the sealed edge, he opened it. Michael smelled plumeria as he withdrew and unfolded the single sheet. He read the solitary word written on the paper.

Yes.

CHAPTER 60

I said yes.

Elise's heart beat so fast and hard she wondered if the audience could hear the rhythm above the orchestra. Sometime during the Allegro con fuoco movement of Dvorak's *New World Symphony*, her note would be delivered to Michael. She wished she could see his face the moment he opened the envelope, but that wasn't possible as she concentrated on the music score and Ava's sweeping direction.

She felt liberty in her decision, yet had no idea what to expect in a future shared with Michael. They were still getting to know one another in so many ways. Completely different from the other men she knew, Michael had a rough discipline. An integrity where she found security. Michael had been peaceful and considerate during the weeks she had taken to work through the maze of what June called the difference between easy and right. She considered thoughts and emotions in the same fashion she discovered colors in the sea and the shells and stones that the Atlantic left like gifts along the shore until one thing became brilliantly clear—there were many paths she could choose, and there were a few people she could make a life with. But there was only one person she could not live without.

The concert was a spectacular success. The music unparalleled. Ava had chosen well when she decided on the line-up for her first concert program in her new position as a full-fledged conductor. Like a porous seashell, the atmospheric theater absorbed the concert's final note into its vast catalog of memories. Tonight would be a lifetime memory for Elise. She'd given her decision to marry Michael surrounded by the people who meant the most to her and in the theater where her parents were still so present in the work they left behind.

Now the audience stood. Applauding.

Shouting "Bravo."

"Bravissimo."

Ava bowed. Then she motioned for her concertmaster to stand and bow. The audience clapped louder. Section by section, Ava recognized the talented musicians in the orchestra. Section by section—the strings, the woodwinds, the brass, the percussion—each stood and bowed to the appreciative crowd.

Ava walked off-stage, and the clapping continued. Someone whistled. Ava reappeared on stage for a second bow and again swept her arm in an inclusive arc of recognition for the players. The conductor bowed and once more disappeared off-stage. As the enthusiastic applause continued, Ava returned to the front of the stage and bowed a third time. Robson placed a large bouquet of flowers in her arms. She smiled her thanks, blew a kiss to the audience, and was gone again.

In that moment, Elise saw Michael. And he saw her. For a split second, he held the envelope where she could see it. Then he tucked the note into his pocket, the one near his heart.

The house lights came on, and the boisterous audience collected programs, wraps, and umbrellas on their way out of the concert hall as the orchestra members gathered their instruments. Several musicians came to the front of the theater to meet and talk with people from the audience. Elise cocked her head to listen. Still people were applauding—at least that's what the sound seemed to be.

"Rain," Robson said. "Come on. Let's pop some champagne with Ava."

Looking off-stage, Elise could see Michael. He threaded his way forward until he stood at the bottom of the stage. Then he vaulted up and came to her. She looked steadily into his eyes and lost herself in the lovelight of his gaze. He cupped her face in his hands and bent to kiss her. His lips were tender. She reached her arms around his neck, the viola and bow still in her hands and now resting against his back.

Someone clapped. Reluctantly ending the kiss, Elise and Michael followed the sound. Bryce stood grinning and applauding at the edge of the stage. Next to Bryce, stood Corbin. Smiling, Dr. Evans wrapped his arm around Keri's waist and gently pulled her close. Robson stood to the side of the stage, hands on hips, looking surprised.

Michael grinned as he looped his arm around Elise's shoulders and brought her to the front of the stage. He jumped down beside Bryce and Corbin, then turned and lifted Elise down to join them. Bryce whistled and thumped his partner on the back.

"Looks like we'll be popping champagne for Michael and Elise too," Robson predicted.

Michael's party followed Elise backstage to put away her viola and catch up with the others who were already in the ballroom for the after-performance celebration. As they entered the festivities, Michael reached for her hand. She blushed when those at the party noticed.

Plucking a yellow hibiscus from an arrangement in the ballroom, June came quickly to her side. She tucked the flower behind Elise's ear with the words "A new beginning." The phrase instantly transported Elise back to the day she listed the cottage for rent.

"You're making this into a goodbye," June had said.

"Isn't it?"

June had flung open the glass double doors and beckoned Elise outside. "By the gods, no! This is a new beginning."

Now June stepped nearly nose-to-nose with Michael. "If you hurt her, I will remove your lungs through your nostrils."

"Yes, ma'am." Michael stood tall. "I believe you."

June harrumphed and turned back to the party. Right behind her, Karl leaned close and kept his voice low. "She'd do it too."

CHAPTER 61

The musicians, season ticket holders, and patrons were a boisterous crowd. Though the brewing storm had kept attendees from neighboring St. Thomas and St. John from attending, the concert had surpassed everyone's expectations. Investors who had previously been reluctant to hire Ava now toasted their decision-making prowess. Corks popped loudly as waiters made the rounds, handing out champagne.

Michael collected two glasses from a passing waiter's tray and handed one to Elise. He leaned close where only she could hear his words. "I love you."

She smiled. "I love you back."

Bryce stepped to Michael's side, his arm companionably around Claire's shoulders. "Look who I found."

"Hello, Claire." Michael rubbed the back of his head. "I never know when I'll run into you."

"Or where. I'm surprised to see you here." She regarded him thoughtfully. "You look different."

"Do I?"

Bryce grinned. "You do." He turned to Elise. "Elise, this is Claire Taylor. Claire, this is Elise Eisler."

"The viola player," Claire put in. "The concert was the best I've heard."

Elise gave a slight bow. "Thank you."

Michael regarded Claire. "What brings you to St. Croix?"

She shrugged. "Some vacation time with my father."

"Your idea or his?" Michael wanted to know.

"Mine, as a matter of fact." Claire glanced to the center of the room where her father stood in the middle of an adoring group. Enjoying the attention, he played the crowd.

Bryce watched the politician reach his arm around the waist of a young, shapely woman and signal for a waiter. "Betcha lunch out he's gonna impress 'em with his private label."

"The first cases were delivered to the hotel this morning," Claire noted as the server leaned close and Senator Taylor gave instructions. "He's been anticipating an event worthy of the unveiling."

Bryce nodded. "Yesterday, he had a staff guy checking the stuff at the distillery."

A waiter brought a tray of drinks around. In the middle of the tray sat an open bottle of Cruzan Rum bearing Senator Taylor's private label.

Claire picked up a glass from the tray. "Daddy didn't bring any staff with him this trip."

Having taken two glasses from the tray, Michael was handing one to Elise, but Claire's words stopped him. Bryce had put his glass to his lips, but froze, his eyes meeting Michael's. He lowered the glass and stared at Claire. "We saw the guy yesterday."

She shook her head. "He wasn't happy with the surprise when I showed up. He came alone. Without staff."

Michael spotted Keri to his right. She clinked her glass against Dr. Evans's and Corbin's and was about to drink. He grabbed her wrist before the rim reached her mouth. Dr. Evans had taken a drink but was too shocked by Michael's actions to swallow. "Spit it out," Michael ordered.

Dr. Evans spit the liquid back into his glass. Corbin smelled the contents of his glass.

Bryce jumped up on a chair and called out to the room, "Don't drink the kind senator's rum just yet."

"What is the meaning of this?" The senator bellowed.

At that moment, Michael saw an older waiter disappear out the ballroom door. As Michael dashed after him, he heard Corbin's authoritative voice address the confused group.

"Bear with us for a moment, ladies and gentlemen. For now, don't drink until we—"

The ballroom door slammed behind him, cutting off Corbin's words. Michael followed the sound of running footsteps down a long, dim hall and around a corner. The runner bolted through an outside door at the back of the theater. Michael crashed through the same door. Outside was unnaturally dark too early in the day and the wind whipped rain against his face. Gathering his bearings, Michael saw a car speed out of the parking lot—the same car that yesterday had been parked in the lot at the distillery.

Running to the closest parked car, Michael wasn't surprised to find the door unlocked and the key in the console. Like living in small-town Nebraska, the islanders usually left car doors unlocked and the keys inside. That way they knew where to find the keys and no one expected a vehicle to be stolen. St. Croix was an island, for Pete's sake, with a half dozen main roads. Where would anyone take a stolen car?

Michael started the engine, shoved the compact into drive, and accelerated after the rapidly disappearing vehicle. Another benefit to being on the island included a limited number of streets and miles for getting lost. Though the wipers whipped at top speed, the pounding rain made seeing the course of the narrow Christiansted roads difficult. Leaning close to the windshield, he pressed the gas pedal. Michael couldn't guess the direction of the car he pursued without its lights on. He took a gamble and aimed for the highway.

Winding through the city streets, he wondered if he'd made a wrong choice. Maybe he should have gone to the harbor instead. Turning onto the highway, he spotted a brief flash of red taillights rounding the bend ahead. Going too fast, the guy leading this race had touched his brakes.

As Michael rounded the same bend, distant lights appeared in his rearview mirror. Friend or foe?

Michael followed the vehicle west. Was the driver in front of him trying to reach the airport? Flying out ahead of the incoming hurricane would be difficult if not impossible. Michael recalled Meatloaf's retelling of the harrowing escape of the crew of the NOAA reconnaissance aircraft.

Closing the distance between himself and the other car, he thought back to his brief glimpse of the man at the Cruzan Rum Factory when Mrs. Nelthropp had waved at him. Older than Michael, the man had been nervous and in a hurry to leave. Was there something familiar about him?

Coming abreast of the speeding car, Michael took a chance that the storm had chased all other traffic off the road. He pulled into the lane for oncoming traffic, driving alongside the other car on the passenger side. Michael steered into the other vehicle, pressing the man off the road. Still the driver raced ahead. With an abrupt twist of his wrist, Michael ran his car into the side of the other. The jolt caused the driver to swerve briefly out of control, then recover and speed to the forefront again.

Stomping on the gas, Michael caught up on the right side and again ran his car into the other. This time, the vehicle spun off the road but before Michael could get turned around, the guy had found another road and sped south. Gunning to catch up, Michael passed the car that had been following him. From the rearview mirror, he could see the shadowing vehicle slow and swing around to join the unceremonious parade. The ferocity of the weather increased in this southerly direction. Ahead, its lights illuminating the approaching car, Michael recognized the Hess Oil Refinery.

In preparation for the incoming hurricane, the gated refinery had evacuated their workers for their safety. The car ahead of him crashed through the wire fence and sped forward, seeking the open avenues between refinery equipment. Definitely a dangerous situation—Michael didn't want to follow this guy into an explosive end. Tonight he had too much to live for.

"Give 'em enough rope and they'll hang themselves," his mother used to say when someone was making wrong choices. Taking his foot off the gas, Michael gave the guy some space.

Sure enough, the driver panicked and took a turn too fast on the slippery wet pavement. The driver's side plowed into a huge round tank. The tank appeared to shudder and groan like an oversized prizefighter taking a punch to his gut.

Michael stopped and cautiously got out of his car. Wind whipped at him and rain stung his face. He was soaked to the skin in the few seconds before he reached the passenger side of the wrecked car and pulled open the door. The driver slumped against the steering wheel. His forehead was bloody and, though his eyes were closed, his face was turned toward Michael.

There was something familiar about the older man.

Michael checked his pulse. It beat steady. He tugged and wrestled the man out of the driver's seat. Balancing the limp man's arm around his neck and fighting against the strong wind, Michael ducked his face away from the rain and dragged him toward the vehicle Michael had driven.

The man's face lolled next to Michael's ear. "Verity," he groaned.

Michael froze.

"My Verity," he cried louder.

Instantly, memories flooded over Michael—remembrances of the father so desperate to help his only daughter that he had disguised himself as a janitor and cleaned floors to reach her.

Bile rose into Michael's throat as he remembered how he had been the one to prevent this caring father from ministering life-giving water to his child—to someone who held a sacred spot in Michael's own heart.

"I killed her," Michael whispered.

Rousing, the man gathered his feet under him and the weight lifted from Michael's sodden shoulders. Michael stepped in front of the man and grasped his upper arms. He stared into his dazed eyes as the pelting rain mercilessly poured over both of them and mixed with the blood from the gash in the man's forehead.

"I'm sorry," Michael yelled above the wind.

Confused, the man stared at him.

"What did you do to Senator Taylor's rum?"

Recognition flickered in the man's eyes. "Murderer!"

The word knifed into Michael's heart.

"He killed her," the man yelled.

"What's in the rum?"

"And that doctor. He killed her."

The newspaper clipping Bryce had mailed to him said Verity's doctor died of a rare illness previously thought contained.

Verity's father whirled and tore from his grasp. Michael lunged at him and missed. With surprising speed and strength, the man ran to the bay adjacent to the refinery. Michael quickly closed the gap between them. When the man reached the dock, he produced a vial from his pocket.

Michael remembered another conversation with Bryce.

Something about a missing virus from Dr. Evans's pharmaceutical company.

Missing? Like lost?

More like stolen is what they think.

Glancing over his shoulder at Michael, the man prepared to lob the tube into the bay.

Could the minute hesitation be the break Michael needed? He ran as fast as he could. Judging the distance, he knew he couldn't make it. Frantic, he leapt and dove onto his side, his arm outstretched over the water in a last desperate attempt. His body slammed to the dock, crushing the air out of his lungs while pain wracked the length of his torso. Michael opened his eyes and followed the length of his arm to his clenched fist. Slowly, he opened his fingers. The vial rested in his palm.

"Drop it!" The man raged and jumped on Michael's outstretched arm. Keeping his left foot planted on Michael's shoulder, the assailant used the other foot to stomp his forearm.

"People are going to die." Michael clenched his teeth against the exploding injury.

The older man tramped on his arm again and again. Michael cried out in pain and tried to roll away, but the weight of the other held him pinned.

"Die like Verity."

Twisting, Michael kicked powerfully against his attacker's legs, throwing him to the ground. Rolling to his feet, Michael fell sprawling again as his opponent tackled him. Claw-like, the man's fingers pried against Michael's closed fist, seeking the vial. A brutal kick to his temple turned Michael's vision to exploding stars.

His assailant bit Michael's wrist, causing the nerves to spasm and his fingers to release their grip. Michael used his other hand to grab the man's hair and wrench him off balance as the vial rolled away from the wrestling men. Michael threw his opponent onto his back. Kneeling over him, Michael wedged his forearm against the man's neck.

Water streamed from his nose onto the man's face as Michael yelled above the wind. "You're going to hurt a lot of people."

"This country murders innocent women." Verity's father shouted back.

"It wasn't right," Michael insisted. "Sometimes the system fails."

The man's eyes blazed with passion. "She was scared."

"Scared of who?"

Frantically, he looked past Michael. "I have to protect her from men who want to kill her."

"Who?" Michael repeated. "Who's trying to kill her?"

The man brought up his knee hard into Michael's crotch. Searing pain permeated his core, momentarily paralyzing him. The man threw him off and scrambled for the vial.

Michael went after him. With trained maneuvers, he quickly pinned the man's arms and muscled him to a standstill.

"Please," he rasped. "She needs me."

"You were there for her." Michael yelled the words into his ear above the roar of the storm.

The man collapsed against Michael. "She needed care." Sobs shook his thin frame.

"I know." Michael's own eyes burned. "When no one else was there for her, you tried."

"Look what they did to her." His voice had become a whimper.

Suddenly, the man twisted and leapt out of Michael's hold. He ran. Michael dove and tackled him. The two fell hard. Michael wrapped his legs tightly about the struggling man. With an iron grasp, he trapped his opponent's arms to his sides.

"The whole incident was wrong." Michael yelled the words as he jerked the man to his feet. Blood from the gray-haired man's nose mingled with tears on his face. Michael put his face close to the old man's and spoke above the noise of the squall. "What they did wasn't right. But what you're doing isn't right, either."

The old man drooped in defeat. Moments before, Michael felt like he struggled with a Tasmanian devil. Now this same man felt fragile and broken in Michael's strong grasp.

"She was my sweet baby." The man turned his eyes heavenward. "I didn't protect my child. What kind of father am I?"

Michael swallowed back the lump in his throat. "You're the kind of father I wish I'd had."

CHAPTER 62

Michael held the sobbing man's face against his chest. Headlights illuminated the two where they had slumped to the ground in the pelting rain and nearly blinded him as the car pulled close and stopped. Doors flew open, and Jerry, Bryce, and Corbin ran to them.

"Who is he?" Bryce bent to help the older man to his feet.

"Verity's father." Michael allowed Corbin to help him to his feet. He wiped his nose with the back of his hand and met Corbin's eyes. "Over there is a vial. Probably Dr. Evans's missing virus."

Corbin hurried to pick up the tube. He examined the small cylinder, made certain the opening was secure, and tucked the vial into his pocket.

"Let's get this party to a safer location." Jerry studied the roiling sky. "This is the last place we want to be during a hurricane."

Driving the vehicle that had brought the friends to Michael's aid at the refinery, Jerry expertly navigated the route back to Christiansted. Weeping, Verity's father sat sandwiched in the backseat between Michael and Bryce while Corbin followed behind in the compact Michael had used. Verity's father shivered and mumbled. Sometimes he appeared to be functioning in the present, but, in a heartbeat, he'd be back to the days when Verity had been in the hospital.

Steering down roads that were nearly invisible in the hard rain, Jerry gripped the steering wheel. "This storm is shaking up worse than we thought."

Back at the Christiansted Theater, Jerry stopped the car in front of the entrance, not bothering with proper parking. Corbin parked behind. Throwing open the car doors, they dashed through the wind and piled inside the theater.

While they had been away, the orchestra members and philharmonic volunteers had moved the instruments and valuable artwork to a safer location in the center of the building. In the middle of the ballroom, Brother Ned had encouraged a group to gather and pray.

Elise and Robson greeted the drenched men. "Are you all right?"

Michael drank in the sight of her and the concern reflected in her eyes. "A bit worse for wear." He wished he'd been wearing the reinforced jump suit when he took that kick in the crotch.

Brother Ned and June brought towels and blankets to wrap about the shoulders of the wet men.

"Holy smokes," Dr. Evans exclaimed as he rushed over.

Corbin raised an eyebrow. "Do you know him?"

"He's one of my scientists. Retired recently."

Corbin fished in his pocket and brought out the vial. "And this?"

"The virus. Thank God!" Dr. Evans searched the disoriented man's face. "I don't understand. Why?"

Toweling his face and hair, Michael spotted Claire. She looked quizzically at Verity's father as Corbin and Bryce helped the dazed man backwards into an oversized suit jacket confiscated from the coatroom. Bryce crossed the arms of the jacket and tied them in the back, straightjacket style.

Jerry signaled to a doctor and a couple others who agreed to keep an eye on the unpredictable patient.

Michael went to Claire. "What do you know about him?" He nodded in the direction of Verity's father.

"My stepmother's father."

Senator Taylor bustled over. "Whoever he is," he demanded, "I want him prosecuted to the fullest extent of the law."

At the sound of the senator's voice, Verity's father's eyes cleared, and he lunged at the politician. "Murderer!" Someone screamed and several onlookers startled and stepped back. Bryce held the man.

In the stunned silence that followed, Michael heard the sound of the blowing wind and rain over the lyrical tones of those in the center of the ballroom who, oblivious to the drama at this end, continued to say their rosaries.

Whatever the senator may have expected, the look on his face showed that seeing Verity's father came as a shock.

Claire stepped between the two men. "Daddy, what is he talking about?"

Staring warily at the straightjacketed man, Taylor dropped his voice. "He's just a crazy man, Claire. Crazy with grief over the loss of his daughter." He shrugged and smiled weakly at her. "Understandable under the circumstances. I'm sure I'd feel the same way."

"I doubt that." She turned to Verity's father. "What happened?"

The senator put a hand on her arm. "Claire, anything you want to know has been in the papers. If you have questions, I'll answer them."

She shrugged him off. Turning to the man who stood with quiet tears on his face, Claire spoke softly. "What happened?"

The man glared at the senator. "He wouldn't let me see her."

"She was brain-dead," Taylor stated.

Fresh tears sprang to the man's eyes. "I'd care for her. I'd give her water."

"Water?" Claire turned on her father. "You withheld water? From your wife?"

He bristled. "She didn't want to be on life support."

Before he could stop himself, Michael spoke up. "She was forbidden people and care."

Out of sight of the senator, Corbin put a cautionary hand on Michael's back.

The senator whirled on Michael. "Just who are you and what do you have to do with any of this?"

"Water is not life support," Claire declared. "But the lack of water is murder."

A thunderous ripping sounded above them. Instinctively, everyone ducked.

"The storm is moving to a level four." Corbin yelled above the din of the tempest and the panicked people. "That means we can lose roofs and lighter structures to the force of the wind."

Brother Ned calmly gathered the frightened crowd into a group where he led them in a prayerful song. As they took up a melody, he gently nudged another man into the leadership position and rejoined Michael's circle.

Corbin glanced at the roof. "This structure sticks up above most of the others. We need to move the people to a safer place."

Michael did a mental check of the structures in the city.

Corbin looked at his watch. "Nearly seven."

"The rectory," Brother Ned suggested.

Jerry spoke up. "He's right. St. Elizabeth's community room has a concrete ceiling and is below the main stairs. That'll be the safest place to stay during the hurricane."

"Let's go." Corbin quickly gave orders. "Divide the group into four. Jerry, you lead the way. Michael, Brother Ned, and I will follow."

Dashing across the street and the few short blocks to the rectory, the groups were quickly soaked from the torrential rain. Michael took Elise's hand as they sloshed through the rushing ground water.

Arriving at the rectory, Michael wasn't surprised to find many others from the parish and community cloistered within. A radio in the center of the room broadcast the news. Many gathered together to pray rosaries. Corbin instructed everyone to stay back from the windows in case any blew in. Michael was relieved to see the windowed walls were inset under a protruding roof that would serve as protection from the ferocious onslaught.

The group kept vigil over the ensuing hours as the storm lashed their island home. A radio gave intermittent weather updates, each sounding more positive than the view through the windows appeared.

"The eye of the hurricane will probably miss St. Croix," the radio announcer reported, and the people gave a collective sigh of relief. Suddenly, as if to contradict the radio's announcement, the air erupted with a devilish ruckus. If he hadn't known better, Michael would swear a locomotive was steaming through the building. Eying the ceiling, most covered their heads with their arms as the sound of objects crashing against the concrete overhead thundered about them. Michael pulled Elise to his chest, sheltering her from the squealing sound of twisting metal that filled their ears.

The frightening noise continued for a long time before finally subsiding. Peering outside through the window, Michael saw an eerie glow. Pieces of building debris and trees swirled around and around like the flurries in a Christmas snow globe—on an island that had never seen snow. Behind him, he heard Brother Ned begin a fresh round of prayer. Many voices joined with his as they corporately brought petitions for safety to God.

Then the radio went silent. Michael glanced at his watch. Two in the morning. The children began to cry and hold their hands over their ears as the air pressure within their cement shelter dropped to nearly unbearable lows. Michael's head ached where he'd suffered a blow during the scuffle with Verity's father.

"Feels like being on an airplane without cabin pressure." Bryce swallowed several times, and then plugged his nose and blew in a futile attempt to clear his own ears.

Several women produced gum and lifesavers from their purses and passed them around. People broke off small pieces to make the meager offerings stretch for others. Somehow, like the loaves and fishes, there was enough for everyone though Michael, Bryce, and Corbin merely tore and stuffed paper in their mouths, chewing like gum.

An hour later, the brutal winds began to subside. Children leaned into their parents and slept. Many adults dozed. Elise sat close to Michael where they could watch through the windows from a safe distance. He noticed how comfortable and warm she felt next to him. He glanced over where Claire sat cross-legged on the floor, her back against a wall. In her lap slept a child. An older sibling leaned on Claire's shoulder. Their mother sat next to them, cradling an infant and a toddler. While those around her dozed, Claire was awake. From her distracted expression, Michael knew she was puzzling out the many questions she had that hadn't been answered.

Close by, Jerry rested in a chair tipped back against a wall. From under a cap he had pulled low, he kept an eye on his resting family and the doctor he had entrusted with the strange patient. He occasionally glanced Michael's way.

The senator slept on a couch.

Able to sleep any place, Corbin and Bryce lay stretched out on the floor. Bryce's hands were characteristically linked behind his neck. Corbin's fingers were laced across his stomach that rose and fell as he snored.

Brother Ned serenely moved between those who were still awake. He smiled at each, patted a shoulder here, and whispered encouragement there. Arriving at Michael's window, he allowed himself a backwards stretch for his lower back. "It is good to be in the house of the Lord and in the arms of the Lord."

Jerry grunted approval. "The worst is finally past."

Claire moved her young sleepers off her lap and settled them in comfortable positions. She crossed the room to where Verity's father sat stone still, staring. She put her hand on his arm and began to talk to him in tones too soft for Michael to hear.

Brother Ned began a new round of prayers, this time in thanksgiving to the heavenly Father who had brought them safely through the eye of the hurricane.

Sound gurgled from the radio once again. Corbin roused and Michael turned as if watching the small box would help it issue information—the information everyone wanted to hear. That they were okay. That the storm hadn't been as horrible as it seemed. Instead, a station from nearby St. Thomas crackled through the static with a steady stream of calls for help. The praying group began a fresh round of petitions to heaven. At one point, the broadcast station issued instructions to the police chief of St. Croix.

"Communications are bankrupt." The winds began to howl in a higher pitch and Corbin pointed to where water dripped through the concrete ceiling. "I hope this holds."

Leaning against one another, Michael and Elise dozed until movement woke him and he glanced up.

Claire stood staring out the window.

"I probably woke you."

"I suspect you meant to." Michael gave her a sidelong glance. "At least you didn't hit me on the head."

Claire chewed her lip.

"What's keeping you awake?" Michael reached for Elise's hand as she shifted her position so her head lay across his knee. He thought about the engagement ring they would shop for, and then turned his attention back to Claire. "Besides the weather. And maybe having your family's skeletons slipping out of the closet."

"The stories don't add up." Claire sighed. "Her father says they withheld life support. The newspaper said Verity overdosed on diet pills."

"Keeping up appearances as a senator's wife?" Michael didn't believe that for a moment as he repeated the explanation the tabloids had circulated.

"You saw her. Verity didn't take diet pills. Her father said she told him she was frightened."

The man had said as much to Michael. "Frightened of who?"

"Daddy."

"Your father. Her husband."

She nodded.

Michael thought of the times he had tried to talk with Claire, but she refused. Now she had come to him—probably the only other person who could help her make sense of what still didn't make sense to either of them. "Did she say anything to you?"

"After mother died, Daddy sent me to boarding school. Before he retired from the military, he married Verity, but we didn't see each other much. I only met her father a couple times during Christmas break." She paced a few steps. "Verity was kind. Sweet. Not at all like Daddy."

"Or you." Michael thought about his own mother and wondered why compassionate women married harsh and bullying men.

The angry stubbornness he had seen before flashed in her eyes. "You called me a chip off the old block. Remember?"

"I did. But I wouldn't say that now."

"I deserved the comment." She glanced over at her dad who slept soundly. "Why withhold life support and refuse visitors. Refuse family?"

"That's my question." Michael looked at Elise, sleeping peacefully. "Not the actions of a loving husband."

"More what someone who is hiding something would do."

Michael raised his eyebrows. "You said it, not me."

She met his gaze. "But you were thinking it."

CHAPTER 63

Elise blinked against the sunlight coming through the window and saw the winds were still blowing, and the rain continued. She crossed to the window where Michael, Bryce, and Corbin stood looking out.

From this view, she could see the roof of the church had been completely blown off. Part of the parish center was a mass of twisted steel. Tables, chairs, and household debris lay scattered everywhere in several inches of water that seemed to cover the island. Looking closer, Elise identified a porch railing, galvanized sheets of roofing, and a bent air conditioner toppled against the building where they had taken refuge.

Corbin whistled. "It's going to be quite a morning after."

And what a morning after—as if the whole island suffered from a monster hangover.

"We've lost most of our material things, but we still have the gift of life from our Creator." Though not as spritely as usual, Brother Ned attempted to encourage everyone who had bunkered in the church. "Thank God for life." This mantra would be repeated many times in the coming weeks throughout St. Croix, both as a greeting and as a prayer.

When the wind and rain dissipated at last, Michael, Bryce, and Jerry ventured outside to assess the damage to the island.

Corbin and Dr. Evans worked with the local police to take the scientist into custody. "We'll probably have to transport this guy stateside quickly," Corbin predicted. "The authorities will want him."

"I suspect he needs medical and mental health support that we can't provide here." Elise felt sorry for the man who hadn't recovered from his eventful night. She didn't know his story but could tell it was deep and sorrowful. "Even without hurricane damage, the island doesn't have a lot in the way of specialized medical services."

Never one to be still, June enrolled Karl, Elise, and several parishioners to help the priest establish St. Elizabeth's as an emergency headquarters where people could come, rest, and get food and water. "Take inventory of whatever remains from the church clothes closet to the food cupboard," she listed. "Check the nursery for cribs and other baby items."

As islanders paraded slowly from their common shelter at St. Elizabeth's, Brother Ned commented, "The church has been our shelter from the storm in more ways than meets the eye." Brother Ned chuckled at the obvious double meaning considering they had experienced the eye of Hurricane Hugo.

Among the first to leave the protection of the rectory, a silent Claire trailed her father out of the building. Moments later, Michael returned with someone slung over his shoulder and Bryce carried something clutched in his arms. Elise came to meet them, but Michael shook his head. "Get Brother Ned."

She did as Michael asked and, with the kindly priest in tow, found Michael in a room down the hall. Someone lay on a classroom table, tangled hair hanging limply off one end and water dripping from a multitude of clothing layers at the other.

"Fran." Brother Ned quickly brushed the leaves from the old woman's hair and face. "Oh, Fran."

Elise reached for Michael as she drew close. "Is she alive?"

"No." Michael tightened his arm around her.

"Where did you find her?" Brother Ned closed Fran's eyes. Elise realized she had no idea how old the woman had been.

"She was curled around these." Bryce held out four tiny kittens, as pitiful looking as Fran except they were very much alive.

"Of course." Brother Ned took the four kittens that began to cry in earnest.

Michael scratched a calico behind its tiny ear. "Looks like a power line went down close by."

"Too close," Bryce added.

The others were quiet while the priest prayed, committing Fran into the arms of the Lord. He gave a great sigh and considered the kittens. "These little ones may be a surprise blessing."

"How so?" Elise marveled at Brother Ned's ability to find silver linings.

"Babies have a miraculous power to bring comfort and hope." He cast his eyes heavenward. "Consider the Christ child."

CHAPTER 64

"Ready?" Elise needed to see the theater. And her home. And the cottage.

Along with so many others, she and Michael had helped where needed. Jerry and his family set out to see how their home had fared, while Ava accompanied Robson to check on the *Day Dream* and the other boats in the floating neighborhood. With the urgent matters finally at bay, Elise grew impatient to be about the important.

Michael nodded and they went out into the city. They picked their way cautiously through the water and debris to the block where the Christiansted Theater had presided like a matriarch. The damage they encountered along their short walk troubled her heart. With each step, Elise vacillated between hope that the theater would miraculously stand spared from the wrath of Hugo and the skulking despair that when smaller buildings were in ruins, there was no possibility the larger site would be unscathed.

When she saw her beloved building, she couldn't hold back a sob.

Michael took her hand. "Let me know when you want to go inside. Once the authorities get mobile, the theater will be off limits."

How difficult to believe they had been here so recently for the celebratory concert that welcomed Ava as conductor. Was it only yesterday? The theater that had been ornate and stately was now a ghostly specter of former glory.

Unable to speak, Elise nodded. She had to see everything—had to know the extent of what had happened. Michael pointed a flashlight and led her inside. In the auditorium where she had so recently played the *New World Symphony* and said yes to Michael's proposal, large sections of the ceiling, which transformed to reflect time and weather, had fallen onto the cloth seats below. The cracked balcony perched at an angle like a lopsided smile. Where she once listened to the echoes of the orchestra and appreciative audiences, she now heard only the sound of dripping water.

Stepping over broken columns, Elise walked to the rooms backstage. Righting a chair, she recalled laughter as well as moans from fellow musicians as they recalled well-played concerts and stretched cramped muscles. She retrieved a violin, a clarinet, and a piccolo from the instrument lockers that sat askew. Michael lifted the timpani drums to a dry section of the room. Sounding like a gunshot, a harp string broke, startling both of them. Elise quickly loosened the taut strings that were being affected by the unusual weather. She wept to see the wood of the grand piano swollen from water that had blown through fissures in the outer walls.

Back out on the stage, Elise surveyed the tiered room that formerly served as the heart of the theater, the center of the city, and the island culture. "It's gone. Gone are the years of music and memories the theater collected."

Michael pulled her into his arms. "Looks pretty bad."

"No amount of money will be enough to repair the wreckage." She balled her fists against his shoulders. "I can't fix this."

"I know." He held her for a long time. "But everything is going to be all right."

Despite standing in the midst of indescribable destruction, she believed him. All would be all right because Michael loved her. She relaxed against him and began to giggle. Then the giggle turned into laughter.

Michael pulled back to look at her. "What are you thinking?"

"Brother Ned," she began. "He told me to trust the process."

"Process?"

She gestured at the mess and felt freedom that she no longer needed or wanted Senator Bennett Taylor's money. "I was so worried about funding for the repairs. All that worry and now it's impossible to—" The laughter dissolved into tears. "It's impossible to fix even with the rest of the senator's money for the painting. Even if my art was popular worldwide, and we had a large trust fund."

"The theater is valuable to you." He lifted her chin. "I'm pretty attached too. This is where we first danced. This is where you said yes."

"It's hard to walk away from my parents' legacy." She moved to the edge of the stage and looked at the mess that covered the second-row seats where she and Michael had first attended a concert together. Where she had a note delivered to him saying she would marry him.

His hands gentle on her shoulders, Michael turned her to face him. "The theater is not your parents' legacy."

She frowned. "But—"

"Robson, June, and Brother Ned all tried to tell you."

"Tried to tell me what?"

He touched her nose. "That it's you."

She frowned, confused. "What's me?"

"Elise, *you* are your parents' most beautiful work of art. You are their greatest legacy."

CHAPTER 65

After inspecting the theater, Michael and Elise set out to see how the house and cottage had fared under Hurricane Hugo's relentless fury. On the drive up the hill, Michael maneuvered around a myriad of obstructions. Six times, he got out of the car to clear the road so they could pass through.

Just before coming over the rise, Michael stopped the vehicle. "Are you ready?"

She took a deep breath. "Yes."

In moments, the property came into view. The sight of the cottage brought a deep moan from Elise. The hurricane had removed windows and a sizeable portion of the cottage roof. Michael parked, and they examined the damage to the house, the cottage, and the grounds. Elise's home had received minor damage compared to what Michael and Elise had seen downtown and along the way to Elise's house. The kitchen windows were gone, and water stood everywhere in that section of the house. Michael suspected some of the damage had come from the cottage roof that had probably been hurled against the home before spinning away to who knew where. Though the greenhouse with its fledgling grape grafts had disappeared and large sections of the lovely gardens had been uprooted, scattered, or carried off—over all, the family property on the hill had fared better than most in the midst of terrible loss.

In the days that followed, the islanders quickly ascertained the natural disaster had damaged ninety-five percent of the buildings on St Croix. Much to the delight of the young scholars, many classroom roofs were missing from St. John's School. The science lab resembled a science experiment gone awry with the schoolroom contents scrambled and marinating on the floor in several inches of green water. Mosquitoes abounded. The pesky insects were the only living things that seemed to thrive in the wreckage.

St. Croix struggled under Hugo's wake nearly as much as the night Hurricane Hugo blew through. Without power, communication on the island and with the outside world remained practically nonexistent.

In the immediate aftermath, Corbin worked with the local authorities to systematically search for missing people, establish communication and support networks, and provide safe drinking water. At one point, he recruited Michael and Bryce to help the police corral a renegade group of vandals. The partners made short work of the assignment as the island afforded the troublemakers nowhere to go. For Michael, the pursuit offered a diversion from the continual damage reports that seemed to deflate the spirit of the islanders.

Fallen trees blocked most of the roads. The sound of chainsaws became prevalent as men cleared the throughways. Gas stations employed generators to provide fuel for heavy-equipment operators. All the while, the thick smell of rotting vegetation permeated the air.

Once Michael was confident Elise and her home were secure, he made his way to Jerry's storefront on the Christiansted pier. Michael passed once beautiful stores that were now empty shells, their previously attractive merchandise and stylish store décor destroyed and decaying in putrid water. Shop owners sorted through the destruction, seeking anything salvageable. He met Brother Ned as the priest exited what remained of the Baptist church.

"Thank God for life." To Michael, Brother Ned looked the picture of island culture. Handsome, caring, and at ease.

"Thank God for life," Michael returned, realizing how much more life meant with Elise in his. "Where are you off to, Padre?"

"I'm gathering all the priests, ministers, and clergy for a meeting today. We'll see how we can work together to help our congregations." He glanced skyward. "Who'd have thought God would use a hurricane to blow away the lines we put up to divide our denominational beliefs? Now we are merely Christ-followers together. Rebuilding together."

Michael nodded. "Now you're organized, what's the plan?"

Brother Ned pulled a list from his pocket. "Staffing the tent hospital. Meet with parents and high school students to distribute service assignments for the students to help out and get credit ..."

"That's a smart idea. I'd have liked those kinds of studies when I was in high school."

Brother Ned's eyes shone. "This will probably be the best school participation we've ever gotten from the boys." He stopped and considered for a moment. "Why does the educational system center around a structure boys don't readily respond to?"

"You mean you didn't enjoy hours in a seat reading Shakespeare and discussing dangling participles?" Michael waved his arm toward the beach. "At least in Nebraska, we had snow and ice during the winter. Here you have perpetual fair weather beckoning kids outdoors."

Brother Ned looked from the harbor to Michael. "I must give that further consideration."

"You do that." Michael indicated the paper. "What else?"

He returned to his list. "A group to see what classrooms we can salvage to resume school for all ages."

"No one is accusing you of being lazy."

He stuck out his hand and Michael accepted the handshake. Brother Ned covered their grasp with his strong left hand. "I'm thankful for you. For your friends. For the work you do."

Michael warmed under the genuine compliment. "You make a guy feel at home."

Leaving the priest to his tasks, Michael continued his walk to the pier. He found Jerry's storefront where previously clients had booked Buck Island tours, rented jet skis, and arranged scuba adventures, roofless and in disarray. The desk had been toppled by the storm. Shelves of snorkeling equipment were scattered about or blown away. The refrigerators lay on their side; the shelves that typically held iced tea, sodas, and bottled water now empty. Snack racks previously filled with chips, pretzels, and gum were bare.

"Thought I might find you here," came a voice from the doorway.

Michael looked up to see Bryce. "What have you been up to?"

Bryce lounged against the doorframe. "Dr. Evans and Keri weighed anchor this morning for the states. They have the mad scientist with 'em."

Michael winced. The label felt offensive.

Bryce shifted, aware his attempt at being cavalier had failed. "What are your plans today?"

"Checking on business here."

Michael and Bryce picked their way to the harbor where Jerry's diving boat was anchored.

"Ahoy!" Michael called. "Anyone there?"

Jerry poked up his head from the engine area. "Wondered when you'd come around. Figured after you made sure that lovely lady of yours was safe."

Michael nodded. "How's things with yours?"

Jerry rubbed his bald head with a meaty hand. Michael decided not to tell him he'd just left grease streaks on that shiny top. "The family is stable. Here,"—he indicated the commercial section of Christiansted—"our whole economic system is collapsed."

Bryce glanced down the dock. "Where's your other boat?"

Jerry followed their gaze to the place where the second member of the St. Croix Adventures fleet normally anchored. "That's a darn good question."

"And the Dive Shack?"

"On my way to find out." Jerry waved them aboard. "The roads aren't passable. You two come along, and we'll cruise over to Cane Bay."

Michael and Bryce boarded the craft and prepared the boat to sail. Untying the line that held the boat to the dock, Michael looked up to see Corbin at the top end of the wharf, shaking hands with the harbormaster. The two parted and Corbin came to the boat.

"What adventure are you three off to?" Corbin bent to unwind the last rope that held the boat to the dock.

"Curious to see what remains of my Dive Shack at Cane Bay." Jerry indicated the empty slip. "Wouldn't mind finding my other boat in the process."

Corbin nodded. "There are a lot of things missing."

"Come aboard." Jerry gazed at the horizon. "We'll see what the sea returns to us."

CHAPTER 66

Standing at the captain's wheel, Jerry kept his eyes on the water, careful to dodge debris from the hurricane. As they cruised past the residential berths, Michael looked for Robson's boat. Despite their efforts to make them secure, vessels were in a tangle. The *Day Dream* looked worse for wear but still livable.

"Those folks probably have better power and water than the island." At the captain's wheel, Jerry kept his eyes on the water, careful to dodge debris from the hurricane. "At least for as long as their portable systems last."

Dr. Evans's yacht no longer occupied the place where he and Keri had anchored for the past week. Jerry hooked a thumb toward the vacant berth. "What happened to your retired scientist?"

Retired scientist, hospital janitor, loving father. The guy remained a question in Michael's mind. He had a lot of questions these days.

"I sent him stateside for medical attention." Corbin shaded his eyes. "And to sort out what he was involved with."

Though he had passed the caution buoys, Jerry maintained a conservative speed as he piloted the vessel west.

At Cane Bay, Michael spotted St. Croix Adventures life jackets floating in the sea. He pointed and Jerry maneuvered close enough for Michael to retrieve them on the port side while Bryce fished out salvageable items on the starboard side. Like participants on a scavenger hunt, they zigzagged to shore, collecting along the way.

Once anchored, the four tramped up the beach and crossed the two-lane highway. The wood-frame snack shack that had stood on the west side of the bay and served the best french fries had blown away. Roofless and missing two walls, the Dive Shack's interior consisted of a jumbled mess of debris and equipment, all wet.

Jerry walked through, kicked a few things, examined a couple of air tanks, and retrieved his favorite regulator. "Well." He put his hands on his hips. "The occasional hurricane is the price of paradise."

Bryce set about stacking the equipment that looked to be salvageable, and Michael joined the hunt. Jerry began a second pile of debris while Corbin inspected the sites where neighboring buildings had stood. They worked for several hours, wet and sticky from sweat and from the perpetual stagnant water that pooled under everything. When they stopped for lunch, Jerry had an idea of what inventory remained to rebuild his business.

"Let's circle Buck Island." Jerry opened the ample picnic Reta had packed and shared the contents. "See what souvenirs Hugo left there."

The ocean no longer bucked and roiled as it had when the storm approached. Like slow moving tankers, uprooted trees floated on the moderate waves. Directionless. Drifting. Plucked up like garden weeds by Hugo's tearing winds.

They anchored at the beach on the south side of the Buck Island and surveyed the devastation. Trees, branches, and coconuts littered the sand and bobbed along the shore. The picnic tables that used to sit in the jungle clearing were gone. Even the old snag that housed the pirate crab was gone. Stubborn and dangerous, the manchineel tree stood.

"C'mon," Jerry groused. "Let's troll around the rest of the island."

He followed the coast, careful to stay in water deep enough to avoid disturbing the magnificent coral gardens surrounding Buck Island. They motored past the rugged north end, and there, on the west side of the island and out of sight of St. Croix, Jerry's missing boat lay anchored near the beach.

Jerry quickly pulled back on the throttle. "Don't believe she blew over here."

"And parked herself," Bryce added.

"How did they come through the hurricane?" Corbin reached for the binoculars.

"Probably took the boat right after we secured everything." Jerry pointed toward the neighboring islands. "While we were at the concert, they dodged the worst of the weather on another island. With St. Croix Adventures on the side, no one was curious about the boat."

Corbin studied the setting through the binoculars. "Three guys. One on the boat. Two on shore. All armed. All Asian."

Michael took the binoculars. "That one guy on the boat is the same one who orbits the senator."

"Bodyguard?" Corbin shaded his eyes and squinted toward shore.

Jerry grunted. "Doesn't have the right haircut."

Michael pulled snorkel equipment from the bins. "Corbin, Bryce, you stay out of sight on the boat. Jerry, just mosey over like you're happy to find your boat. Bryce will cover you if it gets dicey."

Michael strapped a diver's knife to his leg, the MK13 day/night flare taped to the knife sheath. He swung his legs over the side of the boat and slid a facemask onto his head. "Give me some time to get in position." He slipped into the water and swam for the island.

Once on shore and behind a dense tree covering, Michael signaled to Jerry who slowly steered toward his missing vessel. The sound of the motor roused the sleeping watchman aboard the beached boat. Michael recognized him as the Chinese man he'd seen talking with Senator Taylor prior to the concert. Two men came forward from the tree line where Michael had spotted them lounging on the beach under the shade from the jungle. One of the men on shore had a gun tucked in his waistband. The other two wore their weapons in shoulder holsters. All three confidently watched Jerry's boat approach.

When he was close enough, Jerry idled his own craft and called out. "I see you found my boat."

The three seemed to search behind Jerry. When they didn't see anyone else, they exchanged glances. Jerry brought his boat closer and turned the vessel so the motor was facing the island. He stood at the back of his boat, his big arms crossed against his chest, his feet characteristically planted apart for balance.

Michael couldn't hear the rest of the conversation, but he saw Jerry motion toward his stolen boat and saw the man on the beach pull his gun.

Behind the men on shore, Michael poked his head out just enough to catch Jerry's eye. Michael pointed the flare gun.

"Listen. No need to get testy." Jerry reasoned louder for Michael to hear. "I can see I've interrupted your suntan." He took a step sideways. "I'll just get out of your way ..." He took a slow second step toward the side of the vessel.

All at once, Jerry dove behind the equipment bins in the center of the boat. In that moment, Michael squeezed the trigger. The flare gun belched, and like an orange meteor, the flare launched from the barrel and in a flash exploded into a large manchineel tree. Toxic tree bits rained down on the two men who immediately began to howl and scream, batting the blistering sap and tree bark off their bodies.

Aiming in Jerry's direction, the Chinese man aboard Jerry's stolen boat fired once and then turned the gun in Michael's direction. In that instant, Bryce leapt onto the stolen boat. With one hand, Bryce grabbed the man by the hair. With the other hand, he pressed his dive knife against the man's throat. At a word from Bryce, the man tossed his gun to the other boat. Back on his feet aboard Jerry's idling craft, Corbin retrieved the weapon and pointed the gun at the two on shore just as one gave up on removing the manchineel sap in favor of aiming his gun at Corbin. He froze when Corbin fired a shot that tore into the sand at his feet.

Jerry handed a roll of rope to Corbin. "Around here, boat thieves are treated like horse thieves."

"Reasonable." Corbin jumped off the back of the boat and met Michael on the sand.

Jerry regarded the two with manchineel sap on their bodies as they writhed and brushed at their blistering skin. "The most humane thing we can do is drag them behind the boat a ways to wash off the sap."

Bryce pushed the Chinese man from Jerry's stolen boat onto the shore to join the other two.

While Jerry readied the recovered St. Croix Adventures boat, Bryce collected the guns from the two ashore, and Corbin and Michael tied the three men together. Before the Chinese man was secure, he pulled a knife that had been hidden in his clothing. With a sudden thrust, he deeply pierced Corbin's groin. Michael heard Corbin cry out and saw a burst of blood spurt and spurt again. In a flash, Bryce came like a freight train at the assailant, and the two rolled and tumbled away from Corbin followed by a sickening sound of angry fists thudding against flesh.

Corbin dropped to the ground as blood poured from his leg wound. With a shock of dread, Michael grasped the horrible truth. The knife had severed Corbin's femoral artery. In minutes, his friend would bleed to death.

CHAPTER 67

While Corbin writhed in agony, Michael reached for his dive knife. Grasping the handle, Michael sat on Corbin's wounded leg. Holding the leg still, he cursed as he quickly sliced through the flesh to enlarge the wound.

"Holy Mother of Moses," Jerry exclaimed, dropping down next to Michael. "What are you …?"

Ignoring Corbin's anguished cry, Michael stuck his fist inside the man's thigh. The artery spurted his friend's lifeblood like water through a garden hose. Gritting his teeth in concentration, Michael grasped the artery in his fist and squeezed with all his strength.

"Jerry," Michael ordered, "carry him onboard."

Bryce ran back and supported Corbin as Jerry gingerly carried the wounded man. Tossing his head from side to side, Corbin gritted his teeth against pain-filled moans. The short distance to the boat appeared endless as Michael kept pace, his hand still inside his boss's leg, pinching closed the deadly artery rupture.

Lifting Corbin over the side of the boat was tricky, and Corbin yelped in agony as the move went clumsily. Once on board, Jerry laid the wounded man on a bench built along the inside of the boat. Without a word, Bryce slapped Jerry on the back, vaulted back over the side and returned to shore.

Jerry strategically placed life jackets to support Corbin and Michael in as close to a stable position as could be found.

Then Bryce jumped back aboard. "Let's go!"

Leaving the stolen boat behind, Jerry shifted the boat's gears as gently as he could and turned the boat on the shortest route back to St. Croix. The three boat thieves, including the man who had stabbed Corbin, sat tied together in a rescue raft that dragged behind their boat through the water.

Groaning against the pain, Corbin focused desperate eyes on Michael. "Why can't I be unconscious?"

"You've got some threshold," Michael shook his head. "Anyone one else would pass out from the pain."

"Hit me," Corbin pleaded. "Knock me out."

Michael looked at Bryce.

"Tempting." Bryce's eyes were filled with concern. "I just don't know the consequences. They didn't teach us that in medical training."

Michael looked toward St. Croix. "We're making good time."

Finding a bottle of water, Bryce carefully poured as much as Corbin would take into his mouth.

Bryce handed the water next to Michael, who took several large gulps.

Corbin ground his teeth against the pain. Bryce pulled the rubber strap from a snorkeling mask and placed the strap between the Scotsman's lips. He bit down hard on the rubber, his jaw muscles rigid.

Bryce put a hand on Michael's shoulder. "You?"

"My arm is cramped and on fire but I sure can't complain considering what he must feel."

His hand began to shake from the extreme pressure he had to keep on the artery. Corbin's powerful heart pumped mightily to deliver the necessary blood to the lower half of his body. Michael prayed Corbin's rugged health would provide the strength for the man to survive.

CHAPTER 68

Back on St. Croix, a doctor clamped the artery, administered antibiotics and blood, and gave Corbin, who was desperate for relief, powerful pain relievers. Just before he dropped into merciful unconsciousness, Corbin looked at Michael. "Too old. I pushed my luck."

Michael clasped his friend's shoulder. "Heal up. We need you."

Not equipped to handle the magnitude of Corbin's injury, the island hospital stabilized and then flew him to the mainland to be delivered to a critical care hospital.

While Michael and Bryce saw to Corbin, Jerry turned over the three boat thieves to the authorities. Later, Bryce, Jerry, and Michael were solemn and unusually silent as they took Jerry's boat back to Buck Island to collect the stolen boat they'd left there in the urgent need to tend Corbin.

Jerry looked to Bryce. "Can you drive the boat?"

"No problem, mon."

Following Jerry's launch back to the Christiansted pier, Bryce captained the second boat. Michael jumped aboard with Bryce. Two dolphins kept pace beside them, occasionally leaping from the water as if to get a better look. Under the blue sky, the debris in the ocean served as Hugo's calling card.

Bryce glanced sidelong at his partner. "That was the gutsiest move I've ever seen."

Michael flexed his sore arm. "Do you think he'll get back the use of his leg?"

Bryce shrugged. "Hard to say. That was a long time for tissue to be without blood."

"My knife wasn't exactly sanitary."

"Doubt your hand was either."

Michael sighed.

"One thing I do know." Bryce looked somber. "You saved Corbin's life."

CHAPTER 69

The following day Michael and Bryce ventured to the airport. A landing strip had been cleared although commercial flights had not resumed service. Claire and Senator Taylor were awaiting a military transport.

Michael came to Claire's side. "Returning to civilization and communication?"

She eyed her father who paced impatiently out of earshot. "He's been acting like a caged cat since I showed up. But today, he's really agitated."

"A hurricane is not very conducive for a father-daughter getaway." He caught himself. "Oh, yeah, you weren't exactly invited."

She frowned. "I feel like an interruption."

"Rather than a pleasant surprise."

She nodded.

To Michael, she looked the way she had the night they spent in the rectory—the night she spent trying to puzzle together a thousand questions while Hugo furiously tore the island apart.

They watched the jet make its landing and taxi in. Several officials disembarked, sent to help coordinate disaster relief. The senator picked up his briefcase and brushed past.

"Definitely in a hurry to leave." Michael collected Claire's suitcase and walked with her. "Who knows when I'll run into you again? At least this time, I don't have a knot on the back of my head to remember you by."

She chewed her lip and regarded him. "Rather uneventful."

He handed Claire's case to flight personnel. "If you call a hurricane uneventful."

CHAPTER 70

Arriving at Jewel by the Sea, Michael could barely believe this was once the same place where he'd lunched with Bryce and Corbin. Where Bryce had provided the opportunity for him to later meet Elise. Where he'd first seen Elise's talent as an artist.

The previously upscale resort that had catered to the rich, the famous, and the honeymooners, now looked like a military ballistics-testing zone. The volcanic rock wall that separated the pool from the sea had caved in, and the Atlantic waves skipped in and ran back out like naughty Peter Rabbit playing in Mr. McGregor's garden.

The hotel resembled a splendid dollhouse whose contents had been shaken and spilled about. The roof had disappeared, windows were missing, and scattered broken china from the dining room glinted under the tropical sun. Several hotel workers were salvaging anything Hugo had left useful.

Michael found Jacques wrestling the desk in his office and leaned his own weight into righting the stubborn piece of furniture. Jacques nodded his thanks.

Brushing the top of the desk, Michael felt the wood swollen, warped, and sodden with water. "How are you?"

"That's a good question." The Frenchman crossed the room to a cabinet that stood unscathed. From within, Jacques pulled a bottle of cognac and two glasses. He poured a splash in each rounded globe, offered one to Michael, and clinked his glass against Michael's. "My mother declared cognac medicinal."

Michael tipped back his head and swallowed the fiery liquid.

Jacques righted his office chair. Michael found his own seat.

"I enjoyed the open-air dining area of the restaurant but never considered having an open-air office." Jacques put his feet on his desk, a thing Michael was sure the elegantly mannered man had never done before. He reached in a drawer, drew out two expensive cigars, and passed one to Michael. Slowly, Jacques bit the end of his cigar, lit it, and inhaled deeply on the fragrant tobacco.

"Handmade. Shaped on the thighs of skilled women." Jacques held the lit cigar between his thumb and first finger and inspected its seams.

"Elise and I loved this place." Remembering how sick he'd gotten from the cigar Meatloaf handed out when his son was born, Michael merely held his lit cigar between his lips and hoped Jacques wasn't paying close attention.

"Mmm," Jacques murmured. "I did too."

"When will you rebuild?"

Jacques took a long pull on the cigar. He slowly blew the smoke into the island sky. "There's a lovely coastal area in France that has all the elements for a fine resort area."

"You're going home."

Jacques' nod was barely perceptible.

The hotel owner poured another round of cognac, tossed back his own and resumed his position with his feet on the damaged desk. They sat in silence while Jacques savored the cigar, and Michael let his own burn itself away. At last, the older man dropped his cigar butt on the floor and stomped it out. Michael couldn't bring himself to use the resort as an ashtray. Not even with the resort in ruins. Not even for this prized cigar. He ground his out against the bottom of his shoe and dropped the remains in the empty cognac glass.

The restaurateur studied Michael. "I always knew there was more to you. Even when I begin again on the other side of this vast and unpredictable Atlantic Ocean, we will see each other."

"We will, Jacques." Michael shook hands with the genteel entrepreneur. "We will."

When Michael returned to the cottage, Antonio stood in the back of his pickup with a chainsaw, trimming damaged branches from a carambola tree. As they fell, Michael hauled the branches to a growing brush pile Antonio would burn later.

Satisfied with the reconditioned tree, Antonio removed his safety glasses and refueled the chainsaw for the next project. "What troubles you, Señor Michael?"

Michael sat on the tailgate. "I was thinking Jewel by the Sea would be a good place for a wedding."

"It would." Antonio poured water from a thermos and handed the cup to Michael. "I tend the grounds there as well as here."

"Used to, you mean. Have you seen it?"

The gardener rested gloved hands on his hips. "I went by to check on things. It's pretty bad."

"Totaled is more like it." Michael gulped the water and handed back the cup.

"You don't wish to wait until it is rebuilt?" Antonio poured a second cup from the thermos for himself.

Michael sighed. "Jacques doesn't plan to rebuild."

Antonio thoughtfully digested this information. "If Jewel by the Sea is not to be, I know just the place. A place where I worked before Lisandro and I came here."

CHAPTER 71

Six weeks after Hurricane Hugo, three-quarters of the island's roads remained impassable, and power had been restored to a mere twenty-five percent of the island. Eventually, communication was operational once more on St. Croix, and the islanders learned that Hurricane Hugo had battered St. Croix harder than any other location in its destructive path. With one hundred forty-mile per hour winds spurring multiple tornado-like vortices on land while twenty-three-foot waves assailed the coast, Hurricane Hugo had dropped from a category five to a category four when the storm descended on the island. Two people on the island had been killed and eighty injured.

Cisterns were cleaned out and fresh water collected. Brother Ned had done an admirable job of uniting the island's churches and schools to concentrate their combined efforts toward medical help, schooling, and rebuilding.

Bryce received orders to travel to South Carolina. Hurricane Hugo had blown through the Caribbean islands, picked up speed, and bulldozed the state that a hundred years earlier had rocked the Union by firing the first shot of the Civil War across Fort Sumter.

Like a necklace with one hundred seventy pearls, the chain of Sea Islands dot the coast of South Carolina. At midnight on September 21, the eye of Hurricane Hugo passed over the charming community of Sullivan Island. With winds exceeding one hundred sixty-miles per hour, and ocean surges measuring ten feet above sea level, both Sullivan and the neighboring Isle of Palms had been completely destroyed. Michael wondered how the honeymooning couple who had flown home to South Carolina just ahead of Hurricane Hugo had fared.

Along with the rest of St. Croix's inhabitants, Elise and Michael had kept busy clearing debris, rebuilding, and replanting. Weary from another long day, one evening Michael and Elise met in her garden to sit and listen to Dvorak.

"Look what I found." Michael tossed a coconut up and down like a football.

"Is that the one you carried home from our day at Gentle Winds beach? When you found the sea glass?" She lifted the necklace she had made that hung around her throat.

"The very one." He set the brown husk on end and prepared to drop a brick on the drupe the way Elise had taught him. "Occasionally, I find something good in the wreckage from the hurricane."

"With all the water and chaos," Elise said, "it feels like we're searching for surprises and treasure in a tide pool that stretches across St. Croix."

"A giant Easter egg hunt." The brick did its job, and Michael removed the nut from the husk. Another blow from the brick opened a crack in the hairy shell. He poured the concentrated milk into two cups.

"But so much of the island I knew is gone." Elise set a chunk of husk under the sea grapes and filled it with birdseed.

"The first morning I was here, I remember watching the sun rise from the sea." Another blow and the hairy shell broke into pieces. Michael slid the blade of his pocketknife along the hard shell to separate the meat for eating. "Now it seems like the island is rising like a phoenix from a burning pyre and reclaiming its place in the sea."

"I remember that first morning," she said.

He looked at her, surprised. "You do?"

"Of course." She smiled knowingly. "The day we watched the same sunrise and the same jet."

"Chasing sunrise." He studied her. "I didn't realize you'd seen me."

"I may be private." She kissed him. "But I'm not blind."

In the following weeks, island life settled into a new normal, and an envelope arrived from the States. Michael recognized Bryce's handwriting. His friend had mailed another newspaper clipping, this one from the front page.

Bryce had scribbled on the margin. "Wasn't sure if you're getting news from the outside world yet."

The long article told about the arrest of Senator Bennett Taylor. Some internationals had been apprehended with stolen property in United States' territory and were more than happy to trade incriminating evidence about the senator's involvement with trafficking human organs as a plea bargain. The report went on to say Senator Taylor had significant investments in International Dialysis Corporation. While the company did provide dialysis equipment and training around the world, the prime purpose was a cover for subversives to fund terrorist cells by providing transplant material on the black market. Investigators were looking into rumors the transplant materials were collected from political prisoners and orphans.

Michael recalled an earlier conversation with Claire.

Someone tried to kill you. And me. Twice. You might want to figure out who that is.

Or what I'm doing that puts me at risk.

No problem there. You're not exactly home baking cookies. You're putting yourself in the middle of nasty business.

Her eyes had met his. Whose business?

Apparently, Claire had been nosing around the senator's business. Her father's business. No wonder she had lots of questions—why things hadn't made sense.

The story noted that Taylor had been a transplant recipient. When surgery was delayed in the United States, Taylor had faked his collapse overseas and received a new liver through the black market he had since been in business with. Michael recalled the day he carried Verity Marshall-Taylor's luggage to the airport. The day he learned her name.

"My husband collapsed while he was away," she had said then. "He had emergency surgery."

Michael read on. Investigations had reopened in the case of Taylor's second wife's death. Though Verity Marshall-Taylor's father was currently under medical care, the retired scientist had provided his daughter's last communications with him prior to her death. Her messages acknowledged she felt frightened for her safety after she had discovered disturbing information. The scientist had been traveling to see his daughter when Verity was hospitalized.

Michael carried the newspaper clipping outside where he dropped into the same chair he had sat in when Corbin first asked him to once again wear his parajumper insignia. He reread the news story, trying to piece together answers to his many questions regarding Verity and Claire.

Claire. If Corbin and Bryce hadn't talked Michael into returning to work, he wouldn't have met the strong-willed idealist. He probably wouldn't have ever understood what events led to Verity's untimely and tragic death.

Verity must have stumbled upon evidence that connected her husband with unsavory business practices. Simultaneously, Claire had sought to earn daddy's approval by traveling to China to bring back proof that her father's political leanings were valid. Michael recalled his conversation with her.

It's the rhetoric my dad preached all my life. I believed it and planned to vindicate his ideals by documenting the story ... only they traded children for money.

When Claire nearly died on the *Lea*, she had been searching for the American connection who dealt with the black market and who had tried to kill her twice.

He shook his head at the strange realization the connection she sought turned out to be her own father. Did Claire's father know she was the one nosing into his business? Michael doubted the senator understood what Claire had found in China when he asked for military aid to bring her home. But, by then, Claire knew she had stepped into dangerous territory and could no longer be sure who to trust.

When Michael found her on the *Lea*, Claire still hadn't been sure who were good guys and who weren't to be trusted. She had struck out first and asked questions second. Did Bennett Taylor know his own daughter was the inconvenient hostage when he arranged for the destruction of the *Lea*? Again, Michael doubted the senator knew who'd been aboard. The politician probably just arranged for the quick elimination of a potentially explosive exposure. The senator traded his wife and daughter for black-market business connections. Michael held a deep appreciation for the empathetic Verity and admired strong-willed Claire. He couldn't imagine betraying Elise for the likes of guys who pieced out orphans as Taylor had done to his own wife and daughter.

Claire had been on a long quest. She traveled the world and put herself in harm's way to build a relationship with her father. Even during Hurricane Hugo, she had been puzzling through the questions. Whether part of her attempt to follow leads or whether she had truly followed her father to St. Croix in an attempt at some father-daughter time, she had interfered with Taylor's plans to meet with his international business partners—the guys who'd stolen Jerry's boat to keep an appointment on the secluded Buck Island.

Claire had her answers now. Michael understood firsthand the father's absence that felt like betrayal and left a Grand Canyon-sized hole in a child's heart, no matter how old she was.

CHAPTER 72

Though the island eventually became functional again, Michael knew a very long time, probably decades, would elapse before St. Croix returned to being a favorite destination for vacationers and honeymooners.

"It's not all bad," Jerry insisted. "The island will rest and rebuild, maybe not to what it previously was, but certainly to something good. Maybe better."

"Pretty positive philosophy for someone who makes his living on tourism," Michael returned.

Jerry pointed to the surroundings and grinned. "These are the islands, mon. All part of the natural ebb-and-flow. All part of island time."

"No worries, mon?" Michael pressed.

Jerry shook his head. "St. Croix's still an island. People still need good boats, jet skis, and dive equipment. There'll just be a different clientele for a time."

Commercial flights resumed at the airport, and Brother Ned taught school at St. John's. Churches met outdoors, but the Christiansted Theater, like Jewel by the Sea, had been pronounced beyond repair. A melancholy foursome gathered for dinner on Robson's boat to mourn the theater and the closing of an age in the island's rich culture.

"The theater certainly wasn't high on the food chain when islanders listed priorities," Robson noted.

"Not even on the list," Elise clarified.

"That was probably the shortest career a conductor has ever experienced," Ava bemoaned.

"With the current state of the island," Robson reasoned, "there probably won't be many tourists to populate our audience for a long time. We relied on the tourist and transient population to supplement our ticket sales."

"What will you do?" The gentle sway of the cellist's floating home felt soothing to Michael.

"New York has offered me my position back as assistant conductor." Ava tucked her hair behind her ear. "It's serendipitous the position had not yet been filled."

Elise looked to Robson. "And you?"

Robson shrugged. "St. Croix is my home. But I have applied for a position with the New York Symphony."

Michael thought of Dr. Evans and Keri and their yacht. "Plan to park your boat in the residential neighborhood of New York harbor?"

"That's an option." Robson gestured toward the St. Croix Adventures boat pulled tight against her mooring. "Though I know if I leave my *Day Dream* here for a season, Jerry will watch over her."

The stars were plentiful that evening as Michael took Elise home. At her door, she turned to him. "Are you sure you're comfortable at the cottage?"

He glanced over at the former studio, pitifully altered in appearance compared to the first afternoon when June had brought him to see the place. Still, Bryce and Antonio had worked side by side with him to clear debris and make the place habitable until the necessary repairs could be made. In due time. Michael hardly considered the cottage as a priority on the island's repair list.

"I'm safe enough." He touched her nose. "Believe me, I've slept in worse accommodations."

She wrapped her arms around his neck. "I'm sure you have."

With her head nestled against his shoulder, he breathed in deeply. She smelled of plumeria.

CHAPTER 73

The next day Michael's phone rang. The familiar sound was evidence that progress was being made in reestablishing communication.

"Michael, it's Corbin."

"You calling with an assignment?" Even as he asked, Michael felt reluctant to leave with so much to do on the island.

"Not today. In fact, not ever again."

"You decided to reaccept my resignation?"

Corbin laughed. "After all the gymnastics I went through convincing you to come back and play? Guess again."

Michael waited.

"I wanted to let you know I've resigned."

"Resigned?" He recalled his conversation with Corbin on the beach just before the hurricane. When his boss had confided, "I'm getting too old for this."

"Effective immediately."

Michael tried to absorb this new development. "Who's going to take your place?"

"Meatloaf." Corbin let this sink in and continued. "He's ready. As he proved in recent weeks."

"No argument there. He's a good man." Michael dropped into a chair. "So what's next for you?"

Corbin paused. Michael could picture him, his jaw clenched while he weighed how much he wanted to share. "Thanks to you, I have the opportunity to consider options."

The Scotsman's appreciation left Michael strangely uncomfortable. "How is your recovery progressing?"

"Hardest thing I've ever done," he confessed. "Surgery after surgery, so a lot of times I don't know what day it is or how long I've been out."

"Your leg?"

"Lost a muscle in the calf due to lack of circulation. Had some infection to fight."

Michael recalled the unsanitary knife, and certainly Michael's hand had been far from clean. "Sorry."

"I'm alive because of you, Michael. When I get depressed because I can't pee by myself, and I have to learn to walk all over again, I plan what I'm going to do next because I have a next to go to."

"What are you planning?"

"I've been thinking about establishing a sky medic service. Provide medical flights for residents from outlying places. In case of an emergency, I could transport a patient to the hospital of their choice, transport supportive family members, and arrange return."

That made sense to Michael. "Combines your skills as a pilot with your training to handle emergency situations."

"And offer continual on-call availability for a monthly fee." Corbin warmed to the topic. "For those who have medical conditions."

"Like insurance."

"Right."

Michael knew how useful such a service would have been for Corbin when he needed specialized surgery. "You could monitor the national hurricane center's information for alerts."

"I've already thought of that." Corbin's bed squeaked loudly through the phone as he shifted positions.

"I can't picture you lying around while you wait for calls," Michael fished.

"There's some World War II relics I might salvage for museums."

Michael thought of the sonobuoy he had found on his first dive of the wall with Jerry. "That's more than a one-man job."

Corbin cleared his throat. "I might know a guy. A local. Pretty good diver."

Michael smiled and changed the subject. "I saw the news about Senator Taylor."

Corbin grunted. "You're not surprised, are you?"

"No," Michael admitted. "Looks like fish, smells like fish, must be fish. But why were the guys we caught with Jerry's boat more talkative than the one you gaffed out of New York harbor?"

"Your waterlogged assailant didn't say anything because he didn't have to."

"His connections and evidence went up with the boat." Michael was putting pieces together.

Corbin added, "But there were three in the second group."

"An opportunity to play one against another."

"Half a story is enough for a wise man," Corbin philosophized. "Facing consequences regarding stolen property was an added incentive to bargain. Jerry's missing boat and shooting at us was opportune leverage."

Michael processed the bits of information Corbin could tell him and tried to fill in around the information he knew Corbin could not share. "What about Claire? Whose side was she on?"

"Initially, she took a job she thought her father would approve."

"International Dialysis Corporation." Michael recalled her words after their rescue from the shark-infested waters.

"She stumbled onto some things she had not anticipated."

"And the *Lea*?" Michael remembered seeing the boat in two different places with two different names.

"After China, Claire nosed around looking for the American connection. She set up a meeting with the international connection."

"That got her a one-way boat trip to the New York harbor."

"Thanks to you. Or it would have been a one-way trip to the middle of the Atlantic." Corbin paused and his tone changed. "By the way, we never did talk about you being aboard that boat—"

"No sense getting into that now, seeing as you're a short-timer." Michael shifted back to their previous topic. "Any recent update on Claire?"

"Dr. Evans tells me she has developed a friendship with Verity's father."

CHAPTER 74

When their plane landed at the Nashville airport, Elise was delighted to find Michael had arranged for a limo to meet them. The driver took the scenic route to provide Elise with her first tour of the country music capital. Then he turned into the long circle drive to the world's largest hotel, and Elise caught her breath.

"Welcome to the Opryland Hotel," the driver greeted as he opened the door to the lobby.

Their reservations included a suite in the Cascades garden for Elise and a room for Michael above the boisterous Delta Atrium. Under the dome of the night sky, they rode the boat on the hotel's mile-long river before their rehearsal dinner at the Italian restaurant. From the island, June and Karl, Robson and Ava, Jacques and his wife, along with Jerry and his family had come. From the mainland, Michael was pleasantly surprised to see Saundra, whom he introduced to Elise as Corbin's efficient secretary. Elise met Meatloaf and Diane and their lively young son. Exploring the tropical gardens at the first rate resort, Jerry's three children located the large koi in the indoor pond, reminding Elise of the memorable day they had hunted for the small brown sharks on Buck Island.

Michael blinked away tears when he introduced Elise to Rachel Carolynne, his mother's best friend.

And Bryce had arrived. Faithful Bryce.

Tears flooded Michael's eyes when Corbin hobbled into view. He leaned heavily on a cane, and his athletic body showed signs of non-use. Elise could see how much this trip physically taxed the recovering soldier. Michael and Corbin shook hands, and then the older man pulled him into a backslapping embrace. Corbin's arms were strong as he hugged Elise.

Saundra came to Corbin's side, his faithful assistant walking beside the former commander at his slower pace as the wedding party took their seats for the rehearsal dinner.

The food was excellent, the wine plenteous, and a talented musician serenaded the party with a continual stream of love songs on his violin. Late into the night, Jerry's children played hide and seek among the winding paths. The cheery group walked among the gardens until the music from a pub pulled them in.

When Jerry's youngest yawned, Karl lifted her onto his shoulders. "We'll take the children back to the room and watch a movie," June offered to Jerry and Reta. She nodded toward Robson and Ava who were on the dance floor. "You two stay out late tonight and do whatever younger folks do."

A rock-and-roll song from the band touched off a round of razzing between Bryce and Corbin. Sound asleep in his dad's lap, Meatloaf Junior didn't stir as Meatloaf and Michael joined in the good-natured fun.

Diane brought her glass of wine and took a chair next to Elise. "You have to be a particular kind of woman to be the wife of a pararescueman."

Elise looked from Diane to Saundra. "What advice would you give this bride-to-be?"

"Most important," Diane began, "don't waste the time you have together arguing about the time he is away."

"Is that what makes your marriage solid?"

Diane nodded. "PJs show up when someone calls for help. That's what you love about Michael so allow him to be the man you fell in love with. They don't punch a time clock. You won't know where he is or when he's coming back. Sometimes you won't know if he's alive."

Saundra leaned close. "Always believe the best until you hear otherwise."

Looking weary and like his leg probably hurt, Corbin said his goodnights, waving Michael away when he stood to walk the Scotsman to his room. "You guys go share a bottle of whisky and chase women," Corbin winked at Elise, "or whatever you young men do. I need my beauty rest for the big day tomorrow."

Saundra stayed and chatted with the ladies until Meatloaf Junior began to fuss. "Let me put him to bed." She held out her arms for the young boy. "They are playing your song on the dance floor."

Elise didn't know when she'd had such full portions of contented fun as she laughed with best friends and danced with the man she loved. "The Opryland Hotel is not Jewel by the Sea," Michael said as he circled the dance floor with Elise.

"No," she agreed. "But certainly the next most perfect place for a wedding."

He nodded. "Just like Antonio said."

The next afternoon, as Michael had arranged, two stylists arrived at Elise's suite to help her and Ava with their hair. Reta and the ever-opinionated June were there to help Elise into her wedding gown.

"Something borrowed and something old." June handed Elise a pair of earrings. "These were your mother's, which makes them old. She gave them to me as a gift, which makes them borrowed."

When all the preparations were complete, Elise stood in front of the full-length mirror.

June brushed at sudden tears. "Your mama and papa would have adored this moment."

"And they would approve of Michael." Ava hugged Elise. "Some things in life are a sweet surprise."

Elise smiled at her childhood friend. "Like Robson?"

Ava blushed. "We all were convinced you two belonged together."

"We do." Elise laughed. "We merely took a bit of time to understand we belong together like irritating siblings. Not like lovers. He needs you for that deeper relationship."

CHAPTER 75

Michael answered the knock at his hotel door to find Bryce, dressed early, and grinning.

"The big day," his longtime friend announced.

Michael waved him inside. "How do I look?"

Bryce eyed him critically. "I'd like to warn you off this marriage idea 'cuz that's my job as your friend and best man." He met Michael's eyes. "But in this case, if you don't marry that lady, I'd say you were stupid, sucks to be you, and I'd marry her myself."

Michael was pleased but harrumphed anyway. "Like she'd have the likes of you."

Bryce threw out his hands, the picture of surprise. "Are you kidding? Just look at me! What woman could keep her eyes and hands off me in this tux?"

Michael had to admit that his friend looked sharp, but he wasn't going to say so. Instead, he turned to check his own appearance in the mirror.

"Come on, Romeo," Bryce chided. "It's time."

Michael and Bryce rode the glass elevator down to the picturesque gazebo in the hotel's lush Magnolia Garden. A string chamber group, led by last night's violinist, played a repertoire of Elise's choosing. Michael arrived to hear the familiar weave of the *New World Symphony*. Sweeping white bows around arrangements of fragrant magnolias adorned the rows of seats for the wedding guests.

A handsome young man in a dashing suit stepped forward and gave Michael a gallant bow.

"Lisandro!" He grabbed the boy and swung him around.

Lisandro hugged Michael's neck tightly. "Papa and I came with Brother Ned. Papa said you needed a ring-bearer."

Michael laughed. "Indeed I do."

Antonio came to stand behind his son. With the two of them in matching suits and Antonio's hands affectionately on his son's shoulders, the father and son duo were strikingly alike.

Bryce dug a small box from his pocket that he handed to Lisandro. "This is the most important job."

Lisandro's eyes grew wide. "The most?"

"And you're the right man at the right moment." Bryce explained to the eager young man the what and when of being the bearer of the wedding bands.

"Thank you, Antonio." Michael clasped the gardener's hand. "This place is everything you said it would be and more. Now with you here, all the important people in our lives are together."

Antonio jerked a thumb toward Bryce and Meatloaf. "A couple friends said they'd make sure we were safe."

Michael and Bryce greeted guests as they arrived. Looking fresh and rested, Corbin thumped Michael on the back, and Saundra kissed his cheek. His arm around his wife's waist, Meatloaf pumped Michael's hand in an approving handshake. Meatloaf Jr., balanced on his mother's hip, sleepily sucked his thumb. Looking dapper, the soft-spoken Jacques and his sweet wife congratulated Michael, and Jacques slid one of his expensive cigars into Michael's breast pocket.

Once the guests were seated, the musicians began an instrumental rendition of Jesse Barish's "Count On Me." Brother Ned took his place at the front, and Michael made his way to Rachel Carolynne, who waited at the back. For a long moment, they looked at each other. Tears filled her eyes, and Michael brushed at his own. More than a friend, Rachel Carolynne was here to try to satisfy the place his mother would have filled. She reached her arm about his neck and he leaned into her hug.

"I'm proud of you. You look so handsome." Pulling back, she laid her palm against his cheek. "Elise is a lucky girl."

Michael tucked her hand around his arm and escorted his mother's best friend to the seat reserved for the mother of the groom.

Next, with a nod to Karl, Michael held out his arm to June. The spunky redhead smiled warmly as he walked with her down the aisle and to the place traditionally kept for the mother of the bride. Karl followed and sat next to his wife.

With the wedding guests seated, Michael took his position at the front of the gazebo near the grinning Brother Ned.

"Ya' good, mon?" His dark eyes reflecting kind reassurance, Brother Ned stressed the accent as he dropped a reassuring hand on Michael's shoulder.

Michael thought of the first time they had met when the priest had invited Bryce and him to the crab races. Going along had proven to be a smart investment. "I'm good."

"Yeah, mon."

With Bryce at his side, Michael gazed across the group gathered together. They were a mix of lifelong relationships and relatively new friendships made since he had come to St. Croix. Everyone was important to him. And to Elise. They were family.

As the chamber strings began Bach's "Jesu, Joy of Man's Desiring," Elise's maid of honor, Ava, came down the aisle and stood opposite Bryce. Serious and bright-eyed, Lisandro followed to stand tall and important near Bryce. Behind Lisandro, Jerry's two daughters, dressed in ribbons and bows, scattered a path of rose petals from the small baskets they carried. Reaching Ava, the girls turned to see what would happen next. With the wedding party in place, June winked at Michael and stood.

The chamber group began "Pachelbel's Canon." Elise stepped into view, and Michael couldn't breathe. The loveliest woman he had ever seen was smiling at him. On her left, Robson looked tall and genteel, her arm entwined with his, and his left hand protectively cupped over hers—the same way Michael had seen Robson do for Elise so many times before. Now Michael counted the cellist a friend too.

Robson brought Elise up the steps to the white gazebo. Michael came to Elise's right side, and she turned to face him. As bride and groom held hands, Brother Ned began the marriage ceremony.

Before God, the minister, and these close friends, Michael spoke his vows to his bride. "I, Michael, take thee, Elise, to be my lawfully wedded wife. With this ring, I thee wed. This gold and silver I thee give. With my body, I thee worship. And with all my worldly goods, I thee endow. In the name of the Father, and of the Son, and of the Holy Ghost, amen."

Elise repeated the same beautiful words to him, her eyes sincere and full of joy.

Proudly, Lisandro lifted the box that held the rings. Michael slipped the band on her finger, an island design of gold plumeria flowers woven together like a miniature lei and inset with diamonds. She placed a simple gold circle, their names engraved inside, on his left-hand ring finger. Brother Ned pronounced them husband and wife. Michael lifted the wispy veil and sealed their vows with a tender kiss.

"It is my great honor to introduce to you," Brother Ned paused for theatrical effect, "Mr. and Mrs. Elise and Michael Northington." The wedding guests erupted into applause while Bryce and Meatloaf whooped loudly.

Michael and Elise began the recessional to the lively notes of "Sweet Child of Mine."

The ceremony was followed with a catered meal, speeches, and photos. For their first dance as husband and wife, Michael and Elise chose the rich tones of Etta James' most well-known song, "At Last."

Michael and Rachel Carolynne took the floor for the mother-son dance. "She would be pleased, you know," Rachel Carolynne assured him. "Your mother always thought you made good choices. She would be especially pleased with your Elise."

"I wish they could have known one another." Talking with Rachel about his family made them feel closer. "April and Marissa would have been quite taken with her."

Rachel Carolynne laughed. "You would have had to fight for any time with your beloved. I'm not sure who would have been more enamored— Elise with your sisters or your sisters with Elise."

As the wedding guests danced, Michael sought out Corbin. "I've been thinking about your sky medic service."

"So have I." Corbin leaned on his cane. "What's been keeping you awake at night?"

"The cottage will be available. During the repair process, we could remodel the place to suit your needs. St. Croix would be a strategic location for what you want to do."

Corbin nodded. "A flattering offer, Michael. One that bears consideration."

"And," Michael nodded toward Elise talking with Saundra, "I wouldn't mind someone being around the place when Meatloaf finds things for me to do."

Corbin followed his gaze. "Understood."

Meatloaf brought Michael a glass of champagne. "Welcome to the married club."

Michael glanced over to Diane who laughed with Bryce while Meatloaf Jr. perched confidently on Bryce's shoulders. "You and Diane made marriage look pretty inviting."

Robson whirled Elise across the dance floor, and he dipped her low. "They look practiced," Meatloaf observed.

Seeing the two of them together no longer triggered a twinge of jealousy for Michael. "They grew up together, close friends who went everywhere until that someone special arrived."

"Meaning you?"

"Seems he fell first."

"You obviously move faster."

The teammates watched as Corbin escorted Saundra onto the dance floor. Without his cane, he confidently circled her in his arms. To a slow song, he managed to dance without much movement.

"Saundra and Corbin." Michael said their names slowly. "What's brewing between those two?"

"Corbin's been tight-lipped."

"That's a first for the eloquently verbose Scotsman."

Meatloaf nodded. "Which makes the connection all the more interesting, if you ask me."

Michael stuck out his hand to Meatloaf. "Congratulations on your promotion. I know you'll do the position proud."

"Thanks, Michael. I appreciate that from you." Meatloaf's handshake was solid. "Lord knows Corbin left giant shoes to fill."

Diane blew kisses to her son, still perched on Bryce's shoulders, and joined the two men. "This is a beautiful place for a wedding. What gave you the idea?"

"Antonio made the suggestion." Michael inclined his head toward Antonio who sat talking with Robson while Ava danced with Lisandro. "He does the landscaping at Elise's place and apparently he spent some time here maintaining these gardens before coming to St. Croix."

"Works well for a second honeymoon too." Diane looped her arm through her husband's.

Meatloaf excused the two of them to slow dance with his wife.

Michael went to Elise where she stood talking with Rachel Carolynne. "May I have this dance?"

His bride smiled and stepped into his arms. They circled the dance floor several times. When Michael was certain the attention of his guests had returned to their own conversations and drinks, he gently danced her onto a shadowy garden path for a long kiss.

Opening his eyes, he whispered, "I love you."

She met his gaze. "I know."

He took her hand and guided her away from the garden and onto the glass elevator. As they ascended, they could see the reception continuing without them. Michael led the way to a different room. Pulling the key from his pocket, he unlocked the door to the honeymoon suite. Lifting his bride into his arms, he carried her across the threshold.

Inside, Michael kicked the door closed and kissed Elise again before setting her on her feet. He watched her look around the suite, notice their things had been brought over during the ceremony, and listen to the music that played in the background.

"Lovely," she pronounced. "Truly lovely."

"Come see the view." From an iced bottle, he poured her favorite muscatel. "To you."

On the balcony, they sat and watched the sky darken, heard the soothing sounds of the waterfalls, and the distant voices of hotel guests carrying on their lives in the gardens below.

When her glass was empty, Michael stood and took Elise's hand. Back inside the living room, they danced to the soft music. Her head on his shoulder, her body warm against his chest, he breathed the plumeria and jasmine fragrance of her hair. He held her for a very long time, feeling at home.

The music continued to play, and Michael gently kissed the top of her head. He kissed her forehead. Cupping his hand under her chin, he tipped her face and slowly, lightly kissed her nose, her left cheek, and then her right. As he looked at her face, so close to his, Elise opened her eyes.

"Michael," she whispered.

His lips gentle yet eager on hers, he kissed her. Her mouth was welcoming, and her arms slid up around his neck. He kissed her for a long time, never wanting to stop. He kissed her chin and then his lips tasted the lovely skin of her neck and the curve of her shoulder. He could feel her heartbeat under his lips. His eyes trailed the path his lips had taken from her lips, down her neck, and across the silken shoulder. He pressed his lips to her shoulder, her neck, and her mouth. Drawing back, he met her eyes. Elise's trusting eyes. Easily, he lifted her once more into his arms and carried her into their future—

ENJOY A CHAPTER OF BOOK TWO IN THE
CHASING SUNRISE SERIES.

Chapter 1

Through the bustling airport crowd, Elise Eisler Northington saw the man in the distance coming her way. His dark hair disheveled, and with a few days of beard growth, he looked ruggedly handsome. Instantly, her heart leapt with feelings of deep longing that had been dormant during Michael's absence.

She quickened her step. Already she anticipated her husband's lips on hers as he held her in his secure embrace.

A pararescueman with the Air Force, Michael and his rescue team had traveled to South America on an assignment. Depending on arrangements, sometimes Michael returned from a deployment looking fresh and shaved. Other times, his face was shadowed with the beginnings of a beard. With or without a shave, Elise was always elated to see him.

Being married to a man in the military was a completely different lifestyle than she had experienced growing up with her artistic parents. Like an added family member, the military occasionally demanded their full attention for extended periods. That's when Michael would be away and usually out of touch. He had trained to become a parajumper to save lives, and Elise trusted the process. She trusted Michael.

Now the dark haired man came close enough to touch but neither reached for the other. His eyes briefly flickered over Elise and then quickly focused elsewhere as he brushed past. The man wasn't her husband after all. He wasn't Michael.

Disappointed, Elise once again looked for her husband among the disembarking passengers entering the building. Within minutes, travelers in the small airport had swept past the expectant Elise to collect luggage and make their way out of the air-conditioned building and into the island sun.

Still Elise waited. She checked the time on her watch and mentally calculated the date. Yes, today Michael was slated to come home.

Through the picture window, she watched a private plane touch down on the runway and taxi to a stop. She recognized the businessman who flew the little plane. Inside, he nodded to her and signaled to a limo driver listening to the steel drums that beat a welcome to arriving visitors. After the businessman and his driver had departed, the musicians played a final song and packed up their instruments. With no more potential customers, the taxi drivers in their Hawaiian shirts also left. Elise knew that meant there were no more arriving flights scheduled for that day.

Unwilling to surrender all hope, she approached the ticket counter. "Is another flight coming in today?"

Motioning toward the quiet runway, the clerk's bracelet reflected the light. "That was the last."

Elise walked outside where the humidity warmed her. She wasn't sure what to do now. All of her plans were centered around Michael's return.

Where *was* he?

To be continued …

ABOUT THE AUTHOR

P.S. WELLS is the *USA Today* and *Wall Street Journal* bestselling author of twenty-eight titles including *Homeless for the Holidays*.

Program producer, connector, optimistic dream driver, and sought-after inspirational and motivational speaker, she enjoys dark chocolate, Savannah Grey tea, and writing from her home in the 100-Acre Wood in Northern Indiana.

P.S. is the mother of seven and "Mimi" to her grands, otherwise known as her "Grammy Awards."

Made in the USA
Columbia, SC
26 September 2019